BRAVE

BRAVE

ONI FIGHTERS
BOOK ONE

NATALIE GAYLE

BRAVE

Please Note: This is a work of fiction. Names, characters, places, and incidents either are the product of the author's imagination or are used fictitiously, and any resemblance to actual persons, living or dead, business establishments, events or locales is entirely coincidental.

PREFACE

AUTHOR'S NOTE:

Well, Brave is new territory for me. I saw a photo and I had a whole storyline pop into my head. It was tragic and beautiful—a story of being brave enough to face and overcome your fears.

There are parts of this book that some people may find confronting. I apologise in advance if you find those pieces tough. They were probably the pieces I had a hard time writing too.

But even though there are some "tough" and confronting aspects to the book, the overall story is written to be uplifting and encouraging. I want you to be connecting with Eden and Xander and cheering them on.

Like always I have done a lot of research in putting together this book and I have had a lot of expert advice. I hope I got everything "right". If I haven't, it's through no fault of the experts and professionals assisting me—rather a fault of my own.

I hope you enjoy Eden and Xander's journey as much as I did writing it.

Love

Nat

DEDICATION

This book is for every one of us. At some stage in your life the demons inside will start to claw and gnaw. You'll realise the hardest demons to defeat are the ones inside.

To do that—you'll have to be BRAVE.

#Brave

twelve years before

XANDER

The first time I realised Eden Sommers existed I was fourteen years old and she couldn't have been more than ten or eleven. I was still a boy in so many ways, but a young man in others. I remember the day so vividly. It was almost as if, that was the day I started to see the world with variations of colour, texture and emotions. That was the day I realised that everything in this world had a depth to it—one of joy and a depth of despair.

It was a spring afternoon, warm but not hot. She was sitting in the neighbourhood park with a couple of other girls that looked a little younger than her. They sat with their legs crossed, Indian style, joining the little white clover flowers together to make a daisy chain when I first realised what pure beauty was.

Her loose strawberry blonde hair caught the light and cloaked her in almost a halo like effect as she laughed with the two other little girls beside her. She was very young and incredibly pretty in that little girl sort of way. But none of that's what hit me like a cricket ball to the gut.

No, what struck me was the total picture.

The beauty of that moment in time, something I'd never experienced before.

It was as if time had stood still just for me to see this picture.

The sound of her laughter floated across the park to the footpath where I was making my trek to training. It was almost like music to my ears and her face just seemed to light up with joy as she giggled with the other girls.

I realised then, that I was looking at pure joy. Happiness, in its most base and pure sense. It was also innocence, an inner contentment and joy something I'd never seen before that day, or even realised existed.

Here were three girls unknowingly enjoying every facet of life in its purest and most simple form.

They knew, no evil, pain or tragedy in the world. They expected only good.

And there should have been nothing else but good for them.

A hollowness settled deep in my stomach. I knew then that things would never be that way for me. I doubted if I'd ever feel or experience that sort of joy and beauty. I just could never imagine myself feeling like that.

My eyes had suddenly been opened to contrast.

Part of me was jealous; part of me wished I were their age again, free to do something as simple as what they were doing. I wanted to experience the young boy version of what these girls were enjoying. I wondered what it was. But that's the thing with life. You can never go back. Only forward.

"Where the hell you go to, mate?" my friend Dane called and I finally pulled out of my awake stupor.

"Sorry, just daydreaming I guess." I joked.

He laughed and slapped me hard on the shoulder. Dane had been walking beside me when I drifted off into my own head. It was something I did from time to time. My teachers were always complaining about it. A lot of the time my head was the place I preferred to be.

"Best not do that in class. Sensei Ron will have your arse."

Dane was right, we needed to get to class and I needed to focus. Sensei had chewed me out just yesterday for losing focus. We walked on for a little while, but something kept dragging my mind back to the girls. I needed to know more about the girl with the strawberry blonde hair. I didn't know why then, but I just did. I needed to know the name of happiness, I guess. I needed to be able to put a name to the box marked "happiness and beauty" in my head.

"Who were those girls?" I tried to sound nonchalant and relaxed. Dane would think me weird for wanting to know the name of the girl who was years younger than us. He'd had his eye on some cute little red head that was new in our class at school for the last couple of weeks. So far she was ignoring him.

"Why the hell do you care?" He looked at me strangely and suddenly I felt dirty as if asking was something wrong or forbidden. But it wasn't like that. I didn't think of her like that at all. I wanted her name, to complete the picture in my head. It was a moment in time and a picture of happiness. I wanted that to take with me.

Shit, if I'd had a camera I would have snapped it—but I didn't, so my memory would have to do.

I shrugged my shoulders and started to bullshit. "I don't, I just noticed her around the other day and figured she had to be someone's little sister. A few of the older girls were hassling her. Thought I'd mention it to whoever her older sister was."

Dane nodded and seemed to buy my bullshit. Sensei was big on making sure kids in the neighbourhood weren't being picked on or bullied. He was always bashing into us the importance of looking out for those not able to really take care of themselves.

"Her name's Eden Sommers. She doesn't have a big sister that I know of. In fact I think she's the oldest and those two were her little sisters. They moved into the old Johnson place a couple of weeks back."

I cringed at just the mention of the Johnson place. It was the most run down, ramshackle house in the neighbourhood. My dad was always bitching because it hadn't been condemned yet, and that it was dragging the real estate prices down.

Dane went on, "My mum dragged us all over there to introduce us." I could tell this kind of embarrassed him. Dane thought he was a bit beyond that sort of stuff now. He lived right across the street from the Johnson place. Although, I guess it should be called the Sommers place now. "You know how she is." he offered almost in apology.

I did know how Dane's mum was. I also knew that I wished I had a mum—let alone one that gave as much of a shit as his mum did. She tried to mother me at any opportunity she got and I lapped it up. When you didn't have a mum, any woman that showed an interest was welcomed. This embarrassed Dane, but I didn't really care. He didn't know how lucky he was and if his mum was mine, no way would I be so embarrassed.

I never knew my mum. She died when I was just a baby—some sort of complication. I didn't talk about it, because people would just say "sorry" and get all uncomfortable. That would make me feel uncomfortable then, so it was easier to avoid that subject if I could.

My dad said he never regretted having me because having a baby was exactly what she wanted. I'm not sure I believed him. I wanted to, but I just never really felt it. He tried not to dwell on it for my sake. But it was always there in the back of my mind. Just something you know.

So that's how I came to notice Eden the very first time. I was on the way to karate training. That's what dad wanted me to do, so that's what I did. I was good at it. So I did it some more, and some more. In fact, I kept it up for a lot more years—the rest as they say, is history.

three years ago
XANDER

The crowd was deafening, as I headed back to my corner for the minute reprieve between rounds. That minute was both a blessing and a curse. Sure, it gave me a little break, but I'd just about had the guy when the buzzer had sounded. The adrenalin was flowing freely through my body and I felt great—almost euphoric. I wanted this done. That Oceania Title belt was mine. Next step towards the World Championship Title. It was so close I could taste it.

Reggie slapped me on the back as I bounced over to join my corner men. "You okay, Son?"

He was a wily old bastard and had been my corner man since I'd had my first fight a few years ago. His hand shot out and I spat my mouthguard into his waiting palm, in between shuffling from foot to foot. I didn't want to stop. I didn't want to wait. This needed to be over.

My trainer, Reed, towelled my face and shoulders off as Reggie squirted water into my open mouth. I sloshed the first mouthful around my teeth to remove the unpleasant metallic taste of blood, mixed with the rubbery taste of the mouthguard. Mouthguards always seemed to suck the spit right out of your mouth and make your tongue feel like it was three times bigger than normal. Reggie held a bucket and I spat out the offending liquid, before he squirted more water into my mouth, this time to drink.

"Right, Xan, you're doing great. Now you need to finish it off. He's weak on the ground. Take him down. When he goes for the next combination, block and look for the slow retraction of the punch. Use it to step through and take him down to the canvas. Then go to work."

I nodded taking it all in. Reed was a genius at spotting a fighter's weakness. If Reed said he had a slow retraction, then he did, no questions about it. It was my job to find it and find it I would.

"Make sure you stay out of range of the leg kick. It's got a shitload of power and he nearly caught you last round. Don't get suckered in. He's deceptive." Reed got right in my face and his voice was all I heard even though the crowd was chanting my name.

"Pretty Boy, Pretty Boy," they called. The noise was so loud it reverberated around the stadium and the whole place felt like it was experiencing an earth tremor. I normally hated that name Reed had given me, but nothing was going to dampen my spirits tonight.

"Pretty Boy" was the ring name Reed had given me years ago before my first big fight. He'd given it to me, ribbing the shit out of me; claiming I needed to stop worrying about getting hit and just get in and do the business. It'd pissed me off then and it still grated now. Sometimes worse than others—now, funnily enough, wasn't one of those times. Somehow I'd avoided getting my face mangled in all the fights I'd had. I liked to think it was my superior skill and reflexes. Maybe it was just dumb luck, but the "Pretty Boy" moniker still held. Hell, if I won tonight, I was ready to embrace it!

The seconds were ticking down. Reggie pushed the mouth-guard back into place and Reed wiped a little more petroleum jelly over my face.

"You got this. Finish it quick," he got in my face and demanded.

I nodded unable to speak. There was only one acceptable answer.

The buzzer sounded and I bounded into the centre of the cage. "The Cobra" advanced looking a lot fresher than he had at the end of the last five minute round. This was the fourth round. I didn't want to do another five minutes after this. Fuck, I didn't even want to do the full five here.

He came at me with a flurry of punches in quick succession. My arms automatically moved tight to my face and head to guard. I'd learned long ago to keep my hands up and defend. It was the cardinal rule of staying alive in the cage.

The leg kick was coming; I could sense it. I weaved to the left and got my body out of the way a fraction before he could land it. Regardless, I still felt the air rush past my thigh as his leg burst harmlessly through right where I'd just been.

I moved in from the side and landed a solid left hook to his jaw. I felt the satisfying recoil from the force of the connection ricocheting up my arm. There was nothing like the feeling of landing a solid blow on your opponent. This is what we trained for. We were modern day warriors with all the blood lust of our ancestors.

The Cobra swayed slightly and righted himself before I advanced. Rather than defend he chose to attack and then let loose with the punch combination that Reed had been expecting. Reed was right. He was slow with his retraction. That gave me the perfect opening.

I stepped through and wrapped my leg around his, a split second later we were both on the canvas—me straddling his hips. I didn't waste a moment. My fists rained down on his face. Even the lightweight leather of my hand coverings didn't stop the skin from ripping open with the force. I caught him just under the right eye, and a fine line of red instantly formed. Then my next hit was to his nose and I'm sure I broke it before I delivered the third to his right cheekbone.

There was no way he could take much more of this.

Tap out mate.

Let me have my title.

I drew my right fist back and prepared for the knock out blow. If he wouldn't tap out then it would have to be a knock out. I was winning this fight.

My right fist was on its way. In the fraction of a second that blow took to land, I saw desperation, pain and a hint of defeat flicker through his eyes as he turned his head to avoid another front on hit.

I tried to pull it, I swear to God I did! Somewhere deep inside the bloodlust I knew before I even connected.

My fist connected hard to his left jaw and I felt the firmness of the canvas push back at me through the other side of his jaw. It was a sickening feeling and I reeled back with my sweat-laden torso.

I watched The Cobra's eyelids descend over unfocused pools of black surrounded by blue.

It was the knockout blow.

There was no coming back for The Cobra from that one.

I staggered to my feet, all the elation gone.

The title meant nothing now.

I'd just killed a man in sport.

ONE

EDEN

"Hey Eden wait up!" I glanced over my shoulder and saw it was Cindy. Great. Just what I needed—not. Cindy was "that" girl. You know the one. The girl that is just a little too pretty and a little too perky and oh so damned annoying because she knows both of those things and she plays those cards all too frequently. I did my best to plaster a smile on my face, but kept my eyes and face averted down.

"Hey Cindy." My voice was quiet, even to my own ears.

She moved up alongside me with that overly happy and in your face way she has. Her white blonde ponytail even swung with a perky bounce.

I knew there were only two reasons she could be talking to me. Probably one actually, but the other was kind of connected. I waited for it, playing this little internal guessing game with myself, wondering just how right I would be.

"So, Eden, I was hoping you could lend me your notes from our Communications lecture. I know how you love to help out a friend." Yep, I'd guessed it. She wanted my notes. But the way she said it was the bit that really cut. "Help out a Friend." What a load of garbage. Cindy was no more my friend than, Garrett Forbes, the illustrious star of the university football team, was hot for me! Heck, occasionally he'd even offer me a pitiful smile. No girl wants to see pity on the face of the hottest guy around. That's what hurts the most. The pity.

Those looks hurt me more than if he would just ignore me.

Being ignored is easy. Getting the pity smile sucked. That was the one that was hard to take. That was the one that felt like my guts were being ripped out.

What was I supposed to do? Give them a weak arse smile back in return? It always felt weird. So most times, I dropped my eyes and walked on. I never knew what to do, what to say, so I avoided having to do anything.

In fact, now I kept my head down most of the time and just kept walking.

Nobody needed to see my face.

It was just easier.

I kept my strawberry blonde hair long and loose specifically to act as my shield. Out of sight and hopefully out of mind. I wore my non-descript clothes three sizes too big for exactly the same reason. Don't draw attention to yourself Eden, was my mantra. Originally my choice of clothes had been more comfortable after the fire out of necessity. Later, as I'd finally started to venture out of the house, they'd just become part of my armour.

People didn't need to see the burn scars that ran from my hairline, down the right side of my face, over my ear, neck and the right side of my body to my hip. The scars were ugly and red. Raised in some places, shiny and weird in others.

Looking at them just made people feel embarrassed, which made me feel awkward and even more embarrassed, too.

The scars were long healed but I'd carry the memories forever in my mind, and even more so every time I looked in the mirror. Those scars had changed my whole life in a few short seconds. As long as I live, I'll never regret saving my sisters, but that was the night all my dreams went out the window.

The life I had all mapped out went up in smoke along with our ramshackle house.

It's funny how something so quick and unexpected can alter the whole course of your life in seconds. I often ponder the irony of it.

The universe's timing sucked.

I was so close, in fact I had it, but now I'd never taste the sweetness of the dream I'd held since I was a little girl.

That was snatched away from me, along with my face and the perfect skin on my body.

It was laughable really, how fate worked. Just the week before, I'd signed a modelling contract with a well-connected modelling agent when the accident happened. I even had the first advance payment in my bank account.

That contract had been the ticket to my future. It had been my pass to freedom—a better life for my family.

Three minutes and it was all gone.

That's how quick your dreams can disappear.

Three minutes.

Now I'm stuck here in the suburbs of Logan, on the outskirts of Brisbane, where I've spent most of my life. I'm still trying to pick up the pieces of my life and they still don't feel like they fit together; no matter how I arrange them.

There won't be any amazing world destinations for me. Hell, the idea of having my photo taken even for a passport sends me into a cold sweat and I know I'd be fighting off a panic attack. Who wants to go through that?

I've gone from the girl that loved the camera, to the recluse that despises it. Not only does the camera represent the memory of my dreams gone, it also serves to provide constant reminders of just how ugly my face now looks.

Cindy grabbed hold of my wrist and my mind collided back into the present. "So you'll give me your notes, won't you?"

I didn't say anything, warring with myself on what I should do.

"You're the smartest girl in our class; I need your notes." What she didn't say was that I was also the ugliest. The one benefit of having a face like mine, was the lack of distractions. When you had no social life, studying was a cinch. What else was I going to do? It's not as if I had lots of invites to parties...

I really wanted to say no. I wanted to tell her that if she bothered to turn up to class, she wouldn't need to be borrowing mine. I wanted to tell her to get the lecturer's notes from the web. There were so many things I wanted to tell her, including the fact that I absolutely didn't like her and to go and take a very long walk off a very short plank. But I didn't. I did what I always do. I kept my head down and mumbled.

"Sure, I'll email them to you."

She burst forth with, "Thanks Eden. You're the best," and I nearly drowned in her bullshit. She trotted off back to the other beautiful people—mission accomplished.

I nodded and scurried off. I just needed to be gone. I'd been used again. I was hopeless. Why couldn't I just stand up for myself anymore? Why couldn't I be assertive? Sure, I could renege on my agreement with her, but I knew I wouldn't.

I knew the answer to all those questions I asked myself—because it was easier to just be invisible, the little voice in my head kept saying. Don't bring attention to yourself. People don't want to have to acknowledge the ugly girl. The freak.

That's what you soon realise when you're different. People don't know how to act around you. From the time we're born the vast majority of people are conditioned to fit in with the norm. Don't make a scene. Don't rock the boat. Then there are others, the bullies. The cruel people that are so insecure themselves, they build themselves up by cutting others down.

I'd met them, too. I've met them all. In the five years since the fire I'd met all types of people. The carers, the nurturers, the bullies, the uncomfortable, the overbearing—I could go on. I'd taken pigeon holing people to an art form. I could box them up into one of my little categories within a few seconds of meeting them.

I'd seen them all.

I pulled my overlarge jacket tighter around me in defence to the wind and walked on.

From the university grounds I headed down the street a little way, passing a few people, but not once did I look up or make eye contact. The pavement was more than capable of holding my attention. I could describe every crack in that pavement between my house, the university and the coffee shop I was about to enter. I knew them all.

I took a seat in the far corner booth and slunk down into the high backed bench. We chose this café because it was where I felt most comfortable. If you could call it that. Here the high backed booths provided me with a little anonymity, which made me feel more secure.

People couldn't easily or accidentally see my face. It was one of the few places outside of the house I felt comfortable.

As soon as I sat down I felt a little of the tension drain from my body. Mentally and emotionally attending university lectures and tutorials three days a week was very tough. Sure it was easier now than it had been when I started last year, but it was still tough.

I picked up the menu that I knew by heart more out of habit than anything else and glanced down the options. I knew what I was going to have, but I still liked to look even though I never found the courage to order what I really wanted.

"Hey Eden, how you doing today honey?" Sally the middle aged waitress asked. She'd known me for years and I felt comfortable with her. My story was well known around here.

"Well thanks, Sally, and you?"

"Just great honey. I'm off in about an hour and my Dave is taking me out to a movie tonight."

"That sounds like fun." I replied almost automatically because it did. The last movie I'd been to was over five years ago. Don't get me wrong, I was the full bottle on all the latest movies albeit about three to six months behind the times. As soon as they appeared on iTunes, they were mine.

"Oh, it will be. Now what can I get you? The normal?"

"Please, Sally, that would be great."

Just as she was finishing jotting down my order, my sisters Sophia and Tori came rushing in and slid into the seat opposite me.

"Hey, Edie, how you going?" Sophia beamed at me.

"I'm good."

"Do you ladies want me to come back or do you know what you want?"

"Well have our regulars, please." Tori answered with a big smile for Sally.

"What do you have in cakes today, Sal? I'm starving." Sophia asked, her big expressive eyes glittering.

"You're always starving girl." Sally chuckled good-naturedly. "Must be all the exercise you do. We've got a really nice pineapple upside down cake. That would be my pick with a big dollop of whipped cream—people have been telling me it's out of this world."

Sophia's mouth formed into a happy grin and I could almost see her salivating at the idea. My little sister had a hell of a sweet tooth. In fact, I'm almost positive that girl survived on sugar alone.

"We'll take three serves." Sophia confirmed for Sally.

"Sounds good to me. I'm starved, that'll be lunch. I decided to take my lunch break late so I could catch up with you two." Tori sat back and a big growl let loose from her tummy.

Sally turned and raised a brow at Tori. "Guess I'd better hurry that order right up." Before I could protest, Sally turned and was gone.

"There's no way I could eat a piece of cake from here. The servings are huge," I grumbled. "Plus the calories will just go to my hips."

"Why do you even care?" Tori fired back without thinking and her carelessness hit me hard. "It's not like you ever gain any weight. You still fit into the same clothes that you had when you were sixteen."

I let out the breath I'd grabbed when her choice of words had struck. Tori hadn't meant it as an attack. In fact she'd meant it as a compliment, but I was just so damned sensitive to everything—even stuff my sisters said. It pissed me off. I knew in my heart my sisters would never be cruel. Occasionally they could be insensitive, but then that happened in families without people with disfigurements. That was just part and parcel of how families worked. Why did I always flinch? I needed to toughen up. I knew this. I was trying.

"I don't really care about the calories." Once upon a time counting calories was a prominent part of my day. Now I didn't bother and yes, it didn't seem to matter. I always seemed to stay slim. "I'm just not very hungry."

Sophia looked up from the text message she'd been sending. "What happened?"

My younger sister was always intuitive where I was concerned. I didn't need to say a word, she just seemed to know.

I glanced up at the door, trying to avoid eye contact with her.

"Don't pull that avoidance crap with me. Who upset you?" Sophia was the assertive type and she took crap from no one.

I used to be like her once. I used to be a lot of things, confident was just one of those things.

"No one," I muttered more to myself than in answer to her.

"Just tell me, Edie. You know I'll badger you till you tell me what happened." And wasn't that the truth. She really would.

I sighed. "I agreed to give Cindy Tomlinson my lecture notes."

"Why the hell would you do that?" Sophia demanded in horror. Tori just giggled a little.

"Because I'm weak and stupid and it was just easier." My defence sounded totally pathetic even to me. What did you say when you had an indefensible position?

"Just easier. I'm sick of hearing that, Eden. Tell her to bugger off and do her own notes. She just wants a free ride. You don't owe her shit. You need to start standing up for yourself." There was anger and frustration in Sophia's voice.

That's just one of the many things I loved about my sister. Never once through this whole process had she tried to molly-coddle me. Sophia seemed to see me just as she always had.

"You're right I do," I agreed quietly. She was right. I knew it in my heart. I just couldn't seem to break out of the little world the scars had created and I'd perpetuated.

"So do it!"

Fortunately Sally chose that moment to return with our drinks. She passed a tall ice-coffee full of whipped cream to me, an ice chocolate to Sophia and a caramel milkshake to Tori. That was just another sacrifice my sisters made for me.

Ever since the fire I couldn't stand to be near hot things. Particularly things that could potentially burn me easily, like hot drinks or soup. What I wouldn't give to drink a latte, but that wasn't something I saw in the immediate future for me.

Sally returned a moment later and placed a plate with the rich cake and cream in front of each of us.

We ate in silence for a few moments. Sally was right. The cake was out of this world. My sweet tooth was only slightly less ravenous than Sophia's.

A group of young men and a couple of older guys came in and sat down in the back booth on the opposite wall. Instinctively I moved my left shoulder a little further forward to make sure the wall beside me hid my scars and I let my hair fall forward shielding my face.

I saw Sophia and Tori wave across to them from underneath my lashes.

Curiosity got the better of me and I asked but I couldn't keep the uncertainty or edginess from my voice. "Do you know them?"

Sophia let out a little bit of an annoyed huff. "Sure. It's Sensei Xander, Dane and a few of the other guys from the dojo."

I nodded but said nothing more. Sophia had been a regular at the Onigashima Fighters Dojo for the last couple of years. In fact, she did classes four or five times a week and was quickly moving up the ranks in the various martial arts styles she studied.

"You know you really should come and join us, Edie. You'd have a great time and it would be good for you." Tori suggested. Six months ago Tori had joined Sophia. Although Tori only attended classes a couple of times a week because she had late classes the other nights.

Tori was working in retail during the day and studying to be a beautician another two nights a week. I admired her. Tori had basically left school and immediately found a job in one of the more up market boutiques in the local mall. University wasn't for her. Tori knew what she wanted to do and was out there making it happen.

I needed to do the same.

And I was to a degree. This was the first semester I'd taken a full course of subjects. I'd still had nearly a year of school left to finish when the fire happened. The first year after the fire I did nothing but recover from the burns. I was in and out of hospital so many times it all became a blur. Hospital became home and home was some other place where I hung out occasionally when I wasn't in hospital. My family had moved into another rented house in the same neighbourhood.

It took me another two years to finish school part time at home. Then I managed to do my first year of university part time last year, with minimal actual hours logged on campus. Now I'd taken on a full course load and attended all my lectures and tutorials. I needed to force myself out of my shell—but it's not easy.

"Are you even listening to us?" Sophia demanded.

I snapped back to the conversation. Whoops! I was in my head even worse than normal today. I kept disappearing off into my own thoughts. Being in my own head was a double edged sword; my counsellor and I had decided. It was a safe place for me to retreat to, but it was also an avoidance strategy; one that allowed me to disappear and not engage with the people around me.

"Ah sorry. I have been listening, I guess I'm just a bit distant today."

"Well, get with the program, Edie!" Tori joked at me affectionately.

"Working on it short stuff." Short stuff had always been my nickname for Tori although she was now as tall as me at 5'10. It was just one of those things that stuck.

We were all giggling and I guess my guard was a little down because I suddenly realised we were no longer alone at our table. I dropped my head and tilted my jaw slightly to the right to avoid my scars being seen. Suddenly, the half eaten cake on my plate became very interesting.

"Hey Soph, Tori. How are you girls going?" Whoever he was, he surely had a sexy voice. It seemed to slide over my raw nerves and even soothed them a little. I used my hearing far more than my sight now because I chose to keep my head down. This meant that in a lot of ways my hearing had become my primary sense.

"Umm, just fuelling up before you work me over tonight." I could hear the sheepishness in Sophie's voice.

He laughed then. It was a rich, resonating sound that seemed to tickle over me. My skin was starting to twitch just from hearing him. I couldn't resist. Curiosity was screaming at me to really look at him, but to do that I'd have to show my face. I turned my head slightly hoping to catch a glimpse of him in the shiny metal of the sugar dish without looking up and right at him. But my hair was blocking the view. I longed to flick it back but fear squeezed me from the inside out.

"An occasional treat never hurt anyone. And you're right. I've got a big sparring session planned for tonight. You'll work off whatever you eat," he good naturedly ribbed back.

"Can't wait." Sophie's voice was sarcastic but it was easy to tell she was joking and I'd bet my favourite baggy hoodie that she couldn't wait to get stuck into training.

"You should come along and watch, Edie. I'm going along tonight, too." Tori prompted.

Fear struck through me. I hated the conversation directed to me, particularly when there were strangers involved. I could have cursed Tori. She knew better than to put me on the spot like this. I could just see her smirking face across the table from underneath my lashes as my throat started to constrict.

"You're more than welcome to come along and watch. I encourage people to come along and see for themselves what it's all about." Oh, there was that voice again.

I was torn. I didn't want to look up. I didn't want to see the embarrassment and the man with the beautiful voice looking uncomfortable when he realised what my face looked like.

Surely there was a limit to the torture?

Manners, fear, self-consciousness all warred within me.

The silence around me was deafening. I could tell they were all waiting. I could feel three sets of eyes on me watching and wondering if I was actually going to respond. Finally I took a deep breath. What did it matter if he rejected me? It had happened before, and it would happen again. I could do this. It would hurt, but I was no stranger to pain, both physical and emotional.

Very slowly I raised my chin and turned just slightly towards him. I didn't say anything. I couldn't because my throat was closed in fear and uncertainty.

The first thing I noticed was the dark jeans that hung on narrow hips, then a white T-shirt that emphasised his flat belly and defined pecs. Bravely, I raised my eyes a little higher and the pecs ran into a set of wide shoulders. There was a hint of a tattoo peaking out from under one of his short sleeves. It only made his bicep look more delicious and enticing.

I took one final harsh intake of air and allowed my eyes to complete their journey. They travelled up and up the column of his corded neck to his wide angular jaw.

His full lips were slightly turned up in what looked like a half smile or was it amusement? I could only image how it would look once the shock registered when he saw my face.

Above those lips, that looked far too sensual for any man, was a long straight nose with a hint of a flare to the nostrils. The knot in my stomach tightened even further as I finally tilted my head back far enough so my eyes could meet his.

Every muscle in my body was tensed waiting for the shock, horror and embarrassment I was about to see, once my scars registered with his brain. It was an involuntary reaction I realised. Nobody could hide it, no matter how hard they tried. It was just the shock and surprise. I don't blame them for their reactions, it just hurt that was all.

I raised my eyelids that final few millimetres and forced my eyes to focus on his. Right then and there the world stopped spinning for me. Time halted. My sisters faded into the background and I looked into the eyes of one of the most compelling people I had ever seen. Oh, he was handsome, but he was so much more.

But that was not what had me struck dumb—nope that wasn't it.

It was his eyes—those bottomless pools of black onyx. I did a mental double take. For eyes so dark they should have appeared cold and icy.

But they didn't—they weren't cold at all. They were warm and rich. Right then was the first time I could recall in the last five years, a stranger looking at me with warmth in their eyes. Not shock, not pity, not embarrassment. It was warmth.

The shock paralysed me. I didn't know what to do or how to act. My brain was shorting out. Nothing made sense. Somewhere in the back of my mind I registered my leg being kicked under the table, but even that didn't break through my connection with those eyes. I wanted to swim in them, wrap myself in their warmth and burrow down tight.

I have no idea how much time passed.

Finally, he thrust his hand forward to me and without conscious thought, I placed my hand in his to shake. What happened next shocked me even more.

He lent across the table and pulled me into a loose hug and brushed his lips against my left cheek.

My brain was fried and my nerves were all misfiring. Nothing made sense. I was so far out of my comfort zone.

He pulled back slowly and gave me a smile that I'll remember for the rest of my life.

Then he spoke and his words seemed to swirl around me in a caress.

"Hi Eden. I'm Xander Todd."

Suddenly, I realised I had no box to categorise him into.

TWO

XANDER

When I strolled up to the table seating the Sommers girls, I had two clear intentions in mind. One to be polite and say hello. Sophia and Tori were students of mine and I genuinely liked both girls. They were hard workers, always polite and not full of the drama, which seemed to follow most young women around. I didn't have time for drama in my world. It was a distraction and a waste of energy. I couldn't afford it from a time perspective. My days were busy enough as it was, nor did I have the patience.

I taught between twenty and thirty scheduled classes a week. I also had a roster of about a dozen fighters I was in various stages of mentoring and preparing for fights. That was a big workload; plus I did my own training and I took private lessons on request.

The second thing I wanted to do was meet Eden Sommers. Eden had been an enigma to me since that day I first saw her in the park all those years ago. Something about her and that day had touched me deep in my soul. It was hard to fathom and explain, but what I saw, felt and realised that day would stay with me forever. It was a perfect memory—a moment in time that stood out above all others. It may sound sentimental and stupid to some, but not to me. Over the course of my life, I've had a handful of those moments and I remembered them all as vividly. Every single one had touched me deeply and significantly contributed to the man I am today.

Since that first day, there were many times I could have met Eden Sommers but every time, I'd consciously chosen not to. I don't know why. I knew about the fire and I knew about her burns. It was common knowledge in this part of town. But until now, meeting Eden just hadn't felt right. I'm a firm believer in going with my gut and what feels instinctively right to me. For some reason, that only the universe will know, today felt different. Today was the day.

When I walked in and saw the Sommers girls at the table I knew I had to meet Eden and it had to be today. The feeling intensified the longer I sat over on the other side of the café with Dane and a few of the younger fighters I trained. It finally got to the point where I could no longer sit. When I'd glanced across and saw her making a first rate attempt at being swallowed by the wall and the booth, I had to take action.

I couldn't let the girl I knew to be truly beautiful suffer one moment longer in whatever personal prison she was living in. The memory of that day had provided me with comfort and had given me hope as well as something to strive for in my darkest days; it was my turn to return the favour.

Holding her hand in mine and looking down into her eyes I'd felt a knife twist in my heart. Her incredible denim blue eyes hit me like one of Dane's right hooks. As a professional fighter and an instructor, I've learned to read people through their eyes. Their eyes always give them away.

I've seen the genuine fear of physical pain, anger, frustration, lust and humour—every emotion you could think of. But looking into Eden's eyes, I saw something I'd maybe only seen once or twice before. It was deep emotional fear and pain. Emotions collided and merged into one another, as well as her eyes pleading not to be hurt and rejected. The look in her eyes was so raw and real that I just wanted to sweep her into my arms and protect her from all the horrors she must contend with on a daily basis. I wanted to help her fight and slay every one of the demons that hounded her.

In that split second of realisation, I moved forward and tried to give her a friendly hug. Her body felt stiff and tense. But I anticipated it, and wondered when the last time anyone, other than family, had spontaneously shown her any kindness or affection.

Eden's reaction to me was what I'd expected. She was shocked and shaken up—but, not in a bad way. In fact, I think I almost saw a hint of a smile tickle her mouth. I didn't want to upset her but I knew I needed to nudge her out of her comfort zone.

I introduced myself and waited.

There was one of those awkward pauses. I'm sure Eden was trying to comprehend why I'd hugged her and why I wasn't pulling away. Both Tori and Soph were watching, waiting to see how Eden would react.

After what seemed like an eternity, Eden's soft pink tongue flicked out and wet her lips; then she spoke very quietly.

"Hi, Xander, nice to meet you." It was hardly more than a whisper and her eyes lowered a fraction as she finished her sentence.

Oh yeah, the burn scars were noticeable when she looked directly at you, but they weren't hideous. The skin was kind of red and shiny looking. The way her hair fell covered most of it and I could understand why she carried herself that way and let her hair flop forward all the time. The other side of her face was perfect and maybe that's what made the scars more noticeable?

My fingers itched to pull her hair back and really look at the scars. Was that wrong? I don't know. That's just what I wanted to do.

"Come on, Edie, please say you'll come." It was Tori almost pleading with her sister.

Eden dropped her chin and sat further back against the bench.

She was retreating, moving to protect herself from something that she couldn't control or she felt threatened by.

I wanted to reassure her that if she came along it would be fine.

"It's a very low key, no pressure sort of night. These guys won't even know you're there, with how busy I'll have them." I turned my attention to Tori and Soph. They both groaned good-naturedly in unison. "What's the point of training if you don't go hard?"

"Can I get back to you on that?" Sophia joked back at me, with a cringe. I could feel Eden's eyes on the side of my face. I purposely didn't look back towards her just yet. I wanted her to feel comfortable, to see that I wasn't a person to be afraid of, even though I knew most people thought I was one scary dude.

"Sure. You won't change my mind though." I knew just how much Sophia like to train hard so I bought into her humour.

"Yeah, I know. I also know better than to protest too much or my work load will increase exponentially."

"Who said you weren't a smart girl?" We all laughed at that. I think even Eden managed a small chuckle. I needed to wrap this up and head back to the boys before I stepped into that awkward amount of time that turns from saying hello and being polite to lingering like a bad smell. "Okay ladies, I'll leave you to finish." I turned to look directly at Eden and caught her quietly checking me out. "Great meeting you, Eden. I really hope you can make it tonight or any other time you might want to come along. Door's always open and the invitation doesn't expire."

I tried to push as much warmth and openness into my eyes and expression. Just like you would when you're trying to coax a small child or pet into doing something. Eden may be all grown up but after what had happened it was obvious to me; she was well and truly back to square one with meeting new challenges.

"Thank you," she said in a voice that was not much more than a whisper again and I actually wondered if the burns had affected her voice.

"You're welcome, Eden. Your sisters talk about you all the time. I'm sure they'd love it if you came along and saw what they get up to."

She nodded slightly and I could see her really thinking it over. That gave me hope. I may not win this battle but I'd at least have a shot at winning the war. I was a guy that could work with the long term.

I threw the Sommers sisters a "Catch you later, girls," and headed back over to the booth my crew was lounging in.

As I slid up into the bench seat, Dane looked over and rose an eyebrow at me. He didn't need to speak. I already knew he was wondering what I was up to. Problem was, I didn't really know at this stage, either. I just knew I had to try and reach Eden; pull her out of her shell a little—I wanted to see the beautiful girl smile again without the shadows in her eyes.

I wanted her to feel the innocent pleasure that she felt that day when she was laughing with her sisters, just living life.

"Why didn't you ask the girls over?" Micah asked. He was a cocky young fighter that had joined my squad a few months ago when he moved here. I liked the kid, but he still had a lot to learn and manners were one of those things. When he asked why I hadn't asked the girls over, really what he wanted to know was, why hadn't I brought them over for him to flirt with.

"They've got their sister with them."

"So? She looks like a real hottie." And that was part of the problem. From the left side Eden looked absolutely normal. Drop dead gorgeous actually. It was only head on or from the right with her hair back, that anyone would notice. "More the merrier, I say." He nudged his shoulder into Owen trying to get him to join in. Owen glanced at me, looking for my lead. Owen was a local and knew the story of Eden. Everyone here did except Micah. Most people I knew were respectful of Eden and left her to her business.

Conversation at the table had stopped and all the guys were looking to me. That's when Micah realised something was amiss.

"What?"

"That's Eden, Sophia and Tori's older sister. They're having a quiet afternoon together; they don't need you breathing down their necks, Micah."

"Well, why can't they have a quiet afternoon over here with us?" I watched the rest of the table almost groan as Micah carried on with it.

"Just tell him, mate. He's not going to let this go until you explain." Dane sounded frustrated and a little pissed at Micah. Micah was definitely the tenacious type and it served him well in a fight but, by God, it could be a pain in the arse at times.

It wasn't really my story to tell, so that in itself made me feel a little uncomfortable about discussing it.

"Eden has some scars on her face. She was in a fire a few years back. Now she doesn't socialise much. She seems to prefer to keep to herself or just hang with her sisters."

Micah looked shocked and the first thing he did was turn his head to stare at her.

"For fuck's sake, mate. Don't stare." Dane beat me to it, and it came out quite a bit harsher from him than it probably would have from me. Dane had a short fuse at the best of times and Micah often pushed Dane's buttons.

He looked back to me. "But she looks normal."

"She is normal. She just has some scars down the right side of her face." Now that the topic was on the table, I decided now was as good a time as any. "I invited Eden to come and check out what we do. Hopefully she'll take up my invitation. So spread the word through the guys I don't want her to feel uncomfortable. Nobody stares, everybody treats her absolutely normal. Anyone does something to upset her and they'll answer to me. Got it?"

There were nods all round the table and I knew the guys were surprised, but they wouldn't challenge my word or go against my direct instructions. That was one thing I demanded at the dojo—respect. Respect for me, the arts we studied, themselves and their fellow peers.

"Can I ask what your deal is with her?" This time it was

Lincoln. Linc was a quiet one. He didn't say much. Only when he had something to say, or when he wanted to know something. I could appreciate that, but that didn't stop me from feeling a little defensive at being questioned. At this stage I wasn't exactly sure what my "deal" was. I was very much "playing it by ear".

"I'm not intending anything at this stage. I just want her to feel comfortable enough to come along and watch her sisters. Everyone understand?"

I pinned them all with a solid stare. Yeah, they got the message.

I took a deep breath and finished the rest of my black coffee in two big gulps and threw some cash on the table to cover things

"Right. I'm out of here. I've got some stuff to do before class. See you then and bring you're "A" game boys."

They all nodded and Dane got up and followed me out.

He said nothing until we were out on the street. "Want to tell me what the real story is 'Pretty Boy'?"

"Nope." I opened the door to my truck and glared at Dane as he got in the passenger side.

An amused smile broke out across his face. "How come?"

"Because I don't know what it is, yet. I just know I need to see if I can help her."

I glanced over at Dane as I pulled out into the traffic.

"She another one of your projects?" It was a fair enough question. I was known to help out with "strays" and others I felt could use a leg-up. I was fortunate enough to have had a few people help me out along the way. I was just returning the favour. Well, at least, that's the way I saw it.

"Not exactly. She needs to decide she wants help first."

"True." Dane had a knowing smirk on his face. "But we both know you'll work real hard to convince her. Won't you, Pretty Boy?"

This time I grinned and chuckled. My best friend knew me too well and I struggled to stay pissed at him. "Probably."

EDEN

I was still shocked as Sophia dropped me a few streets over at my therapist's appointment. Ever since the fire I'd had therapy, counselling, and shrink sessions. Whatever you wanted to call it. It was all part of the healing process, apparently. Now I only went every couple of weeks and the nature of the sessions had changed.

The sessions were now more about setting goals for me to "join the world" again. It was about setting small steps, to try and get me to where a normal twenty-three year old woman would be. Sounded good right? The only problem with that, was the fact I'd never be normal.

I walked up the stairs and Grace, my counsellor, met me in the reception area. She guided me through into her office and I took up my familiar position on the navy blue sofa. As sofas went it was comfortable, but the room never really felt "comfortable". Sure I liked Grace; she was a good counsellor and I should know. I've had a dozen or more that I could remember over the various stages of my recovery.

"How are you today, Eden?" Grace poured some water from the crystal pitcher sitting on the low table between the sofa and the single overstuffed chair she sat in.

I raised my chin a little. Grace knew how I looked and she never made me feel uncomfortable. I was safe here with her. Or, at least, that's what I kept trying to tell myself. It was really only in the last twelve months or so that I'd been making a real effort to get my life sorted. You don't recover from burns quickly, physically or emotionally. For the first year I was struggling just to get my health back to some level of "normal". Then I had to finish the last year of school, which took me two years by correspondence. My life was very much about small steps.

"I'm doing okay," I said non-committally. I was actually completed freaked out by what had happened at the café with Xander, but I wasn't sure I was ready to talk about it yet.

She smiled at me with a little humour. “Just okay?”

“Well, probably better than okay or compared to how I have been,” I admitted.

“So tell me about what you’ve been up to the last couple of weeks.” This was actually code for “Have you met your challenges?”

“Umm...I’ve been at uni every scheduled day.” And it was true. I hated every second of it. Not the going to school bit and learning. That I loved. It was the having to leave the house and interact with others that I dreaded and deplored.

“Great and how did you feel about it?” I knew the answer Grace was looking for. It was the one they all wanted. Life was great and I was finding it easier blah, blah, blah. Only problem was it never felt like it got easier. I wasn’t big on sugar coating it for shrinks so I went with honesty. I was to the point where I didn’t care if they saw my attitude coming through. Wasn’t this the place where I could be honest?

“I hated it, but I did it.”

She nodded and I saw a hint of disappointment skid across her face before she reverted back to the neutral expression that shrinks were so good at projecting.

“Well, that’s something. Now that you’re managing to at least turn up to school, why don’t we aim to try and make the whole experience a little more enjoyable.”

I laughed a little sarcastically.

“Yeah, I love uni. It’s just the other five thousand people that are there with me at any one time that I hate,” I corrected her. I’d become quite cutting and cynical at times since the fire. Apparently experiences shape your personality and outlook. Well I seemed to have no trouble being “normal” around people I felt comfortable with. It was just everyone else I baulked at and let walk all over me. It was a burr in my side and I hated that I was weak.

“Well, if you’re going to go down that path, let’s be specific. You don’t hate them you just hate the possibility that they’re going to make you feel uncomfortable."

Grace was right. That's exactly how I felt and I was working on it. But it was still hard.

"Yes, you're correct."

She smiled and nodded. "And while we're being honest, it is getting easier, right?"

I nodded annoyed that she was correct even if it was progress. "Yes, you are correct again."

This time her smile had more warmth and she raised her eyebrows at me. Unfortunately, Grace was seasoned at this and knew all the games I played.

"So how did you go with the other aspects of the challenges we agreed? Where was the new place you went?"

"I went to the hairdressers for the first time since the fire. I'm not sure it counts though because I went to Cheryl, my mum's friend's salon, and it was late in the afternoon. There was only one other client there at the time."

Grace looked at me thinking over what I'd disclosed.

"Did you plan to go, organise how you were going to get there, get your hair cut and manage to get home by yourself?"

"Yeah, I did all of those things."

"Then it counts. Sure you might have known Cheryl but the setting was different and you had to make an effort and move out of your comfort zone. It may seem little, but it was a challenge."

"I know but it just seems so stupid. Going to uni is so much more than that. Why can't I just get over it and move on?"

Grace shrugged a little and smiled. I knew what was coming.

"Only you can dictate the pace of how quickly you feel comfortable. Although you may not like it, the physical structure and the process of getting to and from uni is now almost a habit for you. New places and experiences represent new challenges."

I tried to process what she was saying.

"I actually suspect the process of having your haircut was more the issue, than where it was done. How many times have you had your hair trimmed since the fire? And before you start dwelling on it in your head, why don't you tell me about it? It's not something we've talked about before. I'd like to know"

It was uncanny how well Grace seemed to know me sometimes. Yes, I had been about to start "dwelling" on it as she put, it but I guess that was her job. To get me talking about things I didn't want to talk about. I took a deep breath, as the hollow feeling in my guts returned with vengeance. Once again I could smell the odour of my burnt flesh and hair like it had just happened.

"When I woke up from the induced coma I'd been put into I realised my hair had all been cut off. It was singed and matted beyond saving. The doctors had also needed to get access to the burns, so my hair had to go. I was fortunate that it all grew back evenly except for one little spot just in front of my ear." I did something I never did. I pulled my hair back from the right side of my face to show her the spot where hair didn't grow anymore. I also noticed her scribbling on her note pad. I'd said something that she wanted to bring up later. I hated when that happened. Sometimes I'd just slip or say one word and she'd be digging and probing at me.

Grace motioned for me to continue. "So it took ages for it to grow out because they kept shaving it away for the first year. Then Cheryl trimmed it about two years after that to even it up. Last week was the next time."

She looked at me and I knew what she wanted. Grace wanted to know how I felt about it. We'd got to the point where she didn't even need to say the words now—a look would do it.

"I guess I felt in two minds about it. My hair really needed a trim to get rid of the dead ends and to tidy it up. But it's also my shield and I don't like removing any part of it for fear of weakening it or it not covering up as much."

"Before the fire, would you have let your hair get to that state before you trimmed it?"

I laughed. Before the fire my hair was perfect. It was long, thick and the most glorious strawberry blonde colour. In fact, my agent had already lined up a shampoo commercial. Now it was my shield not a damned fashion accessory.

"What's so funny?"

"My hair was always perfect. So perfect, they wanted to do a shampoo commercial with it." My voice sounded bitter even to my ears. Like normal, Grace didn't react just pressed on.

"So why can't your hair be perfect like that again?"

"Because I have a patch missing. The hair won't grow there," I spat out, really annoyed now. Hadn't I just shown her that patch? Wasn't it obvious?

"So that's what's stopping you from having perfect hair?"

"Yes."

"Well, as a woman to a woman, I'd gladly have your thick mane even minus that little dollar sized patch of hair rather than this fine ratty excuse for hair I've got. You mentioned before that you're fortunate to just have that small patch that doesn't grow hair. You're right, you are fortunate that your hair is still glorious and I'm glad you've recognised that everything isn't diabolically terrible."

Ah, so she'd picked up on the word 'fortunate'. That must have been what she'd scribbled down a few moments ago. Fortunate, wasn't something I really thought very often. But Grace was right. It could have been worse. I had a friend Ellie who I'd met in hospital and she'd lost nearly all her hair. She had to wear wigs all the time now.

Yeah I guess I did have one or two things to be thankful for. It was just hard remembering to feel that way. Feeling miserable and down at the world was often a much easier proposition.

I looked over at Grace, feeling a little sheepish. Grace wasn't your average type of shrink. She pushed back and hard at times. Grace made me face my fears and I both loved and hated her for it. At this point in my journey, she was exactly what I needed to push me ahead.

I looked at Grace a little resigned, "And you're right about something else, too."

"What's that?"

"Your hair does suck." She burst out laughing and clapped her hands together, obviously agreeing with me whole-heartedly. Her hair was fine and ratty, now that I really looked. I'd just never bothered. I guess I got so engrossed in my own issues, I often forgot to look at what was right in front of me.

"Oh Eden, the world really does deserve to see your sense of humour and wit."

I grinned slightly. "Yeah, it's just my face that looks like a half chewed Mintie they could do without." I'd meant it as a joke; but there was a level of bitterness and sarcasm that I just couldn't keep out of my voice, no matter how much I tried.

"Eden, we've talked about this before. The first step in having others accept you, is to accept yourself."

And that was the sort of psychobabble claptrap that just pissed me off. Easy to say when it wasn't your face looking back at you in the mirror.

I stiffened my shoulders and turned my head away. It was the equivalent of a recalcitrant child acting out, but I didn't care. That's how I felt. These sessions always made me feel a whole spectrum of emotions and I didn't enjoy that. I much preferred to try and keep my feelings on an even keel.

There was an awkward pause before Grace went on. She'd come back to this topic at some stage. I wouldn't get away with it that easy.

"What about the third part of your challenges? Who was the new person you met?" My mind raced, I hadn't really met anyone except him. But it was something that was precious and mine. I wasn't sure if I wanted to share it. I felt possessive of that memory, that experience. Xander represented so many things that I'd shied away from.

I was contemplating that a little more when Grace pushed me again. "Surely, you must have met someone new in your travels at university?"

Nope, I hadn't. Other than Xander. I don't think the girl who said sorry as she bumped into me in the bathroom counted. She hadn't even looked at me as she careened through the door.

Maybe I could get out of it yet. "I didn't really seek anyone out but I had someone come up to introduce himself to me." Surely that wouldn't count, but at least sounded like I'd completed the challenge.

"Okay, tell me about that. Something interesting happened. I've never seen you fidget so much. I want to know why."

My throat suddenly felt all closed up, just as it had felt when I woke from the coma. My palms were sweating as I opened and closed my fingers and I felt like a silly school girl.

Grace raised her eyebrows at me—a hint to get a move on.

"Umm, just before when I was having afternoon tea with my sisters." Afternoon tea sounded so formal, but I couldn't really say coffee could I? "A guy they know came and introduced himself." That was the truth.

"That sounds very...routine. Now tell me what really happened." It was then I decided that Grace would have been brilliant at prisoner interrogation, because that's kind of how I felt. But another part of me wanted to gush about how this really hot guy had come up to me, just like any other girl my age would do. The only problem with that, was there was no way a hot guy would be interested in me.

I glanced over at Grace and she had that look on her face that said she wasn't going to let it go. Her mouth kind of drew into a straight line and I could see tenacious written all over her face. "We were having afternoon tea as I said; both of my sisters do martial arts. We'd been there at the café a few minutes and their instructor came up to say hello to them. Then he said hello to me..." I paused trying to decide how far I was going to disclose. I closed my eyes for a long moment and ploughed on "and he took my hand and hugged me."

I opened my eyes in time to see the surprise on Grace's face and the little knowing smile twitching at the side of her mouth. "So tell me about this guy. What about him has made you so uncomfortable in sharing?"

"Who says I'm uncomfortable?" Grace gave me a look that said "Please!"

"There was something different about it him. I want you to explain to me what it was."

And yet again I wished my private thoughts could be exactly that—private. Oh I knew logically that this process was supposed to be good for me, but knowing logic and feeling it were two very different things. I knew that better than most.

"He didn't react to my scars...In fact, he didn't even acknowledge them or say anything. I guess he treated me like a normal person." Grace nodded at me, encouraging me to continue. "I even managed to look him in the eye and he didn't look embarrassed, nor did he seem to pity me. He even invited me to come over to the dojo to watch a session whenever—he sounded genuine."

Grace just gave me a knowing smile and prompted me again. "That's great, now tell me about how you felt when he took your hand and gave you a hug."

"I wasn't expecting it. When he looked at me, he just reached out and took my hand. Then he leant forward and hugged me as if it was the most normal thing to do. I guess maybe that's just him." I was still trying to reconcile his actions in my mind.

"Maybe, but Eden this just proves what we've been working on. Not everyone is going to reject you or be embarrassed or make you feel uncomfortable. However, you're never going to accept or realise that unless you give people the chance. Sure you might get an unwanted reaction from nine out of ten but what about the tenth person? Aren't they worth getting to know?"

I thought about that a little. Would I like to get to know Xander? "But what if he was just being polite because I'm the sister of his students?"

"That could be the case but what if he turns out to be something more—a friend, who knows? Every relationship, regardless of the context, starts out with an introduction of some sort. Then the parties take it from there. So are you going to go down to the dojo? That sounds like an excellent series of challenges for your next couple of weeks."

Grace was clearly pleased with the way this meeting potentially opened up new challenges. I wasn't at all sure I was comfortable or on board with it. She glanced at her watch.

"Look, we're almost out of time. How about this? I want you to go down to that dojo and watch a session. I also want you to initiate a conversation with this man and I want you to introduce yourself to another two people there."

I swallowed hard as her challenges swam in my head. That was a lot to take in. "Umm, I'm not sure I feel comfortable...."

"Of course you don't. That's exactly why you're going to do this. Come on, Eden. I know you can do this, but what's more important—I know you want to do this."

Now Grace was a mind reader.

Yes, I wanted to, but that didn't stop me from being close to terrified at the thought or the possibility.

Oh hell, what was the worst that could happen to me? Words and looks. Nothing I hadn't seen before, right.

"Okay I'll do it."

THREE

EDEN

I breathed a sigh of relief as I placed the last dish on the table. Somehow, I'd just managed to get dinner on the table as Tori and Sophia came barrelling through in a great rush. I had to hurry from my appointment with Grace to get home. It was all up to me at the moment. Dad worked as an interstate truck driver. If we were lucky we'd see him for a few hours on the weekend, but it wasn't unusual for him to be gone for weeks, particularly if he was doing a series of runs to Perth or something like that.

Mum had taken a few months' long service leave and was down on the Central Coast with our grandma who'd fallen and broken a hip. Soph and Tori were adults, but I'd gotten into the habit of looking out for them over the years because dad was always away and mum often worked the late shift in the hospital kitchen. They tended to handle more of the chores away from the house; so I'd fallen into the habit of doing the bulk of the ones around the house because that suited me best.

"Geez Tor, you know we can't be late. Sensei will kick our arses. I can't believe how you always seem to get caught with Mel. What can you two possibly gossip about for that long?" Sophia sounded totally pissed off as she stormed through the house, and I caught a glimpse of her stripping off clothes as she went.

"We weren't gossiping. We were closing up the boutique. You know the rules. Two staff members for close," Tori argued back. She was right on Soph's heels and stripping off clothes as well.

"Yeah, I get it. But it's always you and you're always late."

"I can't help it if we have a late customer and close is part of my job description."

Their voices became a little more difficult to hear as they continued to argue all the way down to the bedroom they shared at the back of the house.

After the fire my family had initially moved into emergency accommodation until they found this house. All of this I realised much later. Those first couple of months were really a blur, except for the day I woke up. Even now I do my best to stop my mind from going there.

This house was smaller than the previous one that had burned down, but at least it was sturdier and better maintained by the landlord. Plus it was only a couple of streets over from where we were before. So everything was familiar location wise.

It still took me almost a year to feel comfortable here. For the first several months after the fire I lived in the hospital. Then, I was in and out for weeks at a time as they did all sorts of grafts and other operations to repair my skin the best they could.

I filled glasses with water from the jug in the fridge and sat down. A few seconds later Sophia and Tori appeared. They both quickly surveyed what I'd prepared; then grabbed slices of bread and slapped the cold meat, and salad I'd laid out between them.

They didn't even take the time to sit. Both of them were hoovering down the food and finally looked at me as I placed dainty spoonfuls of coleslaw and potato salad on my plate.

"Just make a sambo. We haven't got time for you to eat a sit down meal," Sophia ordered me in an exasperated voice. She slapped together another sandwich, which I gathered she was going to eat on the way.

"Come on. Edie. You need to hurry," Tori urged, downing food and slapping together another one.

They were just expecting me to go with them. We hadn't talked about it. They'd just assumed and, if I was being fair, it was probably a reasonable assumption. I hadn't exactly said no. But I certainly hadn't said yes.

And the war within me notched up another level.

I'd been fretting over going with them ever since Xander had suggested it earlier this afternoon.

I really wanted to go. I wanted to see what they did, what made them so excited and keen to go back for multiple sessions each week.

I did.

But there was a huge part of me that didn't. I didn't feel comfortable around people my own age. I found them to be far more judgemental then older people. I also didn't feel very comfortable around men. So many times I've watched guys see the left side of my face and make a bee-line for me only to almost shriek away in horror when they see the scars down the right side of my face. You'd think it was something that I'd have gotten used to by now.

No! Hell No!

No one wants to be the ugly girl. The freak.

No girl wants to have guys retreat away from her after making a snap judgment based solely on appearance.

They both looked at me expectantly, mouths chewing. I glanced between them, then stared at my own plate.

"Umm, I'm not going. I have a paper to finish." It was true. I did have a paper to finish. I'd already drafted it. I was at the polishing it stage and I just wanted to make sure it was as perfect as I could make it before I handed it in.

Sophia let out an unladylike snort. "Told you, Tor. I knew it. There was no way she was going to go." With that Sophia spun on her heel and headed from the kitchen, her long braid swishing angrily from side to side.

Tori just looked at me with those big blue eyes of hers pleading. I almost caved...I really did but...

"Come on, Tor," Sophia yelled from the front door.

"Next time, Edie." Tori's voice was barely more than a whisper and I could see, hear and feel the pain this caused her and I felt another wave of guilt wash over me as tears pricked the backs of my eyes.

Fortunately, she turned and hurried off before the first one fell down my cheek. My throat felt dry and scratchy and the plates of food in front me blurred as the tears started to block my vision.

I hated so many things about my life but I couldn't seem to find the door to leave them all behind me. The walls seemed to be closing in around me. I hopped up and ran to my room and threw myself on the bed. The mattress was one of those soft spongy ones and it seemed to swallow me whole and a big part of me wished it was the universe and not just the mattress that swallowed me whole. It wouldn't be the first time I'd wondered if it would have been easier if I hadn't managed to fight my way through the flames.

XANDER

I stood behind the front desk of my dojo, Onigashima, and watched my students file in. It was something that I always got a real kick out of, and a sense of satisfaction. When my fight career had come to an end, I opened the dojo. I needed something to do for the long haul and martial arts was about all I knew. Fortunately, it was also something I loved. It had became such an integral part of me over the years, it seemed like the most natural thing for me to do was to teach it and coach fighters.

Sure, I could have gone back to school and continued my education, but that didn't feel right nor did I have a clue what I would have studied. I did the only thing that made sense to me, and felt comfortable—Onigashima was it.

"Evening, Sensei," my students said to me as they nodded when they came through the front doors. They brought their arms up and across their chests in the bow of respect that I demanded.

"Evening Josh, Cassie." They both headed left through to the main room off reception that hosted the mat and thousands of dollars of floor to ceiling mirrors.

I looked over some paperwork and shuffled a few things around the reception desk, feeling restless and agitated. Would she show? This question kept running through my mind. My belly felt as if it was drawn tight with anticipation, and my head was screaming at me to stop being so damned ridiculous and act cool. For crying out loud, I was the head of this school and I trained a bunch of the most bad arse fighters going around.

We weren't called the Oni Fighters for nothing. Demons is exactly what we were. It perfectly described how we trained, fought and approached everything.

I moved over to grab my water bottle and downed a few mouthfuls, anything to keep my hands busy. Right then, I decided I was going to make tonight's session even more physical. I needed to let off some steam. Dane and I would go a few rounds. Show off some techniques. The release would feel good.

A few more students came in and headed through to the mats. I glanced up and checked the clock for what seemed to be the hundredth time in the last ten minutes—ten to seven.

They'd be here any second. The girls were never late and always left themselves a couple of minutes at least to prepare before class started.

I looked out into the darkness and as if on command, Sophia and then Tori appeared from the shadows cast by the yellowy lights in the car park. It was well lit but this was hardly a good area by anyone's standards, however, having a dojo around seemed to have reduced the crime and incidents in this street at least. At least that's what the local business owners had been telling me.

I looked past them hoping to see Eden's silhouette emerge as well and the tightness in my stomach turned to disappointment.

She wasn't coming.

My brain immediately jumped to "Maybe she'd be along later?" I struggled to understand just how this was happening.

Sophia strode in full of confidence and popped a polished bow, with Tori following suit right behind her.

"Evening, Sensei," they both said, almost in unison.

"Evening, ladies." They went to move off but before they'd even taken a step my mouth opened and the words were falling out. "Eden not joining us?"

Sophia spun around and had a disappointed look on her face. "Not tonight. We tried, we really did but she has some assignment due or something."

We both knew it was a cop out. I nodded in understanding and the girls hurried away to prepare for tonight's session.

Over the next few minutes a few more students passed on their way to class. At a couple of minutes to seven, I slipped the heavy fabric of the gi jacket over my singlet top and grabbed my black belt that was heavily embroided with Japanese symbols and stripes indicating my rank. Without even thinking about it, I tied the belt in a perfect knot, both ends sitting dead level. I stepped out from behind the reception desk and shifted my mind into class mode. The exercise would definitely feel good.

An hour and a half later I had worked my students hard and they were beginning to file out looking hot and tired. Most were taking long pulls from their water bottles as they bowed and exited the doors.

Finally, Tori and Sophia made their way to the reception area chatting to Cassie as they went.

They were about to bow and head out when I did it again.

"Have you got a moment, Sophia?"

She let the heavy duffle bag, carrying her equipment, slide to the ground and she stepped forward towards the desk.

Tori looked between us briefly. “I’ll meet you at the car,” she said, then bowed and headed out with Cassie.

Sophia stood there with expectation on her face but said nothing. Even though class was finished my stature as head of the school remained in place and was respected to the letter, particularly by the lower level students. Sophia was making rapid progress but she’d not made it to brown belt yet.

“I wanted to talk to you about Eden.” I saw the surprise in her face, it was definitely not what she’d been expecting.

“Oh?”

It seemed surreal to me that I’d even started this conversation. What was I thinking?

“I was thinking Eden might like to attend the grading and BBQ afterwards this Sunday. You mentioned earlier that your parents are both away and I was thinking you might like to have some family there for the presentations.” It sounded lame to my ears. Sophia and Tori were both adults so they hardly needed family there. After all, they had each other there. But I couldn’t seem to help myself, so I said it firmly and used every ounce of my standing as the Sensei and pushed it through.

Sophia shifted her weight from foot to foot looking uncertain. “Umm... that’s a really nice idea but I’m not sure she’ll come. You probably guessed—she doesn’t do crowds.”

“I figured that, but surely she needs to get out occasionally?”

Sophia shrugged. “You won’t get any argument from me on that, but Eden doesn’t do anything until she’s good and ready. At the moment the extent of that is going to university. ”

I took a couple of things from what Sophia said. First, she was probably more than a little frustrated with Eden’s progress towards migrating back into society. The other, was that Eden could obviously be strong minded and hard to shift.

“I figured as much. I guess it can’t be easy for her?”

“No, it’s not but she is getting better.” I could tell that Sophia was wary talking to me about Eden and that was understandable. After all, I knew both Sophia and Tori in the capacity of their

Sensei and now I was suddenly asking about their sister.

"Well, I just thought she might enjoy coming along and she could be there to support you both in your grading." God! I was sure I sounded like a sap,

Sophia nodded. "I'll mention it to her."

"You do that. Goodnight, Sophia."

"Night, Sensei." She bowed again, grabbed her bag and disappeared out the door.

I picked up a rubber band and started to flick it between my fingers thinking over what had just been said.

"You've got it bad, mate." I spun around and there was Dane lounging against the door frame that connected my office to the reception area. He'd come in through the other door in my office and I hadn't even realised he'd approached because I was so deep in my head. Dane, being Dane, didn't miss the fact I'd not realised he'd approached.

I said nothing to avoid giving myself away, but I had known that thoughtful look on Dane's face for too long. He saw right through me.

"Nothing, hey?"

I glared at him and he did exactly as I expected. He laughed at me.

"Haven't you got a class to teach?" I reminded him between gritted teeth.

"Yes, Sensei. I do" He was mocking the hell out of me. Dane was only one belt below me and had been my best friend for what seemed like forever. We saw ourselves as equals even if our belts said differently. Dane was a fighter, too, but unlike me he had a few other interests outside the dojo. One of those being a small service station that he'd inherited from his grandfather a couple of years ago. He'd also started an online business selling martial arts equipment.

He fancied himself as a bit of an entrepreneur and truth be told he wasn't doing too badly for himself at all. His desire and success in the ring was coming to him later, unlike me who had been thrust into the professional ranks when I was barely more than twenty.

Still he didn't move, and it was really beginning to piss me off.

"Well? Am I missing something here?"

His mouth twitched. "Rohan's running them through warm-up. I've got a couple of minutes. Ready to tell me what's going on with you yet?"

No, I fucking wasn't ready. God, he could be a pain in my arse! I'd tolerate it from no one else but him.

"Fancy a piece of her, do you?"

My temper flared instantaneously. I didn't like him referring to Eden like that. Let alone thinking that. It was a straightforward enough question and one we'd asked each other many times, but somehow this was different. Eden was different. I wanted to get to know her. I didn't want to fuck her. Well, at least, I didn't think I did. It wasn't like that. It never had been.

"Now's not the time or place," I gritted out.

"Okay, then. You let me know when."

"There's nothing to tell," I protested trying to convince myself as much as him.

He just smiled and nodded. "Keep trying to convince yourself of that." Dane raised his hand in mock salute and headed off to teach his class.

I sat down and tried to make a start on the emails that had rolled in today. Anything to try to stop my mind drifting to Eden Sommers. I feared the chances of that were about a snowball's in hell.

EDEN

Eventually the tears dried up, just like they always did, and I lay there half swallowed by my bed—numb. I tried not to think about anything,—just being in the moment.

My flight to nowhere was rudely interrupted a couple of minutes later by the dinging of the messaging program on my computer. I let it go, three times, then four. After the fifth time I dragged my sorry butt off the bed and slumped myself in the chair in front of my whitewashed desk.

I loved my room.

The walls were the softest shade of mint green and all the trim was a glossy white. The bedframe, nightstand and the desk matched. Dad had helped me paint, sand and distress the cheap pine furniture until it resembled the beautiful pieces that were before me now. The quilt on the bed was white and had almost an old world look to it. I'd piled a mountain of cushions in various shades of green and textures on the bed. I loved cushions. They were my thing. The lamp siting on my nightstand was my absolute favourite. The mirrored base and dangling crystals gave the room a bit of glamour and added to the old world feel created by the quilt.

I loved decorating and making things look beautiful—in fact I'd considered going into interior design when I realised modelling was no longer an option for me. The idea lasted about a whole ten seconds, just until I realised that people would hardly take a disfigured designer seriously. Nor, could I see myself being comfortable in their beautiful homes. Nope accounting and technology would just have to do it for me.

The messaging program dinged again angrily and I typed in my password and the screen came to life. I smiled a little to myself as I realised who was pinging me.

It was Bethany.

We'd met briefly in hospital and immediately become friends—only now we continued it in the cyber world. Beth lived ten hours from me.

I quickly scanned through her messages and focused on the last one.

Beth: Get you backside to the computer Eden. I know you're there. It's after seven and you're always online at night.

I quickly typed out my response.

Me: Sorry Beth, just taking a shower.

It was a blatant lie but better than saying I'd been crying.

Beth: I'll let you off just this once. Can't have you stinking up the place! Geez I could almost smell you from here.

Me: Very true, even my sisters were starting to complain.

Beth: How was the shrinkfest?

I paused, fingers hovering over the keyboard.

How much did I want to tell her? I opened and closed my fists as I debated. Beth really got where I was coming from. She understood me like no one else. She might not have burn scars, but she had her own issues. Beth had lost a leg in a motor vehicle accident. She got what it was like to be different, be stared at. To feel like you never really belonged.

Me: It was okay. Well, yes and no. You see I had something weird happen to me today and then I got myself cornered by Grace and I blurted it out and now she's using it to push me....and I'm so confused and I have no idea what to do...and now I'm rambling and... and....ahhhhhh!!!!

I didn't realise it but while I was furiously typing I'd leaned forward, racing to get it all out. I let out the breath I'd been holding and sat back watching the little curser flash as Beth typed her response. I only had to wait a couple of seconds.

Beth: WTF happened? I want the dets....NOW!

There was no way I could hold back the smile that curled up my lip. Beth would be beside herself wondering what had happened. She was the excitable type! Then suddenly, I found myself anxious to tell her all about it. I took the next couple of minutes to tell her all about meeting Xander and my subsequent "Shrinkfest" session.

I hit the 'enter' key and jumped up from my desk, suddenly feeling thirsty. Well that's what I told myself, but actually I was just restless and anxious—keen to know what Beth was going to say but nervous at the same time.

The kitchen was just the way I'd left it and I hurriedly put covers on dishes and rinsed plates and packed the dishwasher. That was the real bonus of "preparing" rather than "cooking"—clean up was a cinch. I grabbed a diet coke from the fridge and almost bolted back to my bedroom. I caught myself just as I went to go through the door. I was twenty-three, not twelve, after all. I paused, positioned my spine into my best "model strut" and glided the five steps across my room to the chair which I slid into with a graciousness that would make any deportment queen happy.

The message was flashing at me and I dived into the conversation once again.

Beth: OMG! Why the fuck are you here and not there? A hot guy asks you to his dojo and you're sitting here moping—have you lost your mind? (Don't try telling me you're not moping Eden—I know you too well.) Get off your gorgeous butt and get in there! Be gone with you!

I couldn't contain the laugh that rattled around in my chest when I read this. It really was a LOL moment. Beth was a kook, but she was my kook and I loved her for it. I glanced at my watch. It was just after eight-thirty and I knew the girls would be finishing up. I'd dodged a bullet for tonight, and I felt both relieved and also disappointed. A big part of me wanted to go.

Me: Too late. It's done for the night.

Beth: Well that's convenient...When are they training next?

Me: Next Tuesday.

Beth: Right, so I'm making a note right now to ping you at 9:00pm next Tuesday night. I want to know what happens...I'm living vicariously through you! Shit, you know there's not a living breathing male in fifty miles of here other than family or employees, of course! You're it Eden—you need to do this.

That was actually the truth. Beth lived on a cattle property in western Queensland. It literally was miles from nowhere. It was also the truth that she'd ping me Tuesday night. Beth was incredibly organised and punctual. I'd probably talk to her a dozen times before then but she was putting it out there, pushing me into it. She also knew I wouldn't let her down. There was some strange unwritten bond. A sisterhood/brotherhood between survivors. It was okay to let down "normal people" but you didn't let down one of your own—no matter how much it hurt. That was just poor form.

I heard the front door slam then a few seconds later the shower started up in the bathroom—the girls were home.

Me: Okay I'll do it.

There I'd finally agreed. Committed. I'd actually taken it a step further. I'd typed it out and sent it. Committed that notation, a promise to cyberspace for an eternity. There was no taking it back now. Everything on the web lasted forever, even if we thought it didn't. Cybersecurity 101. God, the first technology security course had been dull!

Beth: Oooooo so excited...can't wait to hear what happens. I want pics!

Me: Jesus woman! I'm only going to go along and sit. He was just being polite, don't make this into more than it really is.

Then something occurred to me and my fingers furiously struck the keys.

Me: Are you on another romance novel bender?

Beth: Hahaha...but of course! When have you known me ever not to have a romance novel close to hand? Girl's got to dream...

When we'd been in hospital together, Beth seemed to constantly have her eyes glued to her Kindle app. Devouring romance novels at the rate of one, two or even three a day. I didn't mind reading but I preferred Sci-fi and comics to romance. I guess I shied away from something that was never going to be part of my life.

Me: You're pathetic!

Beth: Nope...just a hopeless romantic. <3 <3

Me: Whatever...

Beth: Laugh all you like...it'll be me laughing my arse off when cupid comes and fires his big old arrow right through your heart.

Me: Are you sure you haven't been drinking?

Beth: No more than normal... ;)

I was about to type something back when Soph was yelling. "Edie, have you seen my new sleep shirt?"

Sophia and washing were a lost cause. The girl, just didn't get it. She could turn whites pink and darks bleach-marked in a second. Socks got "eaten" and lingerie ripped. I had no idea how she managed to achieve it, but it was a serious talent. One that meant, I'd taken over the washing, but I drew the line at folding. This approach, I'd discovered just made everything easier and it also saved us all lots of dollars.

"It's in the basket in the laundry," I yelled back.

"I've looked."

"Did you use your eyes?" I huffed out. Seriously, Sophia had to be worse than a man when it came to finding things.

"Can you just help me, please?" She was getting more and more frustrated.

"I'll be right there." I called back.

Me: Got to go...washing emergency.

Beth: Right, Soaphia...whoops! Freudian slip.....

I giggled a little at this, as I typed a final good night message. Yeah, Sophia could definitely be a bit of a soapy star at times, but she had a great heart. She was a no nonsense sort of girl but she went hard at everything and somehow seemed to make it more interesting, bigger and exciting. It was a true talent...

"Eden..." her voice was getting closer.

Time to go and avert the washing tragedy, before she started stomping. Soph had a short fuse to go along with all that emotion.

"Coming."

I headed through to the laundry, off the kitchen and in less than three seconds flat I'd found her sleep shirt, exactly where I said it was. I had it swinging from my index finger when she came through the laundry door.

"Where was it?" She even looked surprised. I never could tell whether it was the truth or a carefully crafted act. It was kind of amusing, in an annoying sort of way.

"Surprisingly, it was in the washing basket. I mean who would have thought to look there?"

"Ha ha de ha, Edie," she snickered and headed off to the bathroom.

I took out some giant oversized soup mugs and poured milk into them leaving a little room at the top. Then I shovelled heaping spoons of Milo into milk and gave them each a stir. I slid a spoon into each and headed into the lounge room. Tori had just turned on the television.

She looked over at me as I sat down on the worn but cosy sectional sofa beside her. I didn't miss her eyes locking onto my mug of chocolaty goodness.

"Yours is in the kitchen."

Tori sprung off the sofa so fast I would have sworn she'd been zapped if I didn't know better.

I turned my attention to the television as I licked my spoon. It was some reality show that Tori couldn't seem to live without.

A few seconds later both Sophia and Tori returned with their drinks and settled down beside me. We watched the show for a few minutes in silence. Then some annoying redheaded piece started mouthing off.

"Oh, I can't stand that bitch." Sophia grumbled.

"Why? What's wrong with Morgan? She rocks. She's so much

better than that prissy Arianne." Tori flung back.

"You can't be serious? Morgan is so dumb and Arianne is smart. Besides, she's working these people to perfection." Sophia sounded impressed.

My eyes were darting back and forth between them. In actual fact I found my sisters going into bat for their favourite reality stars more entertaining than the actual show.

"What do you think, Eden? Who's the best?" Tori turned to me looking for support

"Oh no. Don't drag me into this. I have no idea and I can't say I really care. In fact I was enjoying watching you two more. I can't believe you two can get so fired up about a TV show. Imagine if it was something really important, like should we eat Tim Tams or Mint Slices with our Milo."

Tori snorted as Sophia disappeared into the kitchen. "That's a total no brainer. You eat them both."

"Exactly," Sophia agreed and dumped a packed of both on the sofa beside me. I passed the Tim Tams to Tori and she quickly helped herself to a couple. I chose the Mint Slices and returned my attention back to the TV.

We munched for a few seconds more. God, I loved chocolate. It was just pure heaven.

"Speaking of important stuff..." My mind struggled back to what Sophia was talking about. She must be referring to my comment from before. "Sensei, or Xander to you, Eden, wanted to know if you'd like to come along to the grading and BBQ after it on Sunday."

My heart immediately started beating faster and I swear I could hear the blood rushing in my ears. Oh God! I'd agreed to go Tuesday night. The girls didn't know about it yet, but I'd decided to do it. Sunday was a whole other story.

"Tell me about it," I asked non-committedly.

"Nothing much to tell. We go do the grading in the school hall in the morning. Then we head to the park and have a BBQ lunch and just hang out. Nothing special. Totally casual." I knew Sophia was trying to downplay it.

"How many people will be there?"

"Probably about sixty students and the same amount of parents or family."

"One hundred and twenty people," I whispered, more to myself than either of them.

"Hey Tor, did you know that Eden can add sixty and sixty together?" Tori burst out laughing and I couldn't keep the smile off my face even if I hated that I needed to ask questions. It annoyed Soph, but I needed to know. I needed to figure out if I could do it and the only way that could happen was by knowing what I was getting myself into.

"So where do the families sit?"

"In the tiered seating off to the side. You remember the hall?" I did. And now that she mentioned it, the layout for the room came whizzing back into my head. I remember the assembly the day of the fire. Mrs Richie called me up to give me a special award and made a big deal out of me getting the contract. I'd been embarrassed and proud all at the same time, if that was even possible. That was the last time I'd set foot in that hall.

"So once we're done at the hall we just head over to the park and plonk ourselves under the trees, eat burgers and hang out. No pressure—all very low key."

I glanced at Tori and her eyes almost pleaded with me.

"Come on, Edie. It would be great to have you there. Everyone is really cool and no one will hassle you." God love Tori. She always cut to the chase in the most innocent of ways.

I spooned the last of the milk soaked Milo out of the mug and half chewed it. I was going to go Tuesday night. Could I manage Sunday as well? I started to work it out in my mind. It was close to home if I felt uncomfortable; it was only a short walk home. Almost everyday I managed to get myself to university; surely I could manage a grading and a community BBQ, I rationalised.

Sophia was scraping the last of the Milo from her mug with the spoon. She was trying not to pressure me but I knew my sister and she really wanted me to go. Not for her sake, but for mine. I really wanted to please them. Make them proud of me. It seemed so stupid given they were younger and everything.

"Okay. I'll give it a go."

Tori thumped her mug onto the side table and smothered me in a hug.

"It's going to be great! You'll see."

Sophia nodded her agreement over Tori's shoulder.

I sure hoped they were right.

FOUR

EDEN

Sunday morning dawned bright and clear—bugger. There was a big part of me that secretly hoped the sky would open up and the rain would pour down. That should at least cancel the BBQ and socialising component of the day, right? No such luck at all.

I looked out the window from the front passenger's seat. Sophia was driving. That was yet another thing I hadn't managed to achieve or motivate myself to do. I was in two minds about that as well. Having a licence would give me vastly more options, but it would also mean I didn't have as many excuses for why I couldn't do stuff. Mmm, that was something I needed to think about a little more. For the moment, I was comfortable with Sophia driving me to the very limited amount of places I need to go other than university, which I could achieve easy enough to achieve by catching the bus.

Both Sophia and Tori were hyped up and were obviously looking forward to the day; they'd bounded out of bed and wolfed down a big breakfast and chatted between themselves. Sometimes

I thought they were more like boys than girls with their carry on, which wasn't a bad thing. Now Sophia had Pharrell William's "Happy" blaring from the stereo and both girls were rocking in their seats. Regardless of how anxious I felt, it was actually hard to keep the smile off my face when that song was playing. The song was just infectious and when I glanced over at Sophia I knew she'd purposely played it to lighten my mood.

The song changed and Maroon Five's "Sugar" filled the car. It was another favourite of mine. We seemed to have music playing in the house all the time and given the closeness in our ages we all tended to have similar tastes.

For the last couple of days I'd been subtly quizzing Sophia on what to expect and how the day would unfold. I was more at ease, if you could really call it that, if I knew in advance what to expect. I didn't like surprises when I was out of my normal surrounds.

The plan was that Tori would come through with me to the seating on the side of the hall and Sophia would get them both registered or whatever they had to do. I started to focus on my breathing, forcing myself to keep it slow and even. Not always easy to do when your stomach felt as if it had been infested with a flock of ravenous butterflies. Anyone who thought butterflies were gentle was just plain wrong!

A few seconds later, Sophia pulled into the parking lot at the side of the school hall and shut off the engine. Both girls sprung out of the small sedan and headed around to get their gear out of the back. At this stage they were just wearing loose training clothes. Tracky pants and floppy T-shirts. Their uniforms were impeccably ironed and folded in their bags. Meanwhile I struggled to steady myself for what I was about to do.

I got out of the car and pulled the chunky, but soft cable knit beanie more securely onto my head and pushed up my huge oversized sunglasses. With some practice, I'd realised I could have my hair loose and sort of pulled forward over the right side of my face. To hold it in place, I could pull the cable knit beanie on. It was hardly cold enough for a beanie but it looked more like a fashion statement than a defence against the cold. This "style" seemed to work well at hiding the worst of the scars. At least from a distance I looked reasonably "normal".

My one "fashion" item today was the indigo skinny jeans I'd worn. They fit me like a glove and on my long legs, they looked mighty fine, but I purposely ruined the effect by wearing a huge sloppy rugby jersey in a pale blue. The jersey was so large it came almost to mid-thigh. I slung the soft leather satchel I always had with me over my shoulder and followed Sophia and Tori. The satchel had become my security blanket in a lot of ways. Just like a toddler has a favourite toy or blanket—I had this satchel. The soft leather fringing on the pockets and flap gave my fingers something to curl into and fiddle with when I felt anxious. Somehow stroking my hand through the soft leather felt reassuring to me.

The walk across the car park seemed to take eons, but I knew in reality it was not more than a few seconds. But that was what fear and anxiety did to you. Time seemed to speed up, slow down and even pause with no rhyme or reason. My ears started to roar with the rush of blood.

"Breathe, breathe, breathe," I silently chanted in my mind over and over again in time to my footsteps.

Sophia pulled open the door and held it. I followed Tori in, staying as close to her back as possible as I tried to hide myself as much as I could. She glanced back over her shoulder and realised I was hot on her heels.

"Come on, Edie." She dropped me a reassuring smile and at times like this I really felt our roles had been reversed and I was the little sister.

The hall was filled with chatter and noise and I tried to take in as much of the room as possible while moving my head as little as possible. I still hadn't taken off my sunglasses and I wasn't sure whether or not I would yet.

Tori, understanding my preferences in seating, headed along the edge of the bank of tiered seating running down the hall, until she came to the end. She then climbed up three rows and sat down. I followed and took up a seat to her right, ensuring there wasn't realistically enough room for anyone else to sit on my right.

"This okay, Edie?"

I reached my hand out and squeezed her thigh. "Sure. Thanks, Tor."

She smiled and patted the top of my hand. "Thanks for coming."

I didn't say anything. To say I was happy to be here would be a lie—or a partial one at least. I was pleased and happy to be able to share something with my sisters, something that was important in their lives, but I wasn't happy to be here. Being out like this challenged me and made me feel uncomfortable.

A few seconds later Sophia bound up the steps to where we were sitting, "We need to get ready, Tor. We're on when the juniors finish in about twenty minutes."

Tori immediately stood and grabbed her kit bag. "We'll be back in a few, Edie."

"Okay." I tried to make my voice sound convincing and confident but it came out more like a squeak. Tori looked a little worried as Sophia grabbed her arm and started to drag her down the stairs. A couple of seconds later they disappeared into the bathroom that I knew were located underneath the slope of the tiered seating.

I took a deep breath and focused on the hall and what I could see in front of me for the first time. The hall was familiar, but also very different. Normally, there were row after row of plastic chairs on the wooden floor. Today, thick heavy grade foam mats in a purple colour covered the worn boards. On the floor was a group of about twenty kids ranging in age from what I figured was about eight to twelve going through a series of drills and moves that a young guy was calling. He wore a black belt around his narrow hips, but he was still young. You could tell by his lanky frame which hadn't filled out yet, and the skin of his jaw that still sported a few tell-tale teenage blemishes.

Behind the action on the floor was a row of men all dressed in gis with black belts. They were holding clipboards and quietly talking to each other as they watched the proceedings on the floor. A couple of young guys who looked to be about fifteen and wore brown belts, moved back and forth at each end of the group, leading and demonstrating moves the black-belt in charged called out.

My eyes skirted back and forth over the group for a few seconds but I couldn't see him. The tinted lens of my sunglasses annoyed me inside and I fought the urge to take them off. I did a quick scan of the people on the seats to my left. No one openly appeared to be paying me any attention at all.

I edged my hand up and pulled the sunglasses from my face and instinctively tilted it a little to the right, just in case my scars were more visible. At home, I could relax, but when I was out I became acutely aware of how my body was positioned in every circumstance.

A few long minutes passed and I tried to focus my attention on the kids doing their grading on the mats. A flash to the left caught my attention and I fought the urge to turn my head. It was the light hitting Sophia's golden blonde hair as she came through the entrance. Tori was beside her and my breath caught in my throat as I realised the person who had filled more of my thoughts for the last few days than I was comfortable with, was right behind them. I noticed just about every head in the gathered supporters turn to look.

How could they not help it?

My sisters were gorgeous, both tall and beautiful. We all favoured our mother's blue-eyed blonde looks, rather than our father's gingery complexion, but we'd all been fortunate enough to inherit dad's colossal height and lithe stature. He was a big man pushing six foot four. Mum wasn't short either but us girls all topped her by about three or four inches.

But my sisters were just part of the picture.

Right behind them was Xander.

The man just oozed presence from every pore. He was

handsome, assured and seemed to have a confidence that made me feel a sense of both foreboding and comfort at the same time. It was a strange combination and I didn't really understand it.

I watched them move a little farther into the hall, where they halted. Xander said something to my sisters and then Sophia turned to look at me and discretely pointed in my direction.

Terror flashed through the pit of my stomach and I felt like every eye in the place had turned to look at whom they were pointing at—me. I couldn't turn my head away quickly enough—Xander's eyes caught mine. A little smile kicked up at the corner of his mouth, as he nodded his head at me in acknowledgement.

Somehow, I dragged my eyes from his hold. I wanted to sink through the floor. Oh no! It was horrible.

Everyone was looking at me.

I sat rigid...frozen stiff...my eyes fixed straight ahead. My heart was thundering in my chest and it sounded so loud inside my head that the noise around me faded to nothing.

How could they?

Didn't they know how hard it was for me to be here today?

What's more I now realised my sisters were heading straight back to where I was sitting with their bags.

Oh this was a disaster...what was I thinking coming here today?

Sophia plonked her kit bag down, sat beside me then proceeded to start rummaging through it looking for something.

I was too freaked out to even feel the anger that I wanted to.

"For Christ sake Edie, breathe and relax would you. It looks like you swallowed a glass of plaster of Paris and you're stuck fast in that position," Sophia hissed at me as she continued her fossicking.

That was exactly how I felt. Petrified to the spot.

"It's fine, Edie. No one's looking," Tori tried to soothe.

And then, the horror started to transform into anger.

I felt angry and annoyed at myself for feeling this way. I was an adult. I had some scars, but that didn't make me worthless or something to be stared at— did it?

Then I started to think some more. Tried to get my brain to react logically. Tried to fight back those inner demons that wanted to capsize me and hold me down.

Focus on the rational.

What was I here for...two reasons: support my sisters, challenge myself.

Sisters, sisters, sisters.

“We’re up in just a sec, Edie. We’re going to warm up.” Tori placed a hand on my shoulder to get my attention.

“Umm okay,” I stammered, still trying to focus on what I was here for.

“You’ll be fine. No one will bother you,” Sophia assured.

They turned to head down to the mats.

“Good luck!” I called.

They both turned and smiled at me.

My breathing had slowed again and I turned my focus back to the mats. Intently, I watched Xander tie new belts around the waists of kids and shake their hands. Their young faces beamed with pride and accomplishment.

I wondered if I’d ever feel like that again.

Everything just seemed to be one struggle after another.

It was easy to tell how proud he was of them. Xander seemed to have a word of encouragement or praise for each of them and my heart sighed a little at his actions.

Many of the parents had moved forward to snap these precious memories of their kids and not for the first time in the last five years, did I wonder if kids would ever be in my future. Something I’d discovered since the fire is that, it’s not until an option that you’ve previously taken for granted almost seems to be impossible, that it suddenly seems to mean something.

Sure, there was no medical reason I couldn’t have kids, but having a relationship with a man seemed about the equivalent of climbing Mt Everest right about now.

The kids walked away from the mats in single file and returned to their parents. Fortunately, this meant that all attention was focused on them and not me.

I watched my sisters warm-up and then their grading started. I was surprised at how good they both appeared to be. They kicked and punched, and performed all manner of other moves with what looked like skill and co-ordination from my untrained perspective. Both of them were naturally athletic and it certainly looked like it helped, particularly the extra reach their long arms and legs provided.

"Hi there."

I jumped at the voice, startled a bit. I'd been so intently watching Tori and Sophia that I'd completely missed a woman approach. What's more she sat down beside me as if she knew me.

My palms started to sweat and I was momentarily overcome with panic. What should I do?

"Umm hi," I managed to squeeze out, desperately trying to avert my face but still be polite.

"I'm Marion. Jacob and Justine's mum. You must be Sophia and Tori's sister. The likeness between the three of you is uncanny."

If only...crossed through my mind. "I'm Eden and yes. I am Tori and Sophia's older sister."

She gave me a warm open smile and I found myself slightly turning towards her friendly nature. I saw the instant she noticed the burn scars flash across her eyes, but rather than retreat in horror or discomfort like so many do, Marion carried on. "Oh, now I remember... you're the one that was caught in the fire. How are you doing after that? I can't imagine what you went through."

I was taken aback. People just didn't come out and say stuff like this—did they? They didn't talk about the elephant in the room.

"Um, I'm getting there slowly," I answered almost without thinking, because I was still too shocked.

"Well, Eden that's great to hear. Took real guts to do what you did."

I just nodded and said nothing. I know that my story had been featured in the press right after it happened but no one ever talked about it now, certainly not openly with me. It was old news. Marion stared at my face almost intently and I was surprised to realise I didn't actually feel self-conscious or anxious. In fact, I think I was too dumbfounded by Marion's reaction to feel anything but surprise.

"Well, those scars healed up pretty good. So are you finished with surgeries or are there more to come?"

In most cases I would have said Marion was being a busy body but somehow she had a caring and interested personality.

"I'm finished for the moment. There are some more that I could have, to try and make the texture of the skin more even, but they're not covered under Medicare and we simply don't have the money to do it."

It was Marion's turn to nod as she took in my words. "Well regardless, you're still a beautiful girl."

I wriggled in my seat, suddenly uncomfortable at her words.

But Marion, just sailed on. "You know that scar kind of looks like one of those port wine birth marks; it's not so bad."

I'm sure she was trying to be kind and to put me at ease, but now she was starting to tread on territory that annoyed me. How would anyone know what it was like unless they'd walked a day in my shoes?

"So which are your kids?" I thrust in before she had an opportunity to talk more about my burns.

"Oh, Jacob is the one on the front right and Justine is in the second row from the left. Second one in." Once she'd pointed them out it was easy to see the resemblance. They both had dark hair and similar features.

"Have they been studying martial arts long? Is that the correct term...studying?" I asked.

Marion chuckled. "Yeah, I think so. Though to be sure you can check with Sensei Xander later. As for the kids, well, I think it's about three years now. Jacob is going for his brown today and Justine her purple."

"What about your sisters?"

Shit, I had no idea? "Um I think Sophia's doing the one before brown and Tori green. Would that be right?"

Marion laughed and patted me on the shoulder. "That sounds about right. Besides these rankings get damned confusing and just when I get used to them wearing one colour, there they go and get another."

"I guess that's true."

We watched the action for a few more minutes and commented quietly on what we saw. The students went through a series of set moves that seemed to be a blur of punches and kicks, then they broke up and did a heap of different stuff with partners in some sort of holds. Finally they put on their shin guards, gloves and mouth guards then got down to some sparring.

It looked savage, and even a bit brutal. I don't really know what I expected, but I guess it wasn't this.

What surprised me even more I guess, was how much my beautiful, graceful sisters seemed to be enjoying punching and kicking at their opponents, even if it was controlled and supervised. It still looked physical and confronting.

Sophia, in particular, seemed to relish the aggression and seemed to be really into it. It was a side to their personalities that I'd never really seen. Just what I'd missed over the last five years hit me really hard. There seemed to be so much about them that I didn't know, even though we lived under the same roof and shared so much.

It'd been all about me and getting over my burns—very little had been about them growing up and becoming the young women I watched before me.

I'd missed so much.

That made me sad. It also made me realise I couldn't continue hiding. By coming out today I was watching and learning about the two people in my life who were the closest to me.

I was pondering all that when Marion's voice cut through. "You coming to get some pictures?" She was already up and pulling out her phone. It wasn't a question but rather a demand wrapped up as one.

My familiar friend, panic, rose up and I could feel my heart start thumping in my chest.

"Ahh...I" my voice stammered looking for an excuse before I even had time to think it through.

"Come on grab your phone and get down there with me. We don't want to miss it."

I reached for my phone and Marion grabbed my hand giving me no chance to procrastinate or think further.

She galloped us down the tiered seating to the floor. It all happened so quickly I didn't even have time to think or assess. A quick glance around confirmed we were just two of many other family members taking photos.

Marion let go of me and stepped forward to take shots of her kids as Xander presented them with their new belts. I could see the look of pride on her face as she snapped away.

Another student stepped up for their belt and Marion's two teenagers fell back into line. Marion was right back beside me.

I was here on the floor, but I couldn't fathom how I came to be. I grabbed my phone and started fiddling with my photo app—anything to allow me to drop my head and blend in.

Suddenly I felt a push in the centre of my back. "Get in there, Eden. Tori's about to get her new belt."

I took a giant step forward to stop myself from tumbling. Then I took another and another until suddenly I was right where Marion had been standing just a minute ago to capture her kid's achievements.

Tori knelt with her old belt folded neatly across her leg. Xander took the belt from her leg and replaced it with a new blue one, shook her hand and passed her a certificate. I captured it all with my phone. Xander stepped back, Tori stood and moved back to her position in the line-up.

Sophia stepped up and repeated the process Tori has just executed; only this time I could have sworn Xander shot me a little sideways grin as he stood back after presenting Sophia with her new purple belt and certificate.

My stomach clenched and I realised then just how good he looked in his gi. Authority and pure masculinity just seemed to ooze from him. There was no doubt he was the man in charge of this whole shebang.

I didn't have the slightest clue what to do. I was so rattled by being on the floor and Xander smiling at me that I turned and fled back to the spot I'd occupied before. My long legs took the steps three at a time as I retreated as quickly as I could, back to my corner. I plonked my butt on the hard bench seat and sucked in a breath then another. I was breathing so heavily, you'd have sworn I'd just run a marathon rather than having walked up a few stairs.

I watched the students go through a series of bows and file out off the mats when dismissed. A few moments later my sisters were headed my way with big smiles on their faces.

"Well done, you two," I said as they dumped their shin guards and gloves into their gear duffles.

Sophia couldn't keep the satisfied and determined look off her face. "Another step closer to black."

This shocked me a little. I'd never really thought about it, but obviously Sophia had. Just then I learned something else—my sister seemed dead-set determined to become a black belt. I was impressed and a little floored.

What was I hell bent on achieving? Sure I wanted a degree and I wanted to not feel like a prisoner in my own body anymore but I knew I didn't have that killer instinct and determination that Sophia had when she said that one simple sentence.

Compared to my sister, I was pathetic.

I kicked that around in my head some more as they chatted to themselves.

"Edie, were you even listening?" Tori demanded of me.

My head snapped up and I mumbled an apology.

She just shook her head in frustration. "We're going to head down to the showers before we go to the BBQ. We'll only be a few minutes."

Sophia held out the keys to her car. "Go hop in the car if you want."

I took the keys and before I could utter a word they were both gone. I looked around cautiously. Everyone was packing up and paying no attention to me. Many people were helping Xander and a few of the other black belts pack up the mats and other equipment that had been used today.

I was torn. I wanted to help. It was the right thing to do, but I didn't know how to go down and get started. I didn't know anyone other than Marion and I couldn't see her. I sat back down and fiddled with my phone some more. It was my security blanket—a way of looking busy when I really had nothing to do.

I waited a few minutes until all but a couple of people remained. Then I gathered my bag and picked my way quietly down the stairs. My foot hit the floor of the hall and I started to move towards the door, when Xander came striding in and moved straight up to me.

"Hey Eden, would you mind giving me a hand for a sec?"

"Um sure, I guess." What else could I say?

He gave me a beaming smile and it felt good. It was that standing in the sunshine where the sun warms your skin on a cool day, kind of good.

"Can you grab my duffle from over there by the wall? That will be the last of it and I can lock up." He motioned to the large red duffle bag with his chin as he easily hefted a large plastic crate filled with all sorts of stuff that they'd used for the grading. It seemed like a strange request but I didn't argue. Xander wasn't really the type you questioned.

I hurried off and grabbed the bag, a little surprised at just how heavy it was. I slipped my phone into the pocket of my jeans, swapped my lighter bag to my left shoulder and settled Xander's heavier bag over my right shoulder and quickly crossed the hall to fall in right behind him.

Once we were on the outside of the double doors he stopped and placed the crate on the ground. Then he pulled the doors shut and locked them. It was only then, that I realised Tori and Sophia were probably still in the showers.

"Wait! I think Sophia and Tori are still in there."

He glanced at me slightly but kept locking the doors. "Nope. They're over by Sophia's car, waiting for you."

I stepped back out from under the stoop as Xander picked up the crate and headed for a shiny black dual cab 4x4 truck that was parked just near the entrance. Sure enough, when I looked up I could see Sophia and Tori. Tori waved her fingers with an amused look on her face. Sophia just shook her head. I knew that expression. It was the one that said she was frustrated with me.

Xander balanced the crate on his hip and hit the button on his key ring remote, the lights of the truck flashed and a distinctive "click" sounded as the door locks disengaged.

"Can you just throw that bag on the back seat please, Eden?" he asked me as he settled the crate into the tray back.

I opened the back door as he asked and slid the bag onto the middle of the seat.

The inside of the truck was spotlessly clean and smelt really good. It had that fresh pine woods sort of scent that I'd noticed on him the other day at the café.

I was just backing out and about to close the door when he opened the front passenger one just in front of me.

"Jump in. You can ride with me." Again it wasn't a question but more like a polite demand.

He stepped back and kind of herded me into the space between the doors, obviously expecting me to comply. The only way to escape the nearness of his body was to get in. It all happened so quickly and before I knew it I was sitting in the front seat of his truck with the door firmly closed behind me.

A second later, he was in and starting the engine and reversing out.

My brain finally kicked into gear and I fished Sophia's keys out of my pocket.

"Xander, wait! I've got Sophia's keys."

He glanced up and took in the situation, before looking across at me and reaching for the keys. The warm skin of his hand brushed mine and little prickles flew up my arm.

Xander halted the truck and opened his door. Standing on the raised running board he pulled his body half from the truck.

"Hey, Soph. Think quick!" he yelled. Then lofted the keys across the carpark.

I watched Sophia register what he'd called and leap forward to snatch the keys out of the air effortlessly.

He settled himself back in the truck and I suddenly realised what I was feeling.

The feeling was something that had deserted me right along with every other one of my dreams. It hadn't visited me for over five years, a feeling that I never expected to experience again. Today with Xander's smile, touch and nearness it had decided to make a return...

It was that warm needy feeling a woman got when she was attracted to a man.

And just as quickly as the feeling registered in my brain, I mentally mocked it.

As if...he'd be the least bit interested in me.

Once upon a time, I had no doubt he'd have thought about it, maybe even acted on it...but certainly not now.

XANDER

I don't know what had possessed me to get Eden Sommers to carry my bag. And if I didn't know that, then I sure as fuck have no idea what I was thinking when I all but demanded and bustled her into my truck. But now that she was sitting across from me staring out at the road I can't say I was feeling unhappy about it.

Nope, not one little bit.

Her spine was steely straight in the chair and I swear she was so tense that if I touched her she'd crumble into a million tiny pieces of rubble. I'd never seen someone so still or tight in their body.

I had no real idea what to do to make it better, but I felt I had to at least try.

"Relax, Eden. You're safe with me." I tried to take the authority I'd been using all morning out of my voice. I wanted to come across as friendly and open to her. I realised then, I wanted to be that person she felt safe with. The one person she had nothing to worry about or fear.

Her breasts rose and fell as she took in my words. Even that huge sloppy rugby jersey couldn't hide those lush curves. Curves, that I had a pretty good idea, were lurking there waiting.

My hands tightened on the wheel at the stray lecherous thought that had slipped into my mind. I wasn't going there. This was about helping Eden out of her shell, wasn't it?

She didn't say anything, just snuck a quick glance my way. Then she pulled off that cute little beanie thing she'd been wearing and let those long thick strawberry blonde waves fall forward hiding the right side of her face from me.

I drove a little way farther and tossed my thoughts around in my head a little more. Finally, I decided just to come out with it. I didn't know what else to do.

"You know you don't need to hide those scars from me. They don't bother me." I tried to sound casual and conversational. I turned slightly to look at her as I pulled up at a red light. I could only describe the look on her face as a cross between terror and horror. What the hell had I done?

"Um, I didn't mean to make you feel uncomfortable. The opposite actually."

She nodded slightly but said nothing.

The silence in the truck was just about killing me.

"So what did you think of the grading? It was your first one right?" There, two questions which required answers.

"It was interesting and yes, I've never been to one before." Again it was that quiet voice that was hardly more than a whisper.

"Tori and Sophia did really well, but I was expecting it. Did you know how good they were?" Both of them had a lot of talent and were naturally athletic. I had no doubt they could go on to a very high level if they chose to.

"Umm no. I didn't know." She paused and I sensed she was about to say something more, but before she did she snuck a little sideways glance my way. "Sophia said something about working her way towards a black belt. I didn't know until today..." There was something wistful in her voice as she trailed off.

"We've talked about it and if she keeps training like she is and progressing, then I think she'll be ready to go for it in about another year."

I heard her gasp a little in surprise. "That's good, isn't it?"

It was obvious that she was interested in her sisters.

"It's great. She's progressed really quickly. In fact, she's at a level now where she can start to compete if she wants."

"Competing can be dangerous, can't it?" I didn't miss the concern that bordered on alarm in her voice.

I'd added the last bit about competing without really thinking and not for the first time I wondered if she knew my story. It was no secret. A quick search on Google and my very public and private demons were right there for the world to see. Did she know about The Cobra? Did it make her feel uncomfortable around me?

"It can be, but no more than other sports. Like anything, proper training and skills are the key." I tried to hold it, but I couldn't stop the image of The Cobra lying at my feet festering in my brain. He'd been trained and he had the skills, but for some reason that night he'd turned. That question still haunted me at all hours of the night.

Why the fuck had he turned his head?

I didn't know the answer to that question. Reed sure as shit didn't and I was almost positive if I could have asked The Cobra, he wouldn't have been able to answer, either. Regardless, the outcome was still the same.

The Cobra was dead and it was my fist that had made it so.

She was looking at me as this all played in my head. I really hoped my face didn't give too much away. Even though I didn't get in the ring anymore I tried my damnedest to make sure my demons didn't flow over into the students I taught. Just because my head was fucked up didn't mean others should be.

What were the chances that freak event would happen twice in my lifetime?

I tried to rationalise it to myself and sometimes I was almost convinced.

It was time to change the topic of conversation as I pulled into the strip parking area running the length of the local park.

"So are you going to find a corner to hide in or are you going to come and join us." No sooner were the words out of my mouth than I realised how harsh and callous they sounded. Fuck, I'd overstepped the mark big time. She wasn't a student. Hell, if I knew what she was, other than someone who I had some probably fucked up sense of responsibility towards and fascination with.

Eden flinched as if I'd struck her and, for all intents and purposes, I probably had. I doubted anyone had spoken so harshly to her, particularly lately. She wrung her hands in her lap and kept her head down.

"It's just easier if I stay on the outside. I make people feel uncomfortable and in turn it makes me feel awful." This time there was a no mistaking her voice. It was a whisper and something told me it was probably the most honest statement she'd made in a very long time.

"Why don't you give it a try, Eden? They're a good bunch of people and they won't make you feel uncomfortable." What I didn't add was that if anyone did or said anything to the contrary, I'd make their life a living hell. The boys had spread the word as I'd asked. A couple of them had even quietly asked me this morning if that was Eden up in the seating area.

She was reaching for the door handle when I took hold of her hand. It felt silky soft and fine in my calloused palm. A heat seemed to shoot between us as she looked down at our hands. Finally, those intense blue eyes looked at me and I swear I saw unshed tears which made me feel like the lowest prick for putting them there. But the girl couldn't hide forever.

"Please." It was about the closest I'd ever come to begging and she seemed to sense that, too.

The heavy lashes shuttered down over her eyes and she nodded slightly.

"I'll try."

I wanted to push her harder, to get a firm commitment but I knew it was too soon. Hell, I'd probably stepped over the line in so many ways, it was unbelievable.

"You do that, Gem."

I released her hand and she gracefully slipped from the truck, leaving nothing but the sweet smell of blackberries and something else as the only reminder she'd been there. I have no idea why I called her Gem but it just seemed to fit her absolutely perfectly.

FIVE

EDEN

Two days later, I threw myself down onto the sofa in disgust. How could I have been so weak and chicken? I'd purposely been late, then I'd conveniently been in the bathroom. I'd done anything and everything to avoid going to the dojo with Tori and Sophia. My stupid fears had taken over again. They wouldn't even have arrived yet and already I felt guilty and knew I'd made the wrong decision.

What was I so damned scared of?

Oh, it was so frustrating. I hated my fears, but I loved them at the same time. They gave me an excuse to duck out. An escape route that was plausible and feasible every single time. They worked not only for me but everyone else as well.

But these fears didn't help me. They kept me a captive.

A captive of my own making.

That's what Grace had been trying to get me to see.

I grabbed the cushion to my left and slammed my fist into it. Just like I'd watched the girls do on the weekend, only they were hitting pads held by their partners.

I did it again and again.

Wow...that felt goooood!

What surprised me was how smashing my fist into the soft spongy cushion had felt so damned good. Maybe there was something to it? Who would have thought? I never would have guessed it.

Sophia and Tori sure seemed to enjoy it.

Lots of other people did, too, if the roll up on Sunday morning for grading was any indication. Maybe I should give it a go?

That got me thinking.

Maybe if I gave it a go, I wouldn't feel so self-conscious because I'd actually be participating and focusing on what I was doing rather than sitting on the sidelines worrying about what everyone was thinking.

Could I do it?

I hadn't done any sport since the fire. The most I'd done was a light weights program in the hospital gym during rehabilitation. I'd not bothered to keep that up once I was home permanently. I walked. That was the extent of it.

Could I do it? Maybe...

Then the logistics of it all flooded me.

To participate, I had to get there.

I hadn't even managed to get myself to the dojo and I'd promised Beth.

Beth, my best friend. I didn't break promises to Beth.

Right—I could fix this.

I leapt from the sofa and ran to my room, grabbed a jacket and my satchel. I didn't know if I could participate tonight but I was dressed in sneakers, leggings and a loose T-shirt. It would do for sportswear.

As I raced out the front door, I glanced at the clock on the wall. Ten to seven. I pulled the door closed behind me and headed to the right. If I cut through the back of the school along the river and came up through the laneway at the bottom of the industrial section of the next estate, I could make it and I would only be a few minutes late. If I went the other way it would add a good twenty minutes to my trip on foot.

I took off and I swear to God it was the fastest I'd walked in what seemed like forever. The wind was cool and I pulled the hood of my jacket up higher around my face to help cut the cold.

As I walked, I played the events of Sunday through my head. It hadn't been so bad. The grading had been fine and I'd even managed to cope for a couple of hours at the BBQ afterwards.

I think it certainly helped that I'd showed up with Xander. It was impossible to miss the looks. I saw surprise but not pity. There was no disgust or that awkward discomfort I was so used to seeing and expected.

He'd been casual and nonchalant about the whole thing. But I couldn't help but wonder why he'd done it. I could have easily grabbed a ride with Sophia and Tori. Was he making some statement to me, to others? I didn't know. I needed to talk it through with Beth and I would have, but she'd been away for the weekend. We were going to talk tonight after the class. It was just too weird to bring it up with my sisters. Xander was their teacher per sé.

Xander had introduced me to a few people, then Marion had taken it upon herself to make sure I was with her which gave Sophia and Tori time to laugh and joke with their friends rather than playing chaperone to me.

Ahhh! It was all too confusing and I knew next to zilch about the finer dynamics of male/female relationships. I wasn't a virgin but I might as well have been; it was so damned long since I'd had anything to do with a male. Even then we'd been nothing but awkward and clueless kids.

Xander was neither.

My mind wandered to him as I moved along the path. The image of him in his gi, demonstrating moves on the weekend played in my mind. He moved with such grace and power. I'd found him hypnotic. Not only in the way he moved, but also in the way he treated me. There was no hesitation. He just seemed to act with such confidence. It was reassuring and I didn't feel so awkward around him.

The dark had all but descended when I popped up out of the narrow laneway that was actually more like a massive stormwater drain and acted as one when we had a lot of rain.

The dojo was only a few blocks up ahead. As I'd expected the rows of industrial sheds and factory type buildings were deserted now that the working day was finished. I actually found it reassuring rather than spooky. The only lights were the street lamps and even those were not the bright white ones, but rather the muted yellow ones. I kept walking and thinking. Xander kept bursting into my thoughts.

For the first time in eonsI was actually interested in someone other than myself. I still hadn't done a Google search on him. After the BBQ, I'd rushed home and buried myself in an assignment and study for a test I'd had earlier today. I was determined to get high-distinctions for both.

As I approached a large silver shed, the big corrugated iron front sliding door opened and three men stood there smoking and drinking beer from bottles. I kept my head down and hurried past, doing my best to blend into the shadows. Not that they'd be the least bit interested in me.

I was almost past the driveway when they noticed me.

"Hey, mate. What are you doing out here now? You casing the place?" one of them called. I said nothing just hurried along, ignoring them.

"We're fucking talking to you, shithead!" one of them called. The urge to run was high but I had done nothing; so I kept my head down and lengthened my stride even more.

The next second I heard footsteps pounding toward me and before I could think or really do anything I froze. Panic flooded me and I stopped dead in my tracks.

A hand grabbed my shoulder painfully and spun me around dislodging my hood at the same time.

"Fuck, it's a woman," one of them said in surprise, but even as rusty as I was with men, I read his lecherous tone through my panic-riddled brain. I dared not raise my face.

"Yeah, and not only is she female; she's also gorgeous."

My gut turned to a massive knot and my mouth was suddenly so dry I could barely draw breath let alone talk.

"What are you doing out here, sweetheart? How about you come and join us for a party?" The voice sounded slurred and I immediately realised he was probably drunk.

The closer they got, the more I could smell them. They stank of stale male sweat, cigarettes and motor oil. One of them threw his arm around my shoulders and I almost gagged at his smell. I tried to pull away but he held me tightly.

"Oh no, sweetie pie. You're ours for the night I think. What do you say, boys?"

Suddenly my mind kicked into action and I realised what was going on. These guys didn't care about anything. They didn't care about my scars. This was getting way out of hand. They were going to rape me or worse.

From deep inside me something sprang into life and ripped upwards through my lungs and outwards. I felt it burn every inch of the way.

I screamed. I screamed so damned loud that my throat instantly felt as if it was on fire from the effort and my ears rang in protest to the noise.

The guy that had his arm around my shoulders momentarily sprang back in surprise. This time I managed to step out of his grasp and I turned to run but not before I ran smack bang into a broad chest and the arms engulfed me.

"Oh darlin', what's the hurry. Join us for a drink."

I screamed again and kept right on going until a massive hand closed over my mouth muffling the sound.

"Shut the fuck up, bitch! It doesn't need to be like this."

Tears were falling down my face and I kept trying to scream. I threw my body from side to side trying to break away. Terror raced through me.

Everything became a blur as they started to drag me back towards the building.

I kept struggling and screamed—powerless to do anything else.

"Let her go."

I wasn't sure if I'd heard that voice or imagined it. All I know is that the guy dragging me seemed to stop and the next thing I heard was fighting. A leg flew through the air and I heard the dull thud of it impacting on a body. Another hit and a grunt sounded. Then I saw first one, then another body land at my feet. This was all I could see within the limited field of vision I had in the shadows and through my hair and my twisted hoodie.

"Let her go." The voice was not much more than a low growl and it seemed familiar, but my heart was beating so fast I couldn't be sure of anything in the shadows. Hope teased me deep down in my stomach.

Was I going to get out of this?

"No fucker. Finders keepers. She's ours for the night," the guy holding me yelled back.

"That's where you're wrong. She's one of ours." The voice was cold and menacing.

My mind whirred. I couldn't keep up. I didn't understand. Ours—what the devil was that all about?

"What the fuck do you mean?" one of the men asked. There was no mistaking the belligerence and posturing in his voice.

"That's Pretty Boy's woman you've got there. You do not want to fuck with him."

I had no idea what they were talking about, but a split second later the arms around my middle released and I crumpled to the ground, too shocked and weak with fear to hold my body up.

Who was Pretty Boy?

I had no idea what they were talking about, but I knew I had to get out of there. With another burst of energy borne of adrenalin, I rolled to my side and brought my sneaker clad feet under me and sprang to my feet.

This time I was going to run.

"Eden, stop. It's me... Dane." The voice rang out around the building and I immediately halted. My body froze—rooted to the spot. "I'll take you back to Xander."

Confusion, relief and about a hundred other things raced around my body, but I did stop. It was something about the voice. The tone. He'd also mentioned Xander. My muddled brain somehow recognised Xander as safe.

One of the guys on the ground rolled and tried to get to his feet. I saw a blur in the dark shadows, then the unmistakeable sound of a kick landing in a belly followed by a pained groan.

"Stay the fuck down. Do not make me put more of a beating on you." Dane's voice was now a growl laced with anger and disgust. "I'd be keeping a low profile if I were you three. Pretty Boy is not going to be happy about this."

"Shit man—we didn't know." I wasn't sure who spoke but I thought it was the man that had held me.

"Well, now you do. But that's no excuse. You don't go attacking women. What the fuck, were you drunken fools thinking?" Dane was furious now and I flinched back from his voice. "Hell, maybe I should beat the shit out of you three as a reminder. As it is Eden is well within her rights to press charges."

"We were just going to have some fun, man," one of them whined from the ground.

"I don't think Eden saw it as fun, and her screams sure as shit didn't sound that way. I'll be telling Xander everything that happened. It'll be up to him what happens. He knows where to find you. Now get the fuck out of my sight."

The two men on the ground staggered to their feet and joined the third. The three of them slunk back towards the building they'd been in.

"Are you okay, Eden?" Dane's voice was softer and reassuring.

Was I okay?

Physically, probably—yes. However, I was shaking like a leaf.

Mentally, I had no idea.

I just needed to sit down. My heart was still racing and

everything seemed surreal and blurry.

Dane gently wrapped his arm around my middle.

"Whoa there, girl. Don't collapse on me. Come on; it's just a little way. Let's get you up to the dojo."

I gratefully slumped against his strong body as we started to move. All I focused on was placing one foot in front of the other. Left, right, left, right I chanted in my head. It was soothing and gave me something to focus on rather than what I'd just gone through.

"What were you doing down there, Eden? Shit, it's dark and cutting through an industrial estate is no place for a woman at night." He rattled on a bit more but I didn't really hear him. I was trying to stay upright when all I wanted to do was lie down.

I heard his voice but the effort to create words and speak seemed too much at the moment. All I could focus on was my feet. Left, right, left, right.

"Please say something to me, Eden. I'm freaking out here," he all but begged me, concern raging through the voice that only moments ago had been so filled with confidence. I fought the exhaustion, and the after-effects of the fear.

"I'm okay, Dane." My voice was nothing more than a whisper, but he heard it.

"Far out, girl. You had me terrified for a moment there," he trailed off with a laugh.

"How much farther?" I managed to croak. I wasn't taking in my surroundings just focusing on moving my feet.

"Just past this building."

Left, right, left, right.

Finally he slid open the door to the dojo and all but dragged me inside.

The last I remember is a sea of heads all swivelling to look at me as everything went dark.

XANDER

"Xander, I need some help here man. She's fainted." Dane's voice was anxious as he called out across the dojo. I'd noticed the second he'd come through the door. He was late. What shocked the hell out of me was when I watched the body he was supporting in his arms, go limp. It all happened at once, as soon as they'd made it through the front door.

There's no way in hell I could miss that curtain of rich strawberry blonde hair. I'd know that colour anywhere.

Fear shot straight to my heart as my brain processed what I was seeing.

"Rohan, take over here," I barked as I ran across the mats. Sophia and Tori hot on my heels, also knew exactly who it was Dane was now holding up.

"What the hell happened?" I demanded of Dane as I scooped her unconscious form into my arms and headed for my office.

"What happened?...How is she?...Eden." Tori and Sophia were both talking at once.

"I found her..."

Too many voices, I needed to know what had happened. "Girls!" I barked out. "Let Dane explain." I knew my tone would silence them.

Gently, I placed her on the sofa in my office and propped the lone cushion underneath her head. I then hooked her lower legs over the other arm of the sofa to raise her feet up slightly, before I moved back to kneel beside her head.

"I was cutting through, down by the river when I came up on some guys outside Heuy's Motor Shop giving her a hard time." My fingers smoothed over the skin of her cheek and I pressed them in to the side of her throat. A little of the fear and tension evaporated from my body when I realised her pulse was strong and steady. As long as she hadn't sustained any other injuries, I figured she'd just fainted and would come around soon.

"What do you mean a hard time?" The fear I was feeling was fast replaced with anger.

"I just saw the end of it. I was walking up the laneway when I heard a woman screaming. I took off running towards it. I'm surprised you didn't hear it. It was loud."

Rage zapped through me. "We didn't hear a thing here. I had the damned front door shut. The wind was whistling round here like a bitch."

I smoothed the hair back from her face and Sophia crowded in at my side.

"Tori, go grab a towel from the tall cupboard in the kitchen area and wet it please," I ordered. She disappeared without questioning me.

"As I came out of the laneway I saw the guys surround her. She wasn't putting up much of a fight, but she obviously didn't want to be going with them. I realised it was Eden as soon as I saw her hair and her height."

A small whimper escaped her throat and a shudder went through her body. She was coming around.

"Did they hurt her?" I had to ask but I was pretty sure she was okay and had only fainted from the shock.

"I don't think so. I think I got there in time."

I could feel the rage pulsing through my body, but somehow I kept my hands gentle as I stroked her hair back from her face again and again. The strands were incredibly soft and silky against my skin. Exactly as I'd known they would be. Touching her somehow seemed to calm me.

"I took the first two to the ground. They were a good way to being shit faced and hardly even put up a fight. The third guy let her go when I told him he had your woman. I didn't want to risk her getting hit if I went after him."

I couldn't help it. I really tried to avoid swearing at the dojo and particularly in front of women and students, but this was different. If ever a situation warranted a curse word it was now.

"Fucking arseholes."

My brain was focused on those fuckers and all I wanted to do was rip them apart. How anyone could think of hurting a woman was beyond me, but Eden? Hell, she was just so damned sweet, beautiful and innocent. And right there was why they'd targeted her. Easy prey.

"What do you mean, she's Sensei's woman?" Sophia asked Dane suspiciously as Tori hurried back in with the wet towel. I took it from her outstretched hands and started to gently press it to Eden's face and neck.

Sensei's woman.

It should have felt weird. Grated on me. Funnily enough, it felt neither. It kind of felt right. I knew Eden Sommers wasn't my woman. But I didn't open my mouth to refute it, either. If those few words had meant Dane could get Eden out of there safely tonight; I'd gladly handle whatever fallout came.

Dane rushed on with a both a hint of defence and a subtle rib directed at me, in the tone of his voice. Something only I'd pick up. "I told him that so he'd let her go. Even those idiots aren't stupid enough to risk Xander coming after them." The words were for the girls, but the tone was all for me.

I said nothing. I was more focused on Eden. Dane's explanation seemed to appease Sophia for the moment.

Eden groaned again and this time her eyelids fluttered open. Those big dark blue eyes of hers were unfocused, as she struggled to figure out what was going on. She tried to sit up and I put a firm hand on her shoulder.

"Just lay there for a minute, Eden. You're safe. I've got you. Try to relax." She half nodded once and collapsed back onto the sofa.

"You're going to be fine, Edie," Sophia assured her, squeezing her hand some more.

She still looked confused and I watched her throat gulp a few times, but nothing seemed to be coming out, so I helped her out. "You just had a little faint. You'll be fine once the shock passes and your body gets a chance to equalise itself. Just try to breathe slowly and evenly. You've had a tough night, but you're going to be fine now."

I kept up with the reassurances a bit longer. It seemed to settle her and we could all see she was starting to get herself back together.

"Could I have a glass of water, please?"

I didn't even have to ask. Dane took off to retrieve it and I kicked myself for not thinking about it sooner.

This time when she started to sit up, I didn't stop her. Her eyes were focused and I could tell she was much more with it.

"Just take it steady, Gem." I slid my arm under her shoulders to help her up the rest of the way.

Sophia and I moved back slightly, to give her some room.

"How do you feel?"

She nodded her head. "I'm okay. I feel a little weak, but I'm okay."

I didn't think she had any other injuries but I had to ask. "Do you hurt anywhere? Did those guys hurt you anywhere else?"

She shook her head slowly no. "They just scared me and tried to drag me off."

I didn't miss the fear in her eyes, nor did her sisters as Dane returned with the glass of water.

"Here you go." He held it out to her and her hand wobbled a little as she took it. Without thinking, I wrapped mine around hers to prevent it spilling. There was a grateful flash in her eyes, as together we moved the glass to her mouth so she could take a sip.

Once she'd had enough, I took the glass and placed it on the low side table beside the sofa, which was covered in the latest martial arts magazines.

I looked directly at Eden, trying to assess where she was at. Her eyes locked with mine, then dropped. Her chin followed her eyes and dipped to her right.

That's about the time that I knew she really was okay, because her self-consciousness had returned in spades. She'd shifted effortlessly from basic survival to a higher level of consciousness. If she could worry about how she looked or how people might be seeing her then, basically she had to be okay. At least, that was my reasoning. I hated the fact she felt the need to constantly shield her face and eyes from view.

And riding right along with Eden's self-consciousness came my anger and frustration at her. I could see the whole incident play out in my mind. This bullshit hiding thing she had going on was a solid contributor to those guys taking a shot at her tonight. Sure, what they'd done was all kinds of wrong, but I'd bet my last dollar that her manner and the way she carried herself had been a huge contributor. It was going to stop. I wasn't going to let her live like this anymore. Next time Dane or I might not be there to save her arse.

"Umm, I'm fine now. I just want to go home." Her voice was a little stronger than I'd been expecting.

"You're not going anywhere for a little while. You just need to take it easy." My voice came out harsher than I'd wanted but, hell now I knew she was all right, I was pissed at the situation and at her.

This crap shouldn't have happened. But I swear to God if it did again, she was going to have a fighting chance and wouldn't be going down so easily. I may not be able to reverse the scars that made her want to retreat within herself, but, by God, I could give her a big shot of confidence through learning to protect herself. If she had that, then I'd bet her whole outlook would change.

That I could give her. I could help her make the change.

"We can take her home now, Sensei." Sophia stood as if to prompt a move. And right there was part of the problem. Eden's family loved her and that love enabled her to stay in her self-imposed bubble. Never really pushing her to move forward. Always being there to pick up the pieces and protect. Sometimes love wasn't so helpful.

I glanced at the clock over my desk. There was still half an hour of the class left.

This was one of those now or never moments. I weighed it up in my head for a split second and went with my instinct.

"You and Tori can get your butts back to class," I all but growled at them. They didn't deserve it but I needed to act now and I couldn't risk anyone interfering if my plan had a chance of working. "Eden and I are going to have a little chat."

They both looked at me, then to Eden and then scurried off with a couple of backwards glances. But Eden wasn't protesting, so they went without any hassles.

Dane looked at me with amusement and that just pissed me off, too. "You can go out there and check on Rohan as well." He grinned knowingly and retreated.

I dragged the hard-backed chair that was in front of my desk across the room and placed it beside the sofa. Then, I threw my leg over, straddled it backwards, my chest pressed against the back of the chair.

Eden shrank into the sofa and I tried to curb the frustration and anger I felt at the situation.

"Tell me what happened." It was a demand, but I managed to soften my voice somewhat.

Her throat was working up and down but no sound was coming out. Confusion flashed in her eyes but at least she looked at me, rather than turning away. I realised then that Eden was not used to being spoken to directly. Everyone danced around her and just let her be.

Well, letting her be wasn't helping at all. In fact, it was achieving the exact opposite of what was needed for her. It was enabling her to remain a recluse and closed off from everything. It could have got her raped or murdered tonight.

I raised my eyebrows and continued to hold her eyes with mine. Finally, Eden dropped her eyes, but at least she started to speak.

"I had planned to come here tonight but as it got closer to the time we needed to leave I started to freak out and I convinced myself to stay at home." I could tell from her tone she was embarrassed, but I sensed she was telling me the truth.

I nodded, encouraging her to go on.

"Then once Tori and Sophia had left I got angry and annoyed with myself. I realised I'd chickened out again and I wanted to fix it. So I decided to come here."

Her head ducked again.

"And you chose to go through the short cut down by the river and up through the back of the industrial estate."

Her head nodded subtly in agreement. "I was going to be late and I thought it would be fine," she protested meekly.

I was hanging onto my temper by a very slim thread. "And it also escaped your notice that it's dark and the industrial areas are hardly a safe place for a woman walking alone."

"It wasn't like that...It was still light when I left. Besides why would anyone want to attack me?"

I locked my hands over the back of the chair and squeezed, directing my anger and frustration out through them. I didn't need to look down to know my knuckles had turned white. I really wanted to pace and kick and hit something but if I lost it like that, she'd be terrified of me. As it was, I knew she was shit scared but still Eden trusted me.

"You really don't get it—do you?" Her eyes looked up at me and I could see them pleading with me, hoping I'd back off. "Well, let me explain it for you. It's really quite simple. You're female and breathing. That's all. No more, no less. Oh, you might think those scars protect you from the animals out there." I saw her gasp and flinch back. but I wasn't stopping she needed to hear this.

"In fact, I doubt you've even thought about your own personal security since the fire, but let me clarify it for you. Guys like that don't give a shit about scars or anything else. You're female and I know exactly what they saw as you walked up. Let me guess what happened. You had your head down and you were trying to blend in with the shadows? Guys like that are predators. Wolves. They pick off the weak and frail. You Eden, would have looked like the perfect little lamb for them to feast on. I bet they couldn't believe their luck when they got a hold of you. Then when they did get a hold of you, I bet you did nothing. You would have frozen. Thank

God, you had the sense to scream. Or hell if I know how this night would have ended up."

I could contain it no longer. I jumped backwards and paced one way then the other in the confined space of the office. "That about what happened?" I demanded of her, pissed off that she was sitting there absorbing it all again, not saying a word to either agree or defend herself.

"Answer me!" I snarled.

Her head shot up and I could see the tears running down her face. "Yes, yes that's what happened," she agreed.

"Do you understand why it happened?" I prodded some more at her, all the time feeling as if I was speaking to a child rather than a grown woman.

She still looked confused, so I decided to explain it again. Eden needed to understand how much danger she'd been in. Somehow she thought those scars protected her from situations like this. It wasn't the case.

"You put yourself in a bad situation when you made the choice to go that way after dark. Then you made yourself an easy target by the way you carried yourself and behaved. No, they shouldn't have attacked you. What they did is all sorts of wrong. But Eden, stuff happens in this life all the time that shouldn't happen. You've got to be able to deal with it and protect yourself." What I didn't say was that she of all people should know that life deals you rough hands at times. I didn't need to rub more salt into the wound.

She looked up at me and more tears were running down her face. That full bottom lip of hers was wavering. "I was coming here to join in. I thought maybe if I did something positive, I'd feel better. Maybe if I was part of the action I wouldn't worry so much about what everybody thought." I was pleased to hear it, but I really wondered if it was the truth or an attempt to deflect my anger away from her.

That's when she broke down into out and out sobs. I couldn't stand it any longer. I could be a hard arse but I also wasn't immune to a woman's tears. I took two steps to the sofa and sat down beside her and pulled her into my arms. She buried her head into my chest and it was both the best and worst feeling.

I'd pushed her hard—too hard, but shit the woman needed to wise up in a hurry. I felt like a heel for doing that to her. Cruel to be kind, and all that bullshit. But at the same time I was enjoying the feeling of her being in my arms just a little too much.

I let her cry against my chest for a few minutes. Just held her. Letting her know she was safe. I might have been a bit harsh, but I gave a shit about what happened to her.

Eden had endured a hell of a night and I probably shouldn't have gone after her as well. But I was a big fan of dealing with wounds and crap immediately, rather than waiting. That way you could get on with setting things straight and healing, without prolonging the agony or stewing over what might happen.

Eventually, she lifted her puffy tear stained face and I passed her the damp towel because I didn't have a tissue in sight.

"Thanks," she mumbled and took it from me.

I gave her a moment to clean up her face a little. I couldn't have cared how she looked right about now, but obviously it was important to her.

"So, how much do you hate me?" I injected a hint of amusement into my voice to try and lighten the situation.

She glanced up at me. "I don't hate you. Can't say I like you much at the moment, but I don't hate you. However, you do make a pretty good pillow to cry into."

I couldn't help the rumble of laughter that rippled out of me. Her last comment was so unexpected and so not what I had expected from Eden. This façade she was hiding behind was obviously also blanking out her personality. With just that one comment, I wanted to know the "real" Eden. What was the person hiding behind the mask really like?

"Well, that's a new one for me."

That earned me a tentative smile from Eden. All I can say is, I felt like I'd just been blessed. Even with those scars, the woman had a smile that lit up a room and I really wondered when was the last time anyone had seen it—most probably right before the fire. I also wondered what it would be like if she smiled big, all the way. I remembered exactly what it looked like when she'd been a child. Now I wanted to see it as an adult. I wanted to see it spontaneous and often.

"Okay, so let's talk some more about what you said before." She looked at me a little in confusion before she dropped her eyes again. "You said you were coming here with the intention of joining in. Which, by the way, I think is an excellent idea. But did you really mean it? I can teach you to fight and look after yourself. I can also teach you how to avoid situations like that and give you tools to use if you find yourself in a situation like tonight again. I think there's a lot you can benefit from by doing some training."

I could feel her eyes boring into the area at the base of my throat. Eden wasn't big on eye contact. That was something else I was going to work on if I got the opportunity.

She nodded a little and I took that as an affirmative. I knew I wasn't going to get much in the way of words from her tonight.

"Right then. What's your schedule like for the rest of the week?"

Eden suddenly started to squirm and looked nervous.

"What is it?"

"I thought I'd just join in with the others," she said in a small voice.

"Yeah, that's one way, but I don't really have a class at the moment that would be appropriate for you to start in. I want to do a few sessions with you to get you up to speed before you start in with the others. I think it will be easier if you know some of the basics, rather than having everything thrown at you at once."

It was a coin toss. There were fors and againsts for putting her straight into a class. Anyone else, I would have slotted straight into a class but I had no idea how she'd react at this stage. My theory was that, at least, if Eden knew the basics she could keep up.

"I'm at uni each morning for the rest of the week. Other than that I'm just studying and doing assignments," she offered.

"Okay, then we'll do something in the afternoons." Then something occurred to me. I'd been railroading her and pushing in all the ways I knew how. But what if I had it wrong? What if I was actually doing her harm? I was acting totally on instinct here. "Eden, do you see a counsellor or something?"

A guarded look filtered her eyes and she nodded slightly confirming this.

"You went through a lot tonight. I think you should see your counsellor before you start here with me. Make sure they're on board with what I'm proposing."

"Okay, I'll call Grace in the morning," she agreed. The class had broken up and the students were starting to file out.

"Good. Now let's get you home if you feel up to it." She slid from my side and stood without wobbling which I took to be a positive sign.

She'd started to move to the door, when she turned and looked back at me. Her lip twitched up slightly and her eyes turned warm. "Thank you," she murmured.

I grinned back following her out into the reception area. "You're welcome. I'd say anytime but I don't think tonight is something you want to be repeating. Text me after you've seen your counsellor and we'll set up a time. Sophia and Tori both have my number."

As I expected Tori and Sophia were waiting anxiously by the reception counter for her. They seemed a little surprised when Eden turned back to me and said with a little smile. "I'll text you tomorrow after I speak with Grace."

"Make sure you do. I'll be waiting for it. Night, ladies." With any other woman it would have sounded like I was needy. With Eden I wanted to make her accountable.

Sophia and Tori both repeated my "Night" and bowed before slipping out, with Eden trailing behind. She gave me a shy little wave from the door as she stepped out into the darkness. As cute as it was, I actually took it for being a positive step. She actually chose to look back rather than scurry off.

I slipped back into my office and found Dane waiting for me, lounging his big frame in the doorway.

"Well, that was interesting." There were questions in his hazel eyes.

"I don't know about interesting. I'd say fucked five ways to Sunday would be a better description, actually." There was something I needed to know. "How close was it?"

Dane shrugged his shoulders. "Hard to say, but I'm real glad I showed up when I did and not thirty seconds later."

"I am, too. She's damned lucky you just chanced upon her. What the hell were you doing coming that way on foot? Where's your truck?" I'd been wondering that since he'd explained what had happened.

"I was helping out a friend. I left my truck with them. I was running late, so I cut through. Fucking lucky I did. What were the chances?"

"You're not wrong. Someone up there was looking out for her tonight," I agreed.

"Is she going to press charges?" My head shot up and I realised I hadn't even thought through that bit. I'd been more concerned about her. She'd never survive a trial or the process with where she was in her headspace. But those guys shouldn't get off scot free either. What they had done was seriously fucked.

"I didn't even ask her about it, but I don't think she'd handle all that attention very well, but it's not really my decision to make."

"No it's not, but we can't just let it go, Xan. That was some fucked up shit those dicks pulled. Why don't I call Mark and have a chat with him. Tell him what happened. At least I can make a statement, then Eden can do whatever. It needs to be on record, but I'm not sure she could even identify them. I never even saw her look at them."

I nodded agreeing with Dane. Mark was one of my higher level students and also a cop. He'd know what to do. I trusted him to know what to do. "Yeah, give him a call, make the statement. Let him handle it. I don't want them to get away with it either, but I don't want to have her dragged through more shit if it's avoidable. If I go down there, I'm not sure I won't lose my shit at them."

Dane nodded in agreement but he looked at me and suddenly I got that "bug under a microscope" feeling. "So what's going on between you two?"

I felt my temper rise a little. It was none of his damned business, but Dane was my oldest and closest friend. Of course he'd ask. "We had a discussion, well that's not quite true, more like I gave her a lecture on the stupidity of what she did and the risks. Outcome is I'm going to start teaching her." It was the abridged version but that's all I felt like telling him. It was between Eden and me—no one else.

A smirk kicked up the corner of my friend's mouth. "What?"

"Nothing man, nothing..."

SIX

EDEN

No sooner had we walked inside than Sophia dragged me into the lounge room and pulled me down beside her on the sofa. Tori was hot on our heels and took up position on my other side. I was surprised they'd actually managed to wait this long. I'd expected this when we got in the car.

"Are you okay, Edie? What the hell happened? I know you've been crying." Sophia opened the interrogation.

"I did something dumb and nearly paid a very big price for it." I was shaken by what had happened and I knew just how lucky I was, but it had also opened my eyes. Xander had opened my eyes. He'd been spot on about everything.

If I hadn't let my demons get the best of me then I would have been safely in the car with the girls; I wouldn't have cut through a bad area and a million other ifs...

"What did Sensei talk to you about? I'm so pissed that he made us go back to class." It was interesting to see just how they respected him and his authority over them. Sophia was headstrong at the best of times, but she hadn't even looked like going against him tonight. I needed to tell them at least some of it. They had a right to know. I was going to be moving into their "territory" so to speak.

"We talked about what happened and he gave me a lecture about personal security and how stupid I'd been." They both winced and I knew then that they'd witnessed that sort of thing before.

"Oooo, brutal," Tori sympathised.

"Yeah, he didn't miss me."

"He made you cry—bastard," Sophia raged.

"He said some stuff that hurt a lot, but he was right. I was an idiot for what I did."

"Still, he didn't need to be a shit about it." Sophia was defending me again. Xander had been tough, but he'd also been fair and kind in his own way. He didn't need the girls having a hate on towards him. This was between him and me. I didn't want their relationship with him affected despite what happened between him and me.

"He wasn't a shit. He was actually pretty nice to me. He just had a few hard things to say and I needed to hear them," I explained.

"But what was with him wanting you to text him?" Tori asked.

"We kind of came to an agreement about me training with him. He wants me to talk to Grace about what happened and if she's okay with it, I'm going to train with him. I have to text him after I speak to Grace." It was right then that I realised how much I wanted this to happen. I was actually excited about doing something. Everything up until this point in time, had been about me needing to do stuff. This was me, wanting something and following through.

"Wow. That's actually really exciting." Sophia had turned from being the fierce one to actually being a little dumbstruck.

"I don't understand? You've never been interested in martial arts, Edie." Tori looked confused. I actually felt a little sorry for her. I knew how much they both worried about me in their own ways.

"Well, after seeing you two on Sunday and everyone else, I thought that it might be something I'd like. Then after what happened tonight...I don't ever want to feel that helpless again." The words came out of my mouth without me actually thinking too much, but I believed them. I didn't ever want to feel that helpless again. I didn't have the first clue how to get myself out of that situation. It didn't need to be like that.

"So you're going to be coming to class tomorrow night with us after you've spoken to Grace? I can't wait." Tori sounded excited like only a little sister could.

"I won't be."

She looked confused. "What do you mean?"

"Xander said he wanted to do a few sessions with me before I joined a class."

"What?" Sophia sounded a little outraged. "He only ever does private lessons with the fighters right before a big fight. New students just get put in with us. We had two last week." She looked at me in a way that was more of a glare. I shrugged my shoulders. I didn't really know or have an opinion.

"That's what he said he wanted to do."

"You're so lucky." Then Sophia went quiet for a second as she obviously thought things over. She turned on me with a look that could only be called accusing. "There's something weird going on. Dane referred to you as "Sensei's woman" or something to that effect and he didn't say a word. Is there something you're not telling us, Edie? Plus you got a ride to the BBQ with him the other day."

"Yeah, what's that about, Edie?" Both Sophia and Tori were putting me on the spot.

"I have no idea. I'd never met him before that day in the coffee shop. You know him better than me! Like I told you on Sunday; he asked me to carry something, then he just kind of hustled me into his truck. Well, you know how intimidating he can be, so I just got in." I threw my hands up in the air in protest.

"We do!" They both agreed with the intimidating comment.

"Maybe he's hot for you!" Tori teased and elbowed me in the ribs.

"That's hardly the case, Tori. I'd say he could have just about any woman he wanted. I doubt he'd have much use for me. He probably just sees me as some sort of project."

"You're too hard on yourself, Eden. A guy would be lucky to have you. You're smart, and caring and well...mostly stunningly beautiful," Sophia teased. We all broke out laughing. I'd noticed, of late, that Sophia had started poking fun at my burns. I didn't mind and it was better than having the topic off-limits. It was something that only happened at home and between us.

"Just don't look at me from head on or the right. Maybe I need a guy that can only see out of one eye? Now let me figure out which one he needs to be able to see out of." We all laughed until we nearly had tears coming down our faces.

"Thanks for trying to make me feel better, Soph, but I doubt Xander has any interest in me as a woman. He's trying to help me and I appreciate his efforts and yeah, I find him kind of intimidating, too." Hopefully they'd drop the crazy idea he was interested in me.

"Well, I don't know. I've never known him to be dating anyone; have you, Sophia?"

"Nope Tori, I haven't. So there you go, Edie. There's hope for you yet."

"Oh yeah, I can just see it now. Xander and I—a match made in heaven. Cue the cupids and the happily ever after. Thanks for trying to be supportive but hey, I need to get myself together and maybe somewhere a long, long way down the track I might find someone that's not too horrified by this face or this body. Somebody that's way lower on the hotness scale than Xander."

Tori looked over at me. "It really isn't that bad anymore Edie. The scars seem to fade all the time and there is that other operation..."

"Yeah, they have reduced but we all know they won't get much better. And as for the operation, we all know that's not in my future. I don't have a spare two hundred thousand so, until it gets covered by Medicare, it's just not an option, so I don't even let myself think about it."

They both nodded. My recovery was about as good as it could be physically, at the moment. It was all about the mental stuff now and that was proving a lot harder to overcome than the physical, in many ways.

"So um if you two are finished with the interrogation, I'm going to go and have a shower." I really felt as if I needed to wash away the night. I could still smell the reek of those guys in my nostrils, just like I could still smell the fire. I wanted it gone.

EDEN

"So how do you feel about what happened last night, Eden? You've given me the facts but there's not been one little bit of information to indicate how you actually feel about it."

Here we go...I thought to myself. I'd expected it. In fact, I was surprised Grace hadn't pressed me earlier but I guess she was waiting to see what I gave away about how I felt.

That was just it. I didn't really know how I felt about what had happened.

I shrugged my shoulders. "I don't really know how I feel, Grace. Sure I was terrified when I realised how much trouble I was in. Horrible stuff flashed through my head. I can still feel them, smell them. But nothing really happened. Dane got there before it did. And I don't know who to thank for that but someone was looking out for me."

Grace just stared at me and I knew she was assessing, trying to decide where to go next. "You said you don't know how you feel. You also said you were terrified when it was happening. How did you feel after? How do you feel now?"

"Well, I didn't really feel much of anything directly after, just a sense of relief and exhaustion. I can just clearly remember chanting left-right in my head. It was like I had tunnel vision and all I could see were my feet. I was shaking like a leaf and well I did faint as I told you before."

"That was the adrenalin." She clarified what I already knew.

"When I came to, it took me a couple of minutes to get my head together, I guess. Then I was talking to Xander, well rather he was lecturing me," I clarified. "It was pretty much a one-way conversation."

"Lecturing you! You said you'd had a chat. How did you feel about that?" Well, that seemed to put Grace on the back foot, which didn't happen very often.

"Well, it was more accurately a lecture. Once he knew I was okay, he kind of lectured me on what a dumb arse thing I'd done. He also said my behaviour and how I carried myself contributed to what happened. Then he just sort of told me he was going to teach me how to fight I guess."

When I finished Grace's mouth was drawn in a tight line. I don't think I'd ever seen that expression before. It was actually kind of amusing.

"You're telling me what happened again. Not how you felt."

I let out a huge breath and snapped my head to the side in frustration and anger. She always had to go poking and prodding. "Well, I guess I felt embarrassed for being so fucking stupid! He was right." My voice was angry now and I couldn't care less. She wanted to know—well, here it was.

"I did do something dumb and it put me at risk. He said I would have appeared weak and an easy target. I'm sure he's right about that. And I damned well know he's right when he said I never worried about my own safety because I stupidly convinced myself no one would be interested in me. He was right about everything he said, and I'm that way because I'm so fucking locked up in my own head, that it's driving me mad. I don't want to be there anymore. It's not a safe place. That place in my head almost got me raped or worse last night. I guess the only benefit is you can't be self-conscious when you're dead!"

Well, if the tight lip line Grace had been sporting before was a new expression than this one was something way past that one. Her eyes were huge and her jaw was actually hanging open a little.

I picked up the cushion on the sofa from beside me and thumped it. Fuck it! It was my appointment, my time and I was done with my own shit.

Just like last night, it felt better to hit the damned stupid stuffed velvet.

Grace let out a little laugh and clapped a couple of time.

"Bravo, Eden! You've had a break through."

"Sure you don't mean a break down?" I snarled.

"Far from it. What happened last night hasn't left you traumatised from what I can gather, in fact it's acted as a catalyst for you to seek positive change. I'm actually convinced after seeing and hearing you just now that you're going to start taking charge of your life."

"What choice do I have?" I smashed back at her.

"Oh, you always have choices, Eden. But you've just told me the way you were is no longer a safe or desirable option. Now it's up to you to decide what you're going to do next."

"I'm going to start living my life and stop hiding. That's what I'm going to try and do."

"And how are you going to do that?"

"Well, for a start I'm going to go and train with Xander. He said he can teach me to fight and look after myself. I don't ever want to feel as helpless as I felt last night. It was a wake up call. I was so lucky. I'm not going to expect to be that lucky again."

"I think that sounds like an excellent idea. So how do you feel about Xander? What makes him different to other people?" I should know. I really should. But again, I'd opened my mouth. Now I had to spill my guts.

"Xander is different. He doesn't look at me with pity. He said the scars don't bother him and well I guess I believe him. He hasn't ever reacted to them yet. And he's not scared to push me. He doesn't treat me like I'm different or made of glass." Then I thought about that fact he didn't want me to go to class with the others and I wondered if I had read that all wrong about him.

"Where'd you just go, Eden? You said all that then something popped into your head and you doubted what you had just said—why?"

"Because he said he wants to do a few one-on-one sessions with me. My sisters said he never does that." I looked at Grace as if she would magically have the answer, even though I knew that wouldn't be the case at all.

"Well, I can't speak for him, nor do I know what his regular practices are, but what do you think?"

"I don't really know. I guess I feel like he's not making excuses for me because of the burns. Kind of like he expects me to get on and do stuff like everyone else."

"I can see that from what you've told me. What do your sisters think? They've obviously spent a lot more time with this man."

"I already told you, they said it wasn't normal. They wondered if there was something else between us and I told them not to be so stupid. As if he'd be interested in me!" Right. There, done. Full disclosure and all that. Grace could make of it what she wanted. "Oh, and please don't ask me how I feel about that. I have no clues where men are concerned and I think the chances of him being interested in me that way are about as good as me winning tomorrow night's fifty million dollar Power Ball. About a billion to one."

Grace let out a laugh. "I'm really enjoying this new side to you, Eden. It's very refreshing. But I think you shouldn't discount someone of the opposite sex being interested in you. You may see scars and dreams lost when you look in the mirror, Eden, but not everyone else does. Men included. Is it really fair that you have already decided what someone will think about you based on how you look to them; before they've even had a chance to get to know you at all? Doesn't seem too fair to me."

I thought about her comment for a moment. Grace did have a point. I did expect everyone to see me a certain way. I'd learned that lesson about safety the hard way last night. Okay, so maybe I just had to be more open-minded.

"Give people a chance to get to know you. Share some of that personality you've just given me with them. You might just be pleasantly surprised."

I saw Grace glance at the clock and I knew she was getting ready to finish up this session.

"So that homework I set last time? Forget it. You've smashed right through all of that. This time I want you to focus on having proper conversations with people. Not just the please and thank you type of thing. Find out about them and their lives. But do try to go to a couple of new places as well."

I stood up and gathered my satchel. "Thanks, Grace."

"You're welcome. I'll see you next week for your scheduled appointment. But if you have any concerns before then give me a call. But something tells me you're going to be just fine."

"Working on it."

•••

Always diligent, Sophia had picked me up from the appointment with Grace. I guess I could have caught a bus or got a cab but Sophia always dropped me off and picked me up an hour later. Then I realised I'd never even asked her what she did in that hour while I was in with Grace. Did she study, go home, get a coffee... what?

That was just one more thing I needed to change. I needed to be more "in the moment" with the people that were important to me. They had lives as well and I had a horrible feeling or rather, a realisation, that I'd been treating each of them like a convenience. A relationship was supposed to be two way and it had been more about solid one way traffic. My way—for far too long.

Now I sat at the little desk I loved so much with my phone in hand. Sophia had shared Xander's contact details with me and all I had to do was type a simple text and send the damned thing. How hard was that really?

But what should I say?

Should I put: Hi, I saw my counsellor and I'm cleared to train

Or something like: All good. Ready to start when you are

I'd never sent a text to anyone but my sisters, Beth and my mum. My dad didn't do text messages. Because he was always driving he liked us to call. He said it helped to pass the time. So I tried to make sure I put aside half an hour every couple of days to have a chat to him. We both enjoyed those calls.

I procrastinated a couple more minutes, but then, as if she knew I needed her, Beth messaged me on my computer.

Beth: What are you up to giraffe?

It was a nick-name Beth sometimes used because of my lanky frame.

Me: Sitting here wondering how to send a text.

Beth: PMSL it's really not that hard. Type the message and press send.

Me: Haha why didn't I think of that?—It's the message bit that's got me stuck.

Beth: Pick up, I'm going to call you!

Next second the little icon at my computer screen started jumping around and buzzing. I clicked on it and immediately Beth was all over me.

"So when the hell did it become so difficult to send a text?" She was ribbing me and enjoying it a little bit too much.

"Since I have to send a text to Xander Todd and I have no freaking idea what to say..."

Her tone changed immediately. "Ohhhhhh. I see the problem."

"Yeah, definite problem."

"Okay, so you need to fill me in. I know I promised to be here last night but we were really late getting back from that thing in Longreach. What a fuck of a weekend. But that's a whole other story. I want to know why you're sitting here struggling over sending a text."

I took a deep breath... "Well a few things have happened..." And I spent the next fifteen minutes bringing her up to speed. I told her everything from what happened at the grading on Sunday to the mess I'd ended up in last night. I told her about 'the lecture', the discussion with my sisters and my appointment with Grace. She now knew everything.

When I finally got to the end I couldn't help but add a "So what the hell do you think of all that?"

"Well hon, when you decided to finally join the world, you did it in a mighty big way!" I heard her laugh. "Well, I'm impressed."

This time I snorted in amusement. "Fantastic Beth, glad to be of service, but I've still got this text message to write."

"Okay, let's figure it out together." This time her voice was more subdued and focused. "I think you need to keep it straight to the point and don't get cute. Text messages are too easy to misinterpret. I think you're tying yourself in knots about nothing." That was good solid sound advice.

But I didn't want to be boring. Hell, I didn't know what I wanted to be. I just didn't want to be scared anymore.

I picked up my phone and typed into the screen as I spoke to Beth. "So I'm going to say this— 'Hey Xander, I'm right to get started with the training when it's convenient for you'."

"Perfect! Go with that. He's just a guy, a person like you or me. Treat him like you would anyone else. Although he is one delicious piece of man–candy."

"What the hell, Beth. How do you even know what he looks

like?" My brain is mush right about now.

"What? Have you not heard of Google images?" Beth squeals at me.

"Of course I have. But I haven't looked." And I hadn't. I'd been busy doing course work, well, at least, that's what I told myself. Beside you couldn't believe everything that was written about someone on the internet could you? And it kind of felt like a huge invasion of privacy when you actually knew the person you were checking out. Well, at least it did to me.

"Well, good thing one of us has done her research and I didn't just study the pics. Although, I could do that for hours." Her voice sounded a little dreamy and suddenly I felt a bit pissed off, as well as being intrigued. There was a part of me that didn't like her enjoying Xander. "He's got a hell of story himself and I'd be surprised if he didn't carry a fair swag of his own demons around."

"Don't tell me. I don't want to know!" I protested sticking to my morals.

"Oh Eden, you're no damned fun. Do you know how dead boring it is living out here? If it wasn't for the internet I'd go stark raving mad." I didn't envy Beth at all. She lived in such isolation. Australia was a massive place.

"Yeah, I get it." I didn't really but she was too polite to correct me. I think living in outback Australia was one of those things you actually had to experience for yourself before you truly understood. It was kind of the same with living with demons.

"So have you sent that damned text message yet?"

"Hang on a sec." I reread the message I'd typed before and hit send. I was done with second guessing it. "Gone." I let out a long sigh. "Oh shit, now I guess I have to wait."

"Hopefully not too long. So you really don't want to know what's on the net about him."

Well, I did want to know. But I wasn't about to admit it. However, it wouldn't seem right to me learning this way. "I'd love to know, but I think people should get the option of telling their story rather than people just sticking it on the internet for it to be interpreted any which way." After the fire people assumed they knew the facts. Thought they knew what happened and why it happened. They weren't there and had nothing to do with the fire, but that didn't stop the rubbish that was peddled on the internet. What was posted was far from the truth, but it was passed off as gospel No, I hated that aspect of the internet and social media.

"Well, suit yourself." She was taking the pissy superior tone. It was a big amusing joke.

"You're just annoyed because I'm not gossiping with you."

"Fucking A, I am. I'm intending to live vicariously through you."

"Well, that could be dangerous and I hope to God you don't mind disappointment."

Before she could make some snarky comeback, my phone pinged with an incoming text. "I've got a text."

"What's it say?"

I opened my txt app and read it aloud. "He says...Awesome—let's do tomorrow afternoon at 2.00."

"That's great."

"Ah no, it's not. I've got a tutorial that goes till 1.30 and I can't miss it."

"Well text him back and let him know. I'm sure he'll be fine. But please no agonising over this one. "

"Okay." I shot back a text, letting him know that I can't do 2.00. Some part of me hopes he'll call the whole thing off if I can't do 2.00pm.

Maybe it will be easier.

"Oh hell...I'm going to have to go. My mum's got some issue I need to go deal with. Drop me a message and let me know what happens. If I don't catch you before. Have fun tomorrow."

"Bye Beth."

"Catch you."

No sooner had I ended the online call than my phone was ringing. I couldn't believe my eyes when I looked down. It was Xander calling.

I flicked my finger across the screen and said hello.

"Hey, Eden. You go to Griffith Uni, Logan Campus, right?"

My mind was racing, why would he want to know? "Yes."

"Cool. I've got a meeting in the City, I'll be coming that way. I'll swing by and pick you up. That'll save some time."

"Okay." Why did my belly feel like it was doing roly polies right now?

"So bring some clothes you can train in. We'll get you kitted out with a gi soon."

"Okay."

"Stay in the grounds of the uni and I'll text you when I'm near. I'll be in my truck." I wasn't sure why he was telling me that, but I guess he had a reason.

"Sure."

"Great, okay I've got to go. I've got a class about to start in a few minutes. But one last thing." He paused and I held my breath wondering what he was about to say. "Relax. I'm strict but I don't bite and I won't hurt you."

"I know." I knew the tone of my voice wasn't very convincing and I heard his low chuckle and it sent little shivers through me.

"Good, get a good night's sleep, drink plenty of water and I'll see you tomorrow."

"Okay. Bye, Xander."

"Bye Eden."

I ended the call and slumped back in my chair a little shell-shocked.

It was really happening.

I couldn't get out of this one.

SEVEN

XANDER

"Fuck," I muttered to myself as I hit the M3 heading out of the City. I had twenty minutes until I needed to pick up Eden. I could be close to the time if I broke a few speed limits.

My meeting with the boring as shit accountant had run over. God, that guy could drone on. Paperwork and particularly the bookwork associated with running my dojo was my least favourite part. I now had a pile of papers I needed to go through and sort out, apparently. Wasn't that what I paid him for? Yeah, I'd get to those papers—later...much! Getting enthused about paperwork was definitely not something that came naturally to me.

I grabbed my phone and illegally whipped out a text message to Eden. I didn't want her standing out the front waiting for me. There'd been at least three attempted abductions of female uni students from around here in the last month. One of my boys had told me about them. After her efforts the night before last, I didn't want to have Eden at risk. I'm not convinced yet, that she understands the concept of personal safety. She will before I'm finished with her.

The traffic was fortunately light where the M3 and the M1 joined at Eight Mile Plains. It could be an absolute shocker. At this rate I'd only be a minute or two late. If I got the lights, I might even make it on time. I took the exit off the M1 and the traffic light Gods were kind to me. Green all the way.

I pulled into the circular driveway at the front of the campus and immediately reached for my phone to send her a text to let her know I was there. Before I could even finish typing it out I recognised her figure walking out. She had stepped from the shadows at the front of the main buildings.

Today she was wearing a big loose long sleeved blue T-shirt and baggy jeans. Both looked to be about four sizes too big. A black knapsack was slung over her shoulder along with her satchel and pair of black converses were on her feet. That distinctive strawberry silk was everywhere, most of it covering her head that was once again down. How Eden could even see where she was going was a complete mystery to me. From what I could tell, she hadn't looked up once. I wanted to rip into her for that. I took a deep breath and schooled myself to have patience. Changing her whole demeanour wasn't going to happen in five seconds.

As she got nearer, I leant over and opened the door. I was in a no-standing zone and the roving campus security guard was giving me evil looks. I would have been even more impressed if he'd come up and asked me what I was doing. Maybe if he did that more often, we wouldn't have some sick fuck trying to abduct girls coming from the university.

She took hold of the door and placed her bags on the floor then looked up at me as those thick dark lashes flirted across her blue eyes. Eden had the most beautiful eyes I had ever seen. The world deserved to see them too.

Before she could hesitate, I reached over and took her hand, giving her a little tug to help her in. My truck was jacked up. Very occasionally she even saw some off road action. Yeah, it was time to plan a trip. I made a mental note.

"Hey Gem, how was class?"

She looked at me a little shyly, but she still looked at me. Yes! I cheered internally—a small victory. "It was okay. Lots of homework but that goes with the territory." Eden had settled herself in the seat and buckled up. I pulled out and headed across town to the dojo. "So how about your day?"

I was surprised. Eden was actually initiating a conversation with me. "Oh, I've had a morning I could have done without. I think I'd even take a trip to the dentist over having to visit my accountant. The guy is as boring as bat shit and I really struggle not to nod off." I glanced sideways and she nodded slightly in understanding and suddenly seemed a little uncomfortable in her seat. I had no idea what I'd said or done to make her feel that way.

We drove a little further until I could no longer stand the uncomfortable silence. "So tell me what are you studying at university?"

She winced and I immediately knew what she'd been uncomfortable about. "Oh no. Tell me it ain't so!" I couldn't help the chuckle that rolled out of me. Fate, you cheeky bitch.

"I'm afraid I can't. I'm studying business with a double major in accounting and information technology." Her voice sounded a little pained.

"Well, if you insist on studying something that dull, then, at least, you're going to have to explain the attraction. Because I just don't get it!" I was joking around trying to keep the mood light and cheery. I wanted Eden to know she could relax and let her guard down around me. Have fun, be free to be herself.

She didn't answer and suddenly I got a horrible sick feeling in my gut. I glanced over and she seemed to have shrunk to half her size in that big leather bucket seat.

"Oh Gem, what is it? What did I say?" I pleaded.

"Maybe we should just forget it, Xander. This...isn't going to work." Her voice was small and broke a couple of times. I checked the traffic and slipped across a couple of lanes and turned into a quiet residential street, pulling up at the curb with a jolt. I punched the gear shifter into Park, unbuckled my seat belt and turned to her.

Eden hadn't looked up; she just sat huddled there.

I reached over and undid her seatbelt and she moved her hand to open the door. She was expecting me to kick her out of the truck. What I wanted to do couldn't have been farther from her thoughts. My reactions were quicker and I hit the auto locking. At that she spun her head up and looked at me. Confusion and fear flashed across her eyes.

"Have I got your attention now?"

She said nothing—just looked at me, poised and waiting as if to be struck. Just how deep did her demons go and what was it going to take to defeat them I wondered for about the thousandth time in the last week.

"This is going to work, Gem, because we're going to make it work. I'm not going to let you get out of this that easily. I'm not going to let you go back and hide. Even if I'm the only one that gets to see the real you, then, by God, that's better than no one at all. You can start by telling me why you study accounting and information technology. That's obviously where I screwed up this conversation."

I could see the tears pooled in her eyes and I knew right then there was going to be a lot more during this journey. "If you need to cry to answer me, do it! Tears are just another form of sweat. They represent hard work and the body cleansing. Have at it, if you need to. But you will answer me. We're not moving from right here until you do."

Her bottom lip was trembling and a lone tear slipped down over the scar on her face. I reached over and opened the glove compartment and deposited the box of tissues in her lap.

She took one and wiped at her eye. "You really want to know?"

"I really want to know."

"I chose to study accounting and information technology because both are professions that allow me to be out of the public eye. I can do both remotely without having to see people."

That was so telling. Here she was planning her life purposely to live in the shadows away from the need to interact with people.

"Do you enjoy accounting and IT?"

"It's okay. I'm getting really good marks. Last semester I got all high distinctions." There was a little bit of pride in her voice but no passion.

"Well, that's a great achievement but let me ask you this. If you could do anything at all what would you choose to do?"

Eden didn't even pause with her answer. "Well, I was going to be a model but that's not going to happen, but my backup plan was always to be an interior designer. I always figured I could do that after modelling as well."

"So why aren't you studying interior design?"

She tilted her head up and looked at me almost as if I was a little simple. "Because who would employ an interior designer that looks like I do?"

"I was under the impression that when someone hired a designer they were paying them to decorate a space. I don't see how your appearance has anything to do with that."

"People like to be around beautiful people, particularly when they're doing aesthetically pleasing activities. Even if I happened to be the best designer ever, I just couldn't see people wanting to hire me." I could see her logic but I wasn't sure whether it was researched or correct. Had she just conveniently come up with that conclusion on her own?

"Did you go to any design companies and talk to them about what opportunities there would be for you?"

She dipped her head. "No." Her voice was back to being the mouse like whisper.

"You just assumed..."

Eden nodded her head.

"Is it what you'd really like to do?"

"I guess..." She didn't sound convincing.

"Well, if it is what you really want to do, you don't give up the dream. You fight and you make it happen." I was in pep talk mode now.

"But I don't have a portfolio or anything even if it was an option. I'd need a portfolio to demonstrate what I'd done. Courses aren't enough; employers want portfolios." Her voice was flat, but I could tell it was pitched that way to mask her enthusiasm for how she really felt.

"So you have to have a portfolio to get into a course. Is that what you're saying?"

"Well, I could get into an okay course but all the best courses and most prestigious courses want a portfolio. Ideally, you'd do a course then try to get an internship with an established designer or company. The better your portfolio, the better the designer you can hope to work for. They want to see progression."

Well, that all made sense, but I didn't have any answers at the moment. "Okay. Well, I don't think you should shut the door on it. Dreams unrealised have a habit of turning into regret." Regret was something I knew all about.

Eden shrugged her shoulders, butI got the feeling she wasn't convinced.

"Anyway, I think it's important that we both acknowledge now I'm going to do things or say things that make you uncomfortable. Whether it's just general conversation or whether it's me teaching you something, stuff will come up. It's going to be tough at times. You do...not...shut down and you do...not...throw in the towel and walk away. You...talk...to...me. Tell me what the issue is, help me understand from your perspective. This sitting here and saying nothing, then deciding that running is easier, stops right now."

Eden was focusing on that point on my collar bones again. I reached out and gently cupped her chin in my hand, forcing her to look me in the eye. "I want your word on it, Eden. I'm happy to put the effort in and do whatever I can if you are. Can you give me your word you're going to work with me no matter how tough it gets?"

Her big eyes blinked slowly a couple of times and I knew she was taking it in and thinking through everything I'd just said.

"Yes."

It was only after I heard that one word did I realise I'd completely tensed my whole body. Eden Sommers was as skittish as a new born fawn, but I was determined to win the day. I also knew that the relationship I had intended to have with Eden was not going to work. I needed to rethink everything in a big hurry.

There was no way my beautiful Gem was ever going to be just a student.

EDEN

Oh my God! Oh my God! What was I doing? I couldn't get those thoughts out of my head as I changed clothes in the ladies bathroom at Onigashima Fighters. I pulled my yoga pants on, then a tight singlet top over my sports bra/crop top thing and my scars. What a laugh. Sports bra/crop top. This thing had never seen a day's action since I bought it a year ago. Maybe that would change today. Then over the singlet top I pulled a big loose T-shirt. It swamped me. Just the way I liked it. I looked in the mirror and started to feel panic rising in my throat.

Why had I agreed to everything he said? What was I thinking? This wasn't for me. This wasn't the life I had.

Breathe Eden. Breathe Eden I chanted.

I could do this. I could. Besides I had a strong suspicion Xander would have no qualms about coming in and finding me if I didn't head out very soon. He'd given me five minutes and by my calculations I was already about a minute over that.

With one last look in the mirror and a deep breath, I pushed open the heavy door, and walked down the corridor towards the main room with mirrors and mats. Xander was already on the floor, his body jack knifed at the waist with his palms flat on the floor. The man was seriously flexible and I knew there was no way I could pull off a stretch even remotely like that.

As he realised I was there he stood and faced me. I hesitated at the edge of the mats and remembered that I was supposed to do some sort of bow thing. I had seen the other students do it.

Xander must have realised my hesitation. "Right fist to left shoulder, left fist to right shoulder over the top. Then bow." I did as he asked and moved forward to him.

He nodded at me. "Well done. I didn't expect you to know that. You were watching. I'm not going to be too formal here at the moment. I just want you to get comfortable with things. But good job on picking up that bow. Just think of this as two friends hanging out at the moment. "

That surprised me, but I nodded my understanding and stood there with my hands by my sides. Xander looked up and down my body and I struggled to stand still as my skin seemed to prickle where his eyes had touched. It was a weird feeling, kind of anxious and tingling at the same time.

"First off you're going to need to tie your hair back. We can't work with it down. It's beautiful as it is, but it has to be tied back for this, Gem."

"I don't have a band," I said almost helplessly. The thought of losing my "shield" sent chills through my blood.

"I can fix that." He jogged over to the reception area—all fluid grace, and returned a second later with a hairband in his outstretched hand.

"There you go. I've learned to keep a supply." He looked at me expectantly. "Come on, Eden, just tie it back already. I've told you the scars don't worry me. We all have some."

I tried to blank my mind and just do it. Slowly I reached behind and tied my hair back into a pony-tail, knowing that pulling my hair back would expose the extent of the scars running down my neck from my face and under the round necked T-shirt. I could feel him watching intently as I did it. I would have worn a turtle neck if thought I could have gotten away with it but the weather was already starting to really warm up. Then, when I finished that task, he kept right on pushing.

"What's the extent of the scarring, Eden? I noticed then, that you moved your right arm tentatively. Does it give you pain? What sort of range of motion do you have?"

I think I flinched at his words. He just came out with it and hit me right between the eyes, so to speak. I hated talking about the scars only slightly less than I hated showing someone. They were so ugly. Sometimes they felt weird—tight, tingly, itchy. So I often moved to compensate and he'd obviously picked up on it. I should have thought about this. Fear and self-consciousness gnawed at my stomach. Why did I agree to this? What had I been thinking in agreeing to this?

"Quit worrying about what I'm going to think and answer my questions. Better still show me so I can really understand."

I gasped in shock. Did I hear him right? Had he just suggested that? Nobody but my family and medical team had ever seen them. The panic I'd been trying to quash before was once again threatening to drown me.

My lips were moving, but I couldn't form words. I didn't know what to say anyway. I felt the tears prick my eyes again and I fought to keep them under control.

"Look, I know this makes you incredibly uncomfortable. I can see it. You're shaking and I know you're fighting tears. Let them go if you need to. Breathe through the panic." He took a couple of deep slow breaths, encouraging me to do the same with him. "You need to understand martial arts training is quite physical by nature. If you don't let me know what we're working with, I can't figure out how best to approach your training. I'm not doing it to make you feel embarrassed or uncomfortable. I'm honestly doing it from the point of trying to understand. I really want to help you; teach you. But I need to know and seeing is probably going to be easiest."

He was looking at me directly. Those deep black onyx pools were full of emotion. I could feel he meant every word he said. Somehow it felt as if this pained him as much as it did me. I felt so exposed and I hadn't even decided what to do.

"What have you got on under that shirt?"

"A singlet and a crop top thing."

He nodded. "Can you do this for me? I know it's a huge step, something tells me if you can do this—everything else after that will be a cinch. Help me; help you, Eden."

I moved my hands to the hem of my T-Shirt, and took a deep breath in through my nose. Come on, Eden, you can do this. You trust him. He's never done anything but try to help you. It's just skin.

Looking back, I think it was probably the same sort of feeling a bungee jumper got as they stood up on the platform as they prepared to hurtle themselves off into nothing. Fear, terror and the promise of freedom and exhilaration.

"Just do it, Eden." And like a jumper that had reached the end of their countdown I lifted the T-Shirt up and over my head as quickly as I could. Jumping into nothingness.

I stood waiting for Xander to say something—my eyes fixed on the spot where his collarbones met the pectoral muscles of his chest. Every now and then a hint of a tattoo peaked out from underneath the collar of his shirt and from the place where his right bicep intersected with his elbow. I wanted to know what that tattoo was about. It looked beautiful and that little spot was a safe place on which to focus. Something to keep me grounded and connected when I felt completely adrift.

"Well done, Eden. That took real guts." He moved a step closer and I knew what he would be seeing, studying—raised, rough, reddened skin in spots, tight, pink and shiny in others. It was ugly and foreign and ran down my shoulder and my side. There was nothing pretty or attractive about it.

"Does it hurt at all?"

Somewhere I found my voice. "Not really. There's some nerve damage on my side. That can annoy me at times if I bump it or sometimes it just pains on its own. It's hard to describe. Sort of a sharp jabbing feeling or even tingles."

He moved another step closer till he was standing so close I could feel the air move between us as he breathed and I could see the pores of his skin in fine detail. I wanted to step back so bad. I wanted to run. His hand came down and rested on my right hip. He did it slowly and I knew it was calculated not to spook me.

"Breathe, Eden. To teach you, I'm going to need to have my hands on you. Martial arts is a contact activity by the very nature of it."

I held my breath and let it out slowly...trying to relax into his touch. His hand on my hip felt so foreign. It was so deliberate. The heat and sensations had my thoughts feeling foggy and disjointed. Was it possible to be terrified and reassured at the same time?

"Are you going to freak out if I lift this singlet up? I want you to show me the spots that give you the most discomfort. I'll try to avoid them, if I can. Just like ripping off a Band-Aid, Eden. Once it's done, it's done."

My eyes scrunched tight and my whole body tensed. I could do it.

I nodded slightly, it was subtle but I was sure I had.

"Give me the words, Eden. Tell me it's okay." His voice was low and demanding. It was the tone he used with his students. The one, that even though he was asking for permission, there was no way you could refuse him.

"Do it!" The words came out before my brain registered I'd done it.

He didn't hesitate. I felt the fabric raise and the air hit my skin directly. Up and up it went, till his hand was level with my crop top bra. I knew what he was seeing. I knew how ugly it was. My lungs were burning and I couldn't seem to draw in any air. I was stuck, frozen to the spot.

Paralysed by my emotions.

"Good girl. You're doing great, Eden. Just focus on my voice. Breathe, don't hold your breath. Breath control is very important in martial arts. We'll do a lot of work on it later. Breathe out slowly." I must have released the breath—I started to feel better. "Okay now breathe in again with me...and out...that's it Eden. You control the moment. Not the other way around."

I listened to his voice. And followed his instructions.

"Okay, keep breathing just like you have been. Open your eyes." Slowly, I raised my eyelids. His face was the first thing I saw, a picture of concern. Not pity. Not discomfort. It was genuine and right then I knew he was feeling every single raw emotion I was. My pain, was his pain. He was guiding me through, helping me face my fear—building me up.

"Okay Eden, now I want you to show me the bits that are the most tender. Don't forget to breathe. It's okay. You're safe."

Somehow after his words, looking down was much easier than I thought. The scars were just disfigured skin. Nothing I could do to fix. I raised my right arm and with my index finger I traced the area down the side and under my breast.

"This area feels a little weird sometimes. The skin seems to be thinner or something. If I move my arm right forward or right up I can feel it pull. It kind of feels like the skin is too tight." I moved my arm to demonstrate.

"Is the skin more fragile?"

"The doctors don't think so. I put lots of moisturiser on it to keep it as supple as possible. And it seems to settle more all the time, but I think I'll always have a few weird sensations there."

He nodded his understanding. "Okay, so that spot we call the floating rib. It's a very sensitive part of the body. Any other spots?"

I pointed to the spot just in front of my right hip. "It's kind of the same." Then I acted on instinct and hooked a thumb into the band of my yoga pants and pulled them down a few inches exposing the area below my hip and sliding into my buttock. "The scars end here."

I could feel his eyes on me during every centimetre of the journey—cataloguing and memorising my scars.

There was no more to show—I'd done it. Relief and something else washed over me. I'd faced my demons and won this round.

I pulled the waistband back up and he lowered my singlet once again. But didn't step back.

Instead Xander moved even closer and pulled me to his body in a hug. He was only slightly taller than me but his shoulders were wide and his hips narrow. There was no mistaking the power and strength in his body as my arms held tight to him. My chest was pressed to his and I could feel my nipples start to pebble against him.

His hand stroked from the back of my head to the middle of my back and I could feel a trail of tingly little prickles in its wake. Then he pulled back from me slightly and captured my eyes with his.

"Thank you for trusting me, Eden. I know how hard that was for you. It's going to get easier from here. I promise. When the next challenge comes up, you're going to remember how difficult it was just now and how good it felt when you managed your fears. Fears rarely ever disappear completely, but they certainly become more manageable. A little bit of fear can be healthy as long as we're the ones managing it."

I could feel the tears about to burst forth again. My emotions were all over the place. I'd gone through a whole scale of them—terror on one end, elation on the other.

"Let them fall if you need to. I'm so proud of you."

How did he read me so well? He seemed to know me better than I knew myself.

Not sure what else to do, I reached down and picked up the T-Shirt I'd discarded before. I went to put it back on but he reached out to stop me.

"Don't Eden. You don't need to cover up. It'll just get in the way. Regardless of the scars you're still a stunning woman with an incredible figure. You don't need to hide it."

I didn't know what to say. Before the fire I was told so many times how pretty I was, how beautiful I was. They were words I hadn't heard in years. I'd forgotten how to respond.

Xander took the shirt from my hand and he had a strange faraway look on his face. "You may not believe me yet. But I'm going to remind you, show you, just how beautiful you are. You gave me beautiful once. I'm going to give it back to you."

I didn't ask, what he meant. Curiosity was screaming for me to, but it didn't feel right for me to ask. It was almost as if he'd unwittingly voiced something that was meant only for himself. Some things were best left unsaid. If he wanted me to know, he'd explain in his own time. Until then I'd wonder.

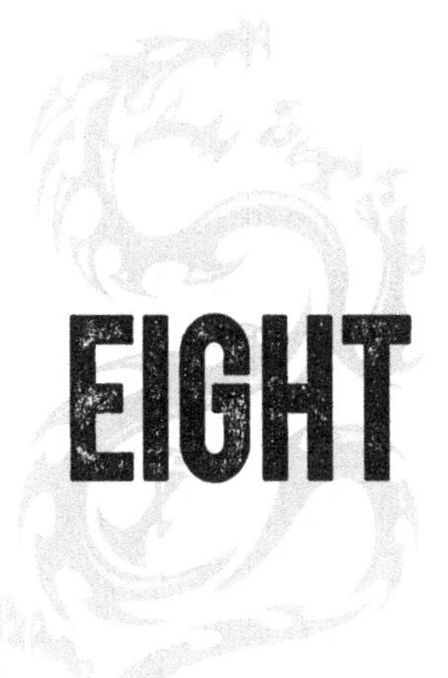

EIGHT

XANDER

Did I just say all that out loud? From the look on Eden's face I had. I hadn't meant to, but she just moved me in ways that had me doing stuff I didn't really understand. I walked to the edge of the mats with her T-Shirt and struggled to get my head together.

I was stunned at how brave she'd just been. How much trust she'd placed in me—I felt the gravity of the responsibility and it was humbling. There's no way I'd intentionally hurt her or let anyone else for that matter.

Eden's bravery wasn't the only thing I was blown away by—the lady was rockin' a killer body under all that loose fabric. My God! I could easily see now how she'd secured that modelling contract. She was all long elegant lines and feminine curves. Her skin, not affected by burns, was satiny smooth and seemed to glow. It was easy to be mesmerised by her—burns or not. There was just something about Eden Sommers that tapped into my heart and wouldn't let go.

Right, time to get started on what I'd planned. I walked back over to where she was standing. "Okay, are you ready to get going?"

She nodded and I noticed her eyes were bright but I think the threat of tears had past. "I'm ready."

I stood in front of her, but a couple of paces back. "Normally we'd run through a warm up routine. I'll show you that next time. But I'm going to keep things light and slow today. We'll let the muscles warm up slowly as we go." Eden nodded her understanding. "Okay, let me show you some basic punches first. The first one I'm going to do is a jab cross. Let me show you."

I demonstrated it at about half speed and half power to give her an idea of what it looked like. Then I went to stand beside her and took hold of her left hand. "So it generally starts with the left hand as you're a right hander. But first you need to make a strong fist." She closed her fingers to make a fist but her manicured nails were going to be a problem for fists, although the thought of them running down my back was a whole other story.

Get your head back in the game, Xan. I mentally chastised myself. "You might need to trim those nails to make it a little more comfortable. Make sure you tuck your thumb under so you don't get it caught or knock it. From experience, it hurts like hell."

Her mouth curled up in a little grin at my words as she focused on what I was showing her with my own fist. "Okay, now I'm going to show you a guard position. So bring your hands to your face. Your knuckles rest on your cheekbones. Your hands stay here all the time unless they're striking or blocking." I quickly demonstrated a couple of other cover positions always starting with my hands on my face. "See how easily I can adjust my cover for incoming strikes if my hands are up protecting my face. I just roll my shoulders inwards and close my forearms and I've made a pretty effective cage for my face. Okay you try it."

She brought her hands up and mimicked what I'd done almost perfectly. I gently moved her hands slightly. "Show me the closed cover." Eden moved her left arm in front of her chest to protect but the right one didn't quite make it in as far or fast.

"Does that give you problem?" Without thinking my hand went

to the spot where the movement was restricted. I could feel the ridge of scared skin below her singlet and she flinched away.

"Sorry, I didn't mean to hurt you." I could feel the heat through the thin material of her singlet, that alone played havoc with my senses.

Then she turned slightly and I could see something new in her eyes—amusement. "You didn't. It tickled!" she said a little shyly.

I chuckled a little with her. "Well, that's better than pain."

"Ah, yes!" Her voice held knowing depth. I doubted the biggest beating I'd ever taken, would have been a hundredth of the pain she must have gone through. It was mind boggling to imagine.

We ran through some more covers and basic punch combinations for the next fifteen minutes until she could throw them comfortably on my call. Eden was a good student. She focused and tried hard to get things exactly right. It wasn't hard for me to understand how her grades were so high.

"Okay, that was great. Now let's do some basic self-defence moves. I want to show you how to get out of some grabs and holds." I moved to stand directly in front of her. I was easily in her "personal space." "Before we get going, I need to warn you, with these ones I will be touching you a lot. There's no other way."

Her eyelids raised a fraction more and I noticed a hint of something in her eyes. "That's okay. I don't think I'll mind too much." What was I seeing? Was it what I thought it was? God, she was killing me. I wanted to touch her so much and not in a strictly professional way.

"Well, okay then, I'm going to start with a front grab. But to start with I want you to place your hands on my shoulders or round my throat and I'll show you how to get out of it. There's several ways. I'll show you a few, then as time goes on you'll figure out which ones work best for you and the ones you feel most comfortable doing."

Eden nodded her understanding and placed her hands on my shoulders about an inch away from my neck on either side. She didn't just rest her hands there, but rather applied a bit of a pressure. It was almost as if she was going to give me a massage and I wondered what that would feel like for a split second before I went about showing her how to remove an attacker's hands from a front grab.

I showed her how to pull fingers back to break the hold, how to drive my arms upwards and downwards with enough force to remove those holding me. We also went through how strikes could be added. Once she had the basics, we reversed the positions and Eden got to work on breaking the holds I put her in. We practised those for a few minutes. I was enjoying the look of achievement she got on her face when she managed to get out of a hold. Eden was really digging this.

"Now let's do some work on grabs from behind." I stood in front of her. "Okay, move in behind me and wrap an arm around my neck." She did as I asked and her arm came around my throat. Her chest was pressed tight to my shoulders and damned if I didn't feel my dick start to stir in my shorts. I knew it was because of the combination of her body pressed tight to me, her warm breath on my neck and the light scent of blackberries that seemed to always be with her. I fucking loved her perfume. This never happened. I taught classes all the time. Men, women, kids, I taught them all. I'd taught women before—stunning, sexy women but none of them had affected me like Eden was now. I could barely think about what I was wanting to show her.

"Is that what you wanted?" Her words came out beside my ear and I shivered from the feel. Focus Xander!

"That's perfect. So this is a really dangerous situation to be in. Doesn't get much worse than this. From here, you have the ability to choke me out really quick if I don't do something about it. You need to stop the arm from tightening around your neck and you need to do it quickly. First off, you need to turn your head into the hold. So if the right arm is around my neck, I turn my head to the right to create some space so I can breathe a bit better." I moved my head to demonstrate. "Now I need to loosen this hold. A backward elbow to the middle can work well." I moved my body a little away from her and moved my right arm back mimicking the strike. “You can stomp on toes, rake your foot down a shin. Strike to the groin. You need to be serious about getting out of here quick. This is a very aggressive hold—you need to show equal aggression to break it.”

I brought my hand up to her arm and indicated that she should let go. “Okay, now you try to get out of my hold.” I moved in behind her and wrapped my arm around her throat and brought my left hand up and interlocked my arms. My left palm cradled the back of her skull but also made the hold that much more aggressive and more challenging to break. Her hair was so soft and silky under my fingers; I had to resist the urge to stroke and massage it.

“What about your hand on my head? I didn’t have that with you before.” She sounded confused and I wasn’t sure whether she was a little put out at me making the hold harder or the feel of my hand on her head. It could be quite intimidating for some people.

“So focus on what you need to do first. Turn your head, give yourself some room to breathe. Don’t panic, I’m just going to demonstrate something.” She nodded slightly. “Okay, you can feel me tightening my arm around you. I could increase the pressure to choke you out easily. So turn your chin to the right. Create the room you need to breathe.” She moved her head slightly. “Good, now do what you need to do to break the hold.” I didn’t want to give her pointers from here. I wanted to see what she would do.

A second later her right arm flew back and connected with my mid-section. The swift blow took me a bit by surprise. I needed to mention to her we weren’t trying to wound each other for practise. She twisted her body around some more and swung backwards with her hand obviously aiming for my groin. I managed to get my right hip and thigh into place to take the hit, rather than my groin. Her hand slammed into my thigh hard enough that I knew it would have left me gasping for breath if she’d connected with her intended target. I loosened my hold and let her struggle some more and break free.

She turned to look at me and I could see colour had pooled in her cheeks and her chest was heaving as if she'd run. It had to be from the emotions that this sort of stuff could stir up. Her attack had only been recent. "You okay, Eden?"

Her eyes closed and she swallowed. I could see she was trying to pull herself together. "Yeah, I'm okay. That was just a bit too real."

I chuckled and thought about my package. "Yeah, I thought you were really going to drop me for a sec. When we do this sort of training, we go at an intensity that demonstrates we know the moves and can break them, but we don't intend to do any damage. We want to be able to keep training." I winked at her and a little grin spread across her face. "Won't be long until a guy would be a fool to mess with you. You're going to be just as fierce as your sisters I see. Must run in the family."

Her eyes lit up and the grin became a smile. There it was. I could look at it for days.

Dane came through the front doors and gave me a wave before he headed down the corridor to the locker room to get changed. His arrival jogged my mind as to the time. It seemed to fly whenever I was with Eden. I also didn't miss that she'd put her body behind mine to prevent him from seeing her.

"Okay, we're going to have to call it quits for today. Dane and some of the guys have a session on these mats in about fifteen minutes. Let me go grab your shirt." I jogged over to the edge of the mats and snagged her shirt.

I passed it back to her and she immediately slipped it back on. "Thanks for understanding." She reached for my hand as she said it and her eyes spoke to me as much as her voice.

"I think you've done amazingly well today, Eden. Why don't you go get changed, then come and find me in my office?"

She nodded and did a perfectly executed bow.

I wanted to hug her, to tip her chin up to me so I could see her eyes and do a hundred other things that would have been inappropriate. Instead I gave her a friendly pat on the back as she walked past me.

I just needed to touch her.

I was in such deep trouble.

EDEN

I felt completely all over the place, wrung out as I left the locker room and headed to Xander's office. Hey, it had been going on for days—ever since Xander Todd had come crashing into my life. But I also felt freer and more alive than I had in years. My emotions terrified, hurt and excited me all at once, but the one that was really playing with me hard was the hope. That scared me the most. Getting a glimpse of something amazing only to have it ripped away—I knew just how gutting that was. I didn't want to feel that level of pain again. I was no stranger to physical or emotional pain. Physical pain could be managed with pain killers—nothing touched the emotional pain.

The door off the corridor was open and I could see him sitting at his desk, his eyes on the computer screen in front of him. His head was shaking from side to side and he looked pissed off.

I stood there for a second, not sure whether to knock or just go or what. He looked really annoyed.

Xander didn't look up. "Are you or aren't you the one that is studying accounting and IT?"

"Yes," I squeaked out.

He pushed back from the desk on his wheeled chair with a move so aggressive my heart almost stopped. "Well, Gem, I suggest you get your butt over here and see if you can make some sense of this. If I have to look at this spreadsheet a second longer, that computer is going to meet an unpleasant end with the road right out front of this place." As aggressive as his actions were his voice was perfectly controlled and sounded totally conversational.

He'd used that word Gem again and I was absolutely confused by it all but said nothing.

Xander moved from behind the desk and stepped forward to herd me behind his desk. My heart thudded in my chest. He plopped his body down on the sofa opposite the desk as I took the seat and ran my eyes over what was causing him so much grief.

It looked to be an expenses sheet.

"Are you trying to get the office expenses column to tally?" I asked very tentatively.

"Yeah, that's the one. Apparently my damned accountant needs this now!" There was no doubting just how he felt about his accountant.

I quickly scanned the column and checked the numbers and then found the problem. Somehow a stray formula had gotten into the column creating an error. I cleared the column and the total popped up happily. Then I linked the expenses column to the overall sheet and it all balanced beautifully.

"Where do you want it saved?" I asked

"You've got it fixed already?" There was no mistaking the awe in his voice. It was nothing really, just a very simple spreadsheeting error.

"Yes, I just need to save it and then you can forward it to your accountant." I hesitated a fraction but turned to look at him. There was a smile on his face and all the tension and anger were gone.

"Just save it to the accountant folder in my documents, please." Then he looked a lot sheepish. "Sorry about that. Bookwork and computers just do my head in. Phones, iPads and xboxes are about the extent of tech I enjoy. Thanks for fixing that, Gem."

I turned back to the computer and quickly found the file path. "Do you want me to send it to the email address it was attached to—your accountant?"

"That'd be awesome." I nodded and sent the spreadsheet on its way.

When I finished, I looked up and could see him staring at me intently. I pushed back from the desk a lot more sedately than he had. I could hear people filing into the dojo and I knew our time was up. I needed to go home and step out of the dream—return back to being Eden.

Xander got up off the sofa as well, as I shouldered my knapsack and satchel.

"Umm... thanks so much for everything you showed me. I'll see you later."

I started rushing for the door but he caught my hand. "Don't rush off, besides I'm going to drive you home. I'm not having you out there wandering around." My stomach danced a little at that but I also felt a little annoyed. I was a nuisance.

"You don't need to worry; I'll be fine to get home."

Then he shocked the hell out of me. For the second time today, his hand took my chin and he forced me to look at him. He did it gently but there was no mistaking his actions or the fact that he had something he wanted me to understand. Strange thing was, when he did this, I didn't feel like a naughty child but rather a woman waking from a very deep sexual sleep.

"You're right. I won't be worrying about you getting home because I'll be taking you. And before you argue some more, understand I want to do it. And I'm the sort of person that doesn't do a damned thing I don't want to."

"Thank you," I murmured staring into his eyes. They were so dark and intense I was positive I could get lost and never find my way out.

He moved in closer to me, and my heart stopped for a split second, wondering what he was going to do. His lips moved closer to me and his eyes were focusing on my mouth. Then he jerked slightly and skimmed his mouth over my forehead.

"You're very welcome." His voice was tight and that confused me. Then I realised what my stupid mind had probably been thinking. No, don't even go there Eden...a man like Xander would never be interested in you in that way. He was just being friendly.

Xander grabbed his car keys from the desk. "Let's go, I need to teach a class in about thirty minutes." I turned and headed from his office. He was right behind me with his hand at the small of my back guiding me.

As we headed down the corridor an attractive little red head with a flirty smile, completely ignored me but beamed at him as we approached.

“Hello, Sensei, are you taking us today?” Her voice almost purred and I knew exactly what she had on her mind.

“No, Clarisse. Sensei Dane is.” Her face fell and bottom lip pouted like a child that had lost its favourite toy.

I kept moving and felt her eyes bore into me as we passed.

A few moments later he was unlocking the door for me and helping me up into my seat before joining me behind the wheel.

We’d been driving for a couple of minutes; he looked to be deep in thought. There was something I needed to discuss with him that had been on my mind for a couple of days. I wasn’t sure how to tackle it, but I needed to raise it. I leaned forward to my satchel and got my purse out.

He glanced across and caught me. “What are you doing?”

“I need to know how much you charge for the lessons.” I really hoped it wasn’t more than fifty dollars. That’s all I had on me and I had barely anymore more money until my next government study assistance payment came in next week.

We stopped at a light and he looked over his gaze serious. “There’s no charge, Eden. I don’t charge friends for my help.”

I was confused. “But we’ve only just met and you’ve been incredibly kind and all, but I wouldn’t have said we were friends yet.” Friends were people you’d been close to for a long time, weren’t they?

“Oh, make no mistake about it. We’re friends, Eden, and I’ve already said I don’t take payments from friends.” The lights changed and he drove off. I didn’t feel right about this. I didn’t want people’s pity or a free ride. My parents had never taken it, nor would I.

“Well, thank you for your generosity, but I don’t feel right accepting your expertise and help without giving you something in return. I mean you run a business; your students pay. Sophia pays. Tori pays." I tried to keep it as unemotional as possible, even though my stomach was in knots again.

"And you don't pay, Eden." His voice was set and determined, but I couldn't leave it there. It wasn't fair to him, nor was it fair to others.

"But what about the other students that pay? We need to sort out something."

He pulled up outside my house and undid his seatbelt, then mine. Just like he'd done earlier this afternoon and I knew we were about to have another one of those conversations. He waited until I looked him directly in the eye, then he started.

"Seems I need to set you straight on a few things. I have rules where my business and private life are concerned. Yes, I train and teach students. But I don't socialise with them. Sure, occasionally we'll do stuff like the BBQ last weekend. But students don't come to my house and I don't hang out with them outside of the dojo. Friends are different. I don't teach them. I help them because I want to. I'm then free to invite them over, make plans with them and hang with them whenever I want. See why you can't be a student and why you can't pay me?"

My brain was suddenly as good as useless. What was he saying? He wanted to spend more time with me. I didn't get it. Why would he want to? I was just a scared girl with some nasty scars. There was absolutely no reason why he'd want to spend time with me...surely? Then the doubts hit me. I knew what it was like to be the brunt of jokes. It had happened before and every time it hurt. Was this some cruel game, some elaborate setup to get me to trust him only so he could make fun of me later?

"Tell me what you're thinking, Eden. I can see your mind ticking over but judging by the look on your face I don't think I like where your thoughts are at."

I dropped my eyes and he caught my chin once more. Not tight or painful—more a reminder of what he wanted, my full attention.

"We're having a serious conversation, Eden. Give me your

eyes." I looked up at him again. "Now tell me what you're thinking. It's killing me."

He asked, so he'd get the truth. "I'm wondering why on earth you want to be friends with me. I'm wondering if it's some sort of sick joke and suddenly a crowd of people are going to jump out and make fun of me. I don't get it, okay? I never wanted anyone's pity. Particularly not yours."

This time it was his turn to turn away. His nostrils flared as he took a deep breath and a few seconds went by; the silence was coming unbearable and I was about to pull away and bolt inside.

Finally he turned back. "That hurt. Eden. A lot..." My stomach clenched and I felt sick. I knew how much I hated pain and the thought I'd caused someone else pain really stabbed at me. I automatically went to say sorry. But he shook his head no... "I get why you'd think it, Eden. I really do. But it's absolutely not true. I'd never intentionally do anything to hurt you. That's a promise. I don't break them. I don't pity you.

I think what happened to you is awful and tragic but I don't pity you. I've seen enough to know how brave you can be, I want to be part of that. I want to see you get your courage back. I want to see you live a full life again, not hiding at home like some recluse. Everyone needs a few good friends and I want to be one of yours. I enjoy spending time with you. There's a lot you're hiding and I want to understand it, experience it."

I knew he was telling me the truth. His eyes told me so—but I still had doubts, it just seemed so unrealistic. I pulled back from his hand cupping my chin. "I want to believe you, Xander, I really do, but are you sure you don't see me as some project or something?"

He shook his head slowly but kept looking at me. "I don't see you as a project. I see you as a woman that's been dealt a shit hand. I see you as someone that is desperate to break out, but just needs some help with the odd sign post along the way. We're all damaged, Eden. We all have fears and demons that eat at our insides. Some are more obvious than others, but they're all there.

We all have them. Anyone that tells you different is lying."

My shoulders shrugged still not convinced. "But you're you and I'm me."

"What's that supposed to mean?" He looked a little exasperated.

"It means...well you know... you're..." I couldn't find the words.

He opened his hands in front of him asking me to explain. "I'm what? What is it you think I am?"

Oh God, he was going to make me say it. He was really going to. I closed my eyes for a second and took a breath to steady my racing heart. "You're some hot professional MMA fighter. You're successful, you're incredibly fit and handsome. You could have any friend you wanted, male or female. Why me?"

Then he nodded. "Well, that's a relief, although hardly true anymore."

Now I was puzzled. "What's a relief?"

"I was beginning to think you weren't interested, didn't feel it."

Now I was hellishly confused. "Look Xander, I have no idea what you're getting at. I'm really sorry but I just don't understand what you're wanting or trying to tell me."

He reached out and stroked a heavy lock of my hair off my face, before he spoke. "Eden, I'm relieved you think I'm attractive because, over the last few days, I've realised I think of you in the same way. Sure the scars are there but I don't notice them. What I see is a woman I want to spend time with and get to know better. There I've said it. That's why you can't be a student. I don't date students."

I shrunk back against the door behind me. What did he just say? Was my hearing and mind playing tricks on me? I did suffer some hearing loss for a while after the fire. Maybe it had come back? I shook my head. My eyes didn't leave his and he looked just as confused as I felt.

I had to know if I'd heard him right. "Did you just say something about dating me?"

He raised his eyebrows at me and nodded his head slowly. "I

did."

There was no mistaking that. I felt so overwhelmed. Dating... hell that meant all sorts of stuff. I wasn't a kid and neither was Xander. That meant a lot more than kissing and holding hands. That meant intimacy and nakedness, an expectation of sex somewhere in the not too distant future. Could I do that? I had no idea.

Oh God! The clock was ticking and I knew he had to get back for a class. I had to say something, do something. We couldn't just leave it at this.

"Xander, I just don't know. I'd like to say yes, but you need to understand I'm such a mess. Hell, today was the first time anyone has seen my scars other than the doctors and my family. I haven't even kissed a man since before the fire. Do you really want to be stuck with that? I just don't know what I'm going to be comfortable doing and not doing and in what time frame. It's all so new to me. I also know you need to be getting back to teach."

He nodded his head. "I do need to get going, Eden. But I want you to know I get what you're saying. I get that it's all going to be new and different and that you're going to be uncomfortable. I guess what I'm asking is—will you at least give it a go? I don't have classes past six tomorrow night. Nobody wants to train on a Friday night—me, included. How about we do another session in the afternoon if you want? Then come over to my house for a bit. I'll cook you dinner and we can just chill out and get to know each other better."

What he was offering was so tempting. I wanted to, I really did but it had to be on my terms.

"Okay, I'll come over." I saw the smile immediately break out on his face. He really was excited. "But...we do this as friends. It's a big step for me. I've not been to anyone's house without my family since the fire. I trust you, but I don't know how I'm going to react or feel. I don't want you to have expectations that I can't live up to."

He took my hand and pulled me forward to him in a hug made

awkward by the console between the seats. His lips brushed my left ear.

"Thank you, Eden. You won't regret this." His arms tightened around me one last time, then he pulled away. "I hate to run when I really think there's more to be said, but I've got to go. We can talk about it more tomorrow night."

I grabbed my gear and opened the door.

"I should be doing that and walking you to the door, will you forgive me just this once? I'm running really late." He pulled a pained face.

I giggled and climbed down waving him off. "I'll hold you to that. Now go and teach!"

"See you, Gem."

"Bye Xander." I closed the door and as I waited for him to pull away, the front door of my house opened and Sophia appeared.

I knew I was going to have some explaining to do.

NINE

EDEN

Far out! What a day! I fell into bed. It was ten pm and I was zonked. First it had been Sophia, then it had been Beth. Then when Tori got the chance she "had to know" as well. I guessed this is what I'd been missing for the last few years—this pouring over conversations, daydreaming and analysing relationships to death. I wasn't sure I really enjoyed it just yet. It felt weird. Besides so far it was just dinner and hanging out at a friend's place.

Relationship...what a strange word! Was that what I was doing? I had no idea. I was excited and terrified all at once. I really hoped he wouldn't be disappointed.

There was a light knock on the door and it opened a fraction. Sophia poked her head around the corner.

"Good, you're still awake." She didn't ask to come in, just came over and sat on my bed. That was so Sophia.

"Something you wanted?"

She looked at me and smiled, but it wasn't her usual type of smile. It was hard to describe, almost a little melancholy "Yeah I just wanted to let you know I'm pleased for you. I can see that you're really trying to make an effort to get out there again and give it ago." She picked up one of the cushions I'd pushed aside and started to cuddle it. "I know how hard it is for you." Then she turned towards me and I could see the tears pooling over her eyes. "I also know that if it wasn't for you, Tori and I wouldn't be alive...right...now." She broke off sobbing so I reached forward and hugged her tight. Tears feel freely down my face as well.

We'd talked about the fire many times as a family. There'd been months of counselling for everyone. It didn't matter. Whenever there was change or stuff going on—the fire always came up. And it needed to be addressed. It was not so overwhelming now, but it would be with us all forever. Each of us had a different haunting memory or different demons to fight from the fire.

Mum and dad beat themselves up about the fact they weren't there. Mum was working a late shift at the hospital. Dad was somewhere on the road between Melbourne and Adelaide. We were hardly little kids when it happened, almost adults.

Sophia and Tori blame themselves.

I blame myself for going to bed early. If I'd been studying for that test like I should have been and not sleeping, then I would have been aware that much earlier. We all got out alive. That's all that matters now.

"Hey, Soph. Shhh... It's okay. It doesn't matter anymore." I held her close to me and crooned to her.

"But it does...if you hadn't have come and got us then you wouldn't be burnt and then you wouldn't be freaking out about a date and...and..." she trailed off.

"Soph, even if I could, I wouldn't change what I did or what happened. Sure I'd prefer there was no fire. But not coming after you two was never an option. I couldn't have lived with myself if I didn't get you out."

She was sobbing up a storm. When Sophia let go, she really let go. I reached over and grabbed the tissues from the bedside table and pushed a handful at her. Then I wiped my own face.

"I know you always say that but then I see how much you

struggle and I just feel so much..."

It was all stuff we'd been through before but I just nodded and held her tight to me. This is how we got through.

My phone chirped from the bedside table indicating a text.

Sophia's head popped up and she looked at it curiously. Then she looked at me, then back at the phone. "Well, aren't you going to find out who it is? I bet it's Xander."

"That's Sensei to you and besides I'm in the middle of comforting you!" I couldn't help ribbing her! She shrugged and rolled her eyes.

"Geez, you've got a lot to learn. A hot guy is texting you at bedtime and you're not even looking. What's wrong with you?"

"There's nothing wrong with me, except I seem to be more concerned about you!" I gave her a playful elbow to the ribs.

"So you do one session with Xander and you think you can take me, do you?" she responded with an elbow back. "Just check the damned message already, would you."

I let out an exaggerated huff, when really excitement and butterflies were whizzing around my body. As I grabbed the screen I made sure she couldn't see, then swiped the face of the phone and read the text. It was in fact from Xander, but Soph didn't need to know that.

"Well, what does it say?" She was almost jumping up and down.

"It's just a message from the phone company to let me know I've used half my plan." I was desperately trying to keep a straight face.

She snatched the phone off me. "Hey. I haven't even read it!" I protested loudly.

"Then how come you know it's the phone company—smarty pants?" I didn't have time to think of something smart. I just needed that phone back.

"It's rude to read someone else's messages," I added and grabbed it back.

"Oh, you're no fun. You finally get a boyfriend and you don't even want to share." This time she really pouted.

I ignored her and read the message.

> **Xander:** Hey Gem, how are you doing tonight? I've been thinking about you all night. I'm really sorry the conversation went down that way. It was one that needed more time. But I'm not sorry I get to spend tomorrow night with you. Where and what time do you want me to pick you up tomorrow afternoon? I'd like to do another session on the mats with you, if you can swing it. Xan ☺

"Far out! Who'd have thought Sensei was capable of writing 'War and Peace?' Can't you read faster...what's he say?"

"None of your business!" I already knew I'd tell her some of it, but not all.

"Oh, come on!" This time it was a whine.

"He just wanted to know where and when to pick me up tomorrow afternoon."

"Bullshit! It doesn't take that many words to say all that. I may not have got a chance to read it but I saw how much text there was."

"Oh, for God's sake," I passed the phone to her. I knew Sophia well. There was no way she'd give up until she got what she wanted. "But this is the only time I'm going to do it and if you breathe a word of this to anyone I'm going to kill you after I ask Xander to show me how."

She let out a little squeal.

"He is so flirting with you!"

This time I rolled my eyes for Sophia's benefit. "I hardly think so."

"He said he's been thinking about you all night then he says he wants to do a session on the mats. Read the double meaning!" She was shaking her head at me.

I shrugged not really sure what to say just at the moment.

"So what are you going to say?" She passed the phone back to me.

Oh shit...this was the bit I hated. I had no idea how to do this shit, but he should know that. "I'm just going to tell him to pick me up at two again from uni."

"Well, at least make it sound like you're excited to see him."

"Okay, okay...pressure much!"

I tapped out a message telling him to come and pick me up the same as today. I added a smiley face as well and sent it before Sophia had time to dissect it. If he didn't like my texts, he could let me know.

"Okay, you seem to be feeling better...I'm going to get some sleep." Nothing like a distraction of the male type to take Sophia's mind off things.

"You want me to go? But I want to see if he texts back."

"I don't care. My texts, my bedroom and it's my sleep time you're interrupting. Now, buzz off."

"Okay, I know when I'm not wanted." She got up and moved from the bed but paused at the door and looked. "I really am pleased for you Eden and proud, too. You've really started to make progress. Night."

"Night honey." I called to her retreating figure.

One more text arrived before I went to sleep. A certain someone wishing me sweet dreams—I replied wishing him the same.

XANDER

Dane followed me into my office after we finished up the last class for the week. There were some guys coming in tomorrow to train, but Rohan was covering that. I might pop in later tomorrow if I felt like it. I tried to keep the weekends fairly light particularly right after a grading.

I went to my laptop; shut it down and started to pack it up. Dane plonked himself down on the sofa.

"Don't make yourself comfortable unless you want to lock-up. I'm out of here in about five minutes." I grabbed a couple of files and threw them into my laptop bag as well.

"Wooo! Hot date?"

I glared at him. "Something like that."

I saw him jerk back in shock then he looked curious. "Wouldn't be a certain long and lean strawberry blonde, would it?"

"Yep, it's Eden." I had every intention of telling him. We didn't keep secrets from each other.

"Okay. I kind of guessed when she was here again this afternoon. Two days in a row!" He looked a little smug. Eden had come in and we'd gone through some more moves. She was doing great. I dropped her home so she could shower and change, then Sophia had offered to drop her back. Like yesterday, Dane had come in just as we were finishing up.

But if he had an issue, I wanted it sorted now. "You got a problem?"

"No man. None at all. Just not your usual type."

I didn't think I had a type but obviously Dane did. It was mute anyway. Eden was the only girl I was interested in at the moment. "Well, Eden's my type now."

"She's always been your type." Dane said under his breath, but he sucked at whispering.

"What's that supposed to mean?"

"Just that you've had a thing for that girl since she first arrived in the neighbourhood. I guess it makes sense. Only a matter of time and all."

I never realised I'd been so transparent, but apparently I had been. I'd never outwardly discussed her with Dane but obviously he's picked up on my actions or interest or something.

"I don't know what's going to happen yet. She's very skittish, as you know. So we'll be taking this very slow." Not that it was any of his business but I just wanted him to understand and not do or say anything dumb. Dane wouldn't but, I was feeling protective.

"It's cool man." He gave me a nod and that's all I needed. We were good.

We talked for a couple more minutes about some of the fighters. There were a few fights coming up. I needed to check the preparation plans for a few of them over the weekend.

I heard the front doors open and I glanced up from my perch on the edge of my desk. It was Eden. Suddenly I felt nervous and more like a stupid high school kid on a first date, than a grown man who'd been doing this for years.

I grabbed my laptop bag and my training duffle full of dirty clothes. "Thanks for offering to lock up man!" I flashed him a grin and bolted towards the reception area. I was lucky to have a best friend like Dane but he was quickly forgotten once I saw Eden there on the other side of the reception desk.

She looked great. Her hair was loose, and she had light makeup on, something I hadn't seen before. Plus she actually looked at me directly and smiled shyly when she saw me. All big pluses.

Once I rounded the counter I didn't hesitate. I moved straight in and looped my arm around her waist and kissed her cheek. "Hey, Eden. Mmm you smell so good." And she did. It was that damned perfume she wore again. It had been playing havoc with my senses all afternoon. It seemed to get into my head and I couldn't think of much else.

One whiff of that and my dick seemed to have all sorts of ideas, all of them inappropriate at this time.

She dropped her chin and smiled a little coyly. It was cute.

"Okay. Dane drew short straw and has to lock up. We're out of here."

I unlocked the truck, threw my gear in the back seat and helped her in. This time I managed to do the gentlemanly thing.

"Thanks," she murmured as she settled back.

"You're welcome, Gem."

I think I managed to get in and get us underway in record time.

"So where do you live?" I was actually surprised. I think this was the first time she'd actually started a conversation.

I glanced across at her and really wished I could put my hand on her thigh but I knew that would be too much, too soon. "Well, I've got a little property south of here, near the river. It's just under five acres. There's a house and a big double story barn. My dad lives in the house and I live in the barn at the moment. Dad's not around at the moment, though. My aunt lives in Sydney and he's down visiting her."

"Wow. Five acres seems a lot."

I shrugged. "We both like the quiet. I get enough of people day in day out with the dojo. Plus, I get to have a few big boys' toys with that much land. If you're very good, I'll let you play with them with me." I turned and gave her a wink.

She giggled a little and looked a bit shy again. "Well, that sounds like fun!"

"Oh I've got all sorts of fun toys: quad bike, couple of dirt bikes, a jet ski and a heap of other non-motorised fun things. I enjoy the outdoors, when I'm not at the dojo."

She nodded her head in understanding and I thought I picked up a little wistfulness. If I was reading this right, Eden was longing to do more.

"So what do you like to do?"

"Well I like to read and I watch movies. It was really all I could do for a long time. Physical activity was restricted to recovery type stuff. I guess there's a lot of stuff I haven't even tried."

That got me thinking and wondering. "So before the fire, what were you into?"

Her face pulled in concentration or was it memories? "Ah, I guess I did school sport stuff. I used to enjoy swimming and I jogged occasionally, but I didn't really have a sport. My main focus was school and modelling I guess. How about you?"

I chuckled a little at this. "Do you mean what was I like at school?"

"Yeah."

"Ummm... not too good. I didn't really like school. I spent every afternoon at the dojo." Eden looked at me a little curiously. "Well, not Onigashima fighters. Dane and I used to train at a place just around the corner. Old Ron Stapleton used to run it. His son Reed was my trainer when I fought." She had questions, I could almost see them.

"Just ask me, whatever you want to know. If I don't want to answer I won't, and I don't just mean about the stuff we're talking about now."

She turned and gave me a little smile and nodded. "Okay."

Maybe if I gave her permission to ask questions, Eden would feel less uncomfortable about talking about things and initiating conversation.

"What does Onigashima Fighters mean?"

This one brought a grin to my face. "Well, Dane and I kind of have a fascination with Japanese manga and folk tales, that sort of thing. Onigashima is the mythical island where the oni or demons live."

I could see Eden thinking this through for a few seconds before she turned to me. "I don't get it. Why would you want to name your business after a place where demons live?"

"Excellent question. And the answer's even simpler. Because Onigashima is where we go to fight the demons. We all carry them inside us, Gem."

"So let me make sure I understand this right. The dojo or Onigashima is the place you go to fight these demons that you say are inside us all."

"That's it. It's kind of a play on the mythical tale. The story goes something like this...the demons or oni lived on Onigashima Island. To fight them you had to go there. We kind of played around with it a little. Remember we're kind of diehard fans of this stuff."

She was still thinking it through. "I like it. It makes sense to me." Then she turned to me as I turned into my driveway. "But you mentioned the demons we all have inside us that we have to fight. What do you mean?"

I didn't answer until I pulled up under the awning off the side of the barn. After I shut off the truck I turned to her "Let's head upstairs and I'll answer that. We're forming a habit of having way too many important conversations in this truck."

I was out and around her side before she even had a chance to answer. Eden took my hand as I helped her out of the truck, but I didn't release her hand.

"It'll be best if you follow me. The light's out under here and I forgot to pick up a bulb for it the other day." I moved forward and let my arm trail behind as I moved around the truck and unlocked the side door of the barn. I flicked the light on just inside the door and she stepped in behind me, her eyes everywhere at once.

"Not what you expected?" I knew it wasn't. Everyone was amazed when they walked in here. The floor was completely concreted. The left hand side which we'd entered through had been polished and lacquered. Down this side of the barn was an open space that housed a big club lounge and a massive television that was mounted on the wall. Connected to the TV was an Xbox and a few other essential toys. Beside that was a little bench and fridge, which cut the area in two. On the other side was my home gym. A few bags suspended from the roof, mats and a rack full of free weights, medicine balls and kettle bells. A variety of different training pads were also hanging from the end wall. The side wall of the barn was fully mirrored.

On the side of the barn that wasn't polished concrete, all my "toys" were housed, and a long workshop bench ran down the other side wall of the barn. This held my tools and all the stuff I needed to maintain the "toys."

She was shaking her head in wonder. "I've never seen anything like this." Her eyes were still roaming around before they turned back to me. "I guess this is what bachelor heaven looks like."

I exploded with laughter because of the way she said it. It really reached somewhere deep in me. But I also knew then what I'd suspected. There was a beautiful joyous person in there just waiting to get out.

"Ready to see the rest of the place?" The stairs went up over the polished concrete area and I could see her looking at them and the door at the top with uncertainty. It felt like I could almost read her thoughts. "It's just an upstairs area Eden. I'll be exactly the same guy up there as the one you've gotten to know a bit about, the one right here. Just that up there, I have a kitchen, a nice bottle of wine and a sofa we can sit on and chat. No pressure."

She gave me a little smile and took one of those deep breaths she always did when she was trying to steady her nerves. "Okay, then show me the top floor."

I didn't hesitate but gave her hand a little squeeze then a tug. We climbed the stairs together and it felt like it was yet another milestone between us. I wasn't quite sure what the milestone was just yet but it felt like it.

EDEN

I was totally transfixed by the barn. It was so different from anything I'd ever really seen before, and when Xander opened the door to the upper mezzanine floor, I was flooded with the potential of the space. It was clean, neat and tidy. The neat and tidy bits I figured were very much to do with the fact that there were next to no furnishings.

When Xander had said there was a kitchen and a sofa upstairs, he'd actually meant it. There was a kitchen, the sofa, a scuffed up tea chest that he was obviously using as a coffee table and another large flat screen TV on the wall. The kitchen was down the far end of the space and a large bench cut it off from the room. Two basic stools sat under the overhang. The sofa and a lot of vacant space were in the middle facing the TV, and a large neatly made king bed was up the other end. A reasonably sized long rectangular room running beside the bedroom area was the only thing that broke up the room. That had to be the bathroom, I guessed.

The whole space was lined with gyprock sheeting and painted a basic white. The floor was covered in oversized pale pine boards, which had a nice honey glow. A couple of windows ran down the long wall and I thought there might have been a door to possibly a balcony off the kitchen.

"So this is home to me. What do you think?"

I stepped away and he let my hand drop, then I moved into the centre of the room to get an even better feel. When I finally stopped my perusal of the room, I could see the anxiousness on his face. At the dojo Xander showed a measure of control all the time. Here, he was something different all together.

"I think this space has amazing potential. You could do so much with it. But I have to ask, where's all your stuff? Did you just move in? There's not one thing I can see here that tells me this is your home."

I watched Xander look around as if seeing the space through my eyes. "I don't actually have that much stuff." He looked a little bit confused at what I was saying. The downstairs area of the barn had been meticulously neat, so was here. It took minimalist to another level.

There was something I was missing here, but I couldn't figure out what it was. "Fair enough. I guess not everyone likes soft furnishings like I do."

"What do you mean by that?" he asked me looking a bit confused.

"Well you know, cushions, throw blankets, pictures, photos, nick nacks that make you happy—that sort of thing. Surely your mum has that sort of stuff around in her house."

I saw him stiffen and I knew immediately I'd said something wrong. I knew exactly that feeling he was experiencing in his gut right now—the one that burns and tightens but feels like dread all at the same time.

"I don't have a mum. She died when I was born." He said the words coldly and unemotionally and I figured he'd had his whole life to practise getting them to sound so flat and lifeless. The tone and delivery were in such stark contrast to the way he normally spoke, which felt more like a rich caress to me.

"Umm... I'm really sorry...I didn't mean to bring up something painful," I stammered out.

"It's hard to feel pain for something you've never known or experienced. Envy, wishing and cheated would probably better describe how I feel."

This choice of words was telling me so much about him and I immediately wondered if this was part of that demon thing he was talking about before. The conversation we'd never finished.

"Does this have something to do with those oni you were talking about before?"

He moved over to the kitchen and around behind the big bench. "Come, take a seat over here and I'll tell you about the oni as I make dinner. Would you like a glass of wine? I picked up a nice Sav Blanc this morning."

"I don't normally drink much, but a glass sounds good." I watched him take two glasses from an overhead cabinet on the wall. Judging by the little stickers on the base, I figured they'd been purchased specially for tonight, but I said nothing. This was all so new to me, so I was hardly in a position to pass judgement and it was sweet that he'd gone to the effort.

He poured the wine and passed a glass across to me. "I would have thought you'd be more of a beer guy for some reason."

Xander chuckled at that. "I'm not much of an anything sort of guy when it comes to alcohol. I rarely drink. Always training," he offered as a way of explanation. "If I have any more than one I'll struggle to take you home later."

I didn't glance behind me but that big bed on the other side of the room was making its presence felt in my thoughts. It felt as if it was staring at me, taunting me with promises, but also fears.

He turned back to the fridge and started to get some food out.

"So I figured we'd have chicken and a rice and veggie dish I can make reasonably well. That suit you?"

"Sounds good to me. I eat pretty much everything, particularly stuff I don't have to cook..." I was fine on this side of the bench, but I was definitely close enough to the heat of the kitchen. I didn't need to be any closer. It hadn't escaped my notice that his stove top was gas. Naked flame. A shiver ran down my spine at the thoughts.

"Cold?" Shit he must have seen me.

"No, umm just another little phobia, I guess." Admitting another hang up I had didn't seem that difficult anymore. Xander had seen the scars from the fire that had created the phobias. This was just another scar, albeit a mental one.

I watched him turn the oven on and then take a large chef's knife from the block beside the stove and a chopping board from a cupboard.

"Tell me about it." He didn't look at me, rather he took an onion and started peeling and chopping it.

"Um, I have an aversion to hot things. If I do anything in the kitchen, it's cold food only. I can assemble, prepare that sort of thing, but I can't dare to touch anything hot. I don't like hot drinks either."

Then he looked up from the slicing, and he had what I was assuming to be a satisfied look, on his face. "That's why you all had milkshakes or something that day. I thought it strange three women would go for cold drinks. Now I know why."

"Yep. It's not easy being around me." I said unable to keep the guilt out of my voice. And it was true, my family had to make many sacrifices to make me comfortable with my little phobias.

'So do you like coffee and teas?" I could see he was thinking about things, scheming!

"Well I used to before the fire, so I'm guessing I do. But I haven't been able to bring myself to try them since. Just the heat from the cup when I bring my hand towards it freaks me out."

"I'm not a huge tea or coffee drinker, but I do enjoy both fairly regularly. So that's something we'll have to work on. What else sends shivers like before, down your spine?"

Now would be the time to say something really flirty and sexy like "You!" but that seemed like a really advanced dating move and I was firmly in the toddlers' enclosure with training wheels on. Besides, I had no idea if this would ever be anything more than two friends having dinner. Xander had a right to know what he was getting himself into initially if he was so intent on being my friend, let alone anything more.

"I'm mostly okay with the hairdryer, but every now and then I'll have a bit of panic attack. It triggers my recollections of the intense heat. Sometimes I need to take a break then go back to it. It's worse on my right side of course."

He'd finished the onions but the strong vapours had wafted across and were making my eyes water. Well, at least that was what I was putting it down to.

I used the back of my T-Shirt sleeve to dab at my eye, trying to avoid smudging my mascara.

"Anything else?" he pushed gently.

Then something occurred to me. "I thought we were talking about oni or whatever?"

He looked up and smiled at me with a grin that was so much softer than what I was used to seeing on his face. Gone was the fierce warrior façade and in its place was a guy casually cooking dinner and chatting. Even his voice sounded softer, less domineering. "We are." I must have looked at him a little strange. He rolled the wrist holding the knife. "Oni are demons. Onigahsima is a play on the whole demon thing. We pride ourselves on fighting like demons in the ring but we also recognise that we all have demons inside us we have to overcome to succeed in whatever we want to do—whether that be fighting or something else. So we go to Onigashima to fight the demons and to become better fighters. How big those oni are varies from person to person. At the moment we're talking about yours." I wanted to take in all that he'd said and think about it. It was simple when he put it like that, but I could also appreciate the thought that was behind the name and the purpose of something that had supposedly been decided by two friends clowning around. I wasn't sure Xander ever clowned around just yet.

"Go on. Get them all out," he urged with his hand.

This one was a bit hard to admit and well it was kind of personal and embarrassing. "Shower, I still can't cope with the water being any more than lukewarm."

"Okay. Well, good thing the weather's warming up and we'll have about seven or eight months to work on that before it's going to be a problem."

I felt my jaw drop and my eyes go wide. What had he just said? He was standing there without a care in the world happily chopping carrots. My stomach on the other hand was sitting somewhere down around my ankles and my mouth had suddenly gone so dry I needed a sip of that wine, desperately.

The cool crisp liquid burst on my tongue and gave me the hint of courage I needed to ask my next question.

"What did you just say?" My voice was hardly more than a whisper but I needed clarification. I needed to understand what he meant.

This time when he looked up he winked at me. "I don't do cold showers." I watched him place the large roasting pan of marinated chicken in the now hot oven. I must have looked like I needed further clarification because he went on. "That gives me seven or eight months to get you comfortable with hot ones."

I dropped my eyes and studied my knees which seemed to have just clamped together even tighter. The denim of my jeans was suddenly so fascinating. Holy shit. My blood was racing through my veins and my palms suddenly seemed to be sweating. This time I couldn't stop it. My brain went there. Xander, me, naked, shower. Could I ever feel that relaxed about my body? Would we ever get to that stage?

"Xander, we talked about no pressure..."

"That wasn't pressure, Gem. That was me planting visuals and scenarios. If we talk about stuff, then it becomes less terrifying." Then he shocked me a little and leaned over the bench and placed a light kiss on my forehead. "I have no expectations, only hopes."

"Okay." I believed him and maybe I was starting to have hopes too.

TEN

XANDER

I was surprised at how quickly Eden was starting to relax around me. Sure there had been a few awkward moments tonight. The hesitation at the bottom of the stairs, then when I'd got a bit playful with the shower comment, and finally when I'd suggested we move over to the sofa to watch a movie just now. I wanted to push her, but not have her afraid or freaking out. I wanted Eden to see that. Sure, I was the guy in charge at the dojo, but I could also be a lot more relaxed away from it.

The microwave dinged and I grabbed the bag of popcorn and poured it into a large bowl. She was sitting over on the sofa watching the previews of a couple of shows before the movie, we'd decided to watch, was going to start.

"Hey, Gem, do you want another glass of wine or something before we watch that movie?"

She turned and looked at me. "Ah, water, please."

I got our drinks and the popcorn and deposited it all on the tea chest I used for a coffee table. Eden was right, the place really could use some sprucing up. I wasn't completely ignorant to what nicely decorated places looked like, but I just had no clue where to start. Decorating was not my thing. It didn't mean I couldn't appreciate it, though.

For instance, I'd bought this sofa about three years ago because it was really comfortable to sit on and great to take a nap on. It would also be excellent to snuggle with Eden on right now. But the rest of the place was devoid of anything else. I guess I'd never realised it until Eden pointed it out tonight.

Before I sat down I moved over and flicked off the lights. I strategically just left the light on over the stove. I preferred to watch movies in the dark and I was interested to see whether the dark made Eden braver or more uncomfortable. I sat down on Eden's right side and stretched my legs out on the chaise section. This was my favourite spot.

Eden was sitting beside me but there was far too much sofa between us. "Come over here, Gem. I won't bite; I promise." I held my left arm up indicating she should move over.

She moved over closer but left about a foot between our bodies. Close, but not close enough. "I meant here." And tilted my head towards my shoulder.

I could see the hesitation in her eyes, but she moved across the distance. "Try it. If you're uncomfortable after a few minutes, then you can move okay."

This seemed to satisfy her that I was still holding up my bargain not to pressure her. She moved over and sat right beside me a little rigidly. There was pressure and there was progress. I was working on progress. I curled my arm around her shoulders and pulled her even closer.

"Put your feet up and your head on my shoulder if you want." I gave her a little squeeze and she did. It was hard to believe I was actually asking a woman to snuggle with me. A few seconds later, she seemed to settle and a lot of the tension released from her body.

"That's it; relax, Gem," I whispered into her silky hair.

"Why do you call me Gem?"

"I don't really know. It slipped out and I've decided it suits you, besides I like it much better than babe. Babe sounds far too common for you. A gem is precious."

That seemed to satisfy her and I reached forward for the popcorn and put it on my lap. We watched the movie for a bit; it was a recent release action/thriller type of thing. The fight scenes were totally unrealistic and had been helped a lot with computer enhancements, but still I was happy to sit here with Eden draped down my side.

Now that she was relaxed, I couldn't help but run my fingers lightly over the gap between her low riser jeans and where her long sleeved T-shirt had ridden up. The silky flesh rippled away then returned as my fingers trailed along, but she didn't pull away or seem distressed in anyway. I did it again, and this time rather than tense her side, she let me stroke the skin. I did it a third time, only this time on the way back down, I opened my palm and slid it downwards over her belly. The skin was silky smooth. I'd purposely sat this way so that her burn scars would mostly be covered where our bodies touched and hopefully lessen any self-consciousness.

I held my hand where it was and tried to focus on the movie. My dick was rock hard under the zipper of my jeans and this bowl was doing an awesome job of hiding the evidence. It was like being back in high school and building up to a make out session with a girl. The slow, almost excruciating, build was something that we seemed to overlook as adults with experience. And that got me thinking about how much experience Eden may have had before the fire. Was she still a virgin? That was a question that needed some finesse. It wasn't one you could just drop on someone.

Then Eden was trying to sit up, pulling away. "Excuse me for a second, but I need to use the bathroom. That's it over there?" She indicated the room off to the side.

"Yes." I followed her up and headed to the kitchen. I put the popcorn bowl in the dishwasher and willed my very uncomfortable dick to subside but I knew that was a wasted effort.

Then on a whim I grabbed a largish bowl and filled it with a couple of different flavours of ice-cream and then I reached for spoons. But instead of two I only grabbed one. I sat back down and waited for Eden to join me. This time I had the ice-cream bowl in my lap. Right about now I could see the merit in the cushions Eden was talking about earlier.

She came out and this time didn't need to be prompted, but curled into my side like a kitten looking to curl up.

"Hope you like ice-cream."

"Everyone loves ice-cream."

"Want to share it with me?"

"Well, it would be rude for you to eat it all by yourself and not offer me any." I chuckled at that. Ooo, there she was!

"You're absolutely right. What was I thinking?" I played along with her. "So what do you want to try first? We have butterscotch, vanilla and of course, the all-time favourite, chocolate."

"I'll go the butterscotch."

I loaded up a spoon and raised it to her lips, and she looked at me in question. "I thought we'd try the full sharing experience."

Eden opened her mouth and closed her lips around the spoon I offered and I wondered if I was crazy putting myself through this torture. Just watching her lips close around the spoon was a sensual overload. "Mmm, this is really good." It came out more as a moan than words. Well, at least that was the way my brain registered it.

"It's one of my favourites." And to prove the claim I loaded a spoon and this time put it to my lips. She was right. The butterscotch was awesome.

"What would you like now?"

"How about some chocolate?"

This time it was chocolate I spooned into her mouth and every time I repeated the process it seemed to get even more sensual and enticing than the last. The movie was playing in the background and I didn't bother to adjust the volume up, neither of us were watching it. We were far more engrossed in sharing ice-cream. It was one of the most erotically innocent things I'd ever done with a woman. Was erotic and innocent even possible at the same time? Because I was sure I'd just experienced it.

When the bowl was gone, I leaned forward and placed it on the tea chest. There was no hiding the evidence of my arousal but, I didn't really want to either. Eden wasn't a child; she knew what happened when men got aroused.

I adjusted our bodies so she was pulled in tighter to me and my arm was around her again. A heavy curtain had fallen across her face, hiding more of her face from me than I liked in the shadowy light. I pushed it back behind her ear and my eyes connected with hers. There was a longing there that I shared and felt, but I'd promised her I'd go slowly—no pressure.

"I'm going to kiss you now, if that's okay with you?"

EDEN

"Yes," I whispered, and the word seemed to hang between us before he slowly moved his body around so he could align his lips to mine. The feeling was foreign and surreal, but oh so good.

Xander had the most beautiful mouth, a perfectly bow shaped upper lip and a full bottom lip and when those lips made contact with mine, all the sensations and female needs I'd locked away for the last five years seemed to flood my body all at once. My skin felt as if it was suddenly supersensitised. There was a whooshing in my ears and an aching need at my core that I hadn't ever felt as intensely as this—for what might well have been forever.

His lips brushed over mine a few more times, teasing and coaxing before they puckered against mine one last time, before he pulled away slightly.

"You okay?" The room was shadowy and I couldn't really see his eyes. They were almost as dark as night, but I could feel them.

It was as if they were searching my soul, seeking to strip me bare.

"Yes." And I knew he was debating what to do next. So I brought my arms up and looped them around his neck and buried my face into his neck. I could feel the warm skin of his neck under my lips and pressed them to him. A shiver racked through his body and a low groan of what sounded like pleasure tickled my ear.

"Are you trying to torture me, Gem? Because if so, your lips on my neck is a really good way to do it." I couldn't help but giggle a little at that and did it some more.

He shivered a little more against me and his breathing was becoming a little ragged.

Then he pulled his head back far enough to move away from my lips but not break the hold I had around his neck.

"Okay, sweets. That's about all of that I can take at the moment. Let's see how you do."

He didn't give me a chance to say anything or even get my thoughts in order before his mouth descended on the left side of my throat. Just like I'd done, his lips teased and tickled me. My body shivered and pressed tighter to him. Then just when I thought it couldn't possibly feel much better, he flicked his tongue across my skin and it felt so incredibly good. This time it was me moaning out my pleasure, and if I thought I was feeling need before, it was nothing compared to what I was feeling now.

My feelings were so strong, they were starting to scare me. It was all happening so quickly; it kind of felt forbidden. I pulled away and gave him a little smile.

"Enjoy that?"

I nodded my head because I didn't think I could form words at this point in time.

"You want to watch the rest of this movie?"

I needed to get home, but I didn't want my time to end with him just yet. "I probably should be getting home soon."

"I can't say I like that idea, but it's probably a good one. If we sit here much longer, we're likely to take things further and I said I wasn't going to pressure you and I meant it."

"Umm... I don't exactly think I was doing much to dissuade you."

He let out a little chuckle. "True. But I want you to get to know me before we go there. And I want you to be comfortable in yourself. That will take a little time."

"Okay..." I didn't quite know what to say to that. Was 'thank you' the right thing? "Thanks for understanding." I hoped it didn't sound too lame.

"I know it will be worth the wait."

A nervous giggle slipped out. "Oh. I hope it doesn't become a disappointment."

"Don't worry about it. We'll be fine." I like the way he said 'we'll'. It gave me hope. I only hoped whatever fascination he had with me didn't wear off. "But before we head out I want to ask you something."

I sat back against the sofa and he took my hand. "I was wondering what you were doing tomorrow?"

I shrugged. "I don't really have anything planned. Probably just do some study and make sure I've got all my assignments in order."

"Well, I've been thinking about what you said and I think you're right." I had no idea what he was talking about. "I think you should come shopping with me and pick out some stuff to make this place seem more like a home."

My stomach dropped and I felt terrible. "Xander, I'm so sorry I didn't mean to offend you before. Forget I said anything. This is obviously the way you like your place and it's not up to me to pass judgement."

He pressed a finger to my lips. "Hush. It's not like that at all. It's not that I don't like the decorating and furnishing stuff you were talking about before. It's more that I have no idea where to start. So I haven't. Hell, I have trouble figuring out what to wear if it doesn't involve training clothes. That's why I firmly stick to jeans and t-shirts. I can't seem to screw that up too much." Everything I'd seen on him so far had looked casual but seemed to really suit him. “Now will you please come out shopping with me tomorrow?”

Shopping centres, people, crowds. “I want to say yes, but I should warn you, I’m not very good in crowds. I don’t like people looking at me and I kind of feel a bit overwhelmed.” I was such a cripple in so many ways.

“I can understand that. I’ve seen you do it. But this time you’ll be with me. Could you at least give it a go? I’d like to spend the day with you. If it gets too much, we can just call it quits—deal?”

He held out his hand as if to shake on it and I reluctantly put mine in his, but before we could shake he leaned in and kissed me on the mouth, quickly and firmly. That crazy heady feeling I’d been struggling with a few minutes ago was instantly back and I wanted him.

“Deal.” There was nothing reluctant about how I answered him.

ELEVEN

XANDER

I stifled a yawn as I sat in the corner booth of the café I'd first meet Eden in a couple of weeks ago. This morning I was waiting for Dane and Reed to arrive. Once a month Dane and I had breakfast with Reed. Things were very different now I wasn't constantly training for a fight, but Reed would always be a special person to me. You can't go through what we had and not have an unshakable bond.

As I looked across to where she'd been sitting last time, I almost expected her to be there. Funny how your mind plays little games, sometimes. I took a sip of the hot coffee the waitress had placed in front of me and my thoughts moved to what she'd told me last night. I guess I'd never thought of all the strange quirky idiosyncrasies that would accompany a trauma like that. When she told me about them they were totally understandable, but I'd been focused on the obvious—the bit that you'd could see and the obvious reactions to it.

I'm sure there was a lot more I would learn along the way and I had every intention of spending the time to get to discover it all.

She was more than just a fascination to me. I was fast realising I enjoyed spending time with her. Unlike most women she didn't grate on my nerves with pointless chatter and crap. Sure she had some hang-ups, who didn't? But she was also very grounded and what had happened to her had made her very unpretentious and kind of an old soul.

If I didn't stop thinking about her and recapping the events of last night, my dick would be hard again. I was tired because I'd spent most of the night thinking about Eden rather than sleeping.

Fortunately, I was saved from my own personal torture by the arrival of both Dane and Reed. I stood as they approached. Reed and I clasped hands in the handshake we'd been using for years. It was more of a grab where you gripped your hand around the person's thumb and wrist, rather than a shake.

"Good to see you, man."

"You too, Reed," I said as we all took our places in the booth.

We did a quick perusal of the menus and ordered before we got down to chatting.

"So what's been happening, Xan?"

"Oh, same old, same old." Dane shot me an amused look and I ignored him. I knew exactly what he was thinking—Eden. "Classes are building. I'm just about to add a few more. I'm thinking about seeing if I can work in with a few other clubs and get more of a regular tournament schedule going for the students that want to train and compete."

"Yeah, that's a good idea. People always love competing and it helps keep them focused at training if they know they've got a competition coming up."

"Yeah, I agree. That's what I was thinking." The waitress turned up with coffees for Dane and Reed, plus a refill for me.

"So what about you, Dane. Have you decided to get serious yet?"

I watched my good friend squirm a bit. Dane had always had plenty of talent and could certainly more than hold his own in any situation, but he'd never been inclined to have the insane "killer instinct" that was needed to be the best in this game.

Ironic really. People joked and referred to the determination to win as "killer instinct"; in my case I knew exactly what it was. I lived with the ramifications of my competitive nature or "killer instinct" every day. There were no visible scars for people to see, but they were there in my heart and head, and they ran deep. I wasn't fighting anymore, was I? They were deep enough to stop me doing the one thing my dreams had been built on.

"I'm toying with the idea." I almost choked on the sip of coffee I'd just taken.

"Since when?" I demanded.

"For a little while now." Well that was news to me. Dane had always been happy to be one of my ring men. Sure, he'd fought in the cage heaps of times, but not at a high level or seriously. Well, things change. He was certainly still young enough to give it a red hot go.

"I might just have something for you in about three months, if you're interested. A promoter out of the US is venturing out here and is putting a card together. It's a big deal. Title fights and lots of coin. I could certainly get you one of the undercard bouts."

Three months would be tight. Dane was in great shape and he could fight but he wasn't a hardened fighter per sé. He'd need a lot of specific skills and serious sparring to get him ready. My mind automatically started to plan a programme in my head as the omelette and bacon I had ordered were placed in front of me.

"When do you need to know?" Dane looked over at Reed as he buttered some toast. Reed was in his early forties and had a light dusting of silver at the temples, but his hair was still thick and his eyes were still bright with that freaky silvery grey colour. Plus the guy was in good nick. He'd looked after himself and he still trained bloody hard. It wasn't unusual for him to pop in and have a rumble on the mats with the boys.

"Ideally Monday, Wednesday at the latest." Dane nodded and looked serious. I needed to have a word to him before he made any decisions like that. There was a lot to consider and think about.

We talked about who the other likely contenders on the card might be as we ate. I had one or two fighters that might be options. I needed to have a think about it and talk to them over the weekend. I didn't take this stuff lightly.

"So how's your family, Dane?"

Dane's family had always been close fixtures in his life and as part of that, they'd been involved with the sports and activities he played.

"Yeah, all good. Mum's still the same, constantly fussing over everyone and dad... Well, he pretends he hates it, but we all know better. Macey's just about to graduate from her nursing degree and Maddie is supposed to be studying hard in year twelve but seems to be more interested in any dickhead that shows her the slightest interest."

And that was a challenge. Maddie was gorgeous. She had long dark hair and a really exotic look about her. A complete dick magnet in more ways than one—she could raise them up with just a look but unfortunately the losers were just as attracted as the good guys.

"That's good to hear. How's your dad, Xan?"

"Yeah, he's okay. Down in Sydney visiting with my aunt at the moment. He'll be back in a week or two, I think." That would create a whole new bunch of issues, well maybe. I wondered what Eden would think of him. He was gruff and very blunt.

We chatted for another half an hour on everything and anything that seemed important. I started to make a few moves to indicate I needed to get going. Then Reed cleared his throat and looked directly at me. I knew there was another reason to this breakfast meet and it looked like I was about to hear it. Sure we caught up regularly, but Reed had a different air about him this morning and I'd sensed there was something he wanted to talk about.

It was nothing more than an intense stare. I'd seen it before and I had a fair idea what was coming.

"That promoter I mentioned, the one who's putting on the card here? Well, he's got an even bigger shindig going down in Vegas a couple of weeks before...They'd like you to be the contender in the feature fight."

His words resounded in my head in slow motion and sort of distorted as if I was in a tunnel or something.

My first instinct was to go with the reply I always did. "I don't fight in the cage anymore." But maybe it was the fact that Reed had never looked more serious, or the fact that he had his hand up as if to combat my rebuttal, that I kept my mouth shut momentarily.

"It's big money this time, Xander, and I know you can take him. In fact you've taken him before." Well, it couldn't have been recently because I hadn't fought in a cage for over three years. It was twelve hundred and seventeen days to be exact since I'd thrown the punch that ended The Cobra's life. And not once had the guilt got easier. Time might dull the pain a little, but it did nothing to ease the guilt. That was a demon I was still fighting every minute of every day.

"Who is it?"

"Luke "Lights Out" O'Donnell and you can't tell me you've not been keeping track of what he's been doing?"

"Yeah, I know what he's been doing but I can't say I've paid a lot of attention." It was a blatant lie. I knew every damned fight he'd had, every strike he'd landed, every hit he'd taken and every knockout he'd made. Once a fighter—always a fighter. It wasn't something that you turned off.

I just had a problem with my conscience or confidence or whatever you wanted to call it. That was my oni to fight. Up until now I hadn't wanted to. I had no incentive, no real reason to fight. Now after my big speech and tough love with Eden, I was feeling like a fraud. How could I be preaching about fighting demons when I was the biggest charlatan of the lot?

"Well, he's still raw over the fact that you took him out for that Pan-Pacific Title a few years back. He wants another shot at you. Only this is a much bigger stage."

"What are we fighting for?"

"The chance to have the number one spot that you walked away from." Well, that was speculation. I wanted more than anything to be number one. Did I still feel that way? I needed to think about that a lot more before I gave Reed my answer. Instead I went for the obvious question that everyone asked. Money was always important, but if I were going to fight again the catalyst for getting me in that cage wouldn't just be money.

"How much are we talking?"

"One million for an appearance. Five for the win—promoters are almost shooting their loads at the thought of getting you two back in the cage." Fuck! That was huge money. I'd done all right from my limited number of professional fights. I'd earned enough to buy the property I lived on now, set up Onigashima and give myself the start of a nest egg but I was far from a rich man.

But, I could just imagine what the publicity was going to be like. "Pretty Boy", the killer up against...Lights Out. They...would... be...merciless. That was something else I needed to think about. Could I handle that level of media scrutiny? As much as you avoided it and stayed away from social media and everything else, there was always something or someone that came up and started a shit storm. And if it didn't happen organically, you could bet your arse the promoters would stir it up—anonymously of course.

However, even if I turned up I'd pretty well be set for life. But, it wasn't about the money. It was about the principle. It was about actually living by the code you prescribed to and preached daily. It was about personal integrity.

Both Reed and Dane were staring at me, assessing me.

"When's the fight?"

"This is the kicker. Eight weeks yesterday!"

Eight weeks was insane but probably achievable.

Eight weeks of hell. Eating, breathing and sleeping the fight. No distractions, no mistakes.

Fight preps especially for a fight like this were insanely brutal. I'm talking hours of training everyday, an incredibly strict diet, eight hours of solid sleep each night and no distractions. I'd probably need to drop about twelve kilos. I fought Welterweight. That meant I needed to be under 77kg at weigh-in. I could do it, but I was going to be as grumpy as fuck getting there and the last week to strip the water was pure torture.

I let out a low whistle. "Eight weeks. That's fucking tight."

"It is. But it was a scheduling and venue thing." I nodded my understanding. It wasn't uncommon.

Reed turned and pegged me with an eye lock. "What are your thoughts?"

It wasn't the first time he'd asked me this question, in fact he'd asked it at least a dozen times over the twelve hundred and seventeen days that had passed. I guess he hoped one day I'd be ready to return. Maybe I was... But I wasn't going to answer today.

I had a lot of soul searching to do first.

"When do you need to know by?"

"Yesterday would have been great. Tomorrow would do, Monday would be cutting it fine. Tuesday is too late."

I understood how these things went down. The promoters needed to lock in fighters to kick start the publicity machine. If they couldn't lock you in for a fight they moved onto the next fighter that they could.

This time it was I who pinned Reed with the stare. "You up for training me?"

"Wouldn't have it any other way man! If you're in the cage, I'm in your corner."

I nodded. "Thanks man." I figured that would be his answer, but you didn't know these things until push came to shove. Last time he'd trained me, I'd killed a man under his watch. I looked at my watch and realised I needed to get my skates on. I'd told Eden I'd pick her up at ten. It was now a quarter to.

"You got somewhere you need to be?" Reed looked at me questioningly. I knew right then he was thinking about and assessing the distractions. I decided then and there if this was going to happen it was going to be on my terms—best to start as I intended to continue. I was three years older and wiser. I made my own decisions.

"Yeah, I've got to go pick up my girl."

Dane just grinned at this and I knew he was amused by the whole thing. My phone would start pinging with texts soon.

"Since when?" Reed looked a bit surprised.

"It's recent."

"She going to be a problem?" I didn't like the tone or the look he gave me.

"It's Eden and it doesn't matter if she is. She's my concern, not yours."

"I need you to be one hundred percent focused on your training if we do this."

I knew the drill. Hell I'd done this before many times. I wasn't some novice kid.

"Save the speech, Reed. I haven't decided yet." I threw some cash on the table to cover my share of the bill and headed for the door. "You can give me the lecture if I decide I'm still a glutton for punishment," I called over my shoulder as I walked away.

I had a lot of thinking to do.

EDEN

"Will you just sit down and take a damned chill pill. You look okay. Not as good as you would look if you wore that new top of mine with those skinny jeans, but I guess Rome wasn't built in a day," Sophia huffed out and plopped down on the sofa. I looked down at the baggy long sleeved T-Shirt. It was casual and fun wasn't it?

"What's wrong with it?"

Sophia shook her head with obvious exasperation. "And they let you stroll down a catwalk. What the hell were they thinking?

I've seen hessian sacks that are sexier."

I paced some more and started to panic about what I was wearing. Was it okay? I just didn't think I could wear something tight fitting.

"You're going to wear a hole in the carpet. I guarantee he'll be here and right on time. Sensei is punctual."

I knew all of that. How could I be so excited and terrified all at the same time?

"What am I doing, Soph? Am I crazy, even thinking we could have something?"

"Oh stop it! For the hundredth time this morning, you're not crazy. He's a good guy and you're doing the right thing. We went through this last night and again this morning. It's just new. Just relax and enjoy the day. He'll look after you." Soph was frowning and shaking her head. I knew she was right, but I had so little dating experience and I was so far behind the eight ball.

"Should I get changed?"

Sophia looked at her watch. "I would, but that's me and I'm not you."

What she was actually saying was she'd never had to contend with the looks that I got. Okay, it was time to focus on what he'd asked me to do. That would hopefully take my mind off what I worried about. I couldn't sleep when I got home, I'd been way too excited after the evening, so I'd spent time online getting some ideas for interior design for his barn apartment. I think I had a really good concept, but I wanted to run it past him first. Then if he was okay, we could go and get started on the shopping.

"What have you got there?" I was flicking through the folder that I'd thrown together with print outs and ideas.

"Xander asked me to help him with a little decorating. So I threw a few ideas together last night, and finished them off this morning," I explained and quickly flicked through the folder for Sophia to see. She was used to me doing things like this. I had all sorts of design concepts that I'd built for various rooms and settings. Nearly every single one remained unimplemented. The only three that had been done were our bedrooms. Oh well, everyone was entitled to a hobby or a dream. Maybe one day I'd have a house of my own to decorate.

"Well, Sensei going home wares shopping. Now that's something I didn't see coming. I'd start texting that around amongst the Onigashima crew, but I can only imagine what my life would be like at my next class if Sensei found out. He has an uncanny knack for finding out things."

"There's absolutely nothing wrong with living and enjoying spaces that are aesthetically pleasing," I argued.

"Except for the fact that shopping for home decorating stuff is a girly thing to do."

"It's not. There are lots of male designers. Just because you like things to look good, it doesn't make you a sissy." I was so busy arguing with Sophia I didn't notice Xander and Tori standing in the doorway until Sophia looked up. My heart leapt into my mouth and I suddenly felt all giddy. What did I do now?

"What do you think about it, Sensei?" Sophia took the opportunity to drag Xander into the conversation.

"Well to start off with Sophia, I have no idea what you're talking about. But good morning." Then he moved over to me and leant in and kissed me briefly on the cheek right there in front of both of my sisters. I could have frozen on the spot. I was actually wondering if I had. "Morning, Gem." His voice was barely more than a whisper beside my ear as he turned his attention back to Sophia's comments.

"We were just talking about shopping for home stuff. I'm saying it's a sissy, girly thing to do. Eden's trying to tell me it isn't."

Xander looked between us as if trying to gauge exactly what side of the argument he should take.

"Why does it matter?"

Both Sophia and I paused for a second.

"It doesn't. Sophia just hates to lose an argument," I clarified and Tori giggled and nodded her head in agreement.

"Oh, stop it. I'm not that bad. And say what you want now. But once you've done a day of home wares shopping, you'll be agreeing with me. I guarantee it."

Xander shrugged his right shoulder in a non-committal way. "I'll take my chances." I saw a little smile pull the corner of his mouth up and I got the feeling that he was amused by our carry on. He turned to me and took my hand like it was the most natural thing in the world to do. "Why don't we make a start on it? Then I'll be able to provide honest feedback, but something tells me if I'm with your sister, it's not going to be too much of a trial." There was a twinkle in the dark pools of his eyes as we headed to the door and I probably enjoyed the gapping open mouth look on Sophia's face just a little too much.

TWELVE

EDEN

"Did you get those measurements I needed?" I asked as we headed into the first large furniture store. We'd discussed my ideas on the way here and when we pulled up out front, I showed Xander some ideas I had put together in my file. He'd seemed genuinely impressed and happy with what I was suggesting so, rather than second-guess it, I was going to run with it.

Last night after Xander dropped me off I sent him a text asking him to get the exact measurements of the space so I knew just how much room there really was and how I could put it together.

"Sure did." He pulled his phone out and showed me what he'd taken down as we got just inside the door. It was hard to focus on what he was showing me because rather than just passing me the phone, he'd opted to pull me into him with an arm around my waist and his head looking over my right shoulder.

"So this is the length of..." Xander kissed my ear a little, the scar not seeming to bother him and I totally forgot what I was saying. All I managed was a little giggle and a bit of a shudder.

"Mmm, you smell really good, Gem. Lucky we're out in public

or I think I'd be spending a lot of time kissing you and I did promise I was going to take it slow." His voice was a sexy whisper and I immediately felt the hormones he'd been slowly awakening kick in. I was also wondering just how lucky it was that we were out shopping. Exploring a lot of kissing with Xander was suddenly sounding like a very enticing option and I was starting to very much wonder about taking things slowly.

"And yes, it is the total length of the space and underneath it I broke it into the three basic sections of bedroom..." He kissed my ear again as if to emphasise that word. "...lounge area and kitchen."

I dragged my focus from his wicked lips and quickly scanned my eyes around the store and realised with a good deal of relief, it was fairly quiet. There were a few other couples looking at various different pieces throughout the store. But what we were here to find was a new bedframe and a dining table and chairs. The basic tubing of the one he had was exactly that—basic. A new bedframe would really add some character to the bedroom portion of the mezzanine apartment and the extent of seating when eating were the two stools at the bench. There was no shortage of scope to work with in his apartment.

"So I'm working from the starting point that you want to keep the sectional sofa you already have—right? The chocolate brown looks good in the room; you just need some other pieces to make it feel like a room. I think that you need to have all the pieces look like they blend and enhance but not necessarily match."

He kissed me again, but this time on the neck. "Sounds good. I like that sofa. But explain to me why we don't match stuff." I pulled away and started heading over to where the bed display was. He let me go but snagged my right hand before I had a chance to take more than a step. His fingers were warm and reassuring as they tangled with mine. The store not having many people in it, certainly helped me feel a little less anxious, and just having him there beside me made everything a whole lot better.

I tried to focus on the task at hand rather than the distraction he seemed to be creating for my body. "The reason you don't match everything is because it's predictable and says "I walked into XYZ Furniture Store and bought the whole suite because I lacked the imagination to put anything else together.""

Xander chuckled a little. "Well, that describes exactly what I would do." Xander didn't seem to be embarrassed about it at all.

"That's not to say that matching pieces wouldn't look nice but, it doesn't show any personality or creativity. It screams someone else had great taste and built a whole heap of really nice furniture. So what we do is look for pieces that complement each other and help to jointly tell a story for your room." I was talking to him over my shoulder as I was walking through the massive store space.

Xander was looking at me intensely. "I just didn't realise there was so much to this whole decorating thing. I knew I had no clues but seriously, now I'm glad I decided to let you guide this process. Because if I thought I didn't know anything about home decorating before, then now I'm absolutely certain I know less than zero."

We moved into the edge of the bedroom furniture display area. "Okay, to start off with let's just have a wander around and look at all the displays." The area was broken into themed areas, showcasing not only the furniture but also linen and other soft furnishings. "If you see something you're drawn to, or you like, let me know. Let's try to get an idea for what you actually like without me influencing the process."

For the first time ever, he looked a little hesitant. "Go on," I encouraged him and motioned with my hand for him to lead the way down the walkway between the little cubicle type areas that had been delineated to represent rooms. He walked past the first room which featured a black lacquered bed frame with matching side tables and a tall boy dresser. He barely even looked at it, which was a huge relief because it was a gaudy looking setting in my opinion, but I thought the black may have appealed to him.

We walked past a few more that showed more promise but didn't seem to appeal to him either. Then he stopped about six displays in.

"I like that." He motioned with his head and pulled me into his side once again, keeping my scarred side closest to his body. Another couple moved past us and I kept my face averted into his chest rather than look towards them.

The bed frame he'd indicated was a stunning piece. It was quite a unique mixture of sleek modern styling but achieved with materials that made the bedframe look like it had aged character. The headboard was quite tall; a solid timber rail ran across the top. It was circular in shape and made from a darker hardwood timber—Jarra, I suspected. Supporting the rail was a very symmetrical steel frame of brushed chrome pipe that had an almost industrial feel to it. The tubing ran across the frame in two distinct panels. The footboard end was a reduced size replica and the timber rail sat at the same height as the mattress.

"It's stunning and a really beautiful piece. It says so many things all at once, but looks so unique and classy." I was trying to describe how I felt about the piece. Instead, I moved forward and touched it. The timber just seemed to be calling out to me to run my hand over. Just as I expected, the timber was warm and smooth to touch. The finish was satiny against my skin and it seemed to encourage me to draw my palm back and forth over it. "It's been really beautifully finished. Touch it."

That was all the encouragement Xander needed and suddenly he was running his hand over the rail along with me.

"It does feel good."

"I don't like the bed linen they've put on it for your apartment though." It was a quilt of purples and blacks—quite striking, but totally the wrong tone for his barn apartment. I bent down and flipped up the floor length valance and noticed the bed frame was designed to either work with a mattress or to connect to an ensemble.

"Do you need a new mattress or ensemble?" I knew without looking at the price tag the bedframe was not going to be cheap; add in the cost of a new mattress or ensemble and it was going to quickly be a very expensive exercise. One thing I hated was waste or spending money when there was no need. I'd grown up respecting the value of every dollar. My parents were battlers and had made every dollar stretch.

"The bed I have is only about twelve months old. I bought it when I moved in and I happen to love it. It's great to sleep on." Well, that answered my question and was plenty good enough for me. Xander moved over to the top of the bed and turned the swing tag to read the price. His expression gave nothing away, and although I didn't see the exact amount, I noticed there were four figures and I felt a moment of anxiousness. I didn't want him spending a whole heap of money because he had some misplaced idea of giving me some sort of project.

We needed to move on. I didn't want him to feel he was pressured to buy this piece. Suddenly the whole decorating thing seemed like a really bad idea.

"Okay then. Your current bed stays. We just need a bed head or frame, but we don't have to get it today. This is more about getting ideas." I tried to make the whole day sound less like a big shopping trip and more like a fact finding mission. I didn't want him to feel obligated to buy anything. "Let's have a look at a few more. There's always the option of attaching a headboard to the wall in a fabric or something. That can look amazing with the right choice of fabric and it can be very cost effective."

I moved down the walkway further and paused in front of an ensemble bed with a padded fabric bedhead. "That's what I was talking about. Well, not that exactly but you get the idea. We'd just find a fabric or even a leather that would look good."

"I don't like that so much. I like the bedframe back there. It feels right for some reason." And I knew exactly what he meant. It was definitely a piece that made an impression and called to you. He moved me back that way, to stand in front of the display once again.

"Would I be committing a decorating sin to get the bedside tables that are beside it?" The tables that had been matched to the frame were gorgeous. They were made from the same timber as the top rails. The drawers and the sizing were done to match the same shapes of the metal rails.

"Not at all. The timber in the bedframe is used as an accent whereas the timber is the feature in the bedside tables. This is one place where it's fine to use matching pieces. The designer has already created the story by just using the rail as an accent. That's the bit that ties it all together." I then stopped because I realised I'd been prattling on about design rubbish and felt embarrassed. Why would he even care? "I'm sorry I didn't mean to bore you to tears with a design lecture. I just tend to get carried away with this sort of stuff. It's hardly like I'm an expert. I just enjoy looking at this sort of stuff and designing rooms in my head."

Xander took my hand again and squeezed it. "Don't be sorry. I was enjoying listening to you chat about it all. I can tell how much you're into this by your voice and how passionate you are about it." He caught my eyes with his. "It's a good thing, Gem, to be passionate about something." Then he took me totally by surprise and leant in and brushed his lips across mine.

The kiss was warm and friendly but I could tell there was a lot more to it than what was on the surface. I could feel the restrained power, the need and desire. It was a wakeup call to the things I'd been missing and a promise of the things to come. Just as quick as his lips met mine, they were gone and he was pressing another light kiss to my forehead. "I couldn't resist, Eden. I've behaved myself all morning so far, but I had to have a little taste." I don't know whether he meant it or whether he did it subconsciously, but either way, when the tip of his tongue flicked out and swept along those gloriously full lips of his, I suddenly wished we weren't here in a public place.

"I've got a good idea I know what you're thinking, Gem, and I promise you it's going to be every bit as good."

I could feel my cheeks heating and my neck felt down right hot. Was the air-conditioning working properly in here? I suddenly started to wonder. I didn't get to think on it much more because a sales assistant finally appeared and on instinct I dropped my face and turned towards Xander to shield me.

"Hey folks, how can I help you today?"

"We'd like to buy this bedframe and those bedside tables." And just like that the decision was made and Xander was buying a new bed, even if he'd politely used the term 'we' to include me. It suddenly felt really good to be part of a 'we' even if it was just for the benefit of the sales assistant.

XANDER

Today had been surprisingly good fun. Shopping really wasn't my thing, but hanging out with Eden had made the whole experience much more enjoyable. I now had a new bedframe, dining suite, coffee table and a couple of other pieces I needed arriving in a few days' time. We'd also gone from store to store looking for the "perfect" bed linen. Eden found it after about the seventh store.

She'd also blushed a beautiful shade of pink when I whispered in her ear how I was imagining her lying in it. When I said I wasn't going to pressure her, I meant it, but that didn't mean I wasn't going to do my best to warm her up to the idea. Eden had been living in a bubble for far too long in all aspects of her life. Although we hadn't talked about it, I didn't need to be Einstein to know she hadn't had any contact with a man since before the fire. I was going to have to broach that with her sometime soon in a non-threatening way.

It was just one of the many things on my mind today. That discussion with Reed was playing heavily on my mind. I was worried about Dane stepping into the pro-ring. It was one thing to fight in club tournaments and interclub stuff. It was a whole other level of competition and commitment to step into the professional ranks. Killer instinct is what it took. I hated that term because that was exactly what I was. I was also torn about what I was going to do. My own personal integrity was weighing on my mind as well. How could I keep preaching to the students I taught and more specifically to Eden if I couldn't live by the code myself. I was supposed to be a role model, an example for the students I taught and the fighters I trained. That was a responsibility I took very seriously. It was something Reed's father and my own had drummed into me since I was small.

Eden chose that moment to slide back into the booth at the café. She'd just been off visiting the bathroom. The café was all but deserted this late in the afternoon. The only other customers here were a couple of middle-aged women out the front.

She was sitting in the seat she always chose. I'd suggested we come here, as I knew she felt comfortable. All day Eden had been doing great with being out and about. I could feel her getting a lot more anxious when we'd ventured into the crowded shopping mall after leaving the larger open area home shopping complexes. We'd grabbed lunch on the run and this was really the first time we'd been able to sit and relax.

"You looked like you were deep in thought?" She smiled at me a little shyly but her eyes were shining and happy.

I gave her a little grin and nod. "Sprung, I guess." Then she looked at me as if she wanted to ask something but wasn't quite sure. "Go on ask. If I don't want to answer, I won't."

"What were you thinking about? Your expression looked intense as I came across the room."

"Yeah, I guess you could say that. I've got a lot on my mind at the moment."

"Oh." Was all she said and she looked a little guilty. "I didn't mean to take up so much of your time."

I reached across the table and took her hand in mine. "That's not it at all, Eden. If I didn't want to spend time with you, I wouldn't. I've just got a few decisions to make about some stuff. Most of it has nothing to do with you, but you've certainly changed my thinking on a couple of things." I could see the curiosity on her face but the waitress chose that moment to come over and looked first to Eden and then to me.

"Hey, Eden, it's great to see you out and about without your sisters or mother. Not that I don't love them, all but it's about time you remembered there was more to life." I saw Eden shrug her shoulders a little and drop her chin coyly.

"Thanks Sally, I'm trying. By the way Sally meet Xander."

Eden turned and motioned to me with her hand.

"Oh, I know who this guy is. "Pretty Boy" has been in here a few times. In fact, I served him breakfast this morning."

The surprised look on Eden's face was impossible to miss. I hadn't mentioned that I'd been here this morning with Dane and Reed. Not because I wanted to keep it from Eden but rather, I hadn't made any decisions yet. I wanted to be sure of what I was going to do before I let her know, but I guess that option had just been removed.

"Oh whoops. Sorry me and my big mouth," Sally apologised and she looked very sheepish.

"It doesn't matter. It was hardly a secret I had breakfast here with Dane and Reed."

"Well, in that case how about I just get on with doing my job which is to take your orders."

I looked over at Eden and nodded my head indicating she should place her order. "I'll have a chocolate thickshake and could I have one of those double choc cupcakes. They're to die for."

Sally nodded and jotted it down, then she looked at me.

"I'll have a black cof..."I heard the sharp intake of Eden's breath and then I realised what I'd done. "Let me change that. I'll have an iced coffee, with extra cream and if those cup cakes are as good as you say, Eden, I'd better have one of those as well."

"I'll get that organised for you right now." Sally turned and headed off to the counter.

"Thank you for understanding about the hot drink." Eden's eyes didn't meet mine as she said the words. I could tell she was embarrassed, but also grateful at the same time.

"It's okay, Eden. You've done really great all day. We'll work on the hot drinks. Besides it might be the last high calorie decadent weekend I have in a while." If I was back in fight training, Iced-Coffees and cupcakes were definitely off the menu. It was eight weeks of hell. The beginning of a campaign like that was always full of mixed emotions. Hard work took on a whole new meaning. I was going to ache everyday in muscles and places I didn't even know I had. Reed and I had always worked on the "Train hard, fight easy Principle". Reed's idea of training hard was total insanity. Part of me relished the challenge again, but another part was filled with dread.

We sat in silence for a few moments. It wasn't uncomfortable, but I was keen to see if Eden would come right out and ask me about breakfast this morning. "You can ask you know. It's not a secret as I said to Sally before."

"Well, you didn't offer it up all day so I figured it's not something you want to talk to me about. Who you choose to have breakfast with is hardly my business."

I nodded in agreement and I watched her retreat more into herself. "But it's not for the reasons you're probably thinking. I haven't told you about this morning because Dane, Reed and I discussed a lot of things. Some of those things have me really asking myself a lot of questions and I'm not sure of the answers at the moment."

Eden was now really intrigued. Her expression had gone from one that almost resembled a whipped puppy to one of open curiosity.

"Dane you know." I watched her nod and a few other emotions flashed across her face too fast for me to easily read, but I figured it was all to do with what she'd experienced the other night. "Reed has been like an older brother to me for about as long as I can remember. He's the son of my old Sensei Ron and then, when I started to fight seriously, he became my trainer."

She nodded her understanding and I went on. "He offered me a big time fight this morning."

I could see the surprise and caution on her face in equal parts. "What does that mean? I understand what a fight is obviously but you don't seem at all happy about it. In fact, the exact opposite." Yeah that about summed it up. I wasn't excited about it. The fight was an opportunity. Nothing more, nothing less. It was an opportunity for me to face my fears and move on. But could I do it? I truthfully didn't know that yet.

"Well, you're right. I'm not that happy about it. I'm not sure I can even do it. I haven't even been back in a cage since the night I killed The Cobra." I said it without really thinking and I'd already retreated back into my head and the events of that fateful night were hammering at my brain.

Then I heard the sudden intake of her breath and the horrified look on her face. Oh God! I'd let my guard down and now I'd blown everything.

How could she not know?

Everyone knew—didn't they?

I watched almost in fascination as her mouth opened and then closed a couple of times. In the end I felt sorry for just dumping that on her. "You didn't know?"

Her head moved "No" in tight jerky little shakes.

"How could you not know? It's all over the internet. I figured you would have Googled me or someone would have said something?" I asked incredulously.

"No, I didn't. I don't like learning about people from the internet. I prefer for them to tell me themselves, so no I didn't Google you." Her words were delivered with a little edge and I knew I deserved it.

Sally chose that moment to bring over our drinks and cakes. "There you both go. If you need anything more just give me a wave." She turned and was gone.

I took a long draw of the iced coffee and suddenly wished it was laced with whisky. I could have certainly used the hit right then.

"First off, before you freak right out, let me explain that it was one hundred percent accidental and it occurred in the cage. The governing body, Occupational Health and Safety as well as the cops carried out an investigation and I was completely cleared of any charges or stuff like that. No case to answer."

Eden nodded and I could see that information had eased a lot of the worry from her face, but I could only imagine what a shock it must have been to her.

"I was in a title fight just over three years ago and I accidentally killed a guy." I clenched my fingers into fists and I could feel the hit, exactly as I'd felt it when I'd connected to his jaw. The sick feeling was sloshing around in my guts and I suddenly wondered if the iced coffee and cupcake were a good idea.

"We'd been going at it for a few rounds and I needed to finish the fight off. My mind was already on the next fight. I knew I had him..." I paused for a second not quite sure how to go on. Eden just sat there and looked at me. There wasn't judgement in her eyes but something else that I didn't recognise. Then she reached over and took my hand.

"Go on, if you want to. Sometimes it helps to talk about it." Then I knew what I was seeing. It was empathy and understanding that only someone who had experienced something terrible happening to them, could understand. It was the firsthand knowledge of the pain that was so deep rooted, you didn't know where it started or finished. It just seemed to be impregnated into every one of the cells that made up your body.

She rubbed her thumb over the back of my hand. It was a tiny gesture, but it seemed to say so much more than words could possibly cover or explain.

"Reed had identified a weakness in his game. He told me what to look for and when the opportunity opened up, I took it. He was slow retracting his punches and I managed to get under his guard and take his legs out from under him. Then I had a strong mount position and I was pummelling his head with punches."

It was the next bit that I still struggled to talk about. My throat felt like it had closed up and I felt like the biggest pussy as the guilt and a thousand other things swamped me. I was stuck because I never expected to have to explain what had happened to Eden right now—if at all. I figured she'd know just like everyone else did. How did I go from having a really great day to my guts feeling like they were being ripped out through my nostrils?

Eden dropped my hand and got up from where she was sitting and I started to panic a little bit. Was she leaving me? Could she not stand to be around me anymore? I didn't blame her if that was the case. There wasn't a much worse thing that one person could do to another.

I was just about to get up and follow her when she slid into the bench seat next to me and laced her fingers through mine and pressed her body right up beside me. Her warmth and caring flooded through me and suddenly the pain seemed to recede a little.

"I know how hard it is to recount what happened. The feelings and the pain don't go away no matter how many times you tell the story. The edge comes off a little, but they still take your breath away and you wonder how on earth you can survive the next few seconds let alone tell someone about what you went through and how you feel about it." That was exactly it—how I was feeling right now. "Take your time."

I nodded and swallowed a few times, desperately trying to make sure my voice didn't crack. "He moved his head. He broke a fundamental safety rule we get taught...By moving his head he increased the impact and I also hit a much more vulnerable area. It all happened so fast. I realised it as I was part way through the strike, but as much as my brain was screaming for me to pull the punch, it was just too late and I couldn't." She squeezed my hand and I knew she was feeling everything I was relating. It was like we were sharing the pain—by touching we were sharing the burden, making it somehow possible to bear.

"I knew as soon as my fist hit his jaw it was going to be bad. He was pretty well gone instantly." For the first time since that night, I felt my eyes get moist and begin to prickle. It was such a foreign sensation. One I'd not felt or experienced in years. My throat was tight and I reached for the iced coffee seeking some sort of lubrication.

"I haven't got back into the cage since. I swore I wouldn't fight again. But now I'm beginning to realise that was me just taking the coward's way out. We all know when we set foot in the cage or the ring there are dangers, but we also know how to protect ourselves. If we don't, we shouldn't be there..." I trailed off and stared at the wall in front of me. It was the first time I'd spoken to anyone about this in a very long time and never quite like this.

Then Eden seemed to snuggle in a little more and rested her head on my shoulder. It was done as form of comfort. From anyone else, I think I would have rejected it, but from Eden it was different. She was a survivor. "I can't even imagine what you must go through living with that. But I do know about replaying the what if's, the if onlys, the why me's and all the logic angles. None of them ever give you any relief from the torment. It's as if somehow applying logic to an awful and totally illogical scenario will suddenly make it all right and give you the permission you need to move on. If only it was that easy..." She let out a jaded little half laugh that spoke a lot of her experience at wrangling with the whole ragged mess.

We just sat for a few moments. Both lost in our own thoughts, but connected by our bodies.

Finally she spoke. "In case you're worried, I don't blame you or think worse of you for what happened. Even though it doesn't feel like it, it was an accident. 'An unfortunate incident that happens unexpectedly and unintentionally, typically resulting in damage or injury.' That's the dictionary definition—unfortunately I know it by heart. But it does nothing to explain the pain and the carnage it leaves behind. It's an empty word that seems nowhere near enough to explain it, but inadequately, that's the best our language seems to be able to come up with. And the victims just live with the consequences."

Eden was absolutely correct. "The Cobra's dead, consequences don't get any worse than that." I said flatly.

"I disagree. Sure he's not here and that's tragic, but you live with the consequences of the accident everyday. That's a heavy weight to carry." And if anyone knew about carrying heavy weights it was Eden.

That was the moment I reversed my whole opinion of Eden. I thought she'd been weak and probably a quitter. But right then I realised I'd just discovered the strongest person I'd ever met. What must she have gone through?

THIRTEEN

EDEN

After a discussion that intense, I thought he'd want a bit of distance. I was certainly ready to head home and call it a day. The day had been great and I'd really enjoyed his company and the hours shared. For the most part, I'd handled my anxiety quite well. At least, I thought so. The mall still bothered the hell out of me, and I wondered if it would ever be any different.

Too many people all seeming to look at me and stare.

We'd not been in his truck for very long when he reached over and took my hand and rested it on his thigh, with his over the top. It felt very intimate and I was both excited and nervous at the same time.

"This could well be my last "free weekend" for a while. I don't want it to end just yet. I've got a proposal for you. Think about it before you answer. I'll respect your decision whatever it is, but I really hope you'll say yes."

My pulse skipped up and I began to really wonder what he had in mind. It sounded serious and I wasn't quite sure if I understood what he meant.

"What did you mean by last free weekend?"

"If I say yes to the fight, training starts immediately. That means things will change for me." He didn't say anymore and I didn't know what it meant for us. Was there even an 'us' or was I living some school girl fantasy? I was really trying not to get my hopes up, but it was becoming more and more impossible the longer I spent with Xander.

When I glanced across at him, he seemed a little unsure which was very un-Xander like. He was always so exact, particular and confident. The fact that he seemed to be procrastinating was making me really nervous. "Are you going to tell me what this is about?"

I noticed his hand tighten on the wheel. "Well, you can always say no. But here goes...So I was thinking if you didn't have anything planned for the rest of the weekend, we could spend it together."

I let out the breath, I didn't realise I was holding. Sure, I had some study to do, but then I always did. There was nothing new there. "That sounds fine, I don't have anything that I can't re-arrange. I was just going to do some study. I've got all my assignments in."

He looked like he relaxed a little and then he took the turn off towards the estate where my house was. "Are you taking me home?" I asked a little confused.

"I am."

"I don't quite understand."

"I want you to go pack a bag. I guess I'd better tell you what I had in mind." My heart had skipped a few beats at "pack a bag". A sleepover wasn't something I'd planned. In fact, I hadn't slept anywhere but at home or the hospital for the last five years.

"Don't freak out. Let me explain what I've got in mind." He obviously knew me well enough to know when I was about to start getting really anxious.

"Okay..."

"So I thought you could grab some stuff for tonight and

tomorrow. Then we could get some takeaway Chinese or whatever, on the way home. Tonight we can just chill out and watch another movie. Then tomorrow morning we get up really early and I'll load up the quad bike. I've got a friend with a property up in the mountains; it's awesome to go quad biking there. How does that sound?" He glanced over at me with a hopeful look and a little grin.

Oh God! That was a lot to throw at me. I'd never spent more than a few hours with anyone. Now he was talking 24x7 for a couple of days. And quad biking. That sounded like fun, but it was something I'd never done or even thought about doing.

"Where would I sleep?" It was the elephant in the room, at least for me.

"You can have my bed. I'll take the sofa. I've slept there before. No pressure Eden. This is not some elaborate plan to push you harder or quicker than what you're comfortable with."

One thing I was comfortable with was his word. He'd pushed me hard in a couple of situations, but Xander had never done anything to make me feel nervous around him, except in a good way. I was sure I could trust him, but maybe I was more of a risk than he was—especially given the way my hormones had been feeling throughout the day.

If worse came to worse, I could always ask him to bring me home and I knew he would. Responsibility and honour were everything to him. I'd never expected that from a fighter. I don't know why. I guess I just assumed they'd all be crass and rough.

"Okay, I'll do it." He immediately flashed me a big cheeky grin. It was the most carefree I'd ever seen him look. There was always such an intensity about him. But this grin was boyish and completely unguarded. "But just realise that this is the first night I've spent away from home or hospital in five years. I know that sounds stupid but I kind of feel like I'm six again and going on my first sleepover." My choice of words might have been considered a little humorous, but there was no humour in the tone of my voice. This was a very big step for me.

He squeezed my hand with his.

"Thank you, Eden, for trusting me. So I guess I'd better pick up some more ice-cream if we're going to have a pyjama party."

We both laughed at that. It was exactly how it felt.

It wasn't Xander I was worried about. Could I trust myself not to freak out, not to have a nightmare or even worse—jump him?

•••

"So tell me about the fight." We were sitting on his sofa with the takeaway Thai food spread out on his makeshift coffee table. I couldn't wait to see what his new furniture would look like when it arrived later in the week.

He loaded up a forkful, but looked across at me and shrugged his shoulders very nonchalantly. "It's a big fight—a rematch to be exact. I beat a guy called Luke O'Donnell a.k.a "Lights Out" a few years back on my way to where I got to last time. He's been busy and has made a big name for himself. I'm the only one who's ever beaten him and he wants another crack at me."

Well, I guess that made sense. This guy wanted his chance to redeem himself. That would also make him very determined, I'd have thought. I also sensed that Xander was nowhere near as relaxed about this fight as he was making out. How could he be? He hadn't been back in the cage in a long time and I knew what was haunting him.

"When is it?"

"Eight weeks."

I must have looked really stunned. "Yeah, that look on your face about sums it up. It's a huge ask but not impossible. I'm in good condition but not fit enough for a fight like that."

Xander kept alluding to the training being really hard; I wanted to know more. "But, don't you train hard all the time?"

"There's training to maintain and learn, but then there's training for a big fight. That's what this will be. I'll be running everyday. Sparring, grappling, bag and pad work, plus a thousand other torturous things that Reed will dream up. But that's only part of it. I'll be exhausted everyday. I'll hurt in places that I don't even know I have. My diet will be totally restricted to specific foods and the further it goes the grumpier and more difficult to be around I'll get—I've got to drop twelve kilos to make weight. It's not easy."

"What?" I was stunned. My jaw dropped open and I fumbled my fork. "Twelve kilos. But there doesn't seem to be any extra on you now." From what I could tell, he was all hard muscle. I'd never seen him without a shirt but I'd felt his arms around me. He was all hard lines.

"Yeah, there's a lot more I can drop. But it's nice of you to think I look okay, if that's what you were getting at?" He winked at me and I dropped my eyes to my plate. Then he put his plate on the tea chest and got up and headed to the bedroom area. He came back with an iPad.

He scrolled through a few screens then turned it around and showed it to me. "That's me at weigh-in for my last fight."

The picture was horrible. His handsome face was sunken and drawn. There were huge dark circles under his eyes and he looked sick. Every muscle in his body was visible and the skin over his muscles looked almost wrinkled and dry. "That's what I look like at about 76.5kg. I fight Welterweight so I need to be under 77kg at weigh-in."

I didn't know what to say, so I went with honesty. "You look terrible."

He laughed and it was easy to tell he was amused by what I'd said. "Not only do I look like shit, I feel like it too, at that stage!"

He flicked at the iPad again and turned it around. "This is me later the same day after I've gone and had a refuel and hydrate." The photo he showed me, barely looked like the same person. His frame looked really full and seemed to glow with health. He looked mega strong and fierce.

"I don't understand, how?" The transformation was nothing short of miraculous.

"I was almost eight kilos heavier there." He said with a little smirk.

I was dumbfounded and didn't understand at all. "The same day?" I asked trying to wrap my brain around it all.

"Yep." He looked a little smug and proud of himself. "Do I look a little better here?"

"Oh, fishing for compliments, are you?" I couldn't help but play along with him. He grinned at me. "Okay, you look incredible," I said shyly and he grinned at me again which just made my temper spark. "There I said it and like you don't know it! But I don't really understand how."

"I basically eat and drink myself silly to build up my strength again. To make weight I have to work out crazy hard and literally sweat every ounce of fluid out of myself. I was so dizzy at that weigh-in, I could barely stand. But there's one more image you need to see to get the full picture of the journey." He turned the iPad back around but rather than show me another image he put it down on the sofa and grabbed the neck of his T-shirt at the back and pulled it over his head. It was one of those sexy moves guys made but this was the first time I'd really seen it happen in front of me, for me.

I'm really glad I had the plate and fork in my hand to give me something to keep them occupied, because it was one thing seeing Xander shirtless in a photo but there was something totally overwhelming seeing him in the flesh just an arms distance away from me.

Then my brain started to register. This was the body that had been pressed up against me while he'd been showing me any number of moves at the dojo, or last night on the sofa. This is who I'd been sitting up close and personal with at the café. His body was so perfect, I didn't quite know where to start to catalogue it. I wanted to look, but I fought the urge to duck my head as well. He was so beautiful with all those lean hard muscles and tattoos that were so stunning and realistic they could only be described as art.

"This is how I start. What you saw is the stages I go through to get to the cage."

The enormity of what he was telling me started to hit. To do what he did he had to put his body through the most brutal hell. Why would he do that to something that looked so perfect and beautiful already?

"Those last few days are hell. I'm unbearable to be around. My body's weak; I'm starving hungry and my thirst is unquenchable." He was telling me all this very honestly and I wondered why?

"What's the motivation? It sounds terrible."

He picked up his plate again and heaped more food on, from the plastic containers. "To know you're the best. As crazy as it sounds, there's actually a hell of a lot of satisfaction to be able to transform my body from this to what you saw. It's the visual proof of my dedication and training. Knowing I can go the distance, make the commitment. Winning the fight is the reward."

I thought about taking another bite and realised my appetite was gone and all my doubts had returned. How could I possibly be attractive to somebody that looked like that? Someone that had such total control of his body and surroundings—someone that was so focused on what he wanted. I just didn't want to be scared anymore.

"Are you finished?"

I nodded but didn't look at him.

"Do I make you uncomfortable sitting here without a shirt?" It was a direct question and cut right to the chase, which I'd come to realise was very much Xander's modus operandi.

"A little."

"So much so you can't even look at me it seems." There was a hint of disappointment in his voice.

"It's not what you think." I blurted out in defence before I realised what I was saying.

"Well, explain it to me then." He came back just as quick with his answer.

I closed my eyes and wondered what the hell I should say. What was the point of continuing this whole thing?

"Overwhelmed. That's how I feel."

I could feel him studying me as I looked down at my hands in my lap.

"How do you mean overwhelmed? In a good way or a bad way?" There was no playfulness now. In fact his voice sounded more cautious than anything.

I flopped back onto the sofa searching for a way to make him understand. "How does anyone explain overwhelmed? You make me feel so many things all at once. Good and bad. You're so perfect and I can't believe I'm admitting this, but I want to run my hands all over you and do other crazy stuff and that scares the living shit out of me. To feel that way, even if it is good and exciting, is just so foreign to me. But then I feel like I'm in some kind of twisted dream when I look at you and then compare it to me...I keep expecting to wake up from this dream and there'll be a crowd of people all laughing and sniggering at me for being so stupid to delude myself."

"I'm not following you, Eden."

The tears were pricking at the back of my eyes and I knew I was only seconds from having a flood. "I'm wondering how someone who looks like you could be interested in someone like me whose body is scarred and ugly. It's beauty and the beast and I'm obviously the damned beast." There I'd said it and the floodgates had opened. The tears were in free fall down my cheeks.

Xander said nothing just got up and fetched a box of tissues from the bathroom, but instead of returning to where he'd been sitting he moved closer and pulled me in tight to his lap.

"You're beautiful Eden, sure you have scars. Everyone does. Yours you wear for everyone to see. Mine I keep hidden away. They all hurt and break us a little along the way. There's no prerequisite to be perfect in order to be beautiful. There's an old saying and I think it's very true. Beauty is in the eye of the beholder, and to me, Eden, you are beautiful, because it's not just about how you look. It's also how you are as a person that makes you attractive to me. So will you please quit worrying about stuff that is just not true? And no, you're not dreaming. Have I given you any reason to think that I'm not interested in you as a woman?"

"No, it just seems so unbelievable to me, I guess."

"Well, believe it. And if I have to spell it out. I will. That's my very hard dick pressed into your backside. You're the one, Gem. No one else here. So you need to start taking note and working with what's real and not what you're making up in your head."

Heat washed through me. I was so much in my own head again, I'd missed the obvious. I was letting my fears and insecurities cloud my thinking on everything.

"I get that you're scared. I get that everything is new, particularly between us, but you need to be open-minded if you can. See and judge things based on what you experience now rather than what you've let yourself be persuaded to believe over the last five years. You have to build a new path in your head on how things should be or are now, rather than what was in the past. You used to have dreams and aspirations. It's okay to have them again."

Then it dawned on me. Somehow we'd gone from talking about him and the crazy regime he put his body through, to me. But wasn't Xander on very much the same path as me? How could he preach to me about doing all of this if he wasn't committed to face his demons as well?

"So what about you?" There was more resolve and steel in my voice and I liked it. I pushed myself off his lap and stood looking down at him.

"What about me?" He looked a little shocked.

"So far you've been pushing me and prodding me to change, to face my fears. But what about you?" I accused. My hand shot out and I pointed right at him aggressively. I think it stunned me just about as much as it did him. Where was this coming from? "Are you going to take the fight or sit here and wonder what if? You didn't lose your career, you're just choosing not to fulfil it. What's worse?"

His face became a mask before he lurched to his feet, pressed one hand to the back of the sofa and vaulted over it with the gracefulness of a cat. He did it to put distance between us and I was damned fine with that right now.

“So that’s how it is?” I nodded my head and glared at him. “Don’t do as I do, do as I say! How convenient.” I could see my words bouncing off him like blows and his face was stormy with emotion. I was seeing him, but feeling me. Not only was I standing on my own two feet, I was questioning and pushing back. I was taking back my power and personality and it felt good—liberating and strong and a huge damned rush all at once.

And in the midst of all those out of control raging feelings, a wild arse crazy hair of an idea popped into my head. I was so damned drunk on my own new found assertiveness and clarity, I went right with it. “If you’re so hell bent on pushing me to fight my demons, then you have to as well. You don’t get to sit back and poke and prod at me, or make me change even if it is for the better. You don’t get to sit there and not be everything you can be because of some accident that happened which you had no control over. If I have to do this, so do you!”

I blinked my eyes a few times, stunned at what I’d just done. Had I really just lashed out at Xander like that? Where the hell had that come from? Part of me immediately regretted what I’d done and wanted to retreat. But a larger part of me knew I was right. Xander had the chance at a career and dream he’d always had, but now he was squandering his ability because of something that wasn’t his fault. It didn’t have to be this way. Sure, he was successful but I doubted it was the path he’d really wanted.

He stood there glaring at me and I didn’t have a clue about what he was thinking. His eyes were totally black. I just knew that this was one of those massive turning points in my life and I was certain that whatever Xander decided to do would affect us both. Somehow we were drawn together, both of us kindred spirits, tied by the gaping wounds we both had. Wounds that only a fellow sufferer really understood.

His jaw twitched and he looked like an angry bull waiting to charge. I'd caused the rage but I knew intrinsically, he wouldn't hurt me. My words had been a catalyst for revealing the rage he'd been concealing but that rage had been festering in his soul for a very long time. I'd been the catalyst, but the rage he was feeling was far more deep-seated than a few words from me had been capable of rendering.

"I need an hour." He said nothing more then stalked to the door and was gone.

I stood there shell shocked, not sure what to do. Stunned at what I'd done but surprisingly, not regretting it. Then I heard the rhythmic smacking of fists into bags and I knew exactly what Xander was doing. It was a sound I was hoping I'd hear a lot more of in the coming weeks. But only he could decide that. That was his journey and his decision to make. However, there was a very good chance my journey with Xander would end right here and now, and that would rip my heart out.

FOURTEEN

XANDER

I took the steps two at a time, and welcomed the sen-sation of being out of control as I descended. Out of control...that was exactly how I felt. The rage was bubbling up and out of me. I moved straight to the heavy bag in my workout corner and started pummelling it.

How could she? How dare she? I hit the bag over and over again, asking myself those very questions. The answer wanted to come screaming into my head, but I blocked it with my rage. Left and right I hit that bag till my arms began to burn and I could no longer maintain the speed or intensity with which I'd started.

Then, the little voices in my head started as soon as my body could no longer keep up the intensity.

She's right, mate. You are a fraud. You preach a code you don't live by. Coward, killer! Over and over they played till I thought I'd go insane.

Then The Cobra's face in death came dancing through my mind, followed by Reed's voice assuring me it was a freak accident; the Commissioner of the sport's Governing Body giving me a slap on the back. "Tough break, Xander. Get over it and get back in the ring."

I saw Carrie, The Cobra's wife, rubbing her pregnant belly beside the ring, then her face distorted in grief as she watched me slaughter her husband in front of her. It all played through my head, slicing me with its claws as it went.

My father: "You're a fucking pussy. Get back in the cage! Like The Cobra would give one fuck about you!"

Flashes of faces and emotions clawed at me from the inside out.

I couldn't stop the pain. No matter how hard or fast I hit something.

I couldn't stop it or make it go away.

My arms hung at my sides, my knuckles dripping blood. Sweat ran in rivers down my body, the waistband of my jeans soaked through, the heavy denim clung to my thighs. And my chest heaved with the effort to suck in as much air as I could.

"Not your fault, man. Not your fault, man." Academically I knew it was true. It was a freak accident—something that shouldn't and didn't happen, but none of that was ever going to change the outcome.

Did I even want to do this again? Could I risk it?

So many questions and no answers.

I stumbled over to the wall and slumped against it, letting my body use it as a guide to the floor. I drew my knees up and rested my elbows on them and cradled my head in my hands.

Then the tears came, great wracking sobs as twelve hundred and seventeen days of bottled up grief came rushing out of me, one tear at a time. The blood on my hands mixed with the tears and I could taste the salty metallic mix on my lips. The room spun through the blur of my eyes and I felt caught, trapped in a cage guarded by demons on all sides. But still the voices raged and fought inside me.

Regret and guilt over what I'd done.

Responsibility and integrity goaded me, taunted me.

Fear whispered to me... "You haven't got it anymore, man. You can't do it. There's no way you can beat him." It was a seductive caress and I wanted to relax into it. Fear offered an option, a way out. "All the pain will go away. Just don't step in the cage again."

Then Eden's face etched in anger and frustration screaming at me. "If I have to do this, so do you!" The scar on her face was a very real and constant reminder of the fear and pain Eden had to live with and overcome everyday. She was trying and making progress. What was I doing other than preaching and attempting to fix other people?

I'd built myself a good life, and yes it was something I loved doing, but it wasn't what I set out to do. I was born and raised to be a fighter. Would I look back ten, twenty years from now and have regrets?

The answer was so obviously YES.

I wouldn't be able to change it then, but I could change it now.

My breathing started to recover and I lifted my head to stare across the room at the quad bike looking all black and shiny, parked over on the other side. I could see my sulking form in the chrome of the exhaust.

I'd been living a broken life, but not willing to face it or change it. How was I any better than Eden? What I'd accused her of being?

I hated myself for it. Another demon to fight.

That thought rattled around in my head for a long while. Long enough for me to realise the polished concrete floor wasn't great on my back and my knuckles were really stinging and my throat felt like I'd swallowed a gallon of acid. My eyes felt like they were more swollen than after a pro fight.

I dragged my sorry arse upright and headed across the room to the small bathroom tucked in the back corner of my workshop. I turned the water on and stripped off my sweat soaked jeans and underwear. I didn't even bother to check the temperature. I just stepped in. It was freezing and I gave a shiver and let the water fall over me.

The water seemed to help. It washed away the grime and the remnants of the demons coming out. Slowly I started to feel human again. I was exhausted, but it was more from the emotional rollercoaster than the pounding I'd put on the bags.

I grabbed a clean towel from under the little sink and dried off a bit before securing it around my hips.

I took a deep breath and headed for the stairs. Right now looking up there, I could have sworn I was about to climb Mt Everest. I knew what I had to do and I was terrified. I only hoped I hadn't misread her.

EDEN

An hour had ticked over long ago. The pounding on the bag had stopped sometime around the hour and fifteen mark. I'd peeked my head out and seen him crumpled on the floor sobbing and I didn't know what to do.

I knew he wouldn't want me to see him like this, but I also felt responsible. Then when he got up and headed across the floor to what I guessed was the bathroom, I retreated inside and cleared away the remains of dinner.

That left me sitting here, flicking at my phone. I could text someone but what would I say? Besides what had happened tonight was deeply personal and emotional for both of us. I'd never tell and I knew he wouldn't either.

I heard his footsteps on the stairs as he slowly made his way up. My heart seemed to climb into my mouth with each one he took. I truly had no idea how he would react, what he'd say, but more to the point, what would I say?

The lock twisted on the door and swung open and in he stepped. The first thing I noticed was how exhausted he looked, wearing nothing but a red towel around his hips. The second was the unmistakable red across his knuckles. Oh God, he'd pounded those bags without wrapping his hands.

His eyes met mine and I struggled to read what they were holding. "Let me get dressed and we'll talk."

Was that good? Or bad? What was it that I wanted? Did I want something with him? Did I even have a right to ask? All of these questions swirled around in my head with dizzying speed as I watched him walk over to a wardrobe tucked behind the bathroom. His back was to me the whole time and I studied every single one of the muscles in his back and shoulders as he moved. He slid the door open and pulled something from a shelf.

Then dropped the towel...

I was staring at his naked arse.

Just like the rest of him, it was perfection. Two tight, hard globes of muscle that had made my fingers twitch and my breath quicken.

He pulled on a pair of track suit pants sans underwear, swiped the towel off the floor and headed into the bathroom. A few seconds later he emerged with a large first-aid box and put it on the tea chest before making his way over to the fridge and dumping a heap of ice from trays into plastic bags.

Finally he made his way back to the sofa and sat down beside me. I didn't have to wait long for him to break the silence.

"We need to talk." His voice forced my eyes to meet his and they looked calm and focused once again. "But while we do, would you mind helping me clean these up?" He gestured to his hands.

"Sure."

He nodded and motioned with his chin to the first aid box. "Everything you need is in there."

I opened the hard outer box, which was more like a small chest than any first aid box I'd ever seen and once I lifted the lid I realised why. There was a small pharmacy inside. Every possible size bandage, sticking plaster, wound dressing, antiseptic and wound cream seemed to be in there.

"I've washed them out. They just needed to be disinfected." I reached for the Dettol which I hoped wouldn't sting too badly.

He shook his head no. "Go the peroxide. I deserve the pain."

I ignored him and grabbed the Dettol. "Peroxide is okay for disinfecting, but crap for promoting wound healing. Apparently, it does something to destroy new cells. You get Dettol." I wasn't up for arguing with him. "Doctors at the hospital told me that."

He said nothing just let me take a sterile wipe and load it with Dettol to dab all over the wounds on his hands. I peeled the plastic bag filled with ice off his left hand and winced. It was nasty. His knuckled resembled minced meat rather than the smooth flesh he'd had not so long ago.

"I heal quick."

"You'd want to. That's going to hurt every time you move your hands."

He shrugged. "It's not the first time and it won't be the last, but I know you're no stranger to pain either."

"That's true, but I do try to avoid it where I can."

Xander let out a low chuckle. "Yeah, well tonight seems to have been one of those unavoidable times, but I can report it was long overdue." I dabbed at his hands, but he didn't wince. I guessed he was used to hiding pain. I figured it wasn't something you wanted to show as a fighter.

"Yep...been there done that. Have the T-Shirt, the sound track and the DVD. And one thing I've learned is that it pops up at the most unusual and often inconvenient times." We both knew I was talking about the demons even though I hadn't directly mentioned it.

He nodded then spoke quietly. "I've buried it so deep for so long. I tried to forget it was there. I'd almost convinced myself I was over it."

"Yeah, I know that feeling well and sometimes I get to the point where if Grace, my therapist, asks me one more time how I feel, I swear I'm going to smack her in the head. It just gets monotonous." I put the Dettol away and then went fishing in the box again looking for something else.

"Just paint some Betadine on. I don't want to cover them. I'll ice them for a bit longer. Try to keep the swelling down." I found the Betadine and got to work with a cotton tip.

"Does talking ever help?" He asked it kind of shyly and I guess he felt a little less than manly asking the question. Did it help?

"Sometimes. I guess it depends on who you talk to. Grace, my current therapist, is about the best I've had. But I always feel obligated or something when I talk to her. I guess she helps but I find I'm getting more and more aggravated each time I've seen her lately. I do find talking to my friend Beth helps a lot. She lost a leg in a motor vehicle accident so she seems to understand a lot better how I feel about things."

I capped the bottle of Betadine and put it back in the box. Then grabbed the rubbish and took it over to the bin I'd found in the kitchen.

"Can I get you a drink?" I figured he had to be thirsty after what he'd been through.

"That'd be awesome. Water is fine." I filled two glasses from the big jug in the fridge and came back to the sofa and passed him one.

I couldn't stand it anymore. I had to know.

"Are we done?"

He looked at me strangely and my stomach lurched. I had no idea what he was thinking or really where his head was at.

"What do you mean?"

"You and me—whatever it is...Is it...done?" My voice cracked a little at the end. It had been a really emotional night and I had a feeling there was more to come.

"Do you want it to be done?" Xander asked the question slowly. Almost as if he was trying to prolong my answer, but it gave me no clues as to where his heart was.

All I could do was go with honesty. If I got crushed in the process, I'd survive. It would hurt because, in the couple of hours I'd waited for him, I'd realised just how much I had come to enjoy being with him. I didn't want to let that go.

"I don't want it to be done." My voice was nothing more than a whisper and I hated that it sounded needy.

He leaned back against the sofa and chuckled softly, shaking his head and suddenly a feeling of dread came over me. Did he not feel the same?

"Stop panicking, Gem. I don't want it to be done either, and I was sure you were about to give me a million reasons why we shouldn't be together any longer."

"And what would you have done?" I really wanted to know. I wanted to have some inkling of just what I meant to him. What did together mean to him?

"I would have spent however long it took convincing you into hanging in there with me."

This time I giggled. He really was relieved and I was beginning to see that the cool confident Sensei persona was a façade he wore like a uniform. It was becoming more and more obvious to me that he didn't feel the need to wear it around me all the time.

"So I need to ask; are you pissed at me? You kind of stormed out before. I'm just trying to figure out where we are."

"Yes, I'm pissed at you." I lurched back a bit, but he went on before I had time to react too badly. "Because you made me face things. But I'm also proud of you. Do you have any idea how few people ever stand up to me?"

That caused a funny sensation in my belly—I didn't quite know what to make of it. "I'm not quite sure what happened. I just kind of snapped and you happened to be close so I unloaded on you."

He snorted. "Well, your aim couldn't have been better targeted. The truth hurts and you dished me a hell of a serving."

"Is that a good or bad thing?"

"Well, neither really, but it was what I needed. You gave me a lot to think about." I'd been burying how I felt about The Cobra for a long time. I guess you can't bottle those things up for ever. I'm just sorry you saw me like that."

I wondered if he knew just how much I had really seen. I didn't think so and I decided it wouldn't serve much purpose to tell him right now. The ground between us was still a little unknown to me at the moment.

"You forced me to make the decision I needed to make. I'm going to take the fight."

He was stepping back in the ring.

And suddenly I didn't know how I felt about that. What if he got hurt? What if he ended up like The Cobra?

If anything happened to him I'd feel so responsible.

"Don't do it for me," I almost pleaded. I couldn't live with any more pain if something happened to him.

"I'm not doing it for you. I'm doing it for me. This is something I need to do. I need to see if I've still got what it takes. You were right. I have to practise what I preach, otherwise I'm nothing but a fraud, a charlatan and I can't live with that. I'd rather be beaten to a pulp or worse than ever be accused of being something less than honourable. To be worthy to stand by your side I have to walk the same line that I've asked of you."

Oh my God. It was intense and I had no idea how to feel. He was bearing his soul to me and it was the most humbling gift. I didn't know what to do, so I did the only thing that felt right.

I covered the distance between us in a split second and threw myself into his arms. I had no idea if that was the reaction he wanted or expected but that was what he got.

My mouth found his and I instigated a kiss so hot I couldn't breathe. This time it wasn't just a gentle lip rub.

This was wild and fierce. We'd jumped about a thousand steps and moved straight to the big leagues. My tongue slashed at his and my hands gripped his shoulders until my fingers began to hurt. Our teeth bumped and I pushed my body harder into his. His hand found the back of my head and cradled it; he guided me to some extent, but let me rule and devour.

He let out a low moan in his throat, and we both went tumbling back onto the sofa. Xander on the bottom, me straddling his hips. There was no mistaking it this time. I was aware of exactly what was pushing up at me between my legs and I wanted it badly.

I pulled my mouth away from his and looked down at him

breathing raggedly. Then it all seemed to swamp me at once.

What the hell was I doing?

I froze and closed my eyes.

Could I go through with this?

Was this what I wanted?

God, what the hell sort of signals was I giving him.

In the end the best I could come up with was "I'm sorry." Before I attempted to scramble off him.

XANDER

Oh no. I wasn't going to let her retreat now.

It was time to have that other talk. The one we needed to have.

I caught her wrist and rolled my knees up to lock around her hips, immobilizing her as gently as I could. I knew more moves than most and I had a feeling I was going to need every one of them to survive the ride Eden was going to take me on.

"Stay right where you are and don't you dare be sorry." Her eyes flew open and I was struggling to read the emotions that were flicking across the beautiful blue pools.

"I didn't mean to lead you on...I just kind of got carried away. What you were saying was so intense and I just kind of acted rather than thought."

"Well, I can't say I'm unhappy about it, Gem, but there's another talk we need to have before we go any further." Her head dropped and her eyes were boring into my collarbone again.

"There's no easy way to say this, honey, so I'm just going to ask...how far have you been with a man, Eden? Have you had sex before?"

She didn't answer for a long time and I was starting to feel very uneasy. Well as uneasy as I could with a raging hard on pressing up into her delectable butt. Not that I had any intention of taking things further tonight.

At last she answered. “Twice, but it was a long time ago. I had a boyfriend before the fire. We’d had sex twice. Then he dumped me when he saw me after the fire.”

Her voice was stilted and I knew that it had taken a lot for her to answer me. I reached up and pulled her down over my body in a hug. She needed it and so did I. Just having her body against mine seemed to make everything better.

“Arsehole,” I whispered into her ear. “Want me to beat him up for you?” I was joking, but many a true word was said in jest. I could only imagine how his breaking up with her would have felt on top of everything else that was going on.

“No, I don’t want you to beat him up for me. I could hardly expect him to stay.” There was something so resigned in her tone. And I felt for her. I was now starting to really understand why she acted the way she did and the true extent of the hurt she’d suffered. Everyone had deserted her except for her family. They’d all judged her based on her scars and decided to cut ties. That had to be hurt upon hurt, from Eden’s perspective.

I needed to lighten the mood and finish this conversation. “So tell me. This sex you had with the douchebag was it any good?” I asked with a little chuckle that had her rolling against me tighter.

“Well, I guess that depends on what scale you’re using to judge. I can’t say I really have enough experience to know, but I’m sure hoping it gets better than him lasting less than a minute and me left wondering what all the big deal was.”

This time I did chuckle for real. Oh my poor Gem—what a disaster! But then teenage sex was hardly stellar. I took her chin in my hand and urged her to raise her head to meet my eyes. I stole a little pecking kiss that was full of fun.

“If you’re prepared to trust me I think I can report with certainty that there’s a lot more to it than what you’ve experienced and it would be my absolute pleasure to introduce you to the finer points.” I dropped another pecking kiss on her lips. This didn’t need to be too heavy. Being intimate was a hard enough subject as it was for her. I was determined to make it as easy as possible and to make her feel wanted and desired. God knew it was true. She was a hell of a heady package for me.

"You on board with that?" I wanted an answer.

"Yes," she whispered against my neck.

I relaxed my knees from around her hips. "Okay then, hop off, Gem. We need to go to bed."

She gasped and I knew what she was thinking.

"Relax, Gem. Nothing is going to happen tonight. We've been on a rollercoaster. But you will be sleeping in my bed with me. If you can stand up to me, yell at me and jump me with a hell of a hot kiss, then you can certainly sleep in my arms. Fair enough?"

It wasn't a question but I got a nod of acceptance anyway.

That was all I needed for now.

FIFTEEN

EDEN

My eyes flew open to a beeping noise. It was strange and for a split second I had no idea where I was. Then it came to me in a rush when I realised for the first time ever I wasn't in bed alone. Xander was pressed against the length of my back and he had one arm under my pillow and the other over my waist.

But it was his hand cupping my breast that really had me coming alert quickly. His fingers tightened for a moment around my T-Shirt covered breast and I sucked in a breath. It felt so good. What felt like his thumb brushed across my nipple and I gave a little shiver.

The damned alarm kept sounding and he rolled away and fiddled with it then, to my surprise, he rolled right back to where he was and replaced his arm and hand. This time I didn't miss the press of his hips into my lower back and the feel of his erection pressed tightly against me.

His mouth settled in to the curve of my neck and he nuzzled a little.

"Good morning, Gem." It was a rough sexy whisper and my

body seemed to flush hot from both his words and the sensation of his lips teasing at my neck.

"Good morning," I croaked out, not really sure what I should do. The hand at my breast was gently massaging and it felt better than anything I could remember. My nipple was hard and pressed into the palm of his hand, seeking contact.

"Relax, Gem. Just feel, enjoy," he whispered into my ear and as if on command my body seemed to go lax, and snuggled back tighter into his. Then the hand that had been teasing my breast descended down over my stomach and I held my breath. Would he go further? Was I okay with it?

Just as I was dying from wondering what would happen next, his hand slipped under the material of the T-Shirt. Then his palm was pressed flat against my belly and I couldn't help but shiver under his touch. The skin of his palm was slightly rough and it set up little trails of hot sensation, which tugged hard on my feminine core.

Then his hand worked its way upward and found my breast again. His fingers teased and massaged until he was cupping me completely in his hand.

"I'd love to see what I've got in my hand. How do you feel about that? But before you answer I should warn you. If I see your breasts I'm going to want to put my mouth on them—to lick and suck your nipples. You decide if you'd like that or if it's too soon."

Fear shot through me. Not at what he wanted to do. That sounded so good and my body was screaming for me to say, "Oh yes please." But I wasn't sure. The scar seeped across my breast. His hand continued to massage and roll my needy flesh.

"Tough question?" he prompted me some more.

Finally I found my voice. "The scar goes across the side of my breast."

His lips found my neck again and nipped at my ear lobe sending another tremor of sensation through me. I could feel how wet I was becoming between my legs.

"Mmm, I figured that when I saw it last time. What did you

decide?" His fingertips lightly pinched at my nipple now and I wondered what it would feel like to have those full, sensuous lips of his, licking and teasing instead.

"I...ahh it's not pretty, Xan," I tried to warn him.

"I've seen nearly all of it, Gem. I'm still here wanting you." He pressed his hips against my back firmer to emphasis his point. "Let me see. Then there's nothing more to hide. You can learn to relax and just enjoy what I do to you."

What he said made sense and my body was begging me to say yes. I just needed to ignore the little voices of uncertainty in my head. "Okay." My voice was small and sounded uncertain.

"Oh, my brave girl." He traced his tongue around the shell of my ear and I rolled back towards him on the wave of a shiver he'd set up. My right shoulder met the mattress and suddenly I was looking into the deep, dark depths of his eyes.

A tiny hint of smile curled up one side of his mouth and his lip seemed to twitch before he dropped a light kiss on my lips. Then he pushed my shirt up with his hand until it was just under my chin. I could feel the cool morning air brush against my heated skin and my nipples seemed to tighten even more.

"Can you sit up for me, Gem? I want to take this off you." Xander rolled back onto his knees and offered me a hand. He pulled me up so I was sitting, then he reached for my shirt and pulled it off over my head.

I watched his face intently and not once did he flinch or retract. In fact his eyes seemed to have gotten hotter and more intense.

"How can you stand to look at that mess?" I truly wondered. Even now, at times, when I looked in the mirror I couldn't hold back the feelings of loss and revulsion at the ugliness of my skin.

"Lay back, honey." He didn't answer but instead followed me down. His hand finding my perfect left breast and his mouth my scarred right. What he did next shocked the hell out of me. Rather than close his mouth around my nipple as he had said he was going to do, his tongue ran the length of the scarred skin on my breast. I wriggled away at the sensation and the surprise.

His head popped up and a slow grin formed. "Tastes just like regular skin but gives me a lot more hills and hollows to explore. And I promise you now I will explore each and every one of them when we have a little more time. But I did promise I was going to suck your nipples, and I decided last night I'm going to be a man of integrity and honesty, one hundred percent from now on."

He said no more, just dropped his head and took my nipple into his mouth and just as he promised, he sucked and licked long and hard. White-hot sensation connected my breasts to my core and it felt incredible. Like nothing I'd ever experienced before and I wanted more. A lot more.

My hand gripped onto his shoulders and my hips seemed to be bucking upwards seeking him.

A low moan escaped my throat and he sucked me deep again before moving across to rain the same shower of pleasure down on the other one.

"Oh Xander that feels so goooood..." My voice was breathy and foreign to my own ears.

Then he pulled away slightly before dropping a kiss on the nipple. Finally, he looked at me. "Your breasts are just as gorgeous as I knew they would be, but I shouldn't have started this, because we don't have time to finish it. Reed is a stickler for punctuality, even if it is a casual social thing."

Before I could say or form any more thoughts, his hand slid down my belly and cupped between my legs. Even through the soft fabric of my sleep shorts, my supersensitised skin seemed to be able to make out every tiny nuance of his hand.

"Next time I'm going to explore down here. You're so hot and I know you're wet for me. It's taking every last bit of my control not to pull these shorts off you and run my fingers and mouth all over you here." He squeezed a little for emphasis and my hips shot up on their own accord. "I think you'd like that. I know I will. Think about it, Eden, as you're sitting behind me on the Quad today, pressed up against me. That's where I'm going to be exploring next. I know I'll be thinking about it."

I was stunned and wanting. Never before had I ever been this turned on and judging by the wicked grin Xander gave me as he pushed up off the bed, I knew that had been his intention. How could he leave me feeling like this?

He headed towards the bathroom, but turned slightly as if he could read my thoughts. Then gestured towards the huge tent in the front of his boxer shorts.

"You're not the only one suffering, Gem. I promise we'll take care of it very soon if that's what you want." With that he turned and retreated into the bathroom closing the door.

For the first time in five years, I felt like a woman and not just the broken shell of somebody that had once been so much more.

XANDER

"Eden, I'd like you to meet my friend and trainer, Reed." Somehow we'd managed to get ourselves organised and out the door. My dick was under temporary control but far from happy with me at the moment. The little knowing glances Eden had been shooting me were a reward in themselves. Her confidence was growing as a person, as a woman. My woman.

I wrapped my arm tightly around her waist. As had become her habit, she always kept me on her right side. In a way I was her shield to the right side of her body. It wasn't ideal but at least she wasn't looking at the floor so much.

She held out her hand tentatively and Reed took it in his. "Hi Reed, nice to meet you," she said quietly. There was still a tentativeness in her voice but she seemed a little more confident.

"Nice to meet you too, Eden. Now I know what had Pretty Boy here racing out on me yesterday like his arse was on fire."

"Pretty Boy?" She looked up at me in confusion.

"My ring name that Reed so kindly monikered me with," I

explained to her.

"Well, you've lived up to it. You haven't smashed up that pretty face yet." Reed gave Eden a playful wink and she giggled a little. Yeah, he was enjoying taking the piss out of me, but I didn't care if it meant Eden got to joke around a little, too.

"I've no intentions of getting this face smashed up. I don't fight to lose." I gave Reed a hard look. I hadn't said I was taking the fight yet and I know he was trying to read me. Taking the fight had to be my decision and Reed wouldn't pressure me. There was no point.

I had to be two hundred percent committed or I would get my face smashed up. That didn't scare me. What did scare me was, not being able to commit. Not being able to go the distance. There couldn't be one doubt in my mind. Fighting was as much mental as it was physical. I had to be prepared to take the pain. Not the obvious pain of being hammered at in the ring, but the pain of the training. I had to be committed to keep getting to my feet when I was beyond exhausted and wanted nothing more than to crawl into bed and sleep for a week. It was going to be eight weeks of the worst hell I had ever faced. Plus, I had Eden to consider now.

Eden looked between us and I knew she was trying to figure out the under currents but was polite enough not to ask. I'd explain it all to her later. Before we got much further into a conversation Reed's wife Carmen came round the house from the side.

A big smile lit up her face and she pulled me straight into a big hug when she reached us. "Hey, Xander good to see you! It's been too long."

She let me go and took a step back. "And who's this?" Her smile for Eden was just as genuine and warm. Carmen was one of those genuinely happy people that saw the best in everyone and immediately made a room feel warmer just by being there. She was short and a little on the rounded side with a puffy cloud of hair just about every shade of brown. It matched her light brown eyes and the whole look seemed to work for her. Reed was a lucky man and he knew it. Not many would put up with his snarly arse. But maybe she had enough smiles for both of them.

"Carmen, this is my girlfriend, Eden." I'd wrapped my arm back around Eden when Carmen had released me from her hug. I felt Eden tense slightly at my choice of words before she seemed to snuggle a fraction closer. I didn't miss the narrowing of Reed's eyes though. Eden went to stretch out her hand to her, but Carmen was having none of that and pulled Eden away from me and into a hug as well.

"Welcome, honey. I'm a hugger even though it pisses off my big grizzly here." Carmen released Eden and dug an elbow into Reed's side playfully. He just growled and shot her a look that conveyed that secret language only couples shared.

"No, I'm a little nervous to be honest." Eden giggled a little and I knew instantly that she was going to be comfortable with Carmen.

"Oh, you're in for a treat. It's such a beautiful morning and we have some awesome trails out here. Plus Xander will keep you safe; just enjoy yourself." She clapped Eden on the shoulder.

"Right, Xan. Let's get going before Carmen talks us all to death." Reed made a move towards the large red quad he was getting out of the shed as we pulled up. Carmen rolled her eyes and flicked Reed on the butt as he walked past. They enjoyed playing games; it was their thing.

"Okay, Gem. Let's get organised." I steered her over to my quad which I had unloaded as soon as we arrived. I loved this bike. It was big, black, large and powerful. What could be better? I grabbed a helmet from the tray of my truck and passed it to Eden.

"Girlfriend?" she asked.

I felt a little self-conscious and covered it with a shrug. "You got a problem with that?"

"No, but I just wasn't sure how you felt." Her words came out hushed and in a hurry.

"Make no mistake. That's how I feel. I figured this morning would have been enough of a clue but obviously not. We good?"

She smiled. "We're good!"

I took the other helmet for myself. I hoped we wouldn't need the helmets but you never know. I strapped a small duffle bag to the bag rack behind the seat, then turned my attention back to Eden.

I leaned in and brushed my lips briefly against hers. "This is going to be fun. Just hang on. I won't let anything happen to you."

"I know." She gave me a grin that said nervous but excited all at the same time. I could see the trust in her eyes and damn, if that didn't make me feel ten feet tall.

I threw my leg over the bike and settled myself then took her hand to steady her as she climbed on.

"Slide in close to me and hang on around my waist. I'll take it steady to start with. Carmen's right, the trails up here are awesome. You're going to love this."

Eden's arms wrapped around my waist and closed tight. She was wearing another of those long sleeved T-shirts she seemed to favour. About three sizes too big. Eden would be a complete knock out in clothes that actually fit. Her body was gorgeous and I knew now without a doubt it was my job to convince her of that.

The scars were there but I hardly seemed to notice them anymore, but I could understand why she would feel differently. Being a beautiful woman and having a scar on your face must be about as bad as it gets, I guessed.

Eden settled herself a little more by wriggling tight to my body. I could feel her breasts pressed up against my back. Those nipples of hers were going to be hard in just a few seconds and I'm sure my dick would be the same. This ride was going to be exquisite torture. She was getting bolder by the minute and I loved it. I had a feeling she would remain a little reserved around most people for a while. But she was really starting to open up to me, and the more I got to know her, the more I was attracted to her as a person. Eden was easy to be around.

Reed and Carmen rode past us and headed out onto the gravel driveway that led up to the house. They lived on a hinterland property about forty minutes from my place. It was beautiful—lush and green, very subtropical looking. The only downside was it was a little far out of town for my liking, but Reed didn't seem to mind the drive and most of his business was done over the phone or via computer connection. Carmen was an artist of sorts and made commissioned pottery pieces. Some of her work was absolutely magnificent. So the seclusion of this property certainly suited them.

Just before the driveway joined the road there was a gate and Reed hopped off and opened it. Once we were all through, he took off again across the ridge top and I followed. I'd been this way many times in the past, but it never got old. The view was incredible. To the left the whole of the Gold Coast and the Pacific Ocean was laid out. It was enough to take your breath away.

The terrain was fairly subdued, a few little bumps, but nothing to really be concerned about. It was all about taking in the view at the moment and it seemed to be the perfect way to start the day.

"Oh wow, Xan! I've never seen the Gold Coast from up here. It looks incredible."

I stopped for a moment and kicked the bike into idle and turned a little so I could look at her better.

"See down there, that really tall building is Q1. Have you done the walk to the top of it?"

"No. How stupid is that? I live less than an hour away and I've never been there."

"Well, it's something we can do together then. I'd love to show you some time. There's a couple of really good Japanese restaurants there and a French one that is supposed to be out of this world. Would you like that?"

She hesitated for a moment. "It sounds really tempting but I haven't really eaten out much beyond the likes of the café." I could tell she was a little embarrassed by her lack of cultural experience.

"Don't sweat it. We'll have an awesome time when we go. Although it won't be for a few weeks. I'm on a diet as of tomorrow." The hard training I could really get into and almost relish, but the highly controlled diet would have me really pissed off by the end of the time. But it was all part of totally committing to a fight.

"Can I help you with stuff while you're training?" Eden squeezed me tighter as she asked the question. I could tell she genuinely wanted to help.

"They'll be plenty of things you can help with. My biggest problem is going to be keeping Onigashima going while I train. I'm going to need to get some of my higher students to step up and lead a few classes. I'll have a chat with them all tomorrow then we can work things through."

She looked at me intently for a few moments. "Have you really got time for us or am I going to be a distraction? You need to answer me truthfully, Xander. I don't want to be a distraction or an inconvenience when you're trying to focus on something."

"Eden, you're neither a distraction, nor an inconvenience. You're important to me. When things are important you prioritise and remove things of lesser importance off your plate. You're right at the top of my priority list."

She seemed to blush a little and dipped her head a fraction, feeling a little self-conscious.

I tilted her chin up with my hand and popped a light, teasing kiss to those sweet lips of hers. I wanted to take it deeper and show her just how serious I was about her being a priority, but Reed had chosen to double back to see why we weren't behind him. As he approached he shook his head and looked annoyed.

"Guess we're busted." I turned back into my seat and kicked the bike back into gear.

"But it was so worth it!" Her voice trailed off on a giggle on the wind. She gave me another squeeze around the middle and there was no way I was going to complain about that.

Yeah, she was right. So worth it.

We rode on for another couple of hours. The terrain was varied. At times it was steep and rocky, sometimes flat and fast. We crossed creeks and popped the odd jump.

Finally, we had come to a little picnic area that Reed knew about. It was in a neighbours' property that all the locals used from time to time. We stopped there and had a drink and a snack from the supplies we'd packed. The four of us relaxed on the grass. It was friendly and fun; something that I knew Eden didn't experience very often.

I could tell Reed wanted to know what my decision was. He'd been eyeing me intently all morning trying to read my decision. When we finally got back to his and Carmen's place, the opportunity presented itself.

Carmen and Eden had headed into the house to organise a late lunch. Reed and I were cleaning up the bikes and I knew that would be when the fight would come up. Reed wasn't a patient man.

"That was a great ride, man. I really needed that," Reed said to me as he hosed his bike.

"Yeah, it was. Pity Dane had something on, he could have used the fun as well," I agreed as I took a cloth and started to chammy off the water from where my bike had been hosed.

"Yeah, he's going to have a big program ahead of him."

"I need to have a chat to him. Make sure he's fully committed to the ride." I was worried about my friend. Dane was a bad ass and a totally capable fighter but joining the pro-ranks was a whole different ball game. The pros took total dedication and commitment. I didn't want him getting disappointed or worse, hurt.

"He'll be fine. I'm more worried about you..."

"What do you mean?"

"Why don't we stop dancing around? Are you taking the fight or not?" If nothing else, Reed was direct.

I stopped my wiping and looked over at him. It was time to come clean.

"I am."

I noticed the hint of surprise flick across his face before it became a stern mask again.

"You up to it? And I don't mean physically. You're not in tip-top fight shape, but in eight weeks you will be. I'm more interested in where your head's at."

And wasn't that the million dollar question?

"Reed, I've never lied to you yet, so I'll give it to you straight. Just between you and me... for the first time ever, I'm fucking terrified about a fight." I heard Reed suck in a breath and his face went dark. "For the first time in twelve hundred and eighteen days I've realised I'm terrified of hopping back into the cage, but the difference now is I actually want to do it. I need to do it." Reed's eyes flew open even wider and I could tell he was wondering what the hell I was doing contemplating a fight.

"Reed, I also realised last night I'm more terrified of not hopping into the cage and not achieving what I've meant to do my whole fucking life."

Reed worked his jaw a couple of times, and considered my words.

"Are you absolutely sure?" His voice was harsh and this was my last chance to back out. After this the wheels would be in motion so to speak.

I paused for a second and searched my soul one last time. There was only one answer that was acceptable.

"Yes. I'm sure."

"What about The Cobra?"

That was the easy bit. "I'll never get over the guilt of what happened with The Cobra, but I can't let it rule me any longer. For three years my guilt has been screwing with my integrity. I've been preaching to my students about fighting their demons, being better people, yada yada. Hell—you know the drill. I learned most of it from you and your dad. But I've been living my life as a fraud and it took Eden to point it out to me. I'm not going to live that life any longer. I need to start practising what I preach. Taking this fight is exactly what I need to do."

Again, Reed was quiet for a few moments and that sort of pissed me off. He liked to run the whole "considered" line and I wondered when I would ever be considered equal in his eyes. It kind of pissed me off that I needed the personal validation, too.

Reed nodded towards the house. “She going to be a problem?”

I saw red and I stood up from where I was lounged against the bike. That comment had really pissed me off.

I pointed towards the house. “It’s Eden. And she’s exactly the reason I’m getting into the cage again. It was Eden who pointed out to me the lie I’d been living. I was asking her to fight her demons but I wasn’t prepared to tackle my own. That’s changed. I’m fighting. And you can fucking well thank her. You know I manage my priorities when I’m training but I will not prioritise Eden. She sits right up there beside this fight. I’ll make this commitment to you. You leave Eden and my relationship alone and I’ll give you everything. Don’t cross me on this, Reed. I’m not negotiable on this.”

Reed glared at me and I knew he wasn’t happy, but I’d made my terms clear. Besides, I wasn’t a kid anymore. I’d been a grown man for quite a few years now and I was a seasoned pro-fighter. I needed a trainer for this fight not a baby sitter.

Finally Reed spoke. “You said you’re going to take the fight—what about winning it?”

This time I pulled the pause thing. “A win is a given. I don’t take fights to lose them. Isn’t that what you taught and drummed the hell into me?”

Reed chuckled a little.

“Besides, as you pointed out earlier, I can’t risk fucking up this pretty face so I’d better be on my game.”

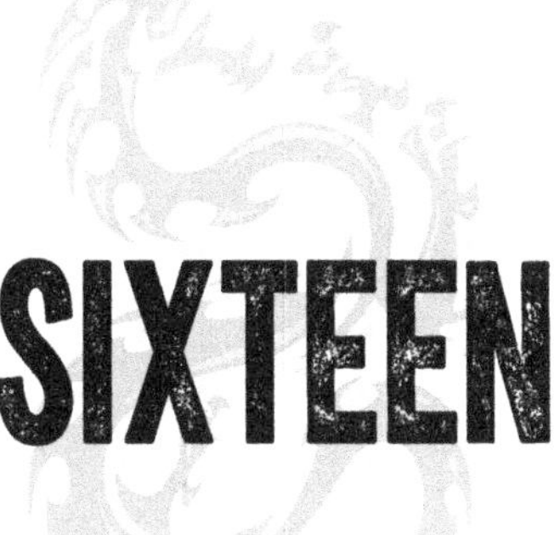

SIXTEEN

EDEN

Thursday afternoon rolled around again and it was time for my appointment with Grace. As I sat in the waiting area I took the time to really reflect over what had happened in the past week. It had been a whirlwind. My life suddenly seemed so busy. Far out, I'd probably come further in that week mentally than I had in the whole past five years. How was that even possible? For once, I was actually looking forward to the fact that I had something to talk about rather than have Grace trying to drag stuff out of me.

A few minutes later Grace invited me in, pulling me from my thoughts. Once we were settled she poured me a glass of water from her crystal pitcher and placed it on the coffee table in front of me.

"Well, you look brighter today? Something tells me you've got lots of news." Grace gave me a genuine smile and I couldn't help but agree.

"You're right. I do have a lot to share." I actually felt a little excited to be telling someone about my relationship with Xander. It wasn't something I wanted to share with my sisters. Xander was their Sensei. No way was I going to talk to them about intimate things. I had Beth of course, but she'd been away visiting relatives. Everyone's timing kind of sucked. I had suddenly made progress and I had news, but I either couldn't tell some people, or the ones I could tell, were away.

Even mum was away and wouldn't be back for another few weeks at least. So Grace was it. At least I didn't have to worry about her getting uncomfortable or telling her stuff that I didn't want told to others.

"Well, tell me what's been going on."

"So, after we last met, I've started to see Xander."

"What do you mean by see?"

"Well he organised to pick me up from uni the first time and we went back to the dojo. He was going to start teaching me some self defence moves." I paused it still shocked me even now. "He made me pull my hair back. Then he asked me about the scars. He wanted to know if they created any restrictions or issues for me exercising. Then he suggested that I show him..." I watched Grace's eyes go wide.

"What did you do?" Uncharacteristically, she wasn't quick enough to hide her surprise at what I was telling her.

"I let him look at them." If Grace's eyes were wide before, then now they were popping out of her head.

"How..." She seemed to be struggling for words for once.

"How did it happen? How did I feel?"

She nodded.

"Terrified, embarrassed, hopeful, liberated. It was kind of an avalanche of feelings all at once. I guess I started to have a bit of a panic attack. The feelings were very overwhelming but Xander made me breathe with him. He kind of talked me through the whole thing, asked me questions."

"You didn't feel embarrassed?"

"Well, at first, but the longer he looked and asked questions, no." Then I got a little embarrassed and heat flashed over me. "He said I was still beautiful even with the scars and I'm sure, now looking back, that he actually meant it."

"That sounds like there's a lot more to tell. Go on..."

I told Grace about what we covered in the self defence sessions then I told her about him refusing to accept money from friends. I spoke about our weekend and what we did. What I didn't tell her was how intimate our relationship was getting. That was a hurdle I was working up to.

"Haven't you been a busy girl? You've gone from having next to no social life to being very busy. So you basically spent the whole weekend with him. What else happened?" Grace gave me a knowing look. "Do you have intimate feelings for Xander?"

I dropped my eyes. Oh yeah, I had intimate feelings for him, but I'd never really talked about my sex life or lack of it with anyone. Xander was the first person I told about what happened with Robert before the fire.

"Yes, I have intimate feelings for him."

"And do you think he reciprocates these feelings...?" Grace asked gently.

I gave a little giggle. "Umm, yeah. We kind of slept together Saturday night."

This time not only did Grace's eyes pop out on sticks her mouth also dropped open in what could only be shock. It was kind of funny to watch actually. Was it wrong to be enjoying actually shocking her for a change?

"Let me explain. We had a very intense discussion about facing our demons. I did something I've never done Grace...I actually defended myself and turned a pretty heated discussion back on him. I guess both of us realised we had a lot of work to do to deal with our own fears. There's more, but I don't think you'll understand how I could possibly have got to where we did, unless I tell you and I'm not entirely comfortable telling you because I feel it will break a confidence."

"It's up to you, Eden. I'm not asking you to divulge every little action and comment. I'm not here to pry into your personal life. I'm here to help you progress. You've told me more today than you ever have before."

I nodded my understanding. I didn't want to tell Grace about what Xander went through. It was his story and feelings. He'd shared them with me and I knew categorically he'd never done that with anyone else. That was a gift and I wasn't about to devalue it by sharing it.

"So after our 'very intense discussion' I was really moved, I guess, by some of the things he'd said. I kind of threw myself into his arms and started kissing him madly. I should mention we had shared a few kisses the night before, but nothing had been intense and Xander made it clear from the outset that he wouldn't pressure me and he hasn't."

Grace smiled and right then I realised she was a romantic at heart. "Go on."

"We kissed for a bit then we headed to bed. He was adamant that he just wanted to hold me. So that's how we slept. Nothing happened other than him holding me while I slept...It was the first time I've ever spent the night in bed with a man. Then the next morning we woke up and his hand was on my breast... and that kind of led a little further. We didn't have sex or anything but he's made it clear that is where it's going ultimately. "

"Oh my, you have had a big few days. Are you okay with all this? I mean just a couple of weeks ago you were struggling to meet new people, now you seem to be in a relationship with a man and intimacy is definitely something that's on the agenda. Is that what you want to talk about?"

I shrugged a little. "I guess it is. I suppose I wouldn't have told you otherwise. Although, you would have probably dragged it out of me anyway!"

"More than likely," Grace agreed with a knowing laugh. "So what exactly do you want to talk about regarding intimacy?"

What did I want to know? "I don't really know. I guess it all just seems to be happening fast and he's been wonderful and I don't feel the least bit pressured. Kind of the other way around to be honest," I realised.

"So, you want me to reassure you that it's okay for you to have a sexual relationship with this man you've started seeing. Is that it?" It felt like Grace was purposely playing dumb and we both knew she was far from it. I guess that was what I was looking for, wasn't it?

"Am I doing the right thing?"

"Does it feel right?"

I couldn't help but smile. It felt more than right whenever I was with Xander. I nodded.

"Eden, you're a grown woman, first and foremost. Yes, you have scars and these have given you a lot of cause to have issues with your confidence and other aspects of social situations. It's not for me to tell you whether you should or shouldn't have a sexual relationship with Xander. That's for you to decide. My advice is take it at your own pace and make sure you're comfortable. It's the same advice I would give any person when entering into a new relationship. Having scars is irrelevant in this case. It seems from what you've told me and the enormous progress you've obviously made, Xander has managed to reach you where we were all previously failing. That's the beauty of being around different people. They bring different experiences, outlooks and approaches. Some people just click. You seem to have clicked with Xander. You need to start making decisions as a woman, rather than as a person with scars."

We didn't talk much more. What more was there really to say? I guess we could have dissected it for hours, but Grace was right. I was a grown woman. As long as I was comfortable with what was happening then that was all that mattered right?

The only person I had to answer to and consider was myself.

That was a little frightening in itself, I'd spent so long trying to hide from the real me.

XANDER

I rolled my shoulders one last time as I finished my warm up. So far today, I'd run ten kilometres, done a killer steps session and then spent a couple of hours grappling with Reed. Now I was supposed to start some sparring drills with Dane. Only problem was the fucker wasn't here!

Reed was off to the side madly texting on his phone and I could see his temper rising with every minute Dane wasn't here.

"This was always my problem with Dane. Everything came too easy for him. Life was one big cruise. It's one thing when his attitude affects himself but it's another when it screws with other people. He gave me his word he was one hundred percent committed to this fight and to be your training partner..." Yep, Reed was officially pissed.

"He's probably hit traffic," I said trying to reason with Reed a little. I'd chew him out when the opportunity arose. But that was between two friends. This was different. Reed was now his trainer too, and Reed wouldn't put up with this.

"This is his one and only chance to screw up. If he's had issues getting here he should pick up his damned phone and let me know." Reed was of course right, but he was also a punctuality Nazi. After sending one last text, Reed tossed his phone onto the bench seat that ran the side of the room. He probably used a little more force than was good for the phone..

"Okay, we'll do some work on the pads while we're waiting." I nodded and checked the fastenings on the gloves I wore.

Reed held up the pads and started calling combinations. I worked through the first few slowly increasing my power and speed as I went, until I was working hard. It was nothing I hadn't done a million times before. Then Reed started to add some feigned counter strikes at random intervals in the combinations. The first caught me a little by surprise, but I managed to get my cover in place before Reed connected. He didn't seem to feel it was necessary for him to indicate he was mixing it up! Well, that was fine by me because I wasn't expecting "Lights Out" to give me a map on where he was going to hit either.

I worked solidly for ten minutes, much longer than a round, then took a break to grab a drink from the water bottle I'd left to the side. Reed moved over to his phone and checked the screen.

"Fuck. Still nothing from him." I could almost see the steam coming out his ears. "Let's keep going. We'll add some kicks and knees." That was code for anything goes. Reed would hold the pads and expect me to follow. He'd also throw in the odd strike. Fighting was as much a game of concentration and strategy as anything else. To win a fight you had to not only have superb technique and stamina, but you also needed to be mentally tough and able to adapt your game plan and strategy to suit whatever your opponent decided he was going to come at you with.

We worked on for another half an hour when finally Dane walked through the door.

He didn't even take his bag to the lockers. Instead he dumped it on the bench seat and started to pull out gloves to get organised.

"What do you think you're doing?" Reed bellowed. Dane looked at him a little sheepishly. "You turn up almost an hour late, you don't answer your phone, you don't contact me or Xander and then you expect to waltz into this session..." Reed shook his head in disbelief.

"It's one thing to put your own training in jeopardy and disrespect me; it absolutely sucks to do it to your best mate when he has the fight of his life in just a few weeks." Reed's tone would have cut toughen steel.

Dane had nothing. What could he say to that?

Finally he went to open his mouth. "Don't even think about offering an excuse." Reed cut him off before Dane had a chance to get a word out. "Xan take a break and rest up. Dane can hit pads for a bit." Reed had an evil glint in his eye and I saw Dane wince. We both knew that what I'd just done was nothing compared to the torture that Dane was about to endure. "Once we're done here, we'll get that sparring done. Dane should be nice and warm by then."

Dane nodded and moved off to warm up; at least he was smart enough to keep his mouth shut.

Reed turned back to me. "Right. Let's keep going for another five minutes while he warms up."

I'd noticed during the last couple of weeks that something was going on with Dane and I needed to have a chat to him. If he had a problem, then I'd be there for him regardless of the fight. I had no doubt he was solid. No way would he have blown me off unless he had a really good reason.

SEVENTEEN

EDEN

My Intermediate Accounting class was dragging. I was sitting in the same seat I sat in every time I was in this lecture theatre. Top row, furthest right. From here I had the option of making a quick get away or I could wait quietly until everyone else had left. Normally I could focus, but not today. Today I just wanted it done. I liked the lecturer. Kevin was middle aged and very "average". Average looking with brown hair, glasses that were fashionable, but not hipster and clothes that were more serviceable than fashionable. His voice was pleasant and normally I appreciated that, but today my heart just wasn't in it. I was counting the time down.

This week we'd managed to carve out a little time together. Xander had been adamant about continuing my training and we'd managed to squeeze in another couple of sessions between his training. I also had assignments to finish and exams to study for. Finals were only a few weeks away and I wanted to do well. So all in all, we hadn't really had anytime to spend together. But that hadn't stopped us from texting or calling late at night when we could.

Poor Xander had been so exhausted last night he fell asleep part way through our call. When he'd told me what Reed had put him through during the day, I'd begged him to go to bed and sleep but instead he'd wanted to talk to me. About ten minutes into the call exhaustion won the battle, and I'd hung up realising what had happened.

One thing I had got better at was texting! No more agonising over a text for me!

I discretely took my phone out and placed it beside my notebook. I flicked the screen and immediately saw a text message from Xander.

> **Xander:** Hey gorgeous, hope your day is going well. Reed's slowly killing me. Can't wait to see you later tonight. :)
>
> **Me:** I'm bored out of my brain. Can't wait to see you either. ☺

I really wanted to put a little heart emoticon at the end of my text, but I wasn't brave enough. Was it too soon for that? I know lots of other girls did that sort of thing all the time but I felt weird doing it unless I meant it.

Xander had been busy. As well as the text, I also had a friend request on Facebook. Social media wasn't really my thing anymore. There was a time before the fire that I lived on it. I'd been actively trying to build my model profile on Facebook and Twitter. Instagram was just starting to get popular when the fire happened. I hadn't updated my fan pages since the fire. Sophia had begged me to keep going with them, but I couldn't bear it. What was I going to do or say? Models were supposed to be beautiful. That was no longer me. For months Soph tried to convince me. Eventually she gave up. In fact I couldn't remember the last time she'd even asked me about it.

Since the fire I'd mostly refused to have my photo taken—but sometimes I couldn't get out of a family snap. However, I absolutely couldn't stand looking at photos of myself. Now I just made posts that contained text or pictures of something else. I didn't need the constant reminders. I lived with that everyday—every time I looked in the mirror.

Eventually my attention returned back to the lecture as Kevin started to run through what the last assignment was going to be and a bit about what would be in the final exam. I jotted down a few notes, and was pleased to see I'd just about finished all the work I needed for the assignment. That would give me more time to study.

Just as I was packing up my things another text came through.

> **Xander:** Don't forget to have Sophia pick you up from the front. Wait inside until she's there. I'm sorry I can't come get you myself.

He was a worry wart! But it was kind of nice to know he cared. I knew he had another couple of sessions this afternoon to get through before he would be finished, so I'd asked Sophia to come pick me up today. I could have caught the bus but I wanted to call past the mall and grab a couple of things and Sophia was always up for a little shopping. I just hoped it wasn't busy. The mall made me uneasy at the best of times. It wasn't too bad with Xander last weekend but that was a whole other story.

> **Me:** Stop worrying. It's all sorted. Soph is picking me up then we're going to the mall and hopefully we can meet up with Tori.

> **Xander:** I like worrying about you ;)

> **Me:** Well then you're a nut and obviously not training hard enough! But thanks anyway ☺

Xander: Breaks over. I'll pick you up from your place as soon as I'm free from here. Pack a bag. XX

Now I was wondering if they were kisses or whether he was signing off his text. I was going to go with kisses. I guess I was also staying over again. That made my heart beat faster and my stomach get even more butterflies. Oh my God, just how far would it go?

Me: See you then XX

My heart was beating quicker and I suddenly felt hot as I thought of being back in that big bed with Xander.

Sophia had been waiting when I walked to the front of campus.

As soon as I got in, she was off. "Hey Soph. What's the hurry?"

"The hurry is I'm getting you to the mall before you change your mind. You never want to go there." Was I really that bad? I didn't even have to think about it. Yeah, I was. Probably worse.

"Sorry. It freaks me out but online shopping only goes so far," I used as an excuse.

"Well, it works just fine if you don't care if things actually fit. To me, internet shopping is about settling. When it comes to clothes I don't settle."

That was certainly the truth and, at one time, it was very much me as well. Up until now I'd been quite content to wear things that provided maximum coverage of the scars. I was thinking of changing that, but I wasn't sure I could do it.

"What are we shopping for anyway?" Soph glanced across asking me.

"Umm, I thought I might see if I can find a couple of tops that actually fit a bit better." I tried to make it sound casual but we both knew that wasn't the case.

"Great idea. I'm sure Sensei will appreciate seeing you in something that actually enhances your rocking body."

"Soph!"

"Oh stop it. I know you've still got a rocking body and I'd lay good money and keep it that he knows, too."

I felt myself blush. I hadn't discussed what had happened between Xander and me with my sisters, but I'm sure Sophia could guess based on my blush and how uncomfortable I felt.

I wanted to say something like "It's really none of your business." But Sophia was my sister and she was so close to me. It just didn't feel right.

"You would keep the money—he knows." She could draw whatever conclusions she wanted from that comment.

"Oh My God! Go Sensei! I wondered if he walked on water, now I know for sure he does. How he managed to get you naked in that space of time is a fricking miracle."

I felt my cheeks get even hotter.

"I wasn't naked, but yes, he has seen the extent of my scars." Hopefully that would be enough information to keep her satisfied.

"And he didn't freak out?"

"No, he didn't. The scars don't seem to bother him... I really don't understand it." And I didn't. Why didn't they act as a deterrent to him? That's what happened with most people. Why not him?

"Sensei's not like a normal douche bag guy. He's all about codes, respect, honour and stuff like that. I still can't believe you've been hanging out with Sensei."

"I can't either to be honest. He even referred to me as his girlfriend when he introduced me to Reed the other day."

"Shihan Reed is so scary."

I giggled a little. "Actually I found him quite nice once I got to know him a little better. His wife, Carmen is a complete sweetheart. We had a lovely time getting some lunch ready."

"You cooked as well?"

"Let's not be hasty here," I joked. "I cut up salad ingredients from the safety of the other side of her kitchen while she handled the stove."

"I was going to say..."

"Yeah. I know."

An hour later we were in the oversized fitting rooms of a department store. I was trying on long-sleeved tops that actually fitted and Sophia was helping me with sizes and giving me her opinion on what looked best.

Finally, we decided on a long sleeved navy top that had a sharp, deep V neck. It was cut so that it hid most of my scars, but it emphasised my waist as well my bust.

"Oh yeah, he'll love that one!" Sophia gave me a big thumbs up. "Guys love tits and you have a great rack, Eden. Get that black shirt as well; it rocked."

"Sophia!" I chastised in mock horror. I knew she was only trying to boost my confidence and I appreciated her efforts.

"Yeah, yeah whatever. Now we need to find you some sexy new underwear."

I gulped, but yes, new underwear had been on my private little mental shopping list.

Another half and hour later and the lingerie was sorted as well. I owed Sophia a big one. She'd left me in the fitting room and had been doing my fetching. I really hoped Xander would like the end results.

Finally satisfied with the underwear and the sexy little shorty pyjamas set, Sophia called it quits.

"Let's go find out if Tori really can get off work on time or whether it's hearsay!"

It would be interesting.

I glanced at my watch and wondered what time Xander would finally make it. He'd said it would be after seven. I was counting down the minutes.

XANDER

Somehow my legs didn't seem to ache as much as I climbed the stairs to the apartment behind Eden. I couldn't take my eyes off her long slender legs or her tight rounded butt in those skinny jeans. I'm sure she'd worn those jeans before, but it was hard to tell. She'd always had a baggy shirt over the top. But not tonight.

When I'd picked her up before, I'd almost done a double take. Her long elegant body was actually in clothes that fit—jeans that looked like they'd been painted on and a navy long-sleeved top that plunged low over her delectable breasts. As soon as I'd laid eyes on her, I'd wondered if it would be inappropriate to reach out and cup one of those beauties. I knew the answer, of course. But a guy could fantasise. I most definitely would have my hands on those breasts and whatever else she felt comfortable with tonight. But first I needed to feed us.

I couldn't wait any longer. As soon as we were inside and I had the door closed, I pulled her into my arms and locked my mouth to hers. That little brush of lips we'd had before when I'd picked her up, wasn't cutting it at all. I wanted her mouth. I was exhausted but I felt raw and needy and the one thing I needed was Eden—against my body and every other way she felt comfortable. Yeah, I needed to rein it in a little. It would be so easy to get carried away.

My tongue pushed into her mouth and I was rewarded with a little throaty whimper. That was definitely music to my ears. Then I stroked my tongue along hers, teasing as I pulled her body tighter into mine. I needed to feel her against me. Eden needed to know how much I wanted her.

She pulled back a fraction and I let her move back—to come up for air, so to speak.

"Oh Xan, that felt way intense."

I nodded my head. Eden was right of course, but I couldn't seem to form words at the moment. Finally, I managed to string a few together. "I missed you this week. A couple of hours here and there wasn't enough for me. I like having you around, close to me."

I didn't miss the coy little smile that formed on her lips. "I missed you, too. I enjoyed the time we had together but I think I know what you mean." She ducked her head into my neck and kissed me just above my shirt.

Right now I was at the point where my dick was throbbing and I could feel the ache there more than the rest of my battered body, which was saying something, but I needed to eat. In order to train as I was, I had to eat regularly and correctly.

"Okay temptation, time you came and kept me company in the kitchen while I get dinner sorted out." Eden giggled and took the hand I extended to her. I was pleased to see she was becoming much more comfortable with my casual flirting.

She took the stool on the lounge room side of the bench and I took the kitchen side. It wasn't a bad idea to have the bench between us until we got food out of the way. Four foot of timber and granite between us might just ensure that dinner actually got cooked.

"You good with a beef and veggie stir fry? Please say yes because I'm really not feeling up to cooking much else tonight." I wasn't too proud to admit I was really feeling it this first week.

"That's fine. Can I help? I know you must be exhausted. If you want to pass me the veggies I'm happy to get started on them. It's just hot things I have an issue with."

I pulled the pre-sliced beef from the fridge and a heap of veggies, which I pushed across the bench to Eden. A few seconds later, I had rice noodles cooking in the microwave and beef sizzling in a wok.

"Um, I'm going to keep mine really bland. I can't do sauces at the moment. But I can make yours more interesting with some Hoi Sin or Teriyaki or something," I offered.

"Whatever you're eating is fine. It would hardly be fair if you're sitting here struggling and I'm hoeing into something yummy. I don't want to make it harder for you than it needs to be. Besides these veggies look great. They should add heaps of natural flavour." She gave me a cheeky little look from under her eyelashes and I wondered if she'd meant to add the double entendre.

"Thank you. Seems I've become more and more acquainted with hard this week."

"Tough week?"

"Yeah, this sort of prep is always really hard. I can't believe I'm admitting this, but I'm aching all over. Well ache is probably not the right word. My limbs just feel heavy." I took the mound of vegetables from her and threw them in the wok with a little stock, a dash of soy sauce and a few fragrant herbs.

"If I'm not mistaken, you've got a bit of a gourmet streak?"

I shrugged. "Well, it was a case of learn to cook or eat the boring stuff dad cooked up. It's not that difficult. There's three million cooking shows on television plus that thing called the interweb! Hey, there's no shortage of places to learn without leaving home."

"I guess. One day I'll give it a go again." I could see Eden was giving herself a pep talk as much as she was talking to me.

"I'm sure you will."

"It's funny how things quickly become a habit and you don't even bother trying. When I realised handling anything hot freaked me out, I quickly started doing everything cold. Now it's a habit and I haven't even thought about making a hot meal. I only eat hot food if someone else prepares it. Even then I can't touch soup unless it's just warm."

I chuckled a little at her choice of words. There was that double entrende again; or maybe it was just my dirty mind having a good time? So far she'd managed to innocently work hot and hard into our last couple of minutes of conversation. I was definitely feeling both of those things.

"Well, I'm hoping we can get you past your fear of handling hot stuff real soon." I turned and winked at her as I dumped the noodles I'd drained into the wok.

Eden looked at me and I could tell she was a little nervous, but she gave me a cheeky grin and I realised she was a wake up to the subtle flirting. "I guess we'll see just how far my fears extend real soon."

Oh yeah, maybe I wasn't as tired as I felt?

I served up great big helpings into the bowls I'd pulled out and pushed one across the bench to her with a fork.

"Don't work yourself up Eden. It'll be fine. We'll just do whatever feels right. That might be nothing or a lot. But would you be terribly offended if we had this and headed to bed early, because I really need a good night's sleep. I don't have a lot of juice left in the tank."

"Sure. I didn't need to be here tonight. I could have caught up tomorrow or Sunday."

"True. You didn't need to be here, but I wanted you here. I needed you with me."

I think my words took her back a bit and I worried a little that maybe I'd come on a bit too strong, but I wasn't one for hiding what I was feeling with people that mattered to me—and Eden mattered a lot.

We ate in silence for a little while.

"You're training tomorrow morning aren't you?"

"Yeah, but I don't need to be in there until ten. So we can sleep in a little bit."

Eden ducked her head and I knew exactly what she was thinking, because it was the same as what I was. We were both thinking about last Sunday morning and my exploration of her breasts. This time I'd be exploring a lot more of her with any luck.

A few minutes later we finished dinner and I loaded everything into the dishwasher and went around the side of the bench and pulled her into my arms. I ran my hands down her sides and dragged my thumbs over her nipples.

"I don't think I told you how much I love this top. It's great to see you wear clothes that flatter your body. Not that you don't look good all the time but Eden, you have an incredible body and you hide it."

She nodded. "I wore the shirt for you. I'm not sure how I'd be, wearing it in front of others just yet."

"I can understand that and I appreciate the effort you went to for me. I'm not sure how I'd feel about other men ogling your breasts either, and they sure will notice them in this shirt." This time I ran my hands from the plains of her chest right down over her breasts and gripped her waist and tugged her closer into me.

"Would it freak you out if I said I really want to take you over to my bed and snuggle up over there?"

She dropped a feather light kiss on my lips. "I think I can cope with that."

"Well, that's the best news I've heard all day."

I led her over to the bed and urged her to sit. She kicked off the ballet flats she wore and I toed off my runners. Then when my eyes met hers, I could tell she was feeling self-conscious but I didn't think it was from her scars so much as not knowing what to do next. Eden might be in her early twenties but she didn't have a lot of experience. I needed to remember that.

"Okay, so I'm just going to come out and tell you what I'm planning here. Then you can let me know if you're on-board with it."

She nodded and I could see the relief on her face.

"So I'm going to strip out of these clothes and lay down in my boxers. I'd like you to join me. It's totally up to you what level of nakedness you choose though."

I turned from her and stripped off my shirt. Before I'd picked Eden up, I'd showered and put on jeans and a T-shirt rather than training clothes. Then I dropped my hands to the button and fly. Shit I was so hard under these jeans. I hope that wouldn't be too much of a problem for her, but there wasn't anything I could do about it at the moment.

"I need to warn you before I turn around that I'm aroused." I looked over my shoulder and I was very pleasantly surprised to see Eden stripping off her jeans as well.

"It was kind of hard to miss, Xander. You were pressed up against me just before. Besides, you're not on your own in the arousal stakes."

So I went from being very pleasantly surprised to being outright stunned. Eden admitting she was aroused was a huge step for her I was sure.

I climbed onto the bed and plumped up the pillows to use more as a backrest. Eden followed wearing the sexiest little pair of ice blue satin boy shorts I'd ever seen with the navy top. Her delectable backside was high in the air as she moved up the bed on all fours. That sight was almost too much for me right then. I needed to be inside her. I needed to feel how much she wanted and needed me.

When she reached me, she turned and snuggled into me, placing her head on my chest. That was fast becoming a spot that Eden seemed to prefer and I couldn't agree more. I brushed the hair back from her face. "I love having you snuggled up to me."

I dropped my lips to her forehead and planted a couple of light kisses there.

Her hand rested on my chest and she started tracing the tattoo on the right side of my chest. I let her fingers wander as I stroked the hair back from her head.

"You've got a lot of these. Do they have any special meaning?"

"Some do. Most are martial arts related; tattoos I've collected or earned along the way to mark some particular point in my career or an achievement. A few I just have because I like them. You don't have any?"

She shook her head no. "I was a little young and I was going to be a fashion and bikini model. It was best not to have reasons why magazines couldn't hire you. Plus they didn't go down well on the catwalk back when I was starting out. Then the fire happened and well, I guess I just haven't thought anymore on it."

Then a glimpse of an idea came to me. "Are you adverse to the idea of tattoos?"

Her fingers kept lightly tracing the outline of the design on my chest. "No, but they have to be good. Yours are incredible, but unfortunately so many look like a total mess and very amateurish.

They kind of all blend together and just look so hotch potch."

I glanced down my body, trying to decide if any of mine fit into that category.

"I wasn't talking about yours. You've got quite a few, but they're more like art and really well done. You can actually see what each of them is about, and the lines and shading are crystal clear." Eden had raised her head and looked at the ones on my right side more critically before returning her head to my chest.

"Well, I'm glad you approve. One of my students is a tattoo artist. He's done most of this work. Not so much fun getting them changed or removed, I hear." Her fingers kept trailing and she traced the one on my floating rib and the muscles in my side rippled at her touch.

"You're ticklish!" she said in what seemed like astonishment. "I would have thought you'd be used to being touched."

I chuckled. "Gem, there's a really big difference between how your fingers are teasing me and what I cop in training or a fight. I've never once mistaken a hit for a tickle. But you can keep touching me anyway you want. It feels great."

She started messing around with changing the pressure of her fingers, sometimes the lightest touch and then a heavier caress. I didn't care. I just loved the feeling of relaxing with her draped over me, touching me.

"So have you thought about getting a tattoo or two?" I wondered.

"Umm, a little. I could never decide what to get or where? I kind of spend my life covered up so it would be for me, I guess."

"That's what the best tats are—something for you."

"Hmm, something to think about I guess."

"I'll hold your hand when you're ready if you want."

"I'll keep that in mind." Then she started to wriggle a little against me. Her hand roved down over my stomach and came back up. Her hand was soft, but firm and it was doing all kinds of things to my exhausted body. She swiped down over my abdomen again and her hips pressed into the side of my body a little harder and her foot dragged up my shin.

Suddenly I felt a lot less exhausted and a whole lot more turned on, if that was possible. I trailed the fingers of the arm I had around her, up and over her hip in big slow circles. She immediately shuddered in my arms and her breath caught in a little gasp of what I took for pleasure.

"As much as I like this new shirt, Eden, I'd prefer it off. You okay with that?"

She said nothing just pushed off me and sat up. Our eyes connected and there was hardly a hint of hesitation as she pulled the shirt over her head. Oh yeah, so that told me quite a bit. Eden was a little shy. She just needed a little suggestion from me. Her body was telling me one thing and her mind was just playing a little catch up.

When she moved the shirt out of the way. I got the full effect and I now knew what she'd been up to at the shopping mall this afternoon. Oh I was a lucky bastard tonight.

"Wow baby, you look gorgeous in that bra. I thought the boy shorts were hot but together with that bra..." I trailed off, needing to get my hands and mouth on her breasts that were covered by the mate to those boy shorts. There was nothing super amazing about either the bra or the panties, but on her body—knockout punch! Sleek, classy, and oh so sexy.

"I have to ask this because I'm a guy...but did you ever do any lingerie shoots?"

She dropped her chin shyly and my heart squeezed tight. "Just one. Mum wouldn't let me do anything like that until I turned eighteen. But a shoot came up and it wasn't really sexy stuff, just some basic pieces for a cotton brand, so she let me." She explained softly. Oh shit! I hope, I hadn't sent her spiralling back into the past and what she'd lost, but every guy had a fantasy about having a lingerie model for a girlfriend, didn't they?

"Well I have no doubt you're even hotter now." I reached out to cup her breasts. "I'm sure these beauties couldn't have looked this good five years ago."

"I don't know, but as long as you're happy I guess..." she trailed off, sounding a little unsure.

"Happy! I'm ecstatic to have my hands on these." I dragged a hand away and gave her a playful little bump on the nose with my index finger. "Now I can't even describe how I'd feel if you moved over here and let me put my mouth on them as well."

She giggled a little, nodded then to my surprise moved over the top of me. Then Eden dropped her lips to mine for a very brief kiss, before she sat back on my hips.

"Now this is the kind of mount position I'm really happy to be on the bottom of Gem. We haven't started any grappling yet, but I'm all good to start your education right now." I rested my hands on her firm thighs and squeezed my fingers a little and she grinned at me again.

"Ha, ha." I got the feeling she was enjoying being on top of me. I wasn't about to let her know I could probably come up with a hundred different ways to have her on her back and under me in the blink of an eye. It was easy to tell that Eden was enjoying being a woman and testing her sexuality. Everything was as good as new to her and I intended to make it all the best I could.

"Any chance I can get a close up of that bra? I'm sure I can hear your breasts screaming to have my mouth on them." I'd issued the invitation; now I'd wait and see what she did.

Her hips ground into mine and I bit back a groan. Her pussy was right over my dick and it was torture, but this was all Eden's show for the moment.

Just as I'd hoped, she leant forward and brought her left breast tantalisingly close to my mouth. I licked my tongue across my lips in anticipation of having her nipple between them very soon.

Then the little tease, waved it across in front of me again. This time I didn't hesitate. I caught both of her breasts in my hands and dipped my thumbs under the silky cups to find her hard nipples. She shuddered over me and I held my breath as her hips ground down again.

"Time to stop teasing me, Gem. Let me take away the ache

you're feeling." I didn't give her a chance to say anything. I pulled the cup down and rose my head to draw her into my mouth. She had the softest, sweetest skin and she tasted incredible. I couldn't describe the taste but I was sure it would be what sunshine tasted like, if that was possible.

I sucked lightly and flicked my tongue over the hard pebble a few more times and she started to moan a little in a low sexy tone. I seemed to feel the moan all the way through me, right down to my insanely hard erection. I wondered then if she'd be loud when I finally plunged my dick inside her.

"Gem, as pretty as this bra is, it has to go."

All I got back in return was another throaty moan as I sucked a little more on her nipple then blew across it.

I could work with that; moans of pleasure were just fine with me.

My hands travelled around to her back and flicked the clasp open. The cups popped forward and I reluctantly released my mouth from her nipple. I eased the straps down her arms, which had begun to tremble a little from supporting her body, and I hoped, the pleasure she was feeling.

In one slick move that was second nature to me I pulled her in tight to my body and rolled her under me.

Last time we were together like this, I'd made her a promise. Now it was time to make good on that.

EIGHTEEN

EDEN

A little squeal of surprise squeezed out of my throat and my eyes flew open. A split second ago I'd been having a lovely time riding Xander's hips as he sucked my nipples. It was so good. Now, I found myself flat on my back beneath him and he had a very knowing grin on his face.

"That was just one of the many escapes for a mount position. In case you're wondering." His eyes danced with humour and I couldn't help but join him with a little giggle of my own.

"I don't think I even put up a fight, did I? So what am I supposed to do now?"

"Well, if it was anyone else but you, I would suggest and show you several easy ways to get out of that submissive position, I've put you in. But given it's me, and I've got you right where I want you, how about you just lay back and relax. I think it's my turn to go exploring." He had a wickedly hot look in his eyes and I knew exactly what he had planned. The thought of him exploring my pussy all but ensured I had no intention of stopping him. My body was screaming for his and this was the next step.

I'd decided to take Grace's advice. Xander didn't seem to care one iota about my scars, so why should they prevent me from enjoying everything he was hinting at doing to me? I wanted to be defined as a woman, not by my scars.

He leaned in further and gave me a heart stopping kiss. I didn't think I would ever get used to the feel of his plump full lips and velvety tongue stroking at my mouth or anywhere else on my body. How could it be so good?

Xander then trailed a line of hot teasing kisses from my mouth, over my jaw and down my neck to my chest, where he once again found my nipples for a little bit.

My breath was coming in hot pants and my core felt like it was wound so tight. I needed relief. I needed to come.

"Xan, please..." I begged, my fingers closing in his hair.

His mouth dropped a little lower to my abdomen and he ran his tongue around my belly button and I couldn't help but buck my hips up to slam into his chest, but he held me firm.

From there his fingers trailed along the edge of my panties, teasing and playing along the line of elastic. His mouth was just above the line of elastic and instead of feeling shy or anxious I needed him to keep going lower.

"Please..." I pleaded again.

"Okay Gem, I'm not going to leave you hanging here, like last time. It damn near killed me as well. I won't do that to you twice." I breathed a sigh of relief and sucked in my stomach as he slid his thumbs under the elastic and ran them from the centre to my hips. A fiery line of sensation prickled in his wake.

Then he sat back on his knees, before rising to stand at the end of the bed. He leaned over and hooked his fingers back into the sides of my panties and smoothly lowered them down over my thighs. I watched the heat flare in his eyes as he uncovered my most private parts.

Funnily, I now realised I was much more comfortable having him see my pussy than my scars. Should I feel nervous, embarrass-ed, or shy? Because I felt none of those feelings, just very needy. I just wanted him to end the ache only he'd been able to create.

"All good, Eden? Because I really want to taste you now." His voice was low and rumbly and his eyelids looked heavy. Every cell in my body seemed to be tingling and resonating with want.

"All good," I whispered.

"Open for me, Gem."

He placed his hands on my thighs and eased them apart as he lowered himself back between my legs and stroked his fingers down over my lower lips. I shivered at his touch and I struggled to keep my lower body still for him.

"So soft," he whispered.

He did it again, but this time he placed a light kiss on the top of my mound.

"I love this tiny little landing strip of hair here. It's like a map."

I giggled a little as I answered, "Something tells me you would have found the way all on your own."

He placed another kiss and gave me a devilish wink.

"That's a very safe bet. I've got a great sense of direction. Particularly when the destination is somewhere I absolutely want to go."

He dipped his head again and this time he used his tongue to trace the line that his fingers had travelled just before. No man had ever had his mouth on me down there before, but it felt so right with Xander. I felt as if I was his to pleasure and be pleasured.

Then he nuzzled in tighter to my pussy and started to tongue my clit.

"Oh God...that feels so incredible." My mind was shorting out and every nerve in my body seemed to be zinging with electricity.

Slowly and gently he licked, then sucked for a few seconds then went back to licking. If I thought the ache was bad before, I had no idea. Now it was the best sort of excruciating need.

He slid a finger inside me and started to stroke me slowly. My hips pushed upward but he held me firm, while his tongue kept up its teasing little dance. It was all too much and not enough at the same time.

My breath was coming in short, uneven pants and every muscle in my body was as tense as a tightrope. I was so close and he knew it. His tongue had slowed and he was holding me at the pinnacle, letting the sensation build even more until finally he decided to suck on my clit and flick it with his tongue all at once.

It was the most incredible sensation I had ever experienced and then I was flying—cast free and falling through huge waves of pleasure.

I gripped hunks of the sheets and my body jerked. My hips slammed into his face uncontrollably and I called his name in a voice that I didn't recognise as mine.

On and on he kept at me, coaxing every last ounce of pleasure from the release, until finally I could take no more and pushed at his head.

"I can't take any more," I begged in a ragged tone.

I fell back on the bed and sucked in a couple of huge lungfuls of air. He planted a final kiss on my mound and my hips flew off the bed in response.

"Someone's sensitive." There was no missing the amusement in his voice as he moved up to lie beside me again. "I wonder where else you're sensitive. Maybe here?" He tweaked a nipple and it had exactly the same effect, nearly launching me off the bed.

"Xander!" I shrieked.

"Mmm...?" he asked knowingly as he nuzzled his face into my neck. I could smell my arousal all over him and I didn't feel the least bit self-conscious. It didn't seem to be bothering him.

"That was..." How do you explain something like that? Words could never quite convey the feeling. "I don't know what—but hell it was good."

"Glad you enjoyed it. I sure enjoyed making you come apart like that for me."

I rolled over onto my side so I could look at him and snuggle closer.

He seemed to sense what I wanted and pulled me in tight to

him. There was no mistaking how aroused he still was. I placed my hand on his hip and stroked it up and down his side. I loved the feeling of all the solid muscle beneath my fingers. Never in my wildest dreams would I have thought I'd be cuddled up to a man as hot and sexy as Xander Todd. I had no idea what I'd done to deserve it, but I wasn't going to look a gift horse in the mouth, nor was I going to give it up easily.

Eventually I found the waistband of his boxer briefs and splayd my palm over his hip. Slowly I lowered my hand wanting to know exactly what he had hidden behind the fabric of his underwear. I'd caught a fleeting glimpse of his rock hard butt last weekend and it had been enough to have my heart skipping a beat. Now I wanted to know that uniquely male part of him that had been pushed so hard up against me.

Xander caught my chin in his hand and drew my face up so our eyes met.

"You don't need to do this, Eden." I could tell by the tone of his voice that he meant it sincerely, but there was no way I was going to go a moment longer without knowing all of him.

"I want you, Xander." My voice was a little husky and seemed to catch in my throat, right about the same time as my hand circled his very erect cock. I ran my palm the length of his arousal but the fabric of his briefs frustratingly prevented me from really feeling him.

"Are you sure, Eden? It's up to you. I'm not going to pressure you, but there is no way I'm going to say no to whatever more you want to do." His breath hitched a little raggedly as I continued to run my hand along the ridge of his arousal.

I hesitated for a split second as doubt flooded me momentarily, but then, I pushed it away. It was time to be the person I wanted to be and not the person I had been.

"I'm sure, Xander. I want to be whole again—a woman. Make me whole. Like only you can do." The fingers of my left hand caught in the waistband and pulled downwards. "I want these off. They need to go now."

There was a little smirk of pride on those beautiful full lips of his and I couldn't help but lean closer and touch mine to his. I swiped my tongue along the plump flesh and tasted myself on him. It was strange and quite heady—not quite what I expected.

"You taste good, don't you?" Amusement flared in his eyes.

I felt heat rise up into my cheeks and I was at a loss for words. "Um, do I?"

"Yeah Gem, you taste incredible. Take my word for it, if you're not sure."

"Okay," I agreed and tugged on his briefs some more. He lifted his hips obligingly and together we worked them down his muscled legs and off.

I pushed him from his side until he was once again on his back. Then I trailed my fingers down over the tight ridges in his stomach until my palm brushed the head of his engorged erection.

His cock jumped against my hand at the contact and I closed my palm around him. I heard him inhale sharply through his nose.

I felt a fleeting shot of fear. "Too tight…?"

He let the breath out slowly. "Too good!"

"Oh, well that's okay then, I guess," I said feeling relieved as I stroked him, learning his size and feel. His cock was just like the rest of him— hardened steel covered in smooth, warm skin. It felt divine, but I was fast learning there was nothing soft about Xander—only his kind words and caring nature. He could be the hardened, brusque warrior or the tender, caring lover.

His eyes squeezed shut and his face contorted in what looked like agony, so I relaxed my grip and slid my hand lower to cup his balls and explore the roughened feel of them.

"Gem, I'm hanging on by a thread here. You need to let me know what you want here, sweetheart? I can't take much more of this torture," he confessed, his jaw clenching in strain.

What did I want? Was I ready to go further? I thought on that for a mere second. Why should I deny what we both obviously wanted?

I drew my leg up and over his hips and slid my body more over the top of his and looked down into his eyes that were dark with need, but warm with tenderness at the same time.

"I want you inside me Xander."

He reached up and cradled my head in his hands and pulled my mouth to his for a kiss that was scorching hot and had the blood racing through my veins again. I couldn't seem to stop wriggling on top of him. I could feel his erection wedged between our bodies, pulsing against my stomach.

I just wanted him to be closer, inside me.

"How about I take over from here?" he whispered into my mouth.

Relief flooded through me as he stroked his hand through my hair. My body knew what it wanted but I was not quite sure how to proceed. It was all so different with Xander—but also very right.

I nodded briefly and he kissed me lightly on the nose, before he nudged me over onto my back again. He turned briefly to the utilitarian bedside table and pulled a condom from the top draw and quickly sheathed himself before rolling his body over mine once again.

"Let's go old school to start with," he suggested.

His lips found mine and he took his time drugging me with kisses so needy and fine I felt as if I was about to come apart again. All conscious thought seemed to evaporate from my mind and I just wanted to sink into him.

Xander shifted a fraction and I felt his arousal glide along the lips of my pussy. I sighed into his mouth as his fingers began to tease me and spread my blossoming wetness over my flesh, before he slid first one then two fingers into me.

"I don't want to hurt you, baby. I know it's been a long time, but you're so wet for me." He stroked inside me and I jammed my hips up and tightly into his hand, enjoying the feeling. His words seemed to inflame the need I was feeling even more.

Finally he pulled his fingers from me and dropped another kiss on my lips.

Then he was probing my opening before he pressed inside me

in one slow smooth stroke—all controlled power before he halted. I sucked in a breath, feeling the burn as I stretched to accommodate his size.

"Relax Gem. I'll just hold here for a second. God, you feel incredible. You're so tight. I'm struggling to maintain control." My hands gripped his shoulders before sliding lower to settle on his butt. The muscles flexed beneath my fingers, two solid globes.

The burn began to subside as quickly as it had started and all that was left was the most incredible feeling of being filled by him. Slowly he began to move, his length stroking every nerve inside of me, but still I needed him deeper.

I drew my knees up and curled my fingers into his butt urging him to go deeper and harder still. The slight change caused his pubic bone to hit my clit and I sucked in air again.

It felt so damned fine. This was what I'd been craving, what Xander had been building up to for days.

"Can you come again for me, Gem?" I looked up into his face and saw the strain and tension it was taking to stop himself from coming.

"I don't know." And I didn't. Tonight had been my first orgasm with a man. It was all so foreign to me. All I knew was it felt so good and I didn't want it to ever end, even though we were both reaching for the climax.

"Okay baby, let me add a little more to this and we'll find out." He pushed up from his elbows onto his hands and rocked his shoulders back but thrust his hips hard into me. I groaned as the sensation of him filling me so deep flashed through me from the centre to every extremity.

Then his lips closed around my nipple and he sucked hard. The spring of need inside me clamped tight and suddenly I was right back on the edge of a climax again, waiting for him to help me jump with him.

"Oh Xan, that feels so good. Right there, just like that." He ground his hips into me and sucked my nipple hard and I knew I was just about done. Then he flicked his tongue over my nipple and gave me a little nip and the spike of pain was all the intense pleasure I needed to go sailing once again.

I cried out a long throaty moan as my body bucked and rolled beneath him. He thrust into me quickly with short fast strokes until he too broke free a couple of seconds later. His hips continued to slam against me as my body absorbed and relished every thrust. I gripped my hands even tighter to his butt and cried out again. My climax rolled on and on, fed by Xander's.

Finally the tension began to drain from my body and I was left with a warm feeling of contentment throughout me. He lowered himself back to his elbows and nuzzled his face into my neck.

Neither of us said anything for a few long moment—both relaxing in the afterglow.

Finally he spoke. "That was something else."

"It sure was. Now I know what all the fuss is about." I agreed. There was no way I could argue with that.

He grinned and gave me a very self-assured and knowing male wink.

"I hope you're not sore tomorrow. I wasn't exactly gentle."

"It was exactly what I wanted and I'll be fine." I was no stranger to pain but if I was sore, this was going to be pain that would remind me of one of my fondest memories.

He slowly pulled out of me and trailed his fingertips down my belly.

"I'll be right back."

I watched him stride across the distance to the bathroom to get rid of the condom. He came back with a wet cloth and a towel. I almost pinched myself in disbelief as he joined me again in his big bed.

Oh my God! I'd just had the most delicious sex with Xander Todd.

He made me feel like a woman once again. His woman.

NINETEEN

EDEN

The weekend flew past in a crazy haze of Xander. I awoke to him tickling his fingers down my side and over my breast. From there things escalated quickly, to us both starting the day in the flush of orgasmic bliss.

Xander had training at ten with Reed and Dane.

Rather than head home, I took my books and spent the time in his office studying. Well, trying to study. I had no idea I would be so distracted watching him and the other two go at it in training. They sparred and did drill after drill. It was totally insane to watch. I'd never seen anything as intense or so physically draining. The sweat was running from both of them for hours on end, but they never seemed to notice or lose intensity. It was a whole other side to professional sport; one I'd had no exposure to or idea about. But the thing that was absolutely evident was the unwavering commitment to what they were doing. Xander wanted to win and this is what he had to do to get there. I admired the hell out of his dedication and focus.

I watched the guys for hours as the days passed. Both Xander and Dane were in amazing physical condition, but there was something that just called to me about Xander, every single time. His presence was commanding and he seemed to know exactly when I was watching him. It was a little unnerving.

More than once he caught me staring at him through the glass of his office door. I was sitting in his chair behind the desk, but I was supposed to be studying. I didn't want to be in the way or be the reason he wasn't focused on his training but I also didn't want to be apart from him, either. I realised something else. During the few weeks I'd known Xander, I'd gone from being unhappy and alone to feeling more positive. I knew that the person who had filled the hole in my soul was Xander. It seemed unreal but everyday I seemed to feel it more.

I wanted to share everything with him. Be with him all the time but it scared me and filled me with excitement and joy all at the same time. What if it ended? Then what? Would I go back to the scared shadow of myself again or would I keep going forward? I didn't know the answer to that question. Xander gave me the strength and encouragement I needed to fight the demons that filled me with doubts. Could I do it on my own? I didn't know, but what's more, I didn't want to know.

Xander had quickly become part of my life now and I was a better person for it.

•••

I was just finishing up my Friday afternoon classes when a notification beeped on my phone. I read it once, then again. My heart pounded and I felt giddy, crazy and happy all at once. Xander had changed his relationship status on Facebook to read

"In a relationship with Eden Sommers".

There it was for all the world to see. Well, his friends at least. I knew this was how he thought of us because he'd introduced me to Reed as his girlfriend, but somehow that stupid little status made everything different. I really was Xander Todd's girlfriend. A big part of me still wondered how the hell this scarred girl could possibly be of interest to him, let alone be his girlfriend.

As I sat on the bus on the way home my phone started to beep like crazy. There were messages coming in from everywhere. Beth was buzzing me incessantly.

> **Beth:** Well, it's official. FaceBook says so! I can't believe my best friend is Xander Todd's girlfriend.

> **Me:** Beth, it's no big deal. It's just social media. Besides you've known this for a couple of weeks now. It's not like I've been keeping this a secret from you.

Social media was not a big part of my life anymore. It was only a way for me to communicate and keep track of the handful of friends and people that mattered to me. When the fire happened, I'd learned a very valuable lesson about fair weather friends.

> **Beth:** Whatever, but that's not going to stop me from being deliriously happy. Besides you give me hope. You've not only found a man but a seriously hot one.

I had, hadn't I! Before I could even respond my phone kept buzzing as friends of his started to comment.

Congrats, man she's a total babe...I guess you like them young.

She's stunning. How the hell did you get her to go out with you?

You're the man, Pretty Boy!

My stomach turned to a knot and I realised they must have checked out my profile. The only photos up there were ones from before the fire. I bit my lip and stared out the window wondering what to do. Should I comment? Did I do nothing? Then another comment came in.

Wasn't she the model chick in that fire a while back?

There was no escaping it. People knew. It would only be a matter of time before they started with the comments. Why would he be with her? Could I cope with that?

For the next hour my stomach churned and I lived in hell. Logic told me it was social media, people could be cruel, but these were his friends.

I was sitting at the kitchen table drinking a glass of juice and wondering what I should do when Sophia came in. She'd just started a new job in real estate and I was excited for her. It was a great opportunity and something she wanted to do. The company was training her and putting her through the necessary courses for the licences she would need. I was proud of her. She'd kept knocking on doors until one finally opened and someone gave her a go. There was no doubt she was going to be super successful.

"What a day! I got to go out on three appraisals and John wanted to know my thoughts about each one as we left. He even included some of my observations in his report!" She was over the moon with good reason, it seemed.

"That's great, Soph. I'm so pleased this job's working out for you. Want a juice?"

"That'd be great!"

I got her a glass and poured one for her from the carton.

"So what have you been up to today?"

"Oh, nothing much. Just school." I hoped my reply sounded casual.

She pulled her phone from her bag.

"Damn! Look at all these messages. I'm supposed to be going out with Rachel and Adelaide tonight." They were Sophia's two closest friends, had been for years. Adelaide also took classes at

Onigashima, I thought. Rachel was more of the princess type and had danced ballet for years.

"That'll be fun. Where are you going?"

"Um, not sure yet. Rachel's brother Seth, has just got back into town. He's been away in the mines for the last couple of years. So apparently we're getting together with him and some of his friends."

"Oh, sounds good. What's Tori up to?"

"No idea." Then she looked up at me from her phone. "Actually I think she mentioned something about catching a movie or something. Why? Won't you be out with Sensei?"

"Sure, I guess." I tried to sound normal but I obviously failed.

Her head flew up. "What's wrong? Did he break up with you?"

"No, why would you say that?" I couldn't keep the defensive tone from my voice.

"Because for the last few weeks you've been floating on cloud nine and now you seem down in the dumps. Or is it just that time of the month?" She eyed me suspiciously trying to figure out what was wrong.

"No. It's not that time of the month!" Oh screw it! I needed to talk to someone and Soph was here. "Xander posted on Facebook that he's in a relationship with me."

"So that's good news, right?" She looked at me as if I'd grown a second head.

"Yeah, but then a whole heap of his friends started to comment and..." I couldn't quite put into words what I was feeling. "Just look for yourself." I thrust my phone at her and she started to scroll through the comments.

"And now you feel like a fraud, perhaps?" Sophia looked up from my phone. "Because you haven't updated your pictures in five years?"

I nodded. I guess that was part of it.

"But Xander knows about your scars and has seen them." She stuck me with a stare that said she knew we'd been intimate. "All of them, I'm guessing, and since he has no problem, then why do you care?"

"I realise I shouldn't care but I can't help feeling like the ugly duckling. I used to be the swan and now I'm the ugly duckling."

Sophia stared at me for a little while longer. "So what are you going to do? It's easy enough to change your profile pic."

"I don't know. That's why I'm talking to you!"

"Have you spoken to Sensei about it?"

"No. He's training until six."

"Well stop worrying about it and talk to him later, if it bothers you that much. Otherwise ignore it. Sensei doesn't do anything, he doesn't want to. If he put it out there–then he's fine with it." It was probably sound advice but it was hard to swallow none the less.

"I suppose." I shrugged my shoulders noncommittally.

"Well I've got to fly. I'll catch you later. Not that you're ever home anymore." She gave me a little eyebrow raise and a naughty smile. "Too busy doing Sen..."

"Sophia Louise Sommers..." I yelled.

All I got back was a cackle. It was probably what I deserved; plus, she was actually telling the truth.

I didn't get to sit and dwell on it for much longer because, not more than a few seconds later, my phone buzzed again with another message.

This time it was Xander and my heart did its little dance like always.

> **Xander:** Gem, you okay to go out for drinks with a few friends of mine. It's a mate's birthday. I'll pick you up around seven.

I'd never met any of his friends before. Sure a few people knew about us from Onigashima. But that was a little different there. Xander was so much in charge and in command of that place, no one would question his judgement or actions. It still shocked me a bit at how "God Like" he was in there. He was so different to the guy I was getting to know more and more outside of Onigashima. I can't say I liked the idea of going out overly much but I knew it was all part and parcel of being in a relationship, so I guess I was okay with it.

> **Me:** Sure, I guess. I'm going to be a little nervous...

I left it at that. I didn't need to say anymore. Xander would understand. As I glanced at my phone I noticed Xander had commented on our relationship thread.

"You're right I'm a lucky guy and Eden isn't as young as you think and yes she is stunning. Oh and BTW if any of you pricks want to disrespect her I'll be more than happy to defend my girl's honour. ☺"

My heart did a little happy dance. His message was playful but there was no doubting his intent. Before I could think on it further he responded to my message.

> **Xander:** You'll be fine. I'll be right beside you. Wear those jeans and that navy top. God what am I saying? My dick's getting hard thinking about you already ;) Reed will kick my arse. Got to go Gem. See you soon XX

I glanced at my watch. I had just over an hour and I wanted to wash my hair. Time to stop worrying and go see what I could do about looking the best I could. It was a strange feeling to want to primp again. Maybe I should try that makeup Tori had brought home from beauty school a couple of days ago? I used to be pretty damned good at putting makeup on.

•••

"Stop worrying; you look gorgeous." Xander pulled me into his side, his left arm around my waist. "I can't wait to take you home and do all sorts of very naughty things to you," he whispered into my ear and then kissed my neck right over the top of my scars.

His words and ticklish breath had me shivering closer to him.

I didn't know about gorgeous, but I did look about the best I could. The makeup Tori had brought home had worked wonders. It hid the red and shiny spots of the scars. No make up could hide the uneven texture of my skin, but at least if the colour all blended then perhaps the scars would be less noticeable. Hopefully the dim lighting in this bar would disguise it a bit further.

Xander spotted his friends and he led me through the crowded bar towards the back of the room where a few tables had been pulled together. I wasn't sure if it was just him or if people actually knew him because they seemed to step aside as he moved through and he got lots of little head nods. Most of which he returned with his own chin bob. It was some strange male language that they all seemed to be fluent in.

As soon as we approached the tables everyone around them seemed to notice him and started getting up to shake his hand, give him a back slap or some other intricate fist bump, hand shake thing. But during all that time he never let me go.

I recognised Dane and a couple of the other guys from Onigashima with him. Dane was by himself but the other couple of guys had girls with them. I think their names were Linc and Owen, but we hadn't been officially introduced.

Xander turned towards me. "Why don't you take the seat beside Dane and I'll get us some drinks? What do you want Gem?"

Dane moved the seat out beside him so I could sit down. "I'll have a lime and soda, please."

"You don't want a wine or something? I'm not drinking but you can if you want. It doesn't bother me."

"No, it's fine. I don't drink much."

"Okay as long as you're sure."

I nodded I was and he waited for me to take the seat beside Dane before heading off.

"Hey Eden, how are you going? Have you met these two delinquents, Xander calls friends?" Dane asked me. I liked Dane, not only had he saved my arse, but I always felt comfortable around him, too. Plus, he wasn't hard on the eyes. He was a little taller than Xander and had lighter hazel eyes. His skin had a deep tan to it and his face had a hint of something exotic in it. He must have some interesting heritage.

"No, I haven't."

The two men and their women were watching me intently and I realised it was essentially because I was "the boss's" woman.

"This is Lincoln." Dane gestured towards the big guy with blonde hair and really blue eyes. He looked serious. "And his girlfriend Alexa." I moved forward and smiled at them and gave a little wave. It was really hard to shake hands or do anything like that because of the table positions.

"My ranga mate here is Owen, and this is Melissa, his girlfriend." I gave them a 'Hi' and wave as well. I'd sort of met the guys before but not their girlfriends. I didn't recall them from the Onigashima BBQ. Well, if they'd been there, I'd not noticed them. What I didn't miss was the surprised look when the women noticed my face. Even though they tried to disguise it, they kind of looked then took another look—as if to see if what they'd first thought was really there. 'I'm not going to let it worry me. I'm not going to let it worry me. Xander doesn't have an issue so why should I?' I kept silently telling myself.

I turned to Dane. "How's the training going?"

"Yeah, really good. Xan's straight back into machine mode. You wouldn't know he'd been out of it for over three years. The guy just eats up the training like it's nothing. God, I wish I had that super power." I wondered just how good Xander was at hiding his pain and acting the part he thought he had to play. More than once I'd seen him at the end of the day with me when his guard was down. He was zonked. Nothing left.

"He seems to be happy doing it," I said non-committally. I didn't have enough knowledge or understanding to really know where he was in the programme and I didn't want to inadvertently give away something about Xander.

Dane looked at me for a bit and I wondered what he was thinking. Since he'd come along that night we'd formed a strange bond. No doubt he'd saved my arse that night. I kind of felt like his little sister or something.

"Can I be straight with you?" he asked.

"Of course."

"This is the happiest and most balanced I've seen him in a long time. I don't know what it is between you two but it seems to work for him. He's really into you. Please don't do anything to change that, particularly with this fight coming up. He needs to be in a stable place." What could I say to that? I had no intention of changing it, but there seemed to be a hint of foreboding in his voice and I started to worry that there was something I should know. I tried to disregard it as my vivid imagination.

I just nodded my understanding and said nothing.

"So how's your training going?"

"Good, I think. He seems to be happy with what we're doing." I shrugged my shoulders. How did I know? Dane smirked a little.

Just then Xander turned up with our drinks. He motioned for me to stand up and I did. Then he took my chair and pulled me down onto his lap. I was the only woman sitting in a man's lap and I felt a little self-conscious, and instinctively snuggled closer to him.

"You all good?" Xander asked me in a low voice against my ear.

I nodded that I was.

"We've just been discussing how training was going for Eden."

"Brilliant. I'm teaching her. How else would it go?" Xander asked Dane.

Dane leant over to me. "He's a cocky bastard, but generally right. Can't help but love his arse, attitude and all."

I giggled at that. "Oh, shut up, Dane. Eden hardly needs you giving an opinion. She'd not stupid."

I turned into Xander and went to change the subject before these guys got more of an opportunity to take pot shots at each other, even though they seemed to enjoy it. "So where's the guest of honour? I was wondering who he was?"

"He hasn't made an appearance yet. Although I'm not surprised. He has a reputation for being notoriously late," Xander explained.

"Oh, I see."

The guys talked about training and a few other things for a while. The bar was noisy. It was one of those moody dark timber kind of places with a combination of booths and tall tables. There was a band over on the little stage preparing for their set. They were just about to start when I was surprised to see Sophia walk in with her friends Rachel and Adelaide. There was a tall good looking man with them. As soon as he noticed us he headed our way.

"Here he is!" Dane stood and moved out from behind the table and pulled the large guy into one of those man hugs. I could feel Xander was anxious to stand as well so I stood and let him up. He too gave the guy a hug. They exchanged a few words then Xander turned to me.

"Seth, this is my girlfriend Eden. She's Sophia and Tori's older sister." Unusually, Sophia had been standing on the periphery. She was usually more of an "in the action" type of girl. "Eden, this is Seth, one of my oldest friends," Xander finished his introductions.

"Hey Eden, pleased to meet you. Soph's told me a lot about you." Seth directed his eyes to me. He had a light hearted and relaxed look about him.

I was still a little stunned. It was one of those small world things. I shouldn't be surprised really. Logan City was big, but not that big. People crossed paths all the time.

"Likewise," I nodded and took the hand he offered.

"Looks like I was a little too late getting home. Left my run too late." Was he flirting with me?

"Yeah, by about a month," Xander cleared up for him.

Seth winked at me. "Well, when you're sick of him being so "buttoned down", look me up. I'll show you a good time."

I felt my face flushing and I didn't quite know how to handle it. "Knock it off, Seth, or I'll be forced to kick one of my best friend's arse. Friend or not you don't mess with my girl." It was all friendly and the tone was light hearted and joking but I had absolutely no doubt Xander would carry through, if he felt it was necessary.

Seth laughed it off. "Noted. I might have to reset my sights on the younger sister. Far out she's become fine since I've been away." Seth let out a whistle and Sophia who had moved closer gave him a backhanded smack into his middle with a little force.

"Like I'd be interested," Sophia corrected Seth.

"Oh, don't be like that, sweetheart."

"I wouldn't push my luck, Seth. Sophia is fast becoming one of my best students. She has some slick moves and a wicked temper to go with it. Word of warning, man," Xander filled him in.

"Thanks for the heads up, man, but I think I'll take my chances. I've been known to have a few moves of my own." And before anything further was said, Seth grabbed Sophia to him and quick as anything dipped her over his arm as if he'd been doing it forever.

Seth leant in as if to kiss her and Sophia came up spluttering, but I knew her well. She was amused and a little cynical of the whole thing if I was any judge of her.

Adelaide turned up about then with a tray of shots, her red hair the colour of fire and her eyes big and blue. She kind of had that orphan Annie look about her. Whatever it was, she rocked it.

The shots were passed around and a toast "to old friends" made before the bottoms went up. I was glad I'd elected to go with the lime and soda. By the look of Seth, and the girls they'd already had a few over dinner.

I was cuddled into Xander and before I knew it I saw the flash of a phone go off. Sophia had snapped us with our heads together. She was looking at the pic and smiling.

“It’s a good one!”

I didn’t know how I felt about it. I hated photos and she knew that, but I also felt tonight was the best I’d ever looked since the fire. Maybe it wouldn’t be so bad?

“Show me,” Xander said, holding out his hand for the phone. Sophia passed it over with a smug look on her face. He looked at the photo and smiled. Then tilted the screen to show me. My heart seemed to be racing and I looked once, then again.

It was hard to believe but with the lighting and the way I had my right side tilted into Xander you could hardly see the scars. I was stunned and pleasantly surprised, I guess. He passed the phone back to Sophia.

“Can you flick that image to Eden and me, please Sophia?” he asked. She nodded and then next second our phones both pinged. A few seconds later and Xander had a new profile picture. I set the photo as my phone wallpaper. It was a big step for me.

The band struck up and the girls went to dance. Seth spoke to Dane and Xander for a while then decided the temptation of Sophia on the dance floor, showing off her lithe body, was too much to take. I watched him move straight in behind her and lock his arms around her middle.

“Mmm, looks like Seth’s keen on your sister,” Xander commented.

“It does.”

“You okay with that or do I need to go read him the riot act. I kind of feel responsible given she’s my girl’s little sister and one of my students.” He nuzzled his face into my neck as he spoke and I started to get very turned on.

“I think Soph can make her own decisions. She’s never had any trouble in the past making it clear to the opposite sex just what she wants. That’s kind of been more my problem,” I said off handedly.

“Oh, I don’t know. We don’t seem to have a problem communicating.” He was speaking in a low voice that told me exactly what he had on his mind.

“You seem surprisingly energetic given how hard you’ve

worked all week." I ran my hand down his face and turned a little more into his body so I could face him.

"Truth...?" I nodded. "I'm exhausted but I'm putting on a good front." He chuckled and I knew it was our little secret. "As I said, Seth's one of my oldest friends. We trained together when we were younger. He had a couple of pro fights but he also had a passion for geology. Now he earns truckloads for one of the mining companies—I couldn't miss tonight. It's kind of double celebration. His birthday and coming home."

"So is he back for a while?" I asked curiously. I was thinking of Sophia. If she was going to get into something, I wanted an idea what it was.

"I don't know. Haven't had a chance to catch up with him yet. I might see if he's free on Sunday or next weekend. I guess we could throw some steaks on the BBQ. Have a little get together. Knowing Seth he'll be hanging out at Onigashima once the weekend's done. I could use another training partner, if he's at a loose end. Seth has wicked ground skills."

I didn't miss the way he said we and my heart skipped a little beat. Xander seemed far more comfortable with our relationship than I was.

Eventually the girls and Seth drifted back to the table. It was starting to get late and Xander yawned. Dane's phone began to vibrate on the table in front of him where he'd placed it. He snatched it up and was busy for a few seconds. Then he stood abruptly and if I wasn't reading it wrong, he had a worried look on his face.

"Got to go, man." He said to Xander and lightly patted me on the shoulder. "Catch you soon, Eden." Before we could say anything more he was gone.

I turned to Xander. "Was that strange?"

He nodded. "There's something going on with him. I'm not sure what, but I'm going to find out. So far he's not talking about it. I tried the other day. "

Seth moved over and took Dane's seat, and they launched into a discussion about Xander's upcoming fight. I really needed to go to the bathroom so I excused myself and rounded the table. As if she sensed my discomfort about moving through the crowded room, Sophia rose and fell in beside me. I moved through the crowd as confidently as I could. Just having Sophia with me, helped me feel a little better. I didn't feel anywhere near as self-conscious now, but old habits die-hard and I was fighting five years of conditioning I'd enforced on myself.

"Crazy night, Edie," she said as she walked beside me. I knew she'd had a lot to drink, but I wasn't exactly sure how much.

"Yeah. You seem to be having a good time." We walked into the bathroom and surprisingly there were stalls available—bonus.

As we were washing our hands, I turned to Soph. "Thanks for looking out for me."

She nodded. "I know you could have gotten here on your own Edie, but I needed to go and I thought you could use the company. You're doing so much better since you've been with Sensei Xander. I'm so pleased for you. Hell, mum won't know you when she finally gets back."

I laughed a little. "It's funny, Soph. Half the time I feel as if I don't actually know myself anymore. I mean look at me. I don't even look the same."

We dried our hands and headed out.

"That foundation Tori came home with really makes a difference. You should keep using that. I really don't know why you didn't try to cover up a little before." She said as she moved in front of me to get through the crowded bar area.

I didn't really know why I hadn't done anything about trying to hide my scars earlier. Well, actually that's not true. I knew exactly why I hadn't bothered. The truth was it was easier to feel sorry for myself and be a victim than make the effort. That was what I was learning to do now. Make the effort. I'd spent five years perfecting my victim persona. Sure, I told myself I wanted to change, but had I really?

As we approached the table I was surprised to see Cindy from uni standing at the table. What was she doing here? It looked like she was talking to Xander?

I stopped just behind and to the side of her, Sophie at my right. She didn't notice us with all the noise and the crowd. "...are you really in a relationship with Eden Sommers? We are talking braniac Eden with the scars, right? Did your Facebook account get hacked or something? I just saw the pic." Her voice sounded overly chirpy and she was doing that exaggerated animated thing she always did. Somewhere along the line she must have thought it was cute or something.

The bottom felt like it had fallen out of my stomach and Soph reached a hand across to hold mine, both of us focused on what Xander would say next. I don't think he'd seen us approach because the crowd was kind of thick. His face looked tight and he had a slight tick at his jaw. I'd only ever seen it once before and that was the night at his place when he kind of lost it.

"No, Cindy. My Facebook account wasn't hacked and yes I am in a relationship with the beautiful Eden Sommers." Suddenly my stomach righted itself and I was feeling much more secure. Now I was far more interested to see what she'd say.

"Beautiful—why?...I don't understand. You have a policy of not dating students, that's what you told me when I trained with you." She genuinely seemed confused. Perhaps she was one of the few females that couldn't do two things at once. It must have really taken some brain power to perfect the hair flick and the pushed out boobs "look at me" kind of gesture while trying to think and talk at the same time.

"That's correct and my policy hasn't changed." His jaw was still clenched tight.

"But you're training her, I heard!" she said in an exasperated voice "And apparently you're sleeping with her. Why would you do that? I made it very clear I was happy not to train and she's well...kind of a freak." The whole table gasped and sucked in a breath. Cindy didn't say it but everyone knew what she was getting at.

Then, it all seemed to happen at once. Sophia dropped my hand and made a lunge for Cindy.

"Sophia, stop." Xander's voice cut through the chatter in his best Sensei tone. At least fifty people suddenly seemed to be very interested in what was going on at our tables. Sophia went as still as a stature. I could tell she wanted a piece of Cindy but she wouldn't go against Xander.

Xander stared right at Cindy and his eyes were absolutely black. If I didn't know him I would have been terrified; the look was so intense. Then he slowly stood, making himself seem even more menacing if that was even possible.

Cindy took a step back as it appeared to dawn on her just how deep a hole she'd dug for herself.

"I've got no idea why you'd come over here looking to start something, Cindy. But let me clear it up for you. First off Eden is not my student—she's my girlfriend. If I choose to teach her or involve her in anything else to do with Onigashima, it's my business and no one else's—but rest assured my no dating students policy is still firmly in place. I've also told you on more than one occasion that I wasn't interested in any sort of relationship with you other than as a student. I'm retracting that offer as well. You are not welcome at Onigashima. You've made it very clear you have no respect for yourself or anyone else. Finally, I don't care how attractive you think you are, beauty is much more than what you see on the outside. You might want to think about that."

She stood there gaping.

Xander moved around the table and came across to me. "It's time Eden and I headed home." Cindy spun around and finally realised I'd been standing just off to the side of her the whole time. The look on her face was priceless.

Everyone else at the table rose as well in a show of solidarity.

By this time I was angry. How dare she be such a bitch? I'd never done anything to her, except help. I been nothing but a doormat—she appreciated nothing. Well, that was going to stop tonight as well.

"Don't bother asking for anymore notes either, Cindy. No way would a 'friend' call me a freak." It was hardly a cutting or defining statement, but it was the best I could do.

Xander put his arm around my waist and left a lingering kiss on my lips. I knew it was all for Cindy's benefit, but I didn't care.

We started moving towards the door when he stopped and turned back to her.

"Oh and Cindy, don't get any stupid ideas of retribution towards Eden. I won't stand for it and I don't doubt that she's more than capable of putting you on your arse right now—but she's too much of a lady and too polite to do that." I could feel the fury radiating off him.

We kept moving and headed out to the car park and were quickly joined by the rest of the group.

Xander nodded at the guys and they nodded back silently as they split to go to their own vehicles. It was that unspoken code again. It was a show of support for me as much as Xander and that felt kind of heady. Other than family, no one had ever stood up for me before.

Sophia looked a little sullen off to the side with Rachel, Adelaide and Seth. I knew she wasn't happy about Xander reining her in. Xander must have figured it out too.

He moved towards Sophia taking me with him.

"Hey Soph. I know you're not happy with me now and I know you were only defending your sister and yeah, I agree she deserved a good smack in the head. But starting something physical with Cindy wasn't the way. She's the type that would have pulled an assault charge on you quicker than blink. If she'd come at you or Eden physically...totally a different story. We don't start it, but by God we will finish it if it's brought to us. Eden's lucky to have a sister like you." He held out his hand for a fist bump that seemed to be the thing with his students. She bumped him back and smiled a little.

He looked around at me. "We're going to head off." Then he

looked back to Sophia, then Seth. "Anyone need a ride?"

"You head home, man. I got this. I just dialled for a cab. I'll make sure the girls all get home safe." Xander nodded and there was that unsaid conversation passing back and forth again. "You training in the morning at Onigashima?"

"Yeah, I'll be in there after ten."

"I'll call in," Seth promised.

"Cool, bring some gear. We'll rumble."

"That's a given." Seth seemed pleased with the idea.

"Just be like old times."

TWENTY

XANDER

I woke up just after dawn. I really struggled to sleep past sunrise regardless of how late I went to bed. Last night was no exception, although I did seem to sleep really soundly when I had Eden in my bed.

That mop of golden hair with fiery streaks was all over the pillows and she was sprawled half over me. I couldn't think of a better way to wake up, but I wasn't one for lying in bed unless, of course, I had a reason to be there. Today I made a bit of an exception, because Eden seemed so comfortable and I didn't want to wake her.

I eased my arm over and reached for my phone and started to scroll through checking out what was going on in the world. There were more comments on my personal Facebook page. I liked a few but didn't post further comments. My relationship with Eden was public, but there was nothing more anyone else needed to know.

I checked my fan page and there was a little more activity over there. I hadn't really done anything with it in over three years but Reed had told me the promoters were looking to fire things up over the next few weeks. I wasn't exactly sure what that meant but the media circus was always the part I least enjoyed about big fights. There was a media meeting organised next week to lay it all out. Typically the last few weeks were the craziest. It's all about whipping the fight fans into a frenzy for maximum return over the last four weeks or so.

My job was to remain focused on the fight and not get dragged into the craziness. I knew it would be crazy because that's how it always went down, plus everyone knew that this would be a grudge match between us.

It was something I needed to talk to Eden about. My life was about to become public property once again; she'd be sucked into that and it scared me almost more than anything else. I didn't want her hurt.

I thought on it a little more and decided to wait until after I met with the media people before I spoke to her. I wanted to be armed with the facts and the plan first. Then we'd figure out how we would deal with it.

The sun was further up now and the light was coming through the window and hitting the bed. I probably should have blinds or something but I really liked waking up to the sun and it wasn't as if I needed blinds for privacy. There was no one living close by who could see anything.

Eden started to wriggle against me and I traced my fingers over the burn scar. The skin was rough and bumpy. She'd never told me anything about the fire and I wondered if she ever would. God, I couldn't imagine how terrifying it must have been.

Her big blue eyes opened and she saw me looking at her and smiled.

"Good morning, gorgeous." I dropped a light kiss on her forehead. She snuggled into me tighter, kind of like a contented cat.

I kept trailing my fingers over the scars absently.

She seemed to be looking at me as if she was trying to understand why I was doing it.

"Does this bother you?" I asked.

"No. But I don't understand why you've never reacted to them. Not once have you ever shied away from them. That's so weird, because everyone else has."

I sighed and wondered if I should tell her. I'd almost come out with it during that first session at Onigashima. If we were going to get through what was to come, we needed some solid foundations. This would be a start. She needed to know the truth.

"You'll always be beautiful to me Eden," I said quietly.

"Thank you. But I don't understand why."

"I'm going to tell you a little story. I'm not sure how you're going to feel about it but just let me run with it, please."

She looked at me curiously and tensed a little before relaxing back into my side. "I first noticed how beautiful you are a long time ago, Eden. In fact, it was only a few days after you moved here."

"What?" There was no mistaking the surprise.

"Yeah. Dane and I were walking to training one day. You and your sisters were in the park down the end of your street. You were sitting on the grass making those little chains from clover flowers. The three of you were laughing and smiling. It sounds really weird I know, but the sun kind of backlit you. Your hair was like a golden halo and for the first time, I knew what beauty looked like."

She took it all in for a few seconds, playing it around in her mind. "I think I was eleven when we moved here. How old were you... fourteen?"

"Yeah, I was."

"What do you mean you didn't know beauty?" I could see her struggling to understand.

"I know it sounds weird, but it's true. My childhood was a hard one, Eden. I don't mean that in a bad way. It was just devoid of anything soft, if that makes sense. My mum died when I was a baby. There was no feminine influence in my life. Dad raised me to be a man the only way he knew how. He didn't beat me and was never awful or cruel or anything like that, but he wasn't affectionate or soft in any way. He didn't really show emotions or stuff like that, well, at least, not to me. It's not his way. That day changed something inside me for the better. Seeing the three of you sitting there kind of peeled back the grey filter I had over my eyes. I saw the beauty in the three of you just having fun, laughing and hanging out. Sure the three of you were pretty enough to paint with all your gorgeous blonde hair and blue eyes but it was more about your happy souls." I looked down into her eyes. "And now I feel like the biggest dweeb...and they'll probably be coming to revoke my man card any second." What was I thinking? I made a show of looking under the cover to see if I still had my balls.

"Still there, but I'm not sure for how long."

She laughed. "Oh stop it...and for your information I think it's one of the most romantic and beautiful things I've ever heard."

"You sure it doesn't sound creepy?...I've never told anyone else." I'd wondered that myself so many times, but it just wasn't the way I saw it.

"Not even Dane?" she asked, surprised.

"Not even Dane, although I think he kind of realised I always had a thing for you."

Now she just looked downright confused.

"But you never approached me before the café, did you?"

"No, I didn't. Plus it was never like that. . You were too young and then the fire happened. I think I was overseas at the time. I remember coming home and reading something about it in the papers. I didn't do anything. It wasn't as if I knew you. It would have been weird if I just suddenly turned up like a creeper."

She nodded seeming to understand.

"Then Sophia walked in about two years ago. I have to say it was a shock when I finally put two and two together a few months later. I got to know her, then Tori turned up. I never really thought much about it. I was building Onigashima and kind of in my own head after that fight. That took up a lot of my time and headspace." I stroked my fingers through her hair. "That afternoon we were in the café, something just made me get up and come over. Have to say I'm really glad I acted on whatever told me to do it. These weeks have been great. I really like what we have here, Eden."

She snuggled in tight and kissed me just over the heart. "Me too, Xander. Thank you for telling me that. I had wondered. You kind of started to say something that first session at Onigashima. And in case you're still worried, I don't think it's weird. I think it's sweet and sentimental. It's also our little secret. I don't want to share it with anyone. I just hope you don't feel some misplaced sense of responsibility to be with me or something? I still can't quite understand why you'd want to be with the girl with all the scars."

"Honestly, Eden, the scars don't worry me. They never have because it's almost as if I could see your spirit right from the start. Your spirit is just as much part of your beauty as your physical appearance." I trailed my fingertips down the scars on her face, neck and finally on to her side.

"I know these really bother you and what Cindy said last night was hurtful and cruel. The make-up sure helped cover up the ones on your face last night, but have you thought about getting a tattoo to cover these ones?" I ran my hand over the scars from her shoulder to her hip

"No. I didn't know you could tattoo burn scars." She looked interested.

"Well I spoke to Jarryd, who's done most of my work. I think I mentioned he's a student." She nodded yes, but she stiffened and I realised she wasn't happy knowing I'd spoken about her scars to someone else. "I didn't mean to break a confidence or something like that. I just wanted to know if it was possible before I spoke to you about it. Please don't be mad at me. He said it can be done and he's done a few before. If you want, he's happy to have a chat to you about it."

She was quiet for a few moments and I hoped I hadn't overstepped the invisible line she'd drawn in the sand regarding her scars.

Finally she spoke. "I'm okay with it. I know you were only

trying to do what you thought was best. But in future, I'd prefer you talk to me about that sort of stuff first. They're my scars after all." I wanted to argue that she was my woman and it was my job to make sure she was okay, but I knew I needed to respect her wishes on this. I was probably lucky she was being so good about it now.

"Okay. I can do that. I really only wanted to see if it was possible. I didn't want you to get your hopes up if it wasn't possible. I'd trust Jarryd to do a good job. Besides he knows I'd kick his arse if he screws up something on my girl."

"Oh you're so scary...if only they all knew you had a soft centre a mile wide."

She had me figured out already, but strangely, it felt right.

"Can this be another of those little secrets?" I asked hopefully.

"Of course...You don't think I'm going to let people know and risk having my sisters give you as much grief as they do me? I do have some sense of mercy." Then she kissed me playfully and wriggled over on top of me.

"Something on your mind, Gem?" My hard cock was already poking at her pussy and I could feel how wet she was already.

"Yep, something on my mind." She looked at me intently.

"Care to share?" I pushed my hips up a little to make sure she knew exactly what she was doing to me although I don't think she had much doubt.

She wriggled back rubbing herself all over my very excited cock. I reached up and tweaked her nipples a little for good measure. And as always she moaned low.

"Why does it always feel so good when you do that? I touch my nipples and it doesn't feel anywhere near as good." I'm not sure whether she meant to admit that or not but the frankness and innocence of the way she said it, made for one heady mix.

"Show me how you touch your nipples Gem. I want to see." My voice was low and raspy which was exactly how I felt right now.

Her eyes flew open with a moment of alarm. "Oh no, don't chicken out. I want to see it. Can't you tell how hot it's making me?" I moved my hips up into her again and she whimpered as I rubbed against her clit.

I took her hands and placed them on her breasts. "Show me, baby. Drive me wild." That was all the encouragement she needed.

She arched her back and thrust her breasts closer to my face and her fingers began to circle and pull at those hard little pebbles. I grabbed hold of her hips and helped her slide along my length. She was so wet. It was crazy torture, especially since I could just slip inside her, straight into heaven, but we both seemed to be intent on driving each other crazy.

Eden threw her head back and I could see the light sheen of sweat start to form on her neck. It was too much to resist. I moved up and licked from her collarbone all the way to her earlobe.

"You're beautiful all the time Eden, but never more than when you're wild for me, baby. Show me how much you want me." I ran the tip of my tongue around her ear then sucked her earlobe into my mouth before nibbling it a little.

Every time my teeth nipped, her hips ground harder into me and she whimpered louder.

She raised her hips a little to break the contact and I went to hold her against me then I realised what she was doing. She was moving to slide me inside her.

I held her firm and pushed my hips down away from the most exquisite temptation. "Let me get a condom, Gem."

"No. Just slide into me," she demanded. "I'm on the pill."

"You've got nothing to worry about from me." I managed to get out before my brain turned to mush and I released the hold I had on her hips. A split second later she was sliding down over me—encasing me in her warm, wet heat. God, it felt incredible.

She rolled her hips a few times and I knew she was close. Her walls were starting to really tighten around me and I could feel everything since I was bare. It was the best feeling ever.

Her hair was everywhere and she had this wild far away look in her half-closed eyes that looked almost drunk with passion.

Sharp little cries started to slip from her mouth in time to the clenching around my cock. My jaws gritted together almost to the point of pain as I strained to hold off my own release. We were going to do this together.

The sensations and build were so intense, I knew that I could only hold a few more seconds. My fingers found her clit and I only needed to stroke her a couple of times before she went wild on my cock. Her body jerked and spasmed and it was the most beautifully erotic thing I had ever seen.

My own release couldn't be contained any longer and it rushed forwarded to join Eden's. Every single muscle of mine seemed to be simultaneously wracked with the opposing sensations of intense pleasure and pain. I thrashed beneath her and she planted her palms on my chest and closed her thighs tightly around my hips.

Finally, our movements became little ripples and eventually stilled. Eden collapsed over me, a complete mess of blonde hair and sweaty skin. Nothing had ever felt better.

"Whoa that was intense," I breathed out and nibbled her neck, my dick starting to relax just a fraction inside her.

"Mmm," she murmured into my neck. Something told me it would be a while before I got anything intelligent out of her. I didn't care, knowing that she was as wrecked as I was from what we both experienced.

"I think I'm exhausted and I haven't even got out of bed yet. Can I just go back to sleep for a few more hours." She tickled my ribs and we both started laughing and wriggling against each other like idiots.

We were so wrapped up in each other that I didn't even realise what happened next until too late. I was that focused on Eden.

The door to my apartment pushed open and in walked my dad.

Eden squealed and I immediately rolled us pinning her under me. Better dad got an eyeful of my naked arse than Eden's.

"Busy here, Dad!" I called out over my shoulder, my voice sounding more like a growl.

"Sorry, son." His tone was gruff like always, but I swore I heard something else.

"Give us a few minutes." The door clicked shut and this time I heard his footsteps retreating.

I lay on top of her waiting to judge her reaction. Eden's face was a horrified mask.

"Didn't you lock the door?" she hissed.

"I guess not. In my defence I was walking up the stairs trailing your delectable backside. Not much else was going through my mind at that time."

"Doesn't he knock?" Good point, well made.

"He's never had a reason to before. I don't have women sleep over."

"What?" She seemed more surprised by that now, than what had happened.

"I haven't had anyone here, Gem. You're the first serious woman I've had in years and I'm liking it." She could ask me all the questions later. Now we needed to grab a quick shower and go talk to dad.

I could only imagine what his response would be. Why couldn't he have stayed in Sydney until all this craziness was over? I didn't need to deal with him on top of everything else. My own demons were hard enough to manage. I didn't need him weighing in as well.

TWENTY-ONE

EDEN

I was just in the process of fastening my jeans, when I heard Xander's dad knock on the door to the apartment. Hell, it hadn't even been ten minutes. We'd both jumped in the shower. Xander first—he liked it hot. Not going there just yet! Thirty seconds later it was all mine and I washed off quicker than I thought possible in the lukewarm water. That was definitely a place we were going to revisit together. Somehow I needed to tackle that fear.

"Just a sec," Xander called out. He'd emerged from the bathroom first. I'm glad I'd chosen to bring my clothes in here, rather than get dressed out in the open.

Xander stuck his head in the door. "You ready, Gem?"

I threw my hands up. "Well, I hadn't really anticipated meeting my boyfriend's father this morning. But I guess I'm showered and dressed now, which is something. He's already seen more of me than I intended. I haven't tackled this mop yet or done anything with my face but I guess it doesn't matter. I only really started wearing makeup again yesterday after all."

He chuckled and gave me a quick kiss. He tasted of toothpaste. “Thanks for being good about this. Just a warning, my dad’s kind of odd and intense. It’s got nothing to do with you and everything to do with me. Just remember that okay.”

I nodded and he was gone. I had a real sense of foreboding as I wondered just what this guy was like.

I pulled a brush through my hair and rubbed some moisturiser into my face.

Finally I took a deep breath and walked out.

Xander was behind the bench fixing coffee by the look of things and his dad was sitting on one of the stools. The new furniture had arrived a few days ago and it looked awesome. All except the bed. There was a shipping problem and it was going to be another couple of weeks.

The place looked a lot more homey, but there was still quite a lot of room for improvement. Some artwork was definitely needed for the walls. Something to break up all the white and bring it together.

Xander saw me approach. “Dad, this is my girlfriend Eden Sommers. Eden, my dad, Len Todd.” Xander’s dad rose from the stool and extended his hand. I took it in mine and shook.

“I’m very pleased to meet you Mr Todd.” I could see him assessing my face and like everyone else, he was wondering about it but he didn’t seem too phased. Len was a man about the same physical size as Xander. He had the same dark eyes and bone structure. He also had the full puffy lips but something told me Len didn’t smile as much as his son. His hair was mostly still dark but the silver had started to set in at the temples. In fact, I think there was a good chance Xander would look exactly like his dad in about thirty years time and that certainly wouldn’t be a bad thing. Len was still a very handsome man.

“It’s Len. Good to see you’ve found a well-mannered one, Alexander.” I wasn’t quite sure how to take that. When Len relaxed his hand we both took our seats again and I kind of looked to Xander for a cue as to what should happen next.

"Thought you weren't due back for another week or two?" Xander asked his father as he pushed a mug of black coffee across the bench. I tried to subtly move a little further away. Hopefully, Len hadn't noticed anything.

"Umph. I wasn't. I was going to head back in a couple of weeks but I got a call from Ron. Could barely believe my ears when he told me my son was getting back in the cage. Reason you didn't bother telling me?" Len narrowed his eyes at Xander.

Xander merely shrugged. "I didn't tell you because I knew you'd come right back here and would be crawling up my arse. Kind of like now."

"You decide to get in the cage after three years and you think it's something you should do on your own? Something you shouldn't tell me?"

I was missing something in this conversation, but I had no idea what and it didn't seem like the time to butt in and ask.

"It wasn't a secret; I just didn't think you needed to cut your trip short. It's not like you can do the training for me."

"No, it's not. But I've always been there..." And then it made sense to me. For some reason Xander wanted to do this fight alone. "But hell, it seems like we're all being kept out of the loop. Reed didn't tell Ron, either. Carmen slipped that you were fighting again to Ron. Ron spoke to Reed and finally Reed filled him in on the details. Then Ron rang me."

Xander nodded, but said nothing. He poured a coffee for himself, then looked over to me. "Juice, Gem?"

"That'd be great." Xander poured my glass and pushed it across for me.

"Thanks," I said, smiling at him.

"Sounds about right, dad," Xander said noncommittally.

"That's all you've got to say?" Len demanded, obviously pissed at Xander.

"What is there to say? I was offered a big fight and I decided to take it. Yes, I haven't fought in a cage for over three years. I've just got to knuckle down and train, be the best I can—like always.

Weren't you the one that kept calling me a pussy for not getting back in the cage? I thought you'd be pleased, but you sure don't sound it." There was an edge to Xander's voice and I knew there was animosity between these two about something.

"I don't know how I feel about it. My son's taken the biggest fight of his life and hasn't spoken a word to me, even though he's been out of the MMA scene for three years. How should I feel? Because right now I have no idea? Why are you doing this now, Alexander?"

Xander was pulling fruit out of the fridge and pushing it across the bench to me. Then came two cartons of eggs. He already had a massive poacher heating up on the stove.

He pulled a container of rolled oats from the pantry as well. "I'm doing this dad because I need to. I can't live a lie any longer." I watched Len's eyebrows draw closer together as he studied his son, and then he looked at me.

"We'll talk about this later." And I knew Len meant when I wasn't around. He obviously thought I was the reason he wasn't getting anything useful out of his son.

"Umm, I can go for a walk or something..."I offered hastily, because it seemed these two really needed to talk.

Xander pinned me with a look that said so many things, but mainly frustrated. "Stay right where you are please, Eden. Dad, we'll talk about this now as it seems so damned important to you that you burst into my place at seven am in the morning while I'm in bed with my girlfriend. Bloody knock in future, will you!"

Len at least had the good graces to look a little embarrassed and mumbled a "Sorry about that! She's got a great arse by the way."

"Dad!" Xander roared and just about leapt across the bench.

A little nervous giggle sort of slipped out from my throat. I didn't know whether to be horrified or flattered.

His father held up his hands. "Didn't mean anything by it. Just speaking the truth."

I heard Xander mutter something that sounded like "Fuck me."

I could also tell he was angry, annoyed and a little embarrassed.

"I just don't understand, why now? I thought there was no chance you'd ever do it again. You were adamant that it wasn't an option. Then out of the blue you take the biggest fight of your career. I don't get it." I almost felt a little sorry for Len. He was obviously concerned and worried for his son.

"There's nothing to get, Dad. It's just something I need to do. I can't keep pushing everyone else to fight their demons and be better people if I can't do the same. Hell, you taught me that, and Ron drummed it in just a bit further."

Xander poured oats into a massive bowl, mixed in almond milk and placed it in the microwave to cook.

Len looked at him sceptically. "I want to know what made you change your mind. When I left to go to Sydney six weeks ago, I would have sworn you weren't getting back in that cage. Then yesterday morning I get a call from Ron and here I am wanting to know the answers."

Xander cracked eggs into the poacher and I sliced fruit, not quite knowing which way to look.

"We do have those things called telephones, Dad. I spoke to you the day before yesterday remember?" It was the first time I'd ever heard Xander sound like a smart arse. It was quite funny, but I managed to bite my cheek to stop the giggle from slipping out.

"Yeah yeah, smart arse. And that's exactly my point. You had plenty of time to tell me on the phone what was going on. You chose not to, so I got in my truck and here I am. I figured face to face, you'd have to tell me." The more they spoke, the more it was all starting to make sense. Any man who would get in his truck and drive over a thousand kilometres in under a day to get some answers, couldn't be all bad. He had to care.

"Can you pass me a plate, please, Xan, for this fruit?" I asked quietly using the tiny lull in conversation to slide in my request.

Xander looked totally frustrated as he passed me a plate. I knew there was a lot he wasn't telling his father or me. I know what I saw that night when he went a little wild downstairs.

He had some serious demons chasing him. Since that night he'd been focused on what he had to do to win that fight. He hadn't described what his fears or issues were; only that he was going to face them. I wasn't going to push him either. For some reason I was confident he'd tell me when he was ready. Just like when he told me about that experience he'd had when he was younger.

"You want to know what changed my mind, Dad?" I could feel the frustration coming off Xander from here. I knew that feeling. So many times I'd been where he was; people asking me to strip bare when it was too raw for even me to understand. People didn't seem to get it. Understand that it wasn't that you didn't want to talk to them about something, but it was more that you didn't know how. Sometimes putting feelings into words was really hard to do. The emotion just seemed to swallow you. This was one of those times.

I tried to catch his eye. I really wanted to go and give him a big hug to let him know I understood his pain and what he was struggling with, but I couldn't think of a way that wouldn't be considered weird. Finally, he looked at me and I tried to push as much understanding into my expression as I could.

His eyes softened a fraction and I knew he was reading me and understanding what I was trying to convey.

"That's the whole point of this, Alexander. I'd rather be in bed, too. It was a bloody long drive!" Yeah his father was just as frustrated.

"The answer is right beside you, Dad." Len glanced at me and looked confused. "Eden's the reason I'm fighting."

Now I really did feel sorry for the poor man. If he looked confused before—there was no doubt he actually was now.

Xander stared at his father for a second and then turned back to the microwave that was beeping. Len kept staring at me and I wondered if I should say something or keep my mouth shut.

Then he looked back to Xander, then me again. "Would someone care to explain?"

I dropped my head and cut up the rest of the melon I was working on.

I could feel Xander's eyes on me. "Eden?" he said quietly and I knew he was asking if it was okay for him to speak about me. How did I feel about Len knowing stuff? I felt for him because the poor man was obviously concerned and confused about his son. What would I even tell him?

Then before I'd even made a conscious decision, my mouth kind of started to move. "I'll tell him, Xander. If he's upset then it should be me he's upset at."

"You don't have to Eden. It's not anyone else's business but ours." Xander was looking to defend me but I could only imagine what Len must have been thinking coming home to all this.

I finished chopping the last of the melon and placed it on the plate pushing it across to Xander. Then I turned to Len.

My instinct was to keep my head down but Len deserved to see my eyes. "I'm sure you've noticed my scars by now." I motioned to my face and Len nodded.

"I'll give you the abbreviated version for now. Just over five years ago I was in a house fire. I got burned pretty badly getting my younger sisters out. The burns extend right down my right side to my hip. If you didn't already see them this morning." I gave him a little eyebrow raise, and he shook his head no. "I spent about a year basically in hospital, then another two doing rehab. With lots of hospital stays." Right about now I realised I hadn't even told Xander any of this and I gave him a look of apology. I felt awful about this. He should have been the first to know. He nodded to me letting me know it was okay—that he understood.

"Then I spent some time finishing my higher school education and now I'm at university studying accounting and IT. They're the facts, of what happened but they don't really tell the story. You see, when the fire happened, I'd just signed with an international modelling agency. I had shows and work booked in New York and Paris." I saw the look of genuine surprise cross Len's face.

"My whole world and my future career, my dreams, it was all

based around my appearance. I went from being...well you know what models look like, to this. By the time I was physically fit enough to face the world I'd retreated so far mentally...I just couldn't do it."

I sucked in a breath and felt the tears prick the backs of my eyes. I didn't want to be a blubbering mess, but I could see Len needed to understand. His son was suddenly going to be doing something very dangerous. I took a sip of the juice and gathered myself to go on.

"It's only been during the last twelve months that I've had the guts to go out in public. I know it might not seem much to you, but let me tell you, it's kind of indescribable when you wake up for the first time and you see this face looking back at you. What hurt me even more was the desertion. People I thought were my friends, my boyfriend even, they all just disappeared. I didn't even hear from them again."

I took another sip of the juice; my throat felt so tight. Xander caught my eye and I knew this was taking its toll on him as well, but I had to keep going now.

"Then when I did eventually start to see people that weren't medical professionals, I'd see the horrified looks on their faces, the discomfort they felt at not knowing what to say or do. I made them feel awkward and uncomfortable and that in turn made me feel exactly that and worse. So it became a self perpetuating thing. I stayed at home and cut myself off. It was easier on everyone. I changed my whole life and picked something to do that wouldn't have me in the public eye because I was too afraid of what people might think or how they might feel basically."

Xander turned off the stove, then came around and stood behind me, drawing me back to lean against him. Just his touch seemed to give me the strength I needed to keep going.

"I was a victim of the fire. I survived, but I have bad scarring as you can see. But I didn't pick myself up and push on, I went and hid. I let people I love enable me to hide. They didn't want to see me hurting so they allowed me to hide, encouraged it even. That doesn't make them bad people—the opposite actually. They were killing me slowly with kindness."

Len watched me intently, but I couldn't read what he was thinking. "I'd been making some progress. I manage to go to uni each day and basically function, but I wasn't living." I paused and pushed my head back to look up into Xander's eyes. I could see the pride and the emotion there. He dropped a soft kiss to my lips and gave me a slow smile of encouragement.

"I wasn't living until this guy, kind of came bulldozing into my life in a good way."

I saw Len's eyes leave my face for the first time and look at Xander, then they were back on me.

"Xander introduced himself to me on one of the very rare occasions I wasn't at the house. I was in a café with my sisters. Xander trains them."

Len looked up at Xander again.

"I'm not sure if you know them Dad—Sophia and Tori. Both knock outs like their big sister." He squeezed me tight and dropped a kiss to the top of my head.

"Then he kind of railroaded me into carrying some stuff at a grading and the next thing I knew I was hopping into his truck. He used that voice on me he uses with his students and I just did as I was told."

A grin spread across Len's face. I had a feeling Len had the same voice tone and Xander was a "chip off the old block" so to speak.

I shrugged and giggled a little. "I've worked it out now. Besides, it doesn't work on me anymore because I'm not his student."

Xander leaned down and whispered in my ear. "I'll remind you of that later in bed, Gem!"

I felt myself blushing and Xander kind of covered it with a chuckle. "I had to do something to get her into my truck, Dad. She was determined to run and seemed to want to ignore all my invitations."

I took a deep breath. "The next bit is kind of the turning point."

I chewed my lip, embarrassed but it was important. “I was supposed to go to Onigashima one night and I chickened out. Then I felt pathetic about the fact that I’d chickened out. So I did something really dumb. Well, I realise it is dumb now; I was probably a bit deluded then.”

Len’s face was ripe with curiosity.

“I headed off from my place on foot, close on dark and I cut through the industrial area down the street from Onigashima. I ran into a bit of trouble...” Xander snorted behind me and I elbowed him in the ribs like he’d taught me.

“Trouble...that’s an understatement.” I obviously didn’t hit him hard enough. He could still talk. I wondered if I should try again.

“Three guys surrounded and grabbed at me—I froze. I truly didn’t think any man would be interested in me.” I saw Len’s eyes narrow and I had no doubt where Xander got a lot of his personality traits from. “Anyway, I was very lucky...Dane happened along and got me out of there and back to his lord and master.” I bumped my head back to indicate Xander.

“Xander kind of set me straight on a lot of things and dished out what I guess you could call some tough love. It didn’t feel good but I needed to hear it. I was so clueless, caught up in my own little world, that I didn’t even realise I was putting myself into danger.”

“She scared the hell out of me that night, Dad,” Xander said gruffly.

“He kind of strongly suggested I start training with him. He also made me see my counsellor before I started. He’s bossy like that!” I was trying to make a tough journey a little more light-hearted.

Len raised his eyebrows. “I thought you didn’t date students, Son?”

“I don’t Dad and Eden has never been a student. I knew from the first day I met her she was going to mean a lot more to me.” Then his grip turned a little ticklish around my ribs. “I just had to get her to come around to my way of thinking.”

I nudged him again with my elbow.

The conversation kind of lulled there for a second and Len looked at us expectantly. Then when neither of us continued, he asked his question. "So how did it go from that to you taking the fight, Son?"

I felt Xander take in a deep breath behind me. "Well Dad, I guess you can say I kept poking and prodding at her, and not like you're thinking. That came later, although thankfully not that much later—I would have waited." I watched Len's mouth twitch in amusement and I felt heat rush over me. I couldn't believe he was spilling our sex life to his dad! This time I struck my elbow back with a lot more force, but Xander expected it and ducked his hips out of the way.

"I guess I went a little too far one night with my pushing her to face her fears. Eden turned around and gave me a fair dressing down." This time Len really did look surprised. "You'd have been impressed. Stunned the hell out of me—rattled my cage to the extent the door flew open."

Xander and I hadn't really spoken about what happened that night—only the outcome. I was curious to know what he was going to say.

"Anyway I kind of lost if for a bit. Went downstairs and beat the hell out of bags for I don't know how long. Carved up my hands pretty bad. Cursed Eden and about everything else I could think of. Then realised, when I hit that exhaustion point, what she said was absolutely right. Eventually I took a shower and came up the stairs fully expecting her to run a mile. Instead it seems to have forged us together even stronger."

It was a lot for Len to take in. I could see him tossing it around in his head.

Finally he asked the critical question. "Can I ask what Eden said to you that changed your mind? I've wondered for years what to say to you. Nothing I ever said moved you an inch."

"Can I tell him, Gem?"

I nodded. Len had the rest of the story; it seemed silly to stop now.

"What Eden said to me Dad, was something along the lines of this. She said I don't get to keep poking and prodding her to fight her demons unless I'm prepared to face mine as well. She also reminded me that I still have a career in the cage, but I was just choosing not to fulfil it."

Xander went on explaining. "It wasn't so much what she said Dad, but who was delivering the message. Eden understands the pain and terror, something you, Ron and Reed will never quite get. I need to do this, Dad. Otherwise I'm nothing but a fraud. I can't live with that nor would I expect Eden to either."

Len looked a little shell shocked, and I couldn't say I blamed him. I was thinking he'd had a hell of a time during the last twenty-four hours.

Finally, Len looked up at Xander. "Are you absolutely sure? This is not going to be a fight like any other you've had. Luke O'Donnell is a lot better fighter than when you last met. They're not calling him "Lights Out" for nothing. Sure, you kicked his arse good and proper, but he wants to prove he's the best. He's cocky and become real familiar with winning. He's not going to want to lose in front of his home crowd. Everything about this fight is in his favour. Not to mention there's five mil on the line."

Suddenly I felt really sick. That was the first time money had been mentioned. It was also the first time Xander's opponent had been mentioned. Now the fight was totally real. My boyfriend was going to step into a cage and go head-to-head with a man that had his reputation at stake and a grudge against him for blemishing his record.

Fear crept through me. Fear Xander might get hurt or worse. Look what had happened to The Cobra. If it happened once, it could happen again; couldn't it? How would I cope if I lost him? Then it dawned on me why I was feeling like this. It washed over me in one giant dumping wave...leaving me in a washed up mess.

I was in love with Xander Todd.

What was I going to do with that?

"You don't think I know all that, Dad?" Xander sounded certain and confident. "I've thought of just about nothing else since Reed spoke to me about the fight. I'm not doing this on a whim. For the last three years I've been living a full life doing what I love, but it still feels hollow. I thought it was hollow because I never did get that World Championship belt. It was always mine. But then I realised this is about so much more than me winning a title, Dad. This is about me truly being the man you raised me to be. This is about me facing all those demons I've got living in me. The doubt, the guilt, the what ifs, the whys. That cuts far deeper than not winning a damned belt, ever has. I've got an opportunity to conquer those fears once and for all. I need to take it, Dad. I need to make you and Eden proud."

"Son, I doubt I could ever be prouder of you than I am now. Don't do it for that reason," Len cut in.

"Let me finish, Dad. But more importantly than you or Eden being proud, I need to be proud of myself. Only then can I truly be the man I want to be."

Len said nothing then slowly nodded. "Fair enough, Son. If you feel that strongly about it, then I'll support you all the way."

Far out, I felt exhausted and a bit numb and stunned all at once. I glanced at Len and I could feel Xander behind me just soaking in our connection.

"Right, Son, stop. Stop cuddling your woman and get some food into you. You've got training to get to." Len stood up and moved behind the bench and started to organise the final preparations on the breakfast.

Xander leaned down into me and whispered, "You okay, Gem? That was intense..."

I nodded. "I'm okay and you're right it was intense but it somehow feels good to get a lot of it out. We've got a lot more to talk about, but it can wait for now. Your dad's right; you need to eat."

I glanced up and realised Len was smirking a little; he'd probably heard every word I'd said.

"Fuck me! I'm going to have both of you riding my arse now and you wonder why I didn't tell you?" Xander accused playfully at his dad.

"Don't swear in front of a lady, Alexander. I taught you better than that. I'm still good enough to take you down and teach you some manners," Len chastised.

"What?" Xander shot back. "You were the one that made the comment about her arse. You need to forget that memory, old man. That arse is mine."

"Haven't you ever heard the expression don't do as I do, do as I say, Boy? And I was only speaking the truth; it doesn't count." Len winked at me and I grinned. Oh, I think I was actually going to enjoy having Len around.

Xander had moved around and was getting eggs on plates and porridge into bowls.

He put a couple of eggs in front of me and a bowl of porridge that was just warm.

"You can't feed her that, Alexander. It's almost stone cold!"

"Actually Len, it's perfect. I kind of have a problem with anything hot. It just about killed me to sit beside you with that hot cup of coffee. I've not been near a hot liquid since the fire."

"I'm the exception to that issue she has with hot of course!"

Len slapped Xander up the side of the head, in fun. Then he turned to me and raised his eyebrows. "Facing your fears." And nodded as if in approval.

"She's a brave one, Boy!"

"Bravest girl I know." Xander winked at me this time and my heart melted a little more if that was possible.

"I'm really not sure about that..." I protested. I had such a long way to go.

Len cut me off. "She can't do a backward elbow strike for shit though, Son. What have you been teaching her?"

"I'm not even going to answer that, Dad," Xander said throwing his hands up in exasperation.

Len turned to me. "While he's off training this morning. I'll show you how to deliver a backward elbow that'll bring down any man."

Xander looked stunned. "You don't train anyone remember? You're too bloody grumpy and bad tempered."

"Well, I'm making an exception. Seems this girl is the one you want, so I'm going to make sure she knows how to look after herself. You, me or Dane might not be there next time."

It was without a doubt the weirdest, most emotionally draining and enlightening morning of my life all rolled into one. I was in love with Xander Todd. How the hell did that happen?

TWENTY-TWO

XANDER

After that crazy arse morning when Dad walked in, things seemed to settle down. I was getting in my morning run, and then we'd be heading back to Onigashima to start the serious training. I liked the opportunity running gave me to be moving, but still having my head clear to think. I seemed to have a lot on my mind these days.

We were half way through the fight prep and it really had become a team effort. Eden and I felt closer, tighter. Even my relationship with dad seemed better. What happened that morning still stunned me a bit. I really wasn't expecting Eden to just offer up all that stuff about her life to a complete stranger. I don't know what she saw in my father, but something must have tripped a switch and they seemed to be getting along famously.

I hadn't intended to include dad in this fight prep, because we just hadn't been "clicking" for the last three years—ever since that damned fight. But something happened that morning and changed it all. Maybe it was because he'd been frustrated because he couldn't reach me and I'd been hell bent on not talking. I just didn't know how to talk about it. I hadn't wanted to rip off that Band-Aid for him to see just how bad the hurt was. He'd raised me to be a man and somehow showing him the hurt went against that grain.

Eden was different. She just knew, because she felt it, too. I didn't need to describe it for her. She knew exactly how it felt. It was just one of the levels we connected on.

It had only taken him a couple of days before Dad had sort of lodged himself back in this fight prep. He wasn't directly involved with my training. That had never been his thing. Reed was my trainer. Dad was the guy in the background making sure it all came together so I could focus on what I needed to do.

For some stupid pigheaded reason at the start, I'd thought I didn't need him to do that this time. I thought I could go it alone, but I had far more responsibilities than last time with Onigashima now. Dad had just sort of stepped in without saying a word and started the organising and day-to-day running. As I jogged along thinking things through, I was genuinely relieved.

Thank God he was retired now and had the time. He'd been a logistics specialist in the army before he retired. Organising was his thing. When I'd come along and mum hadn't made it, he'd switched careers in the Army from Commando to logistics so he could be stationed in one place. It had worked well. Well, at least, that's what he said. Ron had been an old army Commando buddy and when he'd gotten out and started his school, dad had sent me there. He said something about it was better to be taught by Ron than by him.

They were as thick as thieves and that was good. Dad didn't have many people he was close to, but Eden seemed to have really resonated with him. When she wasn't at uni, she'd taken to hanging out at Onigashima. It seemed like she spent just as much time with Dad as she did with me.

Hell, dad was even picking her up from uni and dropping her off. That was another thing. We really needed to get around to teaching her to drive once this fight was done. She'd seemed to have missed out on all that.

Many times I'd look up from training out on the floor and see them in my office going through stuff—organising. I'd hear her soft giggles and his more gruff chuckles. I'd never seen dad so, well "soft". It was times like this I felt a pang of jealousy. A part of me wanted to keep her all to myself, but I knew that wasn't possible. But I also wished he'd be as relaxed and amicable around me. In the end I realised, I was just pleased she was close by me. Eden was also pedantic about making sure I stayed focused on the fight to the point of obsession; that appealed to my dad.

During the week, she'd go home every night, but she would spend Friday, Saturday and Sunday nights with me. Those nights made up for the other four; we both got a hell of a workout those nights. Dad had also learned to knock and so far we'd avoided any further embarrassing situations.

Every time we were together she seemed to get more confident, and a little wilder. It was hot and crazy and I loved every moment of being with her, inside her. But I'd also realised I loved having her around just as much. Who was I kidding? I was in love with her. And now I needed to have a serious chat with her and my dad. We had a lot to work out around this fight.

Reed and I had done a web meeting with the PR people from the fight yesterday. They'd laid out the marketing plan and it was heavy on hype and big on getting every media channel talking about us. That made me uncomfortable.

I explained I had a girlfriend and mentioned she was the shy type and why. I wanted her left out of it. I wasn't foolish or naïve enough to believe they'd respect my wishes, but I wanted my position made clear early. I didn't want there to be any misunderstandings. If they overstepped the boundaries I'd set, there would be problems. Eden was not to be in the public eye.

That thought was weighing heavily on my mind as I picked up Dane along the route. He was not running quite as much distance as me yet.

"Hey, man," I tossed at him as he fell in on my right shoulder.

"Hey." He looked like death warmed up and I wondered what the hell.

"You okay? You look like shit."

"Good, at least I feel like I look," he mumbled. I'd jogged with him enough over the years to be able to make out his speech between breaths.

"You sick?" First he shouldn't be out here if he was. But second, I couldn't risk being in contact with anyone that was sick. I couldn't afford to get a virus or something that might interrupt my training.

"Na man. Just didn't get much sleep."

"How much is not much?" I was worried about him. Three or four times I tried to get him to tell me what was on his mind, but each time he kept shutting me down. Maybe today would be different. He looked worn down and tired enough that he just might crack and let me in.

"Couple of hours," he admitted and I knew he felt guilty, like he'd failed. Eight hours every night was a must. Six at a pinch when we were training like madmen. Even a nap in the afternoon was good, if you could swing it.

"Fuck, Dane, you can't do that to yourself."

"You think I don't know that?"

I guess he did, but I still felt like I needed to look out for him. That's what mates did. "What, you just can't sleep or is it something else?"

He was quiet for a while and we kept running, our strides matching as we ran along the edge of the quite suburban street.

I'd just about given up on him answering me when he finally spoke. "I've met someone." It had to be a woman by the words he'd used, but it didn't sound good.

"Oh?" I left it hanging seeing what he would offer.

"She's not in a good place. Life's tough for her. I've been helping her out." Hell, that could mean anything. He could be helping her financially, emotionally or with maintenance around the house, but somehow I didn't think it was that. Things did make a little more sense now—his odd disappearances, him being late.

"I was coming from her place that night I found Eden." Suddenly I sent up a silent thank you to whoever this woman was. She'd been the reason Dane had broken his routine and Eden had been spared.

"She's got a kid and a dick of an ex-husband."

Wholly fuck! This sounded like it was going to be complicated. "Okay."

"I'm not going to talk about it yet, man. So don't even try, you don't need the worry. Just wanted you to know what was going on. I've got it handled. I'm not doing anything stupid. I just needed you to know I'm more committed than ever, but my fight isn't the only priority in my life. I sure as hell don't want to do anything to fuck up your prep. I already screwed up once being late."

I could tell Dane felt bad about a lot of things, but if he wasn't ready to talk, he wasn't ready to talk. Shit, I knew all about that.

"Thanks for telling me, man," I said and meant it.

He nodded.

"Fight or no fight Dane, if you need me, you talk to me. You're my best friend. I'll always find time for you."

"I know, man."

"You good to pick up the pace. I've got lots of shit to do today. We've got a team meeting later this afternoon, too. Need to sort out the plan for the last few weeks. Need you there, man."

"I'm good on both accounts. Step it up, man."

And we did. By the time we got back to Onigashima there was no more chatting between us. Both of us were heaving, but we'd needed that run in more ways that one.

•••

Reed scheduled the team meeting for two thirty that afternoon. There were no classes at Onigashima until five that day.

"Right, let's get started." I might be the fighter in this fight but Reed was firmly the boss when it came to getting me to the fight.

Everyone shut up and looked to Reed. We'd turned a storage room I hadn't done anything with into temporary fight headquarters. A trestle table had been set up in the middle with a few mismatched chairs we were now sitting on. Reed had a piece of paper the size of a map in front of him, broken into the last four weeks before the fight. A whole heap of things were written into each of the day blocks in different colours.

We were at the pointy end of things. Reed needed to make sure everything was sorted for the last four weeks of prep and the logistics for the fight. A lot of stuff was happening fast.

"I've mapped out the next four weeks the best I can with everything I know about what's happening at the moment. We're exactly four weeks out from the fight today. Everyone in this room is essential in some way to getting Xander to the fight in the best physical and mental condition possible."

I didn't miss the way Reed looked directly at Eden as he said mental. He might be the boss on this gig but if he wanted to start taking pot shots at Eden, he and I would have words sooner, rather than later. She was as much a part of this team as Dane and now Seth. Dad also looked at Reed as if in warning, but it wasn't his place to step in if necessary. It was mine.

"The activities in red are all the training activities organised for Xander, right up until the fight. The blue are marketing activities and press conferences, that sort of thing. The green travel days. The yellow are obvious spare blocks of time, which will probably get gobbled up for more training or promo depending on what needs to be done closer to the fight. Finally, the orange is where the rest of us will intersect on this plan."

I could see Eden studying the plan intensely and I really wondered what she was thinking. This was a whole new level of crazy, but a necessary evil if we had any hope of getting to the fight sane.

"Everyone with me so far?" There were nods all around the table.

"So, now let's look at the key dates. I've got tickets booked for everyone except you Eden, to fly out to Vegas two weeks before." I heard her gasp and I kicked myself for not talking about this with her privately beforehand. I'd just kind of let it all slip by. I was so focused on the training and well 'us' that I forgot. Reed was also about as subtle and diplomatic as a sledge hammer.

"Xan needs the time to acclimatise and finish his preparations where the fight is. He's also going to be needed for a lot of media." I knew Reed was saying this all for Eden's benefit, but unfortunately his tone was always very dictatorial and it came across as harsh. I could see that she thought she'd been excluded and her back had stiffened up and she looked a little sullen.

"Sorry Gem, I should have spoken to you about all this before. I forgot that you've never been through one of these preps. We just need to decide when you can get away. I know you have exams." I looked at the plan and picked up the orange pen. "When do you have exams?"

"This plan is hardly for Eden's exam timetable, Xander," Reed protested.

Right this was going to stop now! "Without meaning to sound like a diva but is or is this not a plan about my life for the next four weeks?" He nodded stiffly. "Well, Eden is my girlfriend and a very big part of my life. Her exam timetable goes on this damned page." I glared across the table to make sure he was absolutely clear. Reed said nothing, but nodded once in understanding.

Eden looked at me and I saw worry written all over her face. Then she pointed to the plan. "My first is here." It was four days before I left. "And the last is here." It was the Friday of the following week. Shit, at best, it wouldn't get her to Vegas until the weekend and the fight was the following Friday night.

"They like to string it out!" I commented.

"They do," she agreed.

"So you could theoretically fly out anytime from Friday night onwards. That might get you to Vegas for at least part of the weekend." I really wanted her there to experience this with me. I needed her. She kept me sane and grounded. I knew I was going to need time out from the crazy. Eden would give me that.

"Look maybe I should just stay here...?" I could see the indecision and the fears starting to rise again. "That way I'm in a familiar environment and you don't have to worry about me."

I could almost feel Reed thinking beside me "Great idea Eden, go with that." He was not the type that liked women around during fight prep.

"Can we just get this sorted and move on? Maybe Eden's right. I think..." Reed suggested.

I cut him off savagely, "Well, it isn't about what you want. It's about what I need. And I need Eden with me as soon as possible." I snarled at Reed. So far he'd heeded my warning about interfering where Eden was concerned. I wasn't about to cop it now.

"I'll stay back and fly with Eden. I don't think it's a good idea to leave this place for as long as we've got planned here anyway. Even though we've got Owen and Lincoln taking over most of the classes and we've cut the schedule a bit, that'll mean I'm around for at least another week to keep an eye on things here," Dad suggested and I could see the relief in Eden's eyes. I'd organised with dad to have Owen and Lincoln help out around here. This was their chance to show they could take on more responsibility. But I was worried about Eden. She'd never done anything like this before; dad was about the next best thing to having me there. Travelling overseas wouldn't be so daunting if she had him with her.

"Thanks, Dad. That would be awesome."

"Not a problem, Son. I want you concentrating on that fight. Eden and I will be just fine here until she's finished her exams." Dad looked over and winked at her. She gave him a shy smile and I hoped that would be fine.

"When do you start school again, Eden?" Why didn't I know that? Simple I'd been so caught up in this fight. I felt like such a shit boyfriend.

"Not till late Feb next year."

"When have you got us coming back, Reed?"

Reed pointed at the plan. "Here, the Tuesday after the fight."

"Make sure Eden and my tickets are flexible. We might head off for a couple of weeks or something after. How does that sound, Gem?" Her eyes twinkled and she gave a little shrug. Oh yeah. She liked that idea. Reed just nodded. Once the fight was over he wouldn't give a shit what I did until the next one was scheduled. And right then I realised there was probably going to be more than just this fight. I really did intend to get back into the saddle, so to speak.

"Okay, if everyone is cool with travel, can we move on to PR?" Reed pressed on. "It's going to go into full swing about now in the US. It'll probably take a couple of days for it to really start to get traction here, but it will. There's a team of people here working with the crew out of the US. You've got the first of the press conferences about the announcement here on Monday. There's another major press conference here, two days after you get to the States and the final one here the day before." Reed pointed out the various time slots on the plan with a pen. "I'd expect others to pop up as we go but those are the scheduled ones so far."

Yeah and that was the problem. "I really don't want to do more than that, Reed. I made that clear yesterday. The media people will create enough hype and bullshit without me commenting every three seconds on stuff. I just want and need to concentrate on the fight." Everyone was tense around the table at the mention of media. It was a double-edged sword. Without it there wouldn't be a fight, but it also took its toll.

"We'll see what we can do, man, but you know what promoters are like. They want to squeeze every last buck out of the fight." Reed shrugged his shoulders as if he was already resigned to the fact it was going to be a circus. This next bit though, needed to come from me.

"I think I need to let you all know to expect this media campaign to be particularly dirty and nasty. They're going to stir up as much crap on me as possible. They haven't said it, but I'm sure they'll also drag up all the stuff about The Cobra to mess with my head and to get more bums on seats. One thing I have been very specific about is that the focus stays on me. I don't want you, Eden, or anyone else being drawn into this. I signed up for it—none of you did. But after saying all this, I can't guarantee it. So I need you all to be really careful with phone calls, social media, and all that sort of stuff. I'd expect the hordes to start descending next week."

I could see Eden starting to stress out. "Try not to worry too much, Eden. But fair warning—it won't be easy."

She nodded her understanding but I could see she was freaking the hell out and she had exams coming up as well. If it didn't rain, it poured.

We spent the next hour going through a lot of other details that needed to be sorted out, but I got the impression Eden was already starting to retreat. We needed some time out before the crazy started.

When we finished Eden disappeared straight to the bathroom and dad stopped me before I headed out.

"You need to talk to her, Son. Get this straightened out now." He didn't bother disguising the worry in his voice.

"Yeah, I know. I think I'm going to need some help with keeping her safe and out of this bullshit. You up for it?" He'd been doing it anyway, but I wanted to make it official.

"Of course. I wouldn't trust anyone else with it."

"You two seem to be getting on great and she trusts you." For the first time since I'd started down this path I was second guessing myself. Was the bullshit I was going to put everyone through worth it? God, I hoped so.

Dad was looking at me closely. "Don't even go there. You need to stay one hundred percent on course. I'll keep your girl safe."

I did something I rarely ever did. I gave him a man hug.

"Thanks, Dad. I appreciate it."

"It's no trouble, Son. I'm just looking out for the mother of my future grandchildren. Besides I like the girl." He had a glint in his eye.

"I think you might be putting the cart before the horse," I said trying to hose him off.

"We'll see." My old man had a very confident look on his face. I'm glad he felt that way, because right now I wasn't so sure.

TWENTY-THREE

EDEN

"Oh, it's going to look incredible. Let me get the new linens to put on it," I said to Xander and Len as they manoeuvred the bed into place and got rid of the old frame. Xander's new bed and side tables had arrived this afternoon. Talk about an afternoon of craziness with this and the meeting. Hell, I didn't know whether I was coming or going, with all this plus exam stress.

Xander helped me with the linens and a couple of minutes later we had the bed looking like something out of an interior design magazine. The three of us all stood back and admired it.

"Wow. It looks even better than I thought." I was so pleased with the effect. The timber and steel created the perfect statement against the timber floor and the big open space. The linens were just gorgeous. Eventually we'd gone with a plain navy quilt and some cream coloured sheets. I'd added a pile of textured cushions that all blended and one in a tangerine colour that just "popped".

"Well, Gem, I have to give it to you sweets. That is genius. When you insisted on that orange cushion I thought "no way" but you wanted it so I went along with it. You were right; it just works." He had a big smile on his face and seemed genuinely pleased—that made me happy! Next thing I know he grabbed me into a hug and kissed me hard.

"Hey Dad, did you know my girl is a decorating genius as well as everything else?"

Len chuckled. "Oh Son, I had no doubt at all. I'm reckoning Eden would be brilliant at just about anything she put her mind too. She puts up with you, doesn't she?"

"Cruel but true, Dad, and on that note the door's that way." Xander nodded his head toward the door. "I want to christen this bed."

"Xander!" I hissed.

"Oh, don't get all bent out of shape, girl. I'd be doing exactly the same thing if I was in his shoes. Have fun kids! I'll see you in the morning." He winked at me and hurried off. Len really was a good sport.

"Yeah. Not too early Dad!"

"I can't believe you two!" I was feeling embarrassed from head to toe. Well, maybe not so much but hey...

"We're guys. We can talk about sex and joke about it as long as it doesn't get too personal and he doesn't walk in on us." Xander was enjoying playing and couldn't seem to help that naughty little grin on his face.

"Yeah, I can do without him seeing my backside again."

He caught me in his arms and backed me over to the bed. The back of my legs hit the frame and Xander kept pushing till we were on the mattress in a tangle of arms and legs, which had me giggling. Although when I finally came up for air, Xander was looking down at me— his face a study in seriousness and intensity.

"What's up?"

"I wanted to apologise for this afternoon, Gem. I blindsided you with all that fight prep stuff and Reed was a dick. He has a thing about women being involved in fight preps, but I told him from the outset I wasn't prepared to compromise when it came to you. If he couldn't handle you being part of my life then I wasn't on board."

He was so sincere as he said it and I knew this was laying heavily on his mind. I was also surprised. Had he really made me a kind of stipulation for him being involved? That was pretty major!

"Yes, you're right. This afternoon did take me by surprise. I guess I never realised the extent of this fight, I didn't realise the magnitude, which was pretty stupid. But I never expected you'd want me to go with you! I mean we haven't talked about it but, I just figured it was something you'd do then come back."

He nodded and looked at me intently

"Before you, yes that's exactly what I would have done, but not now. You're so much a part of this journey and part of me I can't not have you with me—it wouldn't feel right." His dark eyes were intense and I could tell he meant every single word he said. "You don't keep your loved ones at home if you can avoid it and Eden I absolutely love you."

My heart skipped a beat then started to bash against my chest and my stomach felt as if it was doing somersaults. I wanted to kiss him and hug him and tell him I loved him all at once; it was so overwhelming.

Xander Todd loved me!

He grinned and chuckled. "Help me out here, Eden. I've just told you I love you and you're looking at me like a stunned mullet. You're killing me, Gem!"

I grabbed him around the neck and pulled him down for a kiss. It started as a press of lips together. In about point two of a second it had escalated into something that was burning quicker than a wild fire. His hands were everywhere and I knew exactly where this was going to go really quickly, but first I had something to say to him as well. He deserved to know how I felt as well.

I pulled my mouth away and gave him a little nudge to let him know I needed him to back off. "What's up?"

"Nothing. I just need to say something before we get too carried away." A little frown crossed his forehead and I giggled.

"Stop worrying; I just wanted to let you know that I love you, too." His frown morphed into a smile that was so bright, I was sure it could power a city.

Then it morphed from the smile into a very satisfied grin. "Well, what do you know? My girl loves me, too. The day just got a whole heap better. I don't feel near as tired."

I laughed at him. "Oh, you might be tired but so far you've never been too tired. If that's what you're getting at?"

"It'll be a sorry day when I'm too tired to make love to my girl. I'll always find the energy to do that."

"You won't get any complaints from me," I agreed. "But I need to let you know that even though I love you, I'm kind of terrified at the moment."

Xander's face morphed again into concern. "What are you terrified about, Gem?'

I closed my eyes tight and opened them again. "Where do I start? I guess I started to get worried a couple of weeks ago when I realised just how crazy big this fight is you're doing. I never really understood until your dad kind of spelt it out that morning. I haven't said anything because I wanted you to focus, but then when we went through everything today...It was just crazy and the idea of the media really terrifies me, Xan. You know what I'm like."

He nodded his understanding. "Yeah. I'm not happy about it either, but it goes with the territory. There's going to be a lot of crap written and reported about me, Gem, that you just can't believe. You know me. Try to stay away from it all and ignore it. It's just bullshit anyway."

That sounded very foreboding. "What aren't you telling me Xan?"

I saw him start to look agitated and that worried me even more. "They'll bring up about The Cobra for sure. That's half the reason they wanted me to take this fight. Promoters have been begging me to get back in the cage since it happened, specifically because they know they can milk that angle. I'm not happy about that, but that's the price I've got to pay to get back in the cage so to speak. I am concerned about how they represent The Cobra through this. He died doing something he loved. I hope they respect that." He shook his head in disgust and I started to fathom just how distasteful he found this media stuff. Xander really did agonise over a lot of stuff.

"They'll also probably try to do stuff like link me to other women and anything to create hype." I sucked in a breath. The thought of that hurt and it hadn't even started yet. "That always happens. In all the bullshit that's going to happen, about the only truth that'll get reported correctly is that I'm fighting "Lights Out" in a month's time. It'll be so skewed. That's why you can't believe it. Don't even read it or follow it. Or comment on it. It'll drive you mad. Believe nothing unless it comes from my mouth. You can trust me one hundred percent. I might be on the other side of the world and away from you, but that won't change how I feel about you. You need to focus on your exams and try and block the rest out."

He rolled off me and looked up at the ceiling. "What is it Xan?"

"I spoke to dad before. He's agreed to kind of be your unofficial bodyguard. I want to publically distance myself from you if possible. It's the only way to try and keep you safe from the media circus."

I took up my favourite spot with my head on his chest, snuggled into his side and tried to take in everything he was saying. The thought of being away from him cut at me, but I knew he was doing it to try and protect me.

"It's just for the couple of weeks I've got left here. If you're going to uni, then Dad will pick you up and drop you off. Essentially, I don't want you ever out in public without him there. The press are the worst type of vultures. I have no idea what they might pull, but I don't want you left vulnerable to them. I'm not sure if you know this but Dad's ex army. He started life as a commando—he'll absolutely keep you safe."

That explained so much about Len. The pieces all seemed to fit together much better now. That didn't sound so bad. Spending time with Len was no chore—he was funny and kind in his own way. I liked him a lot. He didn't make me feel uncomfortable at all. "Well, it's not like I go out a lot!" I was worried but I didn't want him to worry too much about me; he needed to focus on the fight. "Besides I'll be busy studying most of the time."

"Yeah, that's important. I don't want your grades to suffer because of all this."

"Don't worry about me. I'll be fine. You just focus on doing what you need to do to win that fight." I locked my eyes with his. He needed to know I absolutely meant it. I would be fine.

"Just remember that you are the most important thing in my life now. I love you, Eden."

"I know."

"Good." He closed his arms around me and hugged me tight. I snuggled into him tighter and I wanted more.

"Should we be making the most of the time before the craziness starts?"

"Absolutely. How quick can you strip?" he asked with raised eyebrows.

"A lot faster than when you first met me."

"Excellent answer. I can see the training is paying off!" he teased.

I leapt from the bed and started to shed my clothes. Xander did the same. I was just pulling off my last sock when he tackled me back onto the bed.

"You ended up on the bottom!" He grinned down at me in mock surprise.

"Fancy that! Something tells me it wasn't by accident."

"My girl's not only beautiful, but smart," he said kissing the tip of my nose. There was something about him referring to me as his girl that just made my heart swell. He seemed to be in a playful mood now that we'd waded through all the serious, and I couldn't help but want to play a little more.

"So now that you've got me here, what are you going to do to me?" I gave him what I hoped was a suggestive look, reeling him in.

"Mmm, well there's just too many options. It's hard to pick just one, but I do have something in mind." His eyes went like liquid obsidian and there was no mistaking how turned on he was.

"Well, that sounds intriguing. Care to share?"

"Only seems fair considering you're the focal point of this particular little fantasy I've got." He kissed along my jaw and started to suck and nibble on my ear lobe. Why did that always make me a twitching mess of hormones for him? Then he whispered. "You want to know what I was thinking when I first saw this bed?"

He licked down my neck, over the scars and I could think of nothing but wriggling closer to him. "Yesss...what?"

"I was thinking just how sexy you'd look kneeling with your hands clinging on to the headboard, while I did wicked things to you."

I sucked in a breath and my body arched into his, my core screaming with need for him.

"Fuck Eden, did you nearly just come then? It sure looked like it. Did that little fantasy of mine appeal to you, Gem?"

"Oh, yeah."

His hand slid down between my legs and started to stroke, spreading the pooled wetness everywhere. "You...are...so...wet, and you're becoming such a little seductress. God, how did I get so lucky?"

Then he growled and swiped an arm at all the cushions displayed at the head of the bed. They went flying. Xander grabbed me by the hips and he rolled us till he was under me and I was a bit disorientated. It all happened that quickly!

"Take a hold of the headboard, Gem." It was his Sensei voice and my body tingled even more, my heart pounded harder and my blood seemed to heat even more. He pushed me upwards over his body, guiding me to where he wanted me. My hands latched onto the metal rails under the smooth timber top rail.

He wriggled underneath me and pushed my thighs wider with

his shoulders. His arms locked around my thighs and his hands cupped my butt. I was totally at his mercy by the time I realised what he was going to do.

"Relax Gem, you're going to love this." He reached up and ran his hand down my spine and along the crack of my butt before teasing around my opening as his mouth closed around me.

I didn't have time to feel embarrassed or self-conscious. It just felt so good. My mind went blank of all cognitive thought. All I could focus on was the feel of Xander's mouth and fingers on my pussy. That was the new centre of my universe and I was totally at his mercy.

Every muscle in my body was tightening and stretching, reaching for the pleasure he was teasing and building within me. His tongue rolled over my clit in the most exquisite little strokes and all I could do in response was let out little keening cries in a voice that was totally animalistic.

On and on he teased, coaxing me to the edge...letting me look over, then slowing to pull me back. Then enticing me again. My hips started to thrust harder against his face as he licked and built the pleasure higher. The pressure in my ears and body seemed to be drowning me and still he wouldn't let me go over.

His lips and tongue stilled, and in perfect synchronisation so did my hips. Everything stopped except my focus on his mouth between my legs. The anticipation had me totally attuned to his slightest movement or breath. He drew out the tension to the point of pain; every muscle in my body locked, begging for release. Then he flicked the tip of his tongue over my quivering clit and my world disintegrated around me.

My body thrashed around, only anchored by the railing of the bed and Xander. The more I crashed around, the more he licked and sucked with a new intensity. He dragged every last sensation and feeling from me, until it reached the point where I could no longer hold my head up.

He slipped from between my legs and knelt behind me. His arms wrapped under my shoulders and his fists gripped the bar between my hands, supporting my body. The hard steel of his erection probed at my super sensitised pussy and I bucked with every touch, but still wanted him desperately.

"Oh baby, that was so hot, but I need to be inside you now." My skin tingled and I shivered from his hot whispered breath at my ear.

I bucked against him again as the aftershocks continued to come. He wrapped an arm around my waist and held me firm to him until he was seated deep inside me.

"Ohhhhh." I let out a deep moan of pleasure.

His hips started to thrust against me, carrying me on a new journey of pleasure.

"That's it, Gem, let me take you again."

I pushed down on his erection harder and he ground up into me. He'd never felt this deep. I was oblivious to everything but Xander. He was all around me, in me, part of my being.

The hand at my hip caressed upwards and pulled at my nipple. My hips slammed at his.

"Oh yeah, you're almost there again, Eden. You're squeezing me so tight I can barely breathe." His tongue licked around my ear a little more and he whispered, "I love you, my hot gorgeous girl. Squeeze me tight, make me come for you." And as if on command, every essence of me tightened and I dove into the abyss again.

His hips slapped at me with inhuman speed and a growl ripped from his throat. Stars danced behind my eyes and I floated on rolling waves of pleasure. I could feel him surrounding me, part of me—no beginning, no end.

As if in silent agreement, we both dropped our hold on the bed rail and sank into the plush comfort of the mattress.

Xander finally managed to speak. "Gem, I think you just wiped me out."

"Consider the bed christened," I managed.

That got a low chuckle from him.

XANDER

"No, no, no." The sound eventually penetrated my sleep fogged mind and I woke to realise Eden was thrashing around beside me in the midst of a nightmare. I flicked on the bedside lamp and caught her arms to her body, pulling her to me.

"Shh, Eden. You're dreaming. Wake up, honey. Wake up, Gem." Her eyes flew open and she looked totally disorientated.

"Just a dream, Gem—you're fine. I've got you—you're safe." Then the tears started to free fall from her eyes and her body wracked with sobs. I pulled her tighter to me and stroked her hair.

"It's okay, honey, I'm here. Relax it's not real. Everything's fine."

I wiped the tears from her cheeks and kissed her forehead as she started to relax.

"Sorry to wake you," she said, snuggling her head into my chest.

"It's fine. What had you so freaked out?" It had been one hell of a nightmare.

"The fire," she said simply.

"Okay...you want to talk about it." I didn't expect her to want to but I made the offer just the same.

"What time is it?" she whispered.

I rolled over and picked up my phone. "A little before five. Sun will be up really soon. Does it matter?"

"Sort of. I just wanted to know if there was any point in trying to go back to sleep before I started to tell you about my dream."

Well, that did surprise me. "I'm all ears," I said kissing her again and squeezing her tightly in my arms.

"It was the fire." Her sleep raspy voice caught. "I don't dream of it very often anymore. It used to be just about every night." She shuddered in my arms. "They were very dark days when I woke up from the induced coma."

She didn't say anything for a while and I didn't know whether to prompt her or just let her go. Eventually she said. "The first thing I remember was the screech of the fire alarm. Dad was away and mum was working a late shift at the hospital. She was never home before midnight, but it wasn't as if we were babies." Eden paused again and I could see the pain she was going through remembering. I knew what it was like trying to retell your horrors.

"All I could smell was smoke and I could barely breathe; the smoke was already that thick. We used to live in that place across the road from Dane. You might remember, it was two storeys and I jumped out of bed and ran out into the upstairs hall...The fire was downstairs; I could see it from the stairs, but all the smoke was already rising... Sophia's and Tori's rooms were upstairs. So I ran along the hall and I got Sophia up and out onto the balcony upstairs."

She paused as her voice started to wobble.

"I remember. There was a balcony that ran right across the front, didn't it?" I'd seen that house so many times when I'd visited Dane over the years.

"Yeah, it had holes in it and the railing was rotted through. The landlord wouldn't replace it no matter how much we complained. But it was a balcony and my only thought was to get her outside—she could jump from there."

I glanced down and her eyes were open but they were far away caught in the memories. "I went along to Tori's room, but she wasn't in there. I was so scared. I didn't know where she was." Tears were pouring down her face and I hugged her closer.

"Take a break, Eden. If it's too much, just leave it." I wanted to know, but I hated seeing her so tortured like this.

She nodded but I don't think she had any intention of stopping. "She wasn't anywhere upstairs. I ran from room to room looking. I realised then she had to be downstairs. Oh Xan, the smoke was so thick! My eyes were smarting and I was starting to cough. I was screaming and screaming, calling for Tori but she never called back. The noise of the fire was really loud. Kind of a roaring." She reached for her throat and rubbed it as if trying to ease the pain she was recalling.

"I stood at the top of the stairs—I figured she had to be down there. I was so damned scared. In the end I just took a deep breath and went down stairs as fast as I could...I stumbled and fell the last four steps. My knee hurt like hell, but somehow I got up. The kitchen and dining were just a mass of flames and the heat coming from it was insane. There wasn't any air to breathe and I kind of remember taking tiny breaths trying not to breathe."

The tears were coming faster and harder. Her bottom jaw was quivering as she fought to tell her story. I was horrified with what she was telling me. I couldn't even imagine how scared she must have been.

"I still don't know how, but I kind of stumbled into Tori in the back hall. I think she was coming from mum and dad's room. I don't know, she doesn't really remember what she was doing. I just remember there being fire everywhere; it seemed to be all around us."

She sniffed and took a deep breath then carried on. "Tori was terrified and sort of frozen in fear—kind of glued to the wall. I looked around for something to protect her a bit from the flames. There was mum's knitted woollen rug hanging over the back of the sofa. She used to put it over her legs on chilly nights...I grabbed it and wrapped it around Tori and started pulling her down the hallway to the front door. That was when I first realised my top had caught fire down the right side." Eden was now taking massive big, gulping breaths and I was worried she was going to hyperventilate.

"Easy Gem, slow your breathing...breathe with me for a bit. In, out, in out. You're safe. It can't hurt you anymore." She nodded in acknowledgement.

A few seconds later she continued on. "The pain was insane, I can't begin to describe it—but I could just make out the glass panel in the door and I just kept focusing on it. We were almost there when it burst open. I don't remember anything after that. Well, not really until I woke up a couple of weeks later."

"Apparently, the firemen found us straight away when they pushed through the door. Tori got out with just a couple of superficial burns but my shirt caused all this."

I hugged her harder and I felt like I'd been through a wringer. I couldn't imagine the level of courage it had taken Eden to go downstairs into a fire to find Tori. How they both didn't perish was a miracle. I was so humbled by her bravery I didn't have a clue what to say.

"I popped in and out of consciousness a little, but it's so sketchy. About two weeks after the fire they brought me out of the induced coma. They needed to do a lot of work on the burns so they kept me in it for that long. The next few weeks are a blur in my mind. Even though I was on so many drugs, I could still feel the pain. I had all sorts of dressing and bandages. I remember the day I was with it enough to realise what the burns actually meant. I think it was maybe a month after." She shook her head and fresh tears pooled in her eyes.

"I screamed the place down. When I realised what had happened, I just screamed and screamed. They had to get the doctor to sedate me again. I was such a mess. I remember mum and dad just standing there crying, not knowing what to say or do, or how to comfort me. I was alive, but right then I didn't want to be. I even remember screaming, 'I wish I'd died, I wish I'd died'. Yeah, I was a mess."

I just held her tight and let her settle. Her pain was real—I could feel all of it. The burn, the fear—how had she survived?

"My God, Eden, I can't even imagine what you went through. The fire was horrifying but the recovery must have been indescribable." Nothing I could say seemed to be enough. How could I even respond to what she went through?

"So many times during that first year I just wanted to give up. I had twenty-two different surgeries that year. I had skin grafts and all sorts of things. Burn recovery is a slow process because of infections and basically it's just shit. I wore a pressure suit for months and a plastic mask thing over my face. That was hideous.

My hair was all chopped off because they needed to get to the burns and it had all sort of been singed." She sat up and pulled her hair back from the right side of her face. "This spot here. The hair doesn't grow there anymore." There was a wistfulness in her voice and I felt my own throat tighten.

"I just felt so ugly and inhuman. The person I'd been before the fire seemed to have disappeared that night as well. When I was finally well enough to leave hospital, I was at the point where hospital felt more like home to me than my home. In reality, I didn't even have a home I knew anymore. The place we had lived was destroyed by the fire; my parents were only renters so we had to find somewhere else to live."

The more she spoke the worse it got. I was staggered that she even functioned after what she'd been through. She'd taken hit after hit.

Eden was quiet for a while and I didn't know if she was reflecting or finished. Words just felt so inadequate. I just held her and tried to find something to say that didn't diminish the horrific ordeal she'd endured.

"Do you have any questions? Ask me anything. I'm not sure I'm going to want to talk about this again anytime soon, so now's your chance." She settled back onto my chest and her hand was absently tracing the tattoo of the dragon on my chest.

"What hurts the most? The physical or the emotional pain?"

"Both, but they're different. The physical pain was horrific because the doctors were always messing with the burns to get them to heal, then the rehab and physio. It went on for months. I just wanted to be left alone. I still get twinges now, but at least it goes away. The emotional pain, it doesn't seem to go away. It just seems to go on and on and it morphs. Just when I became numb to one thing, something else seems to trigger it and I'm fighting it all over again." She pressed a kiss to my chest. "I have to admit though that I do feel so much better and stronger since I've meet you. I still feel pain, but I'm not even sure that's the right term. It's more like I'm fighting the fears, and it's hard but I know I'm making progress. Every inch is tough but it's a win. I guess it's another form of pain, but at least it feels like a normal and rational pain. The sort everybody experiences, but it feels positive and I know I'm making ground. Does that make sense? It's hard to explain."

I thought about that for a little while. "I think so. It's kind of where I'm at with this fight. It's still terrifying, but I know I can keep going; that I can beat it. But if you'd asked me to do the same thing a few months ago, there was no way I could have."

She thought on that for a few moments.

"Mmm, I know what you mean. It's almost as if the pain needs to numb a bit. Time seems to do it. Most of the time you can keep it under control but occasionally it just flairs up. Sophia and I had a bit of a melt down a few weeks ago. Something happens in your psyche or a change happens and the emotions kind of get all knocked around. We balled for a bit then I got that text from you after that first day you trained me. That was enough to divert her attention. I think the dream I had tonight is because of everything that's going on. Things are changing between us. My mind needs to work though stuff and process. Bad stuff pops up more than good or when you least expect it."

Eden was right. "It's almost as if you're making progress forward and the demons know it so they make a last ditched attempt to drag you back. Hold you down."

"That's exactly how it feels," she agreed. "I start to make steps forward, then another monster appears. Before you came into my life, I wasn't real fond of facing those demons. I was much more comfortable hiding and hoping they couldn't find me. But they always seemed to find a way regardless of how well I thought I hid or avoided them. It takes a lot of stamina to get through them and I get tired, but I've realised that after being here with you, it's a marathon and I just have to keep going."

There were forty-year-olds I knew that didn't have a handle on stuff as well as Eden did. She understood this stuff and that's what came from being a survivor. But winning and defeating the demons is more than understanding or surviving—it's about taking action, going the distance. That's what Eden was doing now, taking action. So was I. I just hoped we were strong enough together to get to the other side.

TWENTY-FOUR

EDEN

The following days seemed to fly past at warp speed. Every day, I crossed off another box on the cut down version of the plan that Reed had given us all, right after the meeting. Our time alone together was in very short supply now. Xander was starting to get more and more keyed up or maybe edgy was the better word. His body had taken on an even bigger and harder look. Every single one of his muscles felt like hardened steel when I touched him. He seemed to have a new buzzy energy about him and he couldn't remain still , which told me he was feeling the pressure as well.

Just like he'd predicted the craziness started with the first press conference announcing the fight. It was done separately and remotely as Xander had refused to go to the US that early for the fight. I wasn't there at the hotel where the press conference was held, but I'd watched it on YouTube more than once.

Well maybe twice...oh okay—it was more like six times, but I was just so proud of him. But those journalists had been awful. The questions they'd asked! I really didn't understand them or why they'd asked—now I did.

After watching the press conference, I broke my own rule and watched the fight he had with The Cobra on YouTube. I needed to understand what had happened. In my defence, I'd heard it all from Xander before I watched it. Well I thought I did, but I was wrong.

When he told me about the fight and what happened, I had a picture in my mind. An idea of what had happened. Watching was a very different thing.

I'd seen Xan training so many times, but it was nothing like watching him in the cage. Xander in full flight was a thing to behold. Could a person be described as having brutal beauty? Because that's exactly what it looked like to me. Every move was graceful and full of intense and directed power. Never once did it look like he wasn't in perfect control.

I watched the fight from the start. I saw him and Reed talking at the break between rounds with an older man. Then the next round it all happened. The way Xander put The Cobra down on the mats looked elegant in its simplicity, but then I saw the punches to the head—which I found disturbing.

The man I knew and loved was pummelling a guy and I didn't really know how I felt about it. As I watched it, I anticipated the fatal punch. I knew it was coming. The camera angle picked up Xander's face and I noticed the difference straight away. The expression on his face changed before the punch even landed. It was very subtle, but I knew that face very well now. I believe he really did try to pull that punch.

Then the aftermath was harrowing to watch. The crowd went from screaming and cheering for the end to stony stunned silence in a couple of seconds as they realised what had happened. The Cobra's crew were frantically trying to work on him and Xander stood frozen with a million different emotions crossing his face. If that was what was crossing his face, then I could only imagine how his heart felt in those moments.

The next person the camera panned to though was the one that really pulled at me and rocked me to my very being. She was a very pretty pregnant woman, holding her belly and screaming in anguish. Her face was distorted in pain and her grief left a hollow feeling in my stomach. There was no doubt in my mind I was watching the wife or partner of The Cobra dealing with the realisation her man was dead—slain by my man.

I sat and stared at my computer screen long after the video had finished. How did I feel about it? I still don't really know. My heart felt pulled in so many directions. Is it wrong to feel for your man's opponents? Because that's how I feel now that I've watched it.

That poor woman! Her baby would be about three now. Somewhere out there was a little kid running around without a father. I don't know if The Cobra would have been a good father, but he never got the chance to see.

It all made so much more sense to me now. Xander outwardly appeared to be so controlled of not only his body, but his emotions as well. Watching that video gave me the context for how bad the pain really was for him. Now I understood that night down in his home gym so much better. He'd been reliving that fight in his head. We both had demons; they were just different types.

That initial media conference heralded the start of the media flooding on all channels, social media in particular. The fight promoters were in full marketing mode, trying to garner as much support and "buzz" for the fight as possible. Everywhere you looked someone seemed to be doing a story of our local boy taking on Luke "Lights Out" O'Donnell on the world stage. It was intense and surreal all at the same time and certainly not an experience for which I'd had any previous context or baseline.

I'd purposely stayed away from Onigashima, the week before my exams. There seemed to always be media people hanging around, plus I needed to focus on studying for my exams which were starting on the Tuesday so I decided to stay away all week. It had been a a study week after all which meant I'd been cooped up at home. Which until I met Xander would have suited me absolutely perfectly but now—not so great.

I now actually wanted to go out, well I mainly wanted to be wherever Xander was, if I was being truthful. Today was a day to go out. Len had picked me up and dropped me off at my appointment with Grace because with Sophia's new job she didn't have the flexibility to run me around as much.

It was weird but I'd actually looked forward to my last few appointments with Grace. They'd been quite different to "pre-Xander". We seemed to be past the "How do you feel about that?" questions. Now I had experiences to offer and I wanted to talk about them. Today I had a lot on my mind. I wanted to talk about the upcoming fight and how I was feeling.

As always, Grace was punctual as she welcomed me into her office. "And how's my favourite patient, today?" she asked as I took up my regular spot on the blue sofa.

I gave her a sideways look. "Favourite patient?"

"Yes. Hey, you're making me look good! Look at the amazing achievements you've made over the last couple of months. I think a lot has to do with a certain man in your life, but hey, I'll take a little credit. It's not like I can tell anyone anyway!"

I laughed at that. "Very true. It really must be a fairly thankless job you've got here."

She nodded. "At times, yes. But then I see how far someone like you has come and it makes up for every difficult patient. I can only hope that I can open their eyes enough so when whatever catalyst strikes a chord with them, they're in the right place to make positive changes."

"And don't ever think for a moment that the changes you've made in your life are all Xander. Sure he's given you the desire to change, but you had to be in a frame of mind that was open to considering, accepting and then implementing the change. Well done, you!" Grace sounded really proud of me and that actually felt good. She was a nice lady that I believe genuinely cared about her patients.

"So now I've given you all that praise, what do you want to talk about today? Anything worrying you?" Grace looked at me intently and I pushed my jaw from side to side thinking, trying to decide how to start the conversation. In the end I decided to just dive in and see where it went.

"I want to talk about Xander and the upcoming fight of his."

"Okay floor's yours, tell me what's bothering you."

I took a deep breath. "Grace, there's no easy way to say this without it sounding terrible." I watched her eyes narrow but she made no other move or comment. "Xander accidently killed a guy in his last fight and I don't know how I should feel about that." It was one of those "Holy shit!" statements, but so far, Grace was keeping it together. "This upcoming fight of his is also getting bigger than Ben Hur and I'm feeling kind of adrift about the whole thing."

"Well nothing's ever boring with you now. You've certainly jumped in at the deep end, Eden."

I nodded and couldn't agree more. "That's kind of how I feel now. I'm struggling to hold my head above water. Don't get me wrong; our relationship is great and I love him and he's told me he loves me, but all this fight stuff is putting me so far out of my depth."

"I can certainly understand that. Let's start with the first part. Xander accidently killed a man you say..." She paused for a second and frowned, then it was as if a light bulb had clicked on. "I think I remember reading about that somewhere. It was in a Championship Fight a few years back, wasn't it? Very big news for about a week, then it all simmered down."

"That's it."

She nodded. "You're going to have to explain to me what's bothering you. I think you've known about this for a while. So why the issue now?"

"Because the press started in on him about what happened and the questions they asked and stuff they wrote was just horrible and most of it really hurtful. So I went and watched the fight online. Xander had told me what happened, of course, but with the media storm,I figured I needed to know for myself what it was all about."

My throat started to close over and those pesky pricks behind the eyes started, it wouldn't be long before I'd need tissues. Grace nodded at the box on the table beside the crystal water pitcher.

"Oh Grace, it was devastating on so many levels. I watched it all. I saw Xander land that punch and that man die. I then saw the other fighter's pregnant wife beside herself in grief and finally I saw the emotions on Xander's face. But now I think about it, I think I'm actually feeling them. Is that weird?" I reached for a tissue and a sip of water. There had been no stopping the tears falling.

"So what are you feeling the most?"

Wasn't that the question? It almost felt as if I was mirroring his feelings. Was that possible?

"I feel such a strong sense of guilt and regret surrounding him. What happened was an accident, but it was terrible none the less. I can really see how Xander's resisted having another fight. How do you move past that?"

She nodded. "It's certainly an enormous burden to carry, but I think you already know the answer to the getting past question. One day at a time. You know this better than most people, Eden. Emotional healing takes a very long time and many people are never whole again. They're better and can function, but they're never as they were. How can they be? They've lived through something horrific and survived. It's about healing to the best of your ability, and in Xander's case without knowing him, I'd guess it's about forgiving himself as much as anything. He didn't do it intentionally."

I hadn't really thought about the forgiveness part. He'd spoken about fighting his demons and not being a fraud. But a big part of him achieving what he wanted to, was about him forgiving himself to start with.

"How does someone forgive? I mean people talk about forgiveness, but it just seems such an..." I struggled for the words. "I don't know..." I threw my hands up frustrated at searching for what I was trying to say.

"Ubiquitous and maybe over used term?"

"Yes! That's it."

"I get you. Eden, it's about letting go the hurt and the bad feelings. It's accepting what happened and the feeling that go with it. Then consciously deciding that you need to let it go. It's often easier to forgive someone else than yourself. Most people are their own toughest critics and judges."

I nodded and thought on that a little. "I'm starting to see that I think. I used to think everyone was pitying me and uncomfortable around me. Now I'm starting to realise I was projecting my own insecurities. Kind of a self-fulfilling prophecy. If you expect it to be bad, it is. I don't expect it to be so bad anymore and it doesn't seem to be as bad."

Grace smiled. "Exactly. But you need to be in a mental state where you can see the positive rather than the negative. You've got there now, that often takes time. So how do you feel about him fighting?"

How did I feel about that? I'd watched him punch The Cobra in the face on a video. One of those punches was fatal. I'd seen him train and spar.

"I guess I'm mostly okay with it. I don't fully understand it, but it's obviously something he's done all his life and has needed to do. I don't think it's for me to judge if it's right or wrong. It's not like he goes around picking fights. In fact, it seems to be the opposite. " I told her about what had happened at the bar a few weeks ago. "Why? What do you think?"

"It doesn't matter what I think. What's right for me as a person will be different for you. You need to decide if you can handle the life that comes with him—the fighting, the publicity. That's all for you to decide. It won't be easy, but then most relationships decisions aren't." Grace seemed to finish her comment with an off-handed shrug and I wondered who'd broken her heart.

"He wants me to go to Vegas with him. I want to go for him, but after seeing that video I'm scared. I'm scared for him and for me. Oh, who am I kidding. The whole thing terrifies me. Hell, I haven't even been on a plane since the fire. Let alone travelled to the other side of the world."

Grace chuckled a little. "Well Eden, the fear of flying and heading overseas is a very common fear. It's all new and unknown. That one we can work on. As for your fears around the fight, I can help you work through what you're feeling, but maybe you need to start by talking to him about those fears. You're in a relationship with him after all. Do you think he'd want you stewing on something that concerned both of you or talking to him about it? "

Grace was right. I was in a relationship with Xander and he was the one I needed to be talking to. I'd just resisted the urge because I didn't want to burden him with more before the fight, but maybe I was actually making it worse by not talking.

XANDER

I slammed my fists into the pads Reed was holding and imagined it was "Lights Out". Visualising my opponent and choreographing combinations I'd use were just one part of my training. Reed, Seth, Dane and I had watched hours upon hours of footage of Luke "Lights Out" O'Donnell's fights. We'd critiqued what we believed was every last aspect of his technique and Reed had adjusted my training accordingly.

The press was sniffing around everywhere, like the parasites they were. All week we'd been switching it up to throw them off. Some days I trained at home, then I'd pop into Onigashima. Other times I trained at a gym a few suburbs over. It was all designed to keep the press at bay at least for a little while.

I really wanted Onigashima to function as normally as possible, but unfortunately, that was just about impossible with all the press I was now attracting.

The combination I was working on was a high low type of

thing. Hit high, follow up with a low kick to the legs then a mid-section pommeling. Reed was calling a new combination when Eden's image caught my attention in the mirror and I screwed up the combination. I hadn't been expecting her, well more to the point dad and Eden probably hadn't been expecting me to train here today, but I'd wanted to train where I felt most comfortable and Friday was a quiet day for classes.

"What the hell, Xander?" Reed bellowed at me.

I ignored him and ran across the mats and popped a kiss on her lips quickly. She tasted like heaven and I'd like nothing more than to give her a huge hug but I had sweat running off me and I'm sure I smelt worse. "Hey, gorgeous. I wasn't expecting you just yet."

"Obviously! I wasn't expecting you either." Then she dropped her voice. "Reed looks really grumpy!"

"Yeah. I screwed up that combination because I spotted my girl." That got a coy little grin out of her.

"Well get over there. I don't want him yelling at me." She pushed at me to get going back across the mats.

"Okay, Gem." I smiled and dropped another quick kiss to her lips then trotted over to Reed. I watched her and dad who'd been grinning two steps behind head into my office.

"Unbelievable!" Reed growled. "I never thought you were the type to get distracted. I was wrong."

"Oh, for fucks sake! Give me a break. I haven't seen my girl in days. Let's get this done. I'm sick of looking at your ugly mug." He put up the pads and I went to work again pounding as hard as I could.

"Not sure it's a good idea bringing her to Vegas, Xan. You can't get distracted like that!" Reed was grunting between words from the impact of my hits.

"I'll be fine. She either goes or I stay at home!" I said it with as much steel in my voice as I could manage between controlling my breathing

Reed shook his head in annoyance. "I can only prepare you. You need to be in the moment. You've seen the footage. "Lights

Out" has been on a rampage lately. It's going to take all your concentration to take him down, man. Your head must be in the game. Physically you're stronger than ever, but mentally man?"

"You think I can't do it?" I felt my temper flare. Fuck him for doubting me.

"I think you can if you're fully in the game. But I'm not sure you are? You haven't had a fight in over three years. You're bound to have ring rust, every fighter coming back from that sort of lay off does."

I huffed out a breath. "Well, be sure. I'm there. I'm not doing this for fucking fun, ring rust or not." My temper was really starting to run wild and I slammed my fist emphasising every word. "What's your problem with Eden anyway?"

Reed didn't say anything just held the pads as I started to work his mid section with a flurry of fast kicks. My shin was numb from the impact on the pads. Good, I just went harder and faster.

"She's too soft to be a fighter's woman."

That pissed me off to the point of rage. He knew nothing, but was happy to judge. Somewhere I found another gear and seriously started to unleash. My arms and legs flew in a complete flurry. I channelled all my latent rage at Reed into smashing those pads. I could tell he was struggling to hold them up. Perfect. Prick deserved everything I was dishing out.

Eden was a fighter, too, just a different type. I wondered if Reed or I would have been brave enough to go downstairs into a fire to find her sister, if either of us had been in her place. That took some type of guts and love to do that. Eden was exactly the sort of person I wanted on my team—beside me, with me. Maybe Reed couldn't see it, but I knew what my girl was made of. Fuck, if I didn't have this fight coming up I'd deck the arsehole, but then if I didn't have this fight coming up Reed probably wouldn't be behaving like this.

My anger at Reed reached boiling point and I lashed out with a front jam. It was a hellishly powerful kick designed to drive your opponent way back. That's exactly what it did. Reed went back at least three paces and stumbled a bit.

I was done.

"Back the fuck of Eden or we'll have trouble, Reed. This is my last warning." His face registered surprise at the ferocity of my kick. "I'm done for the day." Reed could choke on it right now for all I cared.

I spun on my heel and stormed off to get a shower. As I passed the door to my office I saw dad give me a slight nod and right there I knew he'd witnessed the whole thing. Reed may think I was a dead shit but I knew dad was proud.

That would do me just fine.

TWENTY-FIVE

XANDER

The Saturday before I was due to leave for the USA, Onigashima officially became a mob scene. I'd trained in the morning with Reed and the tension was there between us, but we seemed to have come to some unspoken truce. I was training my arse off. No way was I going to give him a single thing to bitch at me about, but the Eden issue was still hanging between us and neither one of us was going to back down. Well, that was just fine with me.

Dane, Owen and Lincoln had planned a bit of an Onigashima send-off party with my students. Only problem was, somehow the media had got wind of it as well and were now crawling all over the place.

I'd gone in early to train and dad and Eden were coming in later. She'd stayed over last night. God, I'd needed her. Sure I needed to be over her, in her and all around her, but I'd also just needed to spend some quiet time with her to decompress and keep things in perspective. So far I'd been doing well at ignoring all the press. I was making daily Facebook, Instagram and Twitter posts as I agreed, but that was it. I wasn't responding to anything or even looking at my newsfeed, nor was I doing any other internet surfing. The only time I touched my phone was to take a call or respond to text messages. I couldn't buy into all the bullshit.

Seth and I were rolling around on the floor working on my ground game when Dane came through the front doors looking frazzled. Reed was using Seth mainly as my training partner for ground techniques because he was a couple of weight classes above me and had one hell of a ground game which came from his specialisation in Brazilian JuJitsu. Anyway you put it, Seth was a big unit to get through on the ground.

"It's a zoo out there." Dane not only looked a little frazzled, but sounded it as well.

"As long as it stays out there and doesn't interrupt my training," Reed snapped.

I tried to focus as Seth and I fought for a lock up and tap out.

"Well, everyone's going to be arriving in about thirty minutes and the carpark is full of press. What the hell do you want to do?" Dane demanded. He had a point. These sort of things could get out of hand really quickly and I didn't want any trouble with just about every one of my students turning up. The guys had pulled up the mats in the second training studio to create a party room. The caterers were around back now, setting up. I'd decided to make it easy and hire a mobile Asian noodle box company to cater.

Both Seth's and my concentration were slipping and Reed knew it. "Fuck! Cool down fellas. We're shot for anything else useful now."

Seth and I broke apart; neither one of us prepared to admit defeat. We were quite evenly matched despite the weight advantage Seth had over me. Dane glared at me expectantly as if to say "What the hell?"

"Okay, okay, I'll go talk to them. Maybe if I do that, they'll back off. Just give me a few minutes to stretch out." It wasn't likely, but worth a shot. He nodded, but looked about as convinced as I felt.

I stretched out then grabbed my towel from the side of the mat and towelled off the worst of the sweat between taking sips from my water bottle. I felt like facing the "pack" about as much as I wanted to sit through a root canal, but what other options were there?

"I'll come out with you," Reed said to me as he finished up some notes he'd made on my training session.

"Okay."

Together we walked to the door and Reed went through first, and I followed directly behind. The noise was almost deafening. Everyone was shouting and screaming my name. "Xander, tell us how the training's going." "Xander, is it true..." "Xander, what do you think..." Microphones were pushed into my face and cameras were clicking incessantly.

Reed put his fingers to his mouth and let out an ear splitting whistle; then he bellowed in his best drill sergeant voice, "Back up guys!" I knew it well. But it had the desired effect. The pack of fifty or so reporters and photographers all seemed to take a collective step back. They weren't exactly silent, but at least they were quieter now.

I moved to stand by Reed. "I figured you wanted to talk to me. How about I make you a deal?" That created a little bit of stir amongst them. "I'll answer questions for the next fifteen minutes, but then I need you to clear out of here. It's obviously not a secret because you're all here, but my students and I are having a private party. I'd appreciate if you allowed them to enter and exit safely."

There were some nods. I really didn't expect them to agree, but I could hope. Every word I said was being recorded and I wanted to make sure I came across as being responsible and looking out for my students, while still offering these vultures some level of access and respect.

I turned slightly to Reed, "Will you pick them out for questions?"

"Yeah," he growled. "Okay, let's get this done. Anyone with a question raise your hand and I'll pick you out one by one." I kept staring at the crowd, sizing them up.

"Okay, who's got the first question?" Just about every hand in the crowd shot up. "Lady in the blue blouse." Reed pointed to a red head about two back from the front. She looked like she was a TV reporter. Cameramen were clambering from all sorts of positions looking to get a clear view. Hell, a few were perched on the block wall that ran down the side of the building and along the carpark to the street. Another couple were on the industrial waste bin, in the property next door. I counted four standing on top of news trucks. It was quite ridiculous.

"Xander, how's the training going?"

Good an easy one to start with. "Great. Everything's on schedule and we're all very happy with my prep." Reed nodded emphasising the point. Even if my training was going like crap there was no way I'd be admitting to that.

"Bloke in the grey shirt."

"Xander, what tactics are you going to use to beat "Lights Out"?"

As if I was going to answer that one honestly! "Well, we've been watching a lot of film and we think we've got a game plan, just like I'm sure Luke has. It'll come down to who's fitter, and who wants it more."

I answered another three or four innocuous questions about training and my routine. As with all these sorts of things I tried to give them something but really said nothing.

"Bloke in the black cap."

"Xander, there's been a lot said about this fight already. What really made you come out of retirement now? Was it the money?"

I took a deep breath. So we were getting to the more "pointed" questions. "First of all, I was never officially retired. I was otherwise occupied getting Onigashima off the ground. Secondly, I've never fought because of the money. Sure it's nice and it's allowed me to do stuff like build this place and live a pretty good lifestyle for a guy my age, but it's not about the money; never has been. Never will be." I left it at that hoping he'd let it go.

"So what is it then?" The guy in the black cap piped up again.

"I fight because it's always been a part of me. Some people are born to run or play a musical instrument or draw or something. Me, I was born to fight. So that's what I'm doing. I love the challenge—pushing myself."

"What about the last fight." "How can you deal with the..." They were all talking at once again. Reed's shrill whistle split the air again.

"Pipe down or we walk inside and call the cops to have you all moved along. You're standing on private property and Xander is good enough to give you some of his time. Wait your turn," Reed ripped into them and they hushed down a little. "Tall guy over there." Reed pointed off to the left.

"Xander, how do you deal with knowing you killed a man? You've got a confidence problem. Isn't that the reason you really haven't got back in the cage?" I sucked in a breath and forced my expression to remain blank. That one cut close to the bone, but I was expecting it. It wasn't the first time that question had been levelled at me. If I was going to get these scavengers off my tail, then I was going to need to give them something more about the last fight.

"Knowing I killed a man is a burden I'll carry everyday for the rest of my life and I take that very seriously." A hush seemed to descend on the group. "But I can't let it prevent me from being everything I can be, otherwise two lives would have been lost that night. As for whether I have a confidence problem, I guess that's yet to be seen, but let me say this. I thought long and hard before I took this fight and never before have I ever been so committed to not just getting in the cage, but winning. That's all I can give you at the moment. You'll have your answer in a couple weeks."

Reed gave the nod to a woman in a cream suit. "Rumour has it you're carrying a shoulder injury. Is there any truth in that?"

I laughed at that and rolled both shoulders and threw a few jabs. "That one's news to me, folks, so unless you have a crystal ball or something... nope no injuries."

"Man up the back on the right." Reed gave him the nod.

"Xander your FaceBook status says you're in a relationship with Eden Sommers; care to elaborate on that?"

I knew there was no way they could leave my personal life alone. "Well, if you read it on FaceBook it must be true." I emphasised that with an eyebrow raise and pointed look. There were a few light chuckles around the crowd. "But in this case I can confirm that information is correct."

"How does she feel about you fighting?" someone asked.

"She's very supportive of what I'm doing."

"Why don't we ever see you together?"

"Eden is very busy with some other commitments at the moment. She'll be in Vegas with me when it counts." I didn't want to give them anything more than I absolutely had to; otherwise they'd hound her.

Reed was getting even more edgy beside me. He wanted the questions focused on the fight just like I did, but the vultures always wanted to pick over the juicy bits. I could see a few of my students starting to arrive and trying to figure out how to get through the crush of press.

"Final question people, then you need to move along," Reed called out in a very authoritative tone. He gave the nod to a wiry little man in the middle of the crowd.

"Is it true Eden has severe disfigurements from burns?"

Fuck me! How the hell did I answer that question?

I was in two minds should I answer it or not. It was one of those damned whatever way you went situations.

Reed snapped and made the decision for me. "Right that does it. You've got two minutes to vacate the premises before I call the cops."

I really hoped that would be the end of it, but somehow I doubted they'd let it go.

People sucked like that.

EDEN

The party looked to be in full swing by the time I arrived with Len. He seemed to be my shadow these days and it made me realise just how much I missed my own father. Over the last couple of months I think I'd managed to catch him twice between loads. He was working a gruelling schedule and was hell bent on earning as much money as possible to stash away before he retired in a few years. That was just another regret I had.

I'd really hoped a modelling career would have given me the opportunity to better provide for my family. Instead the fire had created more bills and meant that mum had dropped out of working for almost two years to help me with recovery. That put a dent in their finances. One day I'd like to be able to help out a little more. They didn't expect it, but I loved my family and I'd help if I ever could.

"Guess we're fashionably late, girl." Len followed me into Onigashima. I headed straight to Xander's office and popped my satchel in the bottom draw of his desk before I went to find Xander.

I suddenly felt really nervous. Xander was the guest of honour and I was his girlfriend. I'd met some of these people before, one on one over the last couple of months, but never as a big group.

"Well, let's not keep him waiting. He's been blowing up my phone wondering where we were."

"Sorry, Len. I just wanted to finish that review quiz." I felt guilty for holding him up. Since Xander had left this morning I'd been camped out at his new table studying. His stereo system was kick arse and I loved the isolation and vibe his barn apartment had. It was so peaceful but homey now it had been spruced up and I was enjoying studying there. It was kind of like being close to Xander even though he wasn't technically with me.

"No problem. You had important stuff to do just like he has." One thing I'd learned about Len was that he was very fair and practical. He was often gruff, but that was just him. He really had a big soft gooey centre. I walked over to join him at the door to the office. Len's gaze felt assessing as I moved across the space. "Relax Eden, you're amongst friends here." I nodded and knew he was right.

"I just want to make a good impression for Xander's sake."

Len chuckled. "Girl, you got no worries about that. Anyone that spends thirty seconds in your company knows you're top shelf, and don't let anyone tell you different."

I could feel my face grow warm as we headed to the second studio and the party. "Thanks, Len. That's very kind of you."

"I just speak the truth, Girl." He winked at me and we headed in.

The room must have had over a hundred people all milling around eating, drinking and boisterously talking. As to be expected, I found Xander in the middle of the room with a water bottle in his hand. He seemed to realise I was there before I even moved into the circle of people he was presiding over.

His hand reached out and pulled me to him and he dropped his lips to mine briefly in a light kiss. "Hey, gorgeous. I was wondering if you were going to stand me up!"

I grinned at him. "Nothing like that, just wanted to finish my practice quiz. Besides I'm sure you have lots of people that want to wish you well and spend a little time with you today."

He settled his arm around me and whispered in my ear. "True. But none I want to spend time with more than you!" My heart did a little pitter-patter flip-flop thing and I moved in a bit closer.

Sophia and Tori walked over to join us with Adelaide. "Hey Eden, glad to see you finally managed to drag yourself away from the books!" Sophia dug at me like only sisters can do.

"Exam week, Soph. I'm not intending to blow it now," I said a little defensively.

"Your boyfriend's about to go to Vegas and step into the cage with "Lights Out" and you're worried about exams?" She just shook her head at me and grinned at Xander.

"Hey, lay off your sister. She's got lots going on as well. We've got all this sorted between us. Her exams are really important." Xander said it casually, but there was no mistake he was one hundred percent behind what I was doing and that felt good. I'd made a commitment to get good grades. I wasn't about to change that because I now had a boyfriend who was far more of a celebrity than I first realised. I liked the fact we were a team now and he understood that I was committed to my own goals as well.

Not one to be easily swayed, Sophia continued on her path. "Well, don't let her get too buried in the books. Make sure she has some fun in Vegas."

"You can count on it. Once the fight's done Eden and I are going to have a good time for a week or two. I think we deserve it." I hadn't really thought past the fight. In fact, I was trying to keep my head firmly focused on the next couple of weeks and my exams. At this stage, I couldn't let all of Xander's hype affect what I was doing. Once my exams were done, then I was free from uni for about three months. I really needed to see if I could pick up some work. From time to time, I did a bit of virtual personal assistant stuff. I could do some more of that and maybe some web site administration, bookkeeping or that sort of thing. There were a few sites that I'd used in the past to get some casual work. I probably needed to let them know I'd be available in about a month.

A few moments later, Seth sauntered over. He was a rugged cocky sort of guy and I realised immediately who his target was given he spent at least half of his time with Xander at the moment. It certainly wasn't my boyfriend.

"Hey, everyone," he said brightly but I didn't miss that his eyes spoke mainly to Sophia. She glanced at him then turned back to us. Was she playing hard to get?

"So, where are you two going after the fight?"

I had no idea. Xander on the other hand brushed it off. "That's for me to know and for Eden to enjoy the surprise when the time comes."

Sophia squealed a little. “Oh, I’m so jealous. You’re so lucky, Eden.” I could tell her excitement was genuine.

“Why don’t you come on over Soph?” Seth suggested.

I could see Sophia’s eyes light up at the suggestion, then reality hit. “I’d love to but I have a new job and I can’t just blow it off.” Good. I was glad to see my little sister’s head was still planted firmly on her shoulders.

“There’ll be other times. Besides I need someone to let me know that everything is still running here as it should be.” Xander had organised for Linc and Owen to run the place in his absence, but I knew he was still nervous about not being around. Onigashima was his “baby” after all.

Another tall lanky guy approached our group and the first thing I noticed were the tats that covered both of his arms. Sure, a lot of the guys and a few of the girls here at Onigashima sported tats, but this guy had some serious sleeves. He had brown hair that was a little longer than most of the guys’ as well. The guys all tended to have really short styles. Whereas this guy’s hair looked like it had been purposely left messy for the day.

“Hey, just wanted to wish you all the best man.” The guy held his hand out for that weird handshake thing they did.

“Thanks, Jarryd,” Xander said with a nod and dropped his fist. “Hey, this is my girlfriend, Eden. Eden, meet Jarryd.” I held out my hand and he shook it gently. His eyes moved across to my face and I met them. I didn’t feel any discomfort. It was getting easier.

“Nice to meet you, Jarryd.”

“Likewise Eden.”

I felt his eyes subtly drifting over my scars and I figured this was very much due to Xander having talked to him about the possibility of putting some ink over them. I’d been giving it a lot of thought. I liked the idea, I just wasn’t sure what I wanted.

The guys talked about the fight for a bit longer. Sophia, Tori and Adelaide had drifted off and were talking to a couple of people on the other side of the room.

Xander leant over and whispered quietly, “Will you be okay for a second? I just need to check on something and I'll grab you a drink on the way back."

"Sure."

Seth and Xander walked off leaving me with Jarryd.

I wasn't sure whether Xander had planned this or not, but I decided to take the opportunity. "So what do you think?"

Jarryd looked at me thoughtfully and I could tell he knew exactly what I was talking about. "I'd need to see the rest of the scars. But if they're similar to those, I can't see any problem. I'm not sure you'd want decorative ink up your neck and on your face but cosmetic is certainly something to think about. Xander mentioned it's down your side. That'll hurt but I doubt you're any stranger to pain."

Wasn't that the truth in more ways than the obvious. "I may not be a stranger to pain, but I can't say I enjoy it all that much," I joked a little. Strangely I wasn't even completely freaked out about having someone else see my scars. Jarryd just had a very "comfortable" manner about him. I was certainly interested in what he'd mentioned about the cosmetic. I hadn't realised it was an option.

"Haven't met too many people that truly enjoy it," he said with a chuckle.

We stood in silence for a moment, but it felt surprisingly comfortable. Jarryd seemed to be one of those deep reflective types of people.

"Have you thought about what you might like?"

I shook my head no. "That's the problem. I like the idea of having something beautiful on me rather than the scars, but I don't know what I want."

He didn't say anything just nodded thoughtfully again. We talked for a few more minutes about a whole range of stuff. Jarryd was one of those quiet, easy people to be around. Then we both noticed Xander at the door to the studio talking to a few students over there. This seemed to prompt him into action.

"Why don't you let me draw a few things up? I've got a few ideas from talking to you and what Xander has told me." He made the offer casually, but I could tell he meant it.

"Thank you, that's very kind, but I don't want you to go to any trouble. What if I don't like them?"

He shrugged. "I'll have spent a little bit of time doing what I love to do—draw. I don't really see that as a hardship. You never know, you just might like what I have to show you..." There was a quiet confidence in his voice and his strange green eyes seemed very knowing.

"Okay," I agreed.

He passed me a business card. "Give me a call in a few days. I'll have something for you."

Xander moved up to me and passed me a bottle of juice. He looked between Jarryd and me. I knew he'd guessed at what we were discussing, but he said nothing.

If, and it was a big IF, I'd be making that decision.

TWENTY-SIX

EDEN

Another week zoomed past in a frenzied fashion. I'd managed maybe an hour this week with Xander; our joint schedules were just that busy. That hadn't stopped us from texting and messaging all the time though. As Xander had suggested I'd stayed off social media as more and more buzz and hype about the fight swirled around.

The impromptu press conference from last weekend seemed to have earned some favour with the press for Xander. They seemed to have been satisfied with the answers he gave them, but it had also left them hungry. Now they seemed to want to know everything. His profile was going nuts. The number of Facebook fans and Twitter followers he had was growing exponentially every day. He'd been posting once a day as he'd promised the PR people. Usually, it was just a pic snapped at training and a little message about how he was going or some sort of inspirational message.

I might not have been keeping tabs on social media, but Beth had been spending hours trawling through the web keeping tabs on everything. She said it was her duty as my best friend. I told her

I didn't want to know. It was safer that way. What I didn't know couldn't hurt me, could it? But it didn't seem to dissuade her. Beth had far too much time on her hands and nothing to do. Me, I just wanted to focus on my exams and enjoy today. I'd worked my arse off for the last few weeks, so I had a clear day today. It was the last full day I'd have with Xander before his six am flight tomorrow morning. Tomorrow, I'd be back at the books. Today we were going to make the most of it.

And so far the day was good.

Right now I had a view that I knew thousands of woman would probably pay excellent money for. I had a front row seat at a Xander Todd training session—the most private type. To avoid press and a whole heap of fuss we'd decided to stay in today. So training for him was in his home gym. He'd pulled a section of the sofa from in front of the flat screen around and I was sitting watching him. Yeah, not too much of a hardship really, I decided.

"So let me ask you this. How exactly did you manage to blow off Reed today? He's been stuck to you like glue for the last six weeks." I couldn't say Reed was my favourite person. I found him brusque and often rude. How he was married to a sweetheart like Carmen was one of those mysteries of the universe. One thing he was however, was protective of Xander and for that I could almost forgive his attitude towards me. If he got my guy to the cage in the best shape possible and helped keep him safe through the fight, then I could put up with it.

Xander was over on the mats skipping. He just had on a pair of those loose MMA shorts...oh my. I could feel my mouth starting to water and my body starting to tingle. The rope was slapping under his feet rhythmically, but somehow it didn't even appear as if he was doing anything else. Then he started to get a little fancy, doing a couple of rotations of the rope, hopping on one foot then repeating it on the other.

"Carmen told him to be home today or else don't bother coming home. She may not look it, but that woman can be scary fierce when she needs to be."

That made sense. "I dare say she has to be with Reed. The guy is a serious hard arse."

"Yeah, he is. He's the sort that thinks there's only one way—his. Mostly he's right, but times change and so do people." It was disgusting, he'd been skipping for near on fifteen minutes and he wasn't even breathing heavily.

"How long can you do that for?"

"What skip?"

I nodded.

"I don't know, as long as I need to I guess." Then as if to prove a point he started to do some fancy steps with the rope and crossed his hands over with an expertise that was mind-boggling. Yeah, he'd done this once or twice before! His tempo was getting faster and faster, until the rope was no longer visible—just a sensation breaking the air. His feet flew, but barely looked like they were touching the floor.

"Wouldn't be showing off by any chance, would you?" I teased.

"Not at all..." he said straight-faced.

"Because if you are, it's working." I ended on a suggestive giggle. What woman wouldn't be getting turned on watching her incredibly fit and sexy boyfriend put on a private show for her benefit?

"Good to know!"

He twirled his rope for a few more minutes and kept sending me suggestive little looks. Yeah, he was watching me squirm. I was onto his game.

Finally he stopped and put the rope aside then dropped to the mats and started to do push ups. But not just ordinary push-ups—the one handed type. He made it look so easy it was disgusting.

"How can you be so damned fit?"

He laughed but never broke his form. "And I thought you'd been paying attention for the last six weeks."

"You know what I mean."

"Come over here, Gem," he called. I got up from the sofa, a little wary. What was he up to?

Then he lowered his body to the mats, till he was flat. “Want to help me out, gorgeous?”

“Sure...” I wondered what he was up to with this little game.

Xander read my caution but went on. “Won’t hurt, I promise. Lay down on my back very still.”

I got down on the mats beside him glad that I’d pulled on yoga pants and a T-Shirt if I was going to have to do something other than watch.

I hesitated, not quite sure. “Come on, Gem. Hop on my back.” That was all the prodding it took. I stepped over him, and faced his feet. I sat down over his butt and lay back, shoulder to shoulder.

“Okay, good. Now put your legs on top of mine and relax. I’m the one doing all the work here. Count em for me, Gem.”

I did as he asked and then suddenly, we were rising up and then lowering down.

“One.” Every muscle in his body was rock hard under me. “Two.”

What sort of strength did it take to be able to do this? “Three.”

Up this close and personal, I could smell that spicy cologne he wore with the light smell of sweat mixed in. It was a big turn on for me. “Four.”

I wondered how many he’d do. He passed ten and kept going, his breathing was more laboured now, but the movement no less perfect. “Eighteen.”

“Two more,” he gritted out as he completed the set.

Rather than collapse to the floor like most people did on their last rep of a set, Xander lowered agonisingly slowly and I could only imagine the burn he must be feeling in his muscles.

“Twenty...Good job,” I added for good measure. It was what Reed often said to him after he’d finished an exercise or a set of something.

He rolled me off and I ended up on the mats looking up at him. “So you’ve decided to take over as my trainer for the day?”

“I was just sitting over there minding my own business. You were the one that asked me for help,” I reminded him.

"Right. Just sitting over there...not checking me out at all." He dropped a kiss on the end of my nose.

"Well, I might have been. But I thought that was one of the fringe benefits of being your girlfriend."

"Sounds fair. You up for another exercise?" There was a mischievous look in his eyes.

"Maybe."

He rolled to his back and tucked his knees towards his chest with the bottoms of his feet upwards. Then he held out his hands.

"Okay. You'll need to do a bit of work for this one, Gem. So you need to keep your body taut and rest your hips on the soles of my feet. Take my hands and kind of roll forward over me. Then you need to raise your legs up so our point of balance is your hips. Once you're stable, I'm going to raise you up and down."

"Sounds complicated; are you sure it's safe?" I looked at him sceptically and was rewarded with a head roll that might as well have said, "Woman!"

"Na, it's a cinch."

I did as he asked and rolled forwarded onto the soles of his feet.

The grip he had on my hands was firm and I glanced at our entwined fingers. His wrists were so much bigger than mine. At least double the size and every tendon and muscle was tight, supporting my weight. He grinned up at me.

"You ready?"

"Yeah." I braced my body like he'd said and slowly he pushed me up then lowered me down.

"Let's go for ten first up."

First up! I thought. He was the fit one in this relationship, not me!

Up and down we went. The muscles of my tummy, butt and thighs were on fire holding my position.

"One more." He grinned up at me. It appeared to be no effort at all for him.

I gritted my teeth hard as my muscles screamed.

"Ten," he called as he helped me back to terra firma.

My breath was coming fast and I couldn't believe how hard that had been for something that seemed so innocuous.

He grinned knowingly and I poked at his rock hard abs in protest.

"I don't recall seeing Reed doing any of that stuff. He just holds the pads and barks at you."

"Gem, I'm not big on having anyone but you laying along my back. Nor would I want to be looking at Reed's ugly mug or having him balance on my feet. That was a little exercise improvisation."

"Well, consider me exercised," I said plopping down on the sofa again.

"Yeah, have a little rest then you can hold the pads for me."

"What? I've seen how hard you hit those pads. No way can I hang onto them with you pounding away." I realised what I said and my hand flew to my mouth.

He chuckled and that wicked grin was back. "Oh, I don't know. You've seemed to hold up pretty well to the poundings I've given you. In fact, I was under the impression you really enjoyed them."

"Get back to work, Pretty Boy. You're in training." I used my best sergeant major voice and pointed at the mats.

Xander just laughed and grabbed a large kettle bell from the rack. He then started to do a line of walking lunges with the bell in a reverse grip in the centre of his chest. It was an exercise I hadn't seen him do before. It didn't look too difficult but I could see the strain all of his muscles were under as he took each deep step.

"Is that really hard to do?" I called out curiously.

"Grab the small kettle bell and give it a go if you want to know the answer."

Okay, I was feeling a little adventurous.

I walked over to the rack and picked up the smallest kettle bell, which was eight kilos. I took a reverse grip like I saw Xander was doing and I started to try and copy. Immediately, I knew I was in trouble. Every single muscle in my body started to scream.

"The trick is to keep the kettle bell centred in the middle of your body and keep your shoulders back. Posture is everything.

This exercise is as much for the core as anything else. It's also brilliant for developing and stretching muscles in your hips which is exactly what you need for range of motion in kicks."

I grunted out a few more steps, then stopped. My butt was on fire, my thighs were burning and my sides were searing. Okay, now I understood. I caught my breath and promptly replaced the weight in the rack.

"Giving up so soon?"

"Yep. For some reason I think I just started at expert level."

Xander had the hide to laugh! "Yeah, you did. To do this exercise right you need to start with split squats first then work up. It looks easy, but there's a hell of a lot of muscle groups and balance involved. It can take months to build the strength to do it correctly if you've never done it before."

I watched him do another half a dozen runs of the floor. By this stage the sweat was running off him. Then he grabbed two large dumbells and dropped to the mats in a pushup position with a dumbbell in each hand, only his feet were slightly further apart. He then pulled up his right hand till it was level with his chest and lowered it. Then he did the same with his left.

Every single muscle in his back and arms were rippling with the exertion and his butt and thighs were so tight, I could have bounced coins off them. When he had done this thirty times he stopped and then started a series of burpees. Three times he repeated the process and eventually he stopped as his chest and abdomen heaved with the strain of the exercise.

Oh, it was good to be me today and I silently cheered. As soon as he was finished I decided then and there I had another workout for him to complete. This one I hoped he'd be really keen on.

"What was that? That looked seriously difficult but hellishly sexy." I gave him my best sultry look. I have no idea if it was convincing or not but we were both in playful moods it seemed.

"Those were renegade rows and they seriously kill but are amazing for core and just about every other muscle in your body, plus they're a huge cardiovascular exercise. I'm sure you've seen burpees before."

I nodded listening to what he was saying, but seriously getting more and more turned on each second.

"I've got a few more things to do. Why don't you go and hit that heavy bag for a bit. There's some gloves over there then I'd like to work on a few more of your self defence moves. We haven't done much training the last couple of weeks and I feel like I've been neglecting you."

"Do I have to?" I whined and gave him my best puppy dog face.

"Get that delectable arse over to those bags now. If I'm sweating you can, too," he barked in his best Sensei voice. The only thing that gave him away was the twinkle in his eye. His tone alone sent shivers of the best kind down my back.

I picked up some gloves and got to work.

"Keep your wrists firmer as you connect," he called out from where he was going through a series of complicated shadow boxing moves in front of the large mirrors on the wall. Our eyes connected in the mirror as he moved around.

"How am I supposed to concentrate with you doing that?" I whined.

"I don't remember you being so vocal at the start. What's going on?" His top lipped curled a little. He knew exactly what was going on. I wanted him and he was torturing me.

"Fine. I'll just say it then. You've been tormenting me for the best part of two hours. I'm horny. You need to do something about it." I threw the gloves on the rack and stood there glaring at him with my hands on my hips.

He looked at me for a long while and I started to get a little uneasy with my declaration. Then he strode across the mats and grabbed my hand and pulled me into the middle of the mats where he dropped my hand and turned to look at me.

"I think it's time for a little grappling and throws training."

That sounded good, but I did have one surprise I wanted to try. Len had shown me a throw the other day...I wondered if I could pull it off.

Rather than waiting for Xander to deliver his next instruction, I stepped forward into him, but a little to the side. I took my right hand and placed it on his cheek and wrapped my left hand around his bicep just above the elbow. Then I dropped a teasing kiss to his lips. As soon as I knew I'd diverted his attention, I struck!

I pushed down on his elbow and slipped the hand on his cheek to his shoulder, while getting him slightly off balance and onto my right hip. Then it was just a matter of stepping through and taking out his leg. His body went crashing to the mats. Only problem was I was following him down. This wasn't supposed to happen! I was supposed to remain on my feet with control of his arm.

We ended up on the mats in a heap, Xander on the bottom grinning at me with mischief. His legs came up and wrapped around me locking me tight to his body I was at his mercy.

"Not quite what you had in mind, Gem?"

"Mmm, not quite."

"I'm hardly a fair opponent, particularly when I've got something in mind." He reached up and brushed the loose hair that had fallen out of my ponytail back from my face.

"You could have at least let me think I had it right."

"Oh, you had it right, Gem. I just didn't want you still on your feet while I was down here. I wanted you right where you are...over me." He wriggled his hips a little but never broke the lock of his legs around me. There was no mistaking he was fully aroused.

"So now you've got me where you want me. What are you going to do? Talk me into submission?" I said with a whole heap of newly found cheek.

That comment made his eyes flare and a little grin rip at his full lips.

"Nope..." Before he'd even got the word out, we were rolling and I found myself under him again. My first thought was I wanted to learn those moves, but that was short lived as his mouth came down on mine, hungry for my undivided attention. His lips moved urgently on mine and his tongue slashed across and demanded entry to plunder my mouth.

I was feeling needy before, but within about three seconds I'd moved right past needy to full on hungry and, if the way Xander was attacking my mouth was any indication, he was right there with me.

He raised his head a little as if assessing where he was going to attack next. His eyes had that dark wanting bubbling in them that I was now so accustomed to seeing.

"Have you finished training?" my words came out as breathy little whispers.

"Yeah, training's done but I think this work out needs a different type of finish." His hands came to my hips and were pulling at my yoga pants and underwear.

"Xander, anyone could walk in," I reminded him, suddenly a little anxious. His hands stilled for a moment.

"We're fine. Barn's closed to invitation only today. Front gate's locked. Stop worrying. I've wanted to take you here since that first night I brought you home. Let me have this, Eden."

His voice was demanding, but still held a hint of need that was oh so sexy. How could I resist that? He finished pushing my pants down and off.

"Okay." I reached up and kissed his neck, as I caught my fingers in the waistband of his shorts and underwear then pushed them down together. When I could no longer reach with my arms I hooked my toes in to the band and finished the job.

He grinned down at me. "I knew there were benefits to having a girlfriend that had legs that go on forever, wrap them around me Gem and lock them. I want to feel your thighs squeezing me tight."

"Don't you ever get sick of rolling around on these mats, Xander?" I joked as I did as he'd asked.

"Never with you, Gem. Let's get to the good part." He thrust into me hard. It was exactly what I wanted and he knew it. I couldn't help but let out a long low moan. I loved having him inside me.

"Yeah, exactly that Gem...Fuck that feels good," he said on a ragged growl, shaking his head and sucking in air through his teeth. "Woman, you push me to the edge so quick—each time, every time."

He set up a slow rhythm with deep strokes that hit every single sensitive spot, then some; my fingers gripped tight to his butt pulling him into me. I wanted to feel every last ounce of pleasure and sensation he could give me. It was more of the torturous slow build we'd been dancing around for the last couple of hours. Wonderful, but I wanted more and needed to feel the race to the end. I pushed at his shoulders and he sat up to his knees grabbing my hips tight to him to keep me locked around his hard cock.

"Something you wanted?" He raised his eyebrows in question.

"Yeah, you deep and hard." My voice sounded low and raspy.

He held tight to my hips and thrust hard. "Like that?"

"Like that." I wriggled my spine and shoulders trying to get even closer.

"Hold for a second, sweet thing." I went to protest but he cut me off as he leant forward for a kiss. "Let's get this shirt off you. I want your breasts."

His hands had the shirt over my head and they were undoing the clasp on my bra before I could form words. He dragged the straps down my arms and flicked it to the side, then he locked his lips around my right nipple. Oh, so good. The sensation shot straight to my feminine centre and I felt myself clench tight around him.

He pulled his head back and he looked liked he'd been scorched. "Woman, you make it damned difficult not to come."

"Isn't that the point?" I asked innocently and wriggled letting him know I wanted him to move.

"Ahhh! It is but not so soon. I want this to last," he gritted out as I rocked my hips, enjoying the feeling of being so full of him and teasing him.

"We can always do it again, you know."

It was as if the idea hadn't occurred to him until then. His hips sprang into action and he thrust deeply, every stroke pulling me closer to the edge. He raised his body up and pulled me with him. I wrapped my arms around his shoulders and held tight.

"Take what you want, baby," he growled out in a low whisper against my ear.

That was my cue and I didn't miss it. I rocked my hips hard against him to catch every single spot that brought us both pleasure.

I threw my head back and he nipped at my neck, then licked up to my ear. The soft tickling sensations mixed with the hard rhythmic build of my hips moving on his solid length. Everything seemed to be moving around me as I climbed higher pulling Xander with me.

"Oh. I'm so close," I stuttered out between breaths and thrusts.

"Yeah Gem, just there." He growled again biting down on my earlobe.

The world went fuzzy as the sensations flooded through me and we jerked and thrashed while clinging to each other. We toppled back and landed on the mats with Xander on the bottom once again. I lay on his heaving chest, not caring about the sweat that we were sharing between us. I could hear the rapid beating of his heart, then it slowing as he brushed the hair from my face.

We lay there for a few minutes, neither of us saying anything nor needing to—just experiencing the connection of being together and sharing. Neither of us had spoken of him leaving tomorrow. It was almost as if we didn't talk about it, it wouldn't be true. It was only going to be for a week, but for some reason it seemed to feel much longer.

"Want a shower?"

Mmm tempting, but I wasn't sure. "What did you have in mind?"

"Today, I'm prepared to make an exception. Lukewarm it is, but you'll have to keep me warm if I start to get cold," he joked.

"Sook, my big bad fighter boy doesn't like cold showers." I ran my hands down his ribs tickling him. He bucked underneath me and caught my hands. "I suppose I could be enticed to keep you warm if it's that much of a problem." I huffed making it sound like far more of an issue than it was. No way would I pass up the opportunity to be naked next to Xander.

"I've got a big fight in a couple of weeks, Gem. I need to keep my muscles loose and limber. Can't have them freezing up." He popped a little kiss on my lips punctuating his words.

"I thought ice therapy was good for muscle recovery?"

He shook his head in mock annoyance. "This is what I get for having a brainiac for a girlfriend?"

"All part of the package." I shrugged.

"Ice therapy is great for muscle recovery, but didn't say I liked it. My dick doesn't either." He gave me a look that was all suggestion.

I giggled. "Well in that case ice therapy is off the menu for today."

"Good plan. No cold water. I've got serious plans for my dick today."

"You can partake in ice therapy as much as you want once you get to Vegas."

"If it was up to me—never. I think Reed and my physio have other ideas though."

My brain started to switch gears. As much as part of me tried to ignore it, he was heading off tomorrow. Sure we'd only be apart for about ten days, but why did it seem like forever?

"I know Gem, I feel the same," he said quietly, stroking his hands down my shoulders and back.

I looked down into his eyes and could see what I was feeling reflected in his obsidian depths.

"I know it's only about ten days but it just seems so long. I know we're both going to be stupidly busy but still..."

He nodded his head. "Reality and how we feel don't seem to be meshing at the moment. I wish you could come with me, but you need to get these exams done. You can't blow off all you've worked for. I'd feel awful about that."

I nodded and I knew he was right. "Okay. Then I guess we'll just need to double our texting and messaging for the next ten days until we can do this again." I tried to sound light and breezy.

"We will." He was back to being positive. "I guess it's just kind of hitting me how much I'm going to miss you and it's sort of surprising the hell out of me, but in a good way."

My heart squeezed tight. There was something about being loved and needed by Xander that just touched me in the deepest of ways.

"We're a hopeless pair because I feel the same. Normally I don't mind studying, but at the moment it's really bugging me. I just want to spend time with you. I know that isn't practical all the time but that doesn't make how I feel change any."

"I know. What a pair we are?" We both laughed and rolled around a little more.

TWENTY-SEVEN

EDEN

Just one more exam. 'Today was it,' I told myself as I looked at my notes one last time before Len dropped me off at my mid-morning exam. I was ready—I had this one in the bag. My mind drifted from accounting principles to Xander.

As soon as this exam was done I was going to relax, then pack the last few things I needed and Len and I would be off to the airport to take a midnight flight to the US. It was all happening so fast and slow at the same time, if that made sense.

I wondered if Xander would still be up by the time I finished the exam. I'd spoken to him earlier and I really wanted to chat to him later when I was finally done, but with the time difference, he should be asleep.

He'd said he was well, just fighting jet lag a bit and starting to really cut on his diet. The hype over there was pretty full on, apparently and he'd said getting to and from the training facility from the hotel was harder and harder each day.

I thought back to the morning he left. It really had flown by, even though it didn't seem like it would then. His time to leave had rolled around all too quickly and I'd bid Xander a teary goodbye. It was a little easier today, but that was because we were only just over a day away from seeing each other again. I knew as soon as I was done with exams and as I let my mind focus on him again, my stomach would start doing its little happy dance.

He'd left for the airport just after three in the morning to make his six am flight. We'd spent what there was of the night wrapped in each other's arms. More than once I'd suggested he should sleep.

I doubt he'd done more than nap before waking me to snuggle and make slow tender love. He kept saying it would be good to be tired because then he might have a better chance of sleeping away most of the twenty hours travel time it took him to get to the USA.

Len had driven him to the airport and I had tried to go back to sleep. We'd all decided it would be better if I was at home as the paparazzi were bound to be out in force.

It was ridiculous really when I thought about it. We'd be back together again in just over a day. If this was what love felt like then it sucked at times. I tossed and turned all the while hugging his pillow to me.

Finally, I couldn't stand it any longer and I got up and started studying. I'd needed to do something productive. I'd used that same approach to survive the last ten days. I'd never been better prepared for exams.

There was a sharp rap at the front door and I quickly gathered my things. Len was right on time as always.

"Morning, Eden. All set?" he asked as he guided me to his truck.

"Hey, Len. Yeah. I guess I'm as ready as I'll ever be."

"You'll do fine, girl. I've never seen anyone study harder." There was admiration in his voice and that felt good.

"I have up until recently, because it was all I had in my life," I admitted a little shyly.

"That may be the case, but even though your life is a lot fuller now, you haven't lost your focus on your studies. That's a job well done," he said as he pulled from the curb.

"Len, you always say the nicest things."

He gave me one of his slow grins. "Just speaking the truth, Girl."

It was time to change the subject. "I spoke to Xander before."

Len nodded. "Figured you would have; that's why I didn't bother calling him."

"He says he's well, just fighting a bit of jetlag at the moment. He also said something about really starting to cut now."

"Yeah, he will be. By the time we get there you'll get to see him in the worst kind of mood," Len warned with a little chuckle. "Glad you're the one sharing a room with him and not me. Although he might be more even-tempered with you around."

"What do you mean?"

"He's going to be on a really strict diet, low carbs, and heaps of cardio work to strip the last of the weight off him. He's going to be like a bear with a sore head. That boy loves to eat," Len said with a chuckle.

"He said something about that. He showed me a photo at his last weigh-in as well. I hardly recognised him. Thanks for the heads up."

"Oh, my pleasure. I'll let you take care of his every wish and command this time round."

I burst out laughing. "Stop trying to wind me up, Len. There's no way Xander could be that bad."

"Don't say I didn't warn you, Eden. I'll remind you of this conversation next week when he's snapping your head off."

It didn't sound like Xander at all, but regardless it was only for a few days. I could cop a few ordinary days. I knew what it was like to be uncomfortable and irritable. I'd had months of it.

We pulled up outside the Uni a few minutes later.

"Good luck," Len called as I went to get out. "I'll pick you up in three hours, right? I won't be far anyway, I've got a few last minute errands to run before we leave tonight."

"Yep, that's it. I'll text you if I finish early and no I won't leave the building until I see you pull up." I added that bit before he had a chance to.

"Make sure you do. All looks good." Len said as he finished surveying the area. He was looking for any stray paparazzi. There hadn't been any around since Xander left for the US, which was a bit of a relief, but Len wasn't taking any chances.

"Thanks again," I called as I got out and headed to the exam hall. I was a little early, but that was my plan. I wanted to be at the head of the cue to get my favourite seat. I pulled my summarised notes out of my satchel and ran through them one last time.

A couple of minutes later a few other people started to arrive and a couple said hello. I murmured hello back but dropped my head back to my notes. Today wasn't the day I was going to start making new friends. I just wanted to get this exam done and head out.

Finally, the doors to the exam hall opened at a quarter to ten. I moved to the table that the exam attendants were sitting at and gave my name so I could have it marked off on the roll and, in return, the woman handed me a big yellow envelope with my name on it. "Do Not Open Until Instructed" was printed in large text across the front. I moved quickly to my favourite seat—back row, far right.

I placed my water bottle and a couple of pens in front of me, then pushed my satchel under the desk. All around me the scrap of metal chairs on hard flooring and smashing of table legs and chair rang out. There was a quiet din as everyone took their seats.

At exactly ten the person overseeing the exam stood at the front of the room and instructed us that all mobile phones and devices had to be turned off and stowed out of sight in our bags. Nearly everyone had done that. None of us were completely new to the rules. Then we were advised the three hours allocated time was starting now and to open the envelopes.

I opened my envelope and pulled out the contents. On top was the answer page. There were one hundred multiple choice questions. Underneath that was the question booklet. I opened it up and my stomach dropped and my hand flew to my face.

Tears pricked my eyes and I reached for my water bottle to take a sip before my throat closed right up. I couldn't believe what I was seeing.

I leafed through the pages. They were screen shots of social media sites and my scarred face was front and centre in each one. Right there. I couldn't have looked worse. How could this happen? My eyes couldn't help but read the comments below the photos.

"Can you believe he's seeing this freak???"

"She must be amazing in bed to make up for that face."

Then someone had put underneath

"All cats look grey at night. Hehehe!"

"Dump her Pretty Boy. I'll fuck you so good."

"No wonder we haven't seen her before now. Who'd want to take her out in public?"

The more I read, the more the tears started to fall. I wiped my sleeve angrily across my eyes. Who had I been kidding? How could I really do this? I dropped my head and tried to shut it all out.

What should I do? What should I do?

Should I call the exam overseer or should I just get on with it? I had an exam to do after all.

Rage and equal parts hurt, burned through me.

Then I realised something. Previously I would have wanted to flee and hide. Not anymore. This time I was angry.

I wanted to fight. Fuck them!

I wasn't doing anything wrong here. This was on them. Not me.

I could do this. To fail or hide would let them win.

This time I was winning.

With shaking hands I turned the offending pages face down and pushed them to the left of my desk. I tried to focus on the questions and do what I was here for. I knew I could answer every question correctly. I'd studied until this stuff was second nature. I'd done the hard work. I wouldn't let them beat me.

The words blurred in front of my eyes as I tried to read the questions; emotions ripped through me. All the while I thought about what I'd seen and read. Who would do this to me? I kept playing it over in my mind? Why would anyone be so hurtful? How could people do this? Had this been going on the whole time? Surely, Beth would have told me?

Then I started to think this through a little more as I answered the questions on autopilot. How had those pages gotten into the envelope? They had to know me. Who would do this?

I snuck a glance out from under my eyelashes, everybody seemed to have their head down. Well, someone was guilty. I kept at the questions, going with my first instinct—today, I wasn't going to second guess myself. Whatever I thought was the right answer was going down on the page.

What did they have to gain from this? Who were they anyway? I ticked off a few more questions and I was about to start on the last twenty five when I felt the sensation of eyes on me. There was no one behind me or to my right.

I glanced up from my pages but didn't turn my head—only my eyes. It was a skill I'd become incredibly proficient at over the last few years.

And there I had my answer. Half a dozen seats down and in the row in front was Cindy and the look on her face told me everything I needed to know. I may not know all the details about this yet, but she was certainly involved. I was that good at reading faces. I'd been hurt by so many.

I flew through the last twenty five questions—my mind whirring with everything, but the exam. I closed the exam booklet and didn't even bother to review my answers. I glanced at my watch. A little over an hour and a half. I put my hand up and an exam supervisor came over to me.

"I've finished." I passed my exam papers over to a woman who looked like a librarian that had swallowed a tart lemon; the expression on her face was that pinched. She glanced down and noticed the other pages on my desk.

"What are these?" she motioned down in an accusing whisper.

Exactly what the hell were these? I picked them up and passed them to her. She looked at them and a few seconds later shock settled over her face. She motioned for me to join her outside the exam hall and signalled to the other exam supervisor that she was leaving the room.

"How did these get into the room?" she said with a little too much attitude in her tone. I mean really, why would I bring something like that into an exam? I wasn't the perpetrator here. I was the victim but I'd be damned if I was going to act like it any more.

"Excellent question. I opened the envelope and those pages were in the question booklet. I'd like an explanation as to how that happened."

That seemed to set her back. "Why didn't you say something earlier?"

"I came here to do an exam. I've taken it. Now you need to deal with this. How did this happen?" I demanded.

"I can't explain it, but I will lodge an official incident report."

"You're damned right you will and I want a copy of those before I leave."

The woman hurried off and came back with a form and a copy of the pages. I filled out the form and she notarised the bits she needed to.

"I'll submit this immediately."

"You do that. I don't think I need to mention to you that this is bullying and victimisation. I thought this university had a nil tolerance policy for such. The university had better get to the bottom of this or I'll be considering my options."

She nodded her understanding and hurried away. My phone beeped with a text from Len letting me know he was outside. I'd text him while I was waiting for the woman to document the incident.

I strode from the exam hall and down to the front where Len was waiting for me. I got in the truck and pulled the door closed with a little more force than was probably necessary. Rage still burned through me. How dare people try to screw with me like this? But what did I do about it?

Len looked at me with questions in his eyes. “What happened? Did you blow the exam?”

“I didn’t blow the exam,” I seethed. The more I thought about it the crankier I got.

“Well then, what the hell’s wrong, Girl? I’ve never seen you pissed like this.” I didn’t answer just pulled the pages from my satchel and handed them to him.

He popped his reading glasses on and scanned through them while I gritted my teeth.

Len said nothing, but he got a twitch in his jaw that I’d seen on Xander a couple of times. He put the pages on the console between us then took off his glasses and tightened his hands on the wheel. He was just as pissed as I was.

Finally he spoke. “You got some work out gear at Onigashima?”

“Yep. I do.”

“Let’s go. We’ve got a date with some bags. We’ll work out the mad, then figure out what to do.”

“Sounds good,” I agreed.

•••

As my gloved fists smacked into the bags I realised what Xander had been feeling that day down in the barn. This is what it felt like to work your demons out on the bags. The physicality and burn felt good. It fed the rage, but exhausted it at the same time.

Each hit was a punch to everyone that had doubted me or been unkind. I didn’t ask to be the way I was. This was the badge I wore because I’d survived. I’d toughed it out and made it through not only the fire but the years of rehab.

Screw them all.

Now they were pissed at me because I dared step above some imaginary line or that was the way it seemed. They were jealous because me—scarred Eden, was with Xander the "Pretty Boy." Some people sucked so badly. I thumped the bags harder. My hands were numb, but I didn't care.

Len was beside me doing exactly the same. It was as if we were in some unannounced fight with everyone else. I laughed inwardly at the change in my life. Before, if this had happened someone would have wrapped me in a hug and cooed words of encouragement and I'd have hidden away and not come out for weeks until I'd worked up the courage again.

The thought of Len doing anything like that was laughable. He'd dealt with it the only way he'd known how. He'd thrown me a set of gloves and told me to get to it and he was right there with me smashing bags as well. Now I was facing my demons in a whole different way. A way that actually felt productive.

I didn't last as long as Xander had that night. After fifteen minutes, I couldn't keep going. And the last few had been a serious effort. I pulled off the gloves and walked over to the bench seat that ran the length of the room. Len joined me shortly after, thoughtfully grabbing a couple of bottles of water for us.

We sat in silence for a few minutes sipping at the water and getting our breaths back. Well, I was getting my breath back. Len seemed to be in really good condition for an older guy. He looked like he was deep in thought, but he was still fresh.

"So you want to tell me what happened now?" he asked after a while.

There was no escaping it. "Yep. I do," I said and went on to tell him the whole thing including my suspicions about Cindy and how I'd submitted the incident for investigation. My temper was still boiling.

"I just don't get why people need to be so damned horrible, Len," I finished.

"One of life's mysteries for sure. In my experience they're

generally the type that feel entitled and instead of respecting hard work and dedication, they get a kick out of trying to bring other people down. Not worth knowing or wasting energy on." There was an edge to his voice and we were both a lot calmer but still pissed about the whole thing. "Don't let 'em worry you, Girl. You're so much better than that."

"Thanks, Len. For the first time since the fire I actually feel angry at being treated like this. I don't deserve it and I'm not going away. It's their problem not mine. I've done nothing wrong except dare to be with a guy that they think is above me, apparently."

"You're probably right, but pay them no mind. I raised my boy to think for himself and make his own mind up. He sees a hell of a lot more than a few scars when he sees you. Pity the rest of 'em haven't taken the time to look as well." Len was defending me and complimenting me all at the same time.

"Thanks, Len, your support means a lot to me." I gave him a shoulder bump, which earned me a wry grin. Len wasn't really the hugging type.

"So what are you going to do about it?" he looked at me and asked.

"I don't know. I doubt this will be the end of it. I'm guessing they're looking for me to crawl back into my hole and not come out. It feels like they want me to run, but not this time. I'm not going to do that. We're happy in our relationship; I'm not going to let these people undermine it." I let out a huge sigh. "I really have no idea what they hope to achieve. Do you have any ideas?"

He thought on that for a minute. "Well, haters will always be haters, so there's probably some of that. It's also crossed my mind that this is some sort of stunt to get Alexander off his game. But I am very glad that you're not going to back down. I knew you were made of tough stuff the morning I met you."

"Thanks for the vote of confidence. I wondered whether this was some sort of stunt against Xander. Do you think it is?" That concerned me. I didn't want his attention distracted from the fight.

"I don't know. The internet isn't really my thing. I know how to do my computer banking and check my emails and find stuff, but as for that social media crap. No idea. But that doesn't mean I don't know people that are real good at it." A little twinkle came into his eye and I got the feeling Len had a plan coming together in his head.

"I haven't been into it really either since the fire." He nodded in silent understanding and was silent for a bit longer.

Eventually I couldn't stand it any longer. "What are you cooking up, Len?"

"I'm going to call a buddy of mine. But we're not going to do anything different, Girl. We'll head out tonight as planned."

"Okay. I'm not sure whether I should tell Xander about this? It's not that I want to keep it from him, I just don't want him distracted or worried about me. What do you think?" Len nodded and rubbed his hand over his bristly chin. It was obvious he hadn't bothered shaving this morning.

"I agree. Let me get my buddy on it before we mention it to Alexander. I want his opinion first." Len stood. "Okay let's get moving. I'm sure you've got stuff to do and so do I." I nodded.

"Don't worry too much Eden. We'll set this straight somehow." I really hoped he was right. There was such determination and certainty in his voice, I was hard pressed not to believe him.

TWENTY-EIGHT

EDEN

"Vegas, Baby!" Xander lifted me off my feet and spun me around when he saw me in the foyer of the fancy hotel we were staying at. I squealed a little, then giggled like an idiot. I was so excited to see him.

Then he was kissing me and my mind went numb and all I could think about was him. Why did everything suddenly seem better?

Through the jet lagged and excited fog in my brain, I finally registered someone clearing their throat to get our attention. Reluctantly we broke the kiss and Xander put his arm around my waist pulling me in tight to him. It was so good to feel him up against my side again.

"Son, I'm not sure you want to be putting on a show for the press," Len said as he moved in closer.

"Noted, Dad." Xander looked around. "Let's get out of here before the vultures really descend. I didn't think your arrival time was common knowledge. Obviously, I was wrong." I now realised what he was referring to. Just across the room, there was a little group of photographers snapping away. The photos would be all over the media in no time. I was really glad I'd taken the time to put on some make up and make myself look the best I could after the flight. My hair was down and forward. Hopefully, that was covering the worst of things. Although my scars were hardly a secret anymore.

Xander guided us over to the lifts and nodded to the concierge to take care of the luggage. Once in the lift he passed a room card to his father. "You're a couple down from us."

"Everything going okay?" Len asked.

"Yeah, everything's fine. Just on the final cut, you know how it is." Len nodded.

The lift stopped and we all got out. Xander motioned to a door. "You're here, Dad. We're two down on the corner. Ring before you come a knocking." Len gave Xander a playful slap on the back of the head.

"Let this old man get some sleep. You should do the same," Len suggested as he headed into his room.

The door closed behind Len and we moved down the corridor to the last door. Xander opened the door and I looked around. It was one of those hotel suites like you see in movies. It was huge and plush. The door opened into a combined lounge room/dining room and there was a door to the left that I gathered led to the bedroom. It looked like there was a compact kitchen tucked over to the right as well.

"Wow. I didn't expect anything like this."

Xander grinned. "Yeah, the promoter organised it. I wasn't about to complain." I walked over and looked out the windows. The bright lights of the strip stretched out both sides below. It really was just like you saw on TV.

A moment later there was a knock on the door and my luggage was delivered. Xander tipped the guy and moved my luggage through into the bedroom. Then I stood there a little awkwardly. Xander seemed a little distant and I didn't know if it was him or me?

I followed him through into the bedroom. Just like the rest of the suite, the bedroom was no exception. The bed was massive and covered in white linen with a heavy gold brocade throw, crisply placed across the bottom. The curtains were in a heavy gold fabric as well and the bedhead was a dark timber inlay.

Xander placed my suitcase to the side and looked across at me. His face looked thinner and there was a tiredness around his eyes. “Come over here, Gem. I need to hold you.” I didn’t need to be asked twice. I moved around the bed and straight into his outstretched arms.

I buried my face against his neck and inhaled the smell I’d come to love. “I missed you so much,” I whispered.

“I missed you too, Gem. It’s been a long week and a bit.” His hands ran up and down my back and I just enjoyed the feeling of being close to him.

“Do you want to take a shower? I need to head to bed. It’s getting late.” My body clock was so screwed up I had no idea what time it was. It could have been morning, noon or night.

“I’d love a shower. I feel blah.” He chuckled.

“Yep, I know that feeling.”

We broke apart and I grabbed a few things from my suitcase before heading to the bathroom. I purposely left the bathroom door open hoping he’d join me. When it became obvious he wasn’t going to, I hurried through the last of my bedtime routine.

I found Xander propped up in bed flicking through channels on the TV. He turned the TV off and flicked back the covers on my side of the bed. I crawled under and immediately curled into his body; his arm came around me and he kissed me on the top of the head.

My hand went to his chest and started tracing the tattoo which was one of my favourite things to do. The muscles in his chest and abdomen seemed even more defined and hard than when I’d last seen him and I wondered what he’d been through in the last week to make that happen.

“You’ve got more road bumps here.”

He chuckled a little as I trailed my fingertips over them with the lightest of touches. “I do. They’ll get even more defined over the next few days.”

I might be struggling with jet lag, but that didn’t make my body want him any less. His arm tightened around me and he pulled me closer. My fingers travelled lower to the waistband of the loose cotton shorts he wore and started to tease along the edge. His hard erection was impossible to miss in the tenting fabric.

“You are impossible to resist,” he muttered more to himself rather than me. It was a strange thing to say.

I pushed up off him and looked him in the eye. “Why would you resist? I want you, too, in case I didn’t make it clear enough.”

He drew in a frustrated breath and threw himself back into the pillows against the headboard.

Xander went to say something then stopped. I looked at him a little puzzled and started to get an uneasy feeling. What had happened in the time we’d been apart to make him feel this way? Was he having second thoughts about our relationship? I glanced down at the little strapy satin nighty I was wearing and suddenly wished it was a baggy T-Shirt.

“It’s not you; it’s me,” he said. Well, if there was ever an ominous line that was it!

My heart shot into my mouth and my stomach dropped. This was it.

His hand reached out to stroke the hair back from my face and I saw the pain in his eyes. “Just say it, Xander,”I whispered.

“You don’t know how hard this is for me...” I closed my eyes waiting for the rest. “But I can’t...” My heart was thundering now. “...I can’t make love to you until after the fight.” What did he just say? Did I hear him right?

My eyes flew open and I saw the worry etched in his face. “Did you hear me, Gem?’

I nodded slowly. “I think I heard you? Did you just say I can’t make love to you till after the fight?”

“Yes.” His voice was raspy.

I let out the breath I didn't realise I'd been holding and giggled before I collapsed back onto his chest. "Phew. I thought you were going to say something else."

Then I felt his body rise and fall under me in a chuckle. "What did you think I was going to say?"

"Well, when you said 'It's not you; it's me,' I figured for sure you were breaking up with me."

He squeezed me tight to him. "Why would I do that when all I've thought about is getting you back over here with me?"

"I don't know. Just my over active imagination or something..." I trailed off.

"Well, stop worrying. My feelings haven't changed; I've only realised how much more I've missed you. I'm just not sure how to tell you what I need to tell you."

My mind started to get over its self-imposed shock. "Words generally work pretty well," I teased and nipped playfully at his neck.

He pulled away chuckling. "Stop it. That's the problem. I want you so much and I can't have you till after the fight."

I looked up at him curious. "Why? Is this some strange rule of no sex before the big event because it might affect your performance or something? Has Reed made this stipulation?"

He shook his head no. "No. On both accounts, although I have no doubts Reed would prefer I abstain. But that's not the reason."

I started to reach for the band on his shorts again. He caught my hand in a tight grip and shook his head from side to side. I pouted in mock disappointment.

Once again I settled into his side, my head on his chest. "Well, you'll just have to use those words and tell me I guess."

His arm tightened around me. "I guess." There was a little pause before he went on. "You know how you have those little quirks like hot drinks and showers and stuff because of the fire?" I nodded yes. "Well I have one, too, because of the fight. It's about the possibility of leaving behind a child."

Then I understood what he was talking about. This had to be

something to do with The Cobra's wife being pregnant. I didn't say anything just waited for him to go on.

"Carrie was seven months pregnant at the time Colton passed. I'm not sure if you know but Carrie was The Cobra's wife." He explained.

"I watched the video of the fight online after the reporters started asking all those questions. I saw her in it." I wasn't sure how he'd feel about me seeing it but I thought he should know I had watched it.

He just nodded. "One of the things I'm struggling with the most is that what happened, left a child without a father. I'm responsible for that and it eats me up."

I could feel his pain. It wasn't something that could just be smoothed over with a few words. Xander felt things deeply. It was part of what made him the person he was. He had a deep sense of responsibility.

"It's a terrible thing and unfortunately part of the tragedy of what happened." Words were always so insufficient in these circumstances.

"It is. I don't want there to be a possibility that I could leave you like that, in that position." He was worried about me being pregnant.

"Xander, I'm not pregnant. I'm on the pill. I'm not going to get pregnant. I've got no reason to believe there's any reason to think otherwise. Everything happened just like it should last week..." I trailed off.

"I know and that's why I said before. It's me, not you. This is my screwed up idiosyncrasy and I know it's ridiculous but let me have it. Okay? I need to not have any concerns about this come Friday night." I could feel the depth of his conviction and pain in the tone of his voice. If this is what he needed, then I'd happily accept it. I really, really wanted him, but I was more concerned about his needs than some sexual satisfaction. Just being here with him would be fine.

I reached up and popped a light kiss on his lips. "Stop worrying. I get it and it's fine. It's hardly a terrible idiosyncrasy as they go. If that's what you need to go into the fight in the best head-space possible, then that's what we'll do. I'm just happy to be here with you."

He grabbed the back of my head and pulled me in close. His lips locked with mine and his tongue invaded my mouth with so much feeling and passion I immediately felt swamped. A groan escaped from my throat and I grabbed hold of him harder and let him have his fill. His hand found my breast and started to caress. I slid my hand down over his abs and underneath the waistband of his shorts. I'd just closed my hand around his silky length when his hand locked on my wrist.

"No, don't."

"There is other stuff we can do that doesn't risk pregnancy you know." I nipped at his lip.

"I'm aware of that. But if I'm going to give up sex for the next few days I might as well give it right up. Then there's no way Reed can hold that against me. He hasn't said anything, but I don't want him to have anything to use against me." I was surprised by the extent of his convictions, but I understood.

"If that's the way you want it..."

"I do," he said emphatically and started to push up my nightie. Before my brain registered what I was doing, I slapped at his hand, too.

He looked at me in surprise. "What? Just because I'm not partaking, sweets, doesn't mean you should miss out." He kissed my neck and I sighed.

"It's only a few days and if you can't enjoy yourself, then I won't either."

"I was looking forward to seeing you go all wild with passion," he whispered and kept nibbling at my neck. Ahhh, he was so tempting. My body was screaming for him but my conscience and brain had other ideas.

"Then, you'll just have to wait till later on Friday night. That'll be your incentive not to get beaten up too bad. Know that I've got a big night planned for you when you get done and I want this face and body just as it is now."

"Mmm. Well that sounds like a great incentive. Now I'm curious, what are you going to do to me?" His fingers tickled up my side as he said it.

I had no idea just now but I was going to run with it. "That's for me to know and for you to wonder about." I teased then turned over and snuggled down into the pillows. "How about making yourself useful and snuggling into my back, seeing all we're doing is sleeping."

He chuckled and pulled me back into his front. "I can definitely snuggle with you. That is absolutely not off the menu. Night, Gem. Thanks for understanding and I love you so much." His voice was a teasing whisper across my ear.

I wriggled back against him for maximum contact. "I love you, too, Xan."

TWENTY-NINE

EDEN

Trying to kill time in Vegas when you couldn't go out in public without fear of becoming a media spectacle became old very quickly. Xander was at training with Reed and the boys. Today was Xander's last real day of training and they wanted to get in a solid session—whatever that meant? They were training this morning, then there was some sort of briefing with the PR people this afternoon before tomorrow. Tomorrow was weigh-in and a big press conference. Then Friday was D-Day—fight day. I kind of wondered what life would be like on Saturday.

I wasn't into shopping or gambling and I refused to go on the net and see what was being written about me. Len had spoken to his "guy" and the recommendation had been to do nothing. Apparently the "thinking" was to let these social media troll fests die a natural death. It was thought that responding would only breathe more air onto the fire. Doing nothing, didn't seem like much of a solution, but that's what the expert recommendation was.

So ever since last Friday I'd been trying to pretend it never happened and went about living my life. Which surprisingly wasn't too hard to do as long as I avoided my phone, television and the internet. In other words, a total technology black out. I'd even reverted to old school phone calls from the room phone to my parents, sisters and Beth. Mum and Dad were totally okay with that approach but my sisters and Beth—not so much. They wanted to have more access.

I picked up a copy of a new release romance and read a few pages before I realised I hadn't taken a word in. Who the main characters were, I had no clue. This was so strange for me. Normally I could read something and retain almost perfect comprehension. A sharp knock sounded on the door and I leapt from the bed. I glanced briefly through the peep hole and saw Len standing there looking surly.

I opened the door and stepped aside to let him in.

"Get your stuff together, Girl. We're getting out of here." Even though the guys all toddled off to go training multiple times each day, Len stayed close to me. I didn't know if it had been jointly decided between Xander and Len, I hadn't asked. But that's what had been happening. He must have been as bored out of his brain as I was. Len was the sort of guy that needed to be doing something all the time.

"Where are we going, Len?"

"Where going to check on how the boy's coming along," he growled. Yeah, he was struggling with cabin fever, too.

"Are we allowed?"

He looked at me a little strangely. "Fuck allowed, 'scuse my French. I'm his father and you're his woman. That gives us admittance anywhere he is in my book."

"I didn't think Reed..."

"Reed can like it or lump it. I remember when he was nothing more than a snotty nosed little kid. I won't have a problem reminding him."

I couldn't help the smile that was fast spreading across my face. Len was the shit! "Let me get my bag and a hat."

Somehow we managed to make it through the hotel and out into the black SUV that was waiting for us without creating too much of a fuss. A few minutes later the driver pulled up out the front of the gym the fight promoters had organised for Xander's use. There was a crowd of press mingling around outside and I could see the buzz that whipped through them when they realised something was going on when they saw us pull up.

Len got out first and helped me out. "Head straight for the door. I won't let them touch you."

I wasn't concerned, I knew Len would absolutely make sure I was okay.

"Eden, how's Xander feeling?"

"How do you feel about all the things that they're saying about you, Eden?"

"Are you worried Xander's going to find someone more attractive?"

The questions flew around and I ignored them all and focused on putting one foot in front of the other. Len wrapped an arm around me as if to shield me from the horrible words and snarled a few choice words of his own at them.

A few seconds later, we made it through the doors and into the seeming sanctuary of the gym. A big blonde guy that looked like an ex pro wrestler walked towards us. His hand extended to Len.

"Hi, I'm Mike Torrens. This is my place. Glad to have you here."

"Len Todd." The men shook hands.

Then Mike turned to me. "And this is Alexander's girlfriend, Eden," Len introduced. Mike took my hand and gently shook it.

"Pleasure to meet you both. I was wondering if we'd see you two down here. Sorry about all that." He nodded his head towards the press out the front. "They've been haunting my doorstep ever since Xander arrived in town."

"Vultures. I find it hard to believe they actually get paid for that." Len shook his head in amazement.

Mike just chuckled a low deep rumbly sound. "Well, your son is just about the biggest news in Vegas right now."

"Apparently," Len said unimpressed.

"Can I offer you two a cold drink or coffee?"

"Coffee, would be good." Then Len looked at me. "Actually, make it a cold drink. I can't say I've got a taste for the way you Americans make it yet." I knew immediately that Len had changed his mind on my account.

"Eden?"

"Water, or something like that, would be great, thanks."

"I'll be right back. Then I'll show you to a little area where you can watch." Mike turned and headed off.

"Thanks, Len." I said quietly.

He just grinned. "No problem. I haven't had a decent coffee here yet anyway."

We both laughed.

"I don't currently have that problem."

"Might be wise to avoid it for a bit longer," Len suggested.

"Noted." I was fast getting the feeling that Aussie taste in coffee varied to American taste!

Mike returned with bottles of some sort of flavoured water and showed us to a little seating area off the gym floor. Xander, Dane and Seth were all involved in some sort of intricate sparring. Reed was watching on and yelling instructions from the side.

We sat and watched for a few minutes.

"What are they doing, Len? I don't understand."

"Dane's strength is strikes. So Xan is working those with Dane. The intent is to get through the strikes and get Dane to the ground or get a knock out on him. Although it won't be a real one here." I watched Xander throw a combination then step in and do some sort of throw.

"Now Seth on the other hand; his strength is the ground. Alexander's aim is to either pin him to tap out or get up. Reed's using the strengths of both of the guys to hone Xander's."

Xander's was continually fighting either Dane or Seth, whereas each of them got a break while the other one was fighting Xander.

What I was watching was intense and none of them seemed to be going easy on him.

"Xander hasn't said much about his opponent, Len, and I haven't wanted to ask, but his name kind of terrifies me," I admitted in a low voice.

Len chuckled. "That's exactly what his ring name is supposed to do—incite fear. He's known for winning by a knockout; that's why he's called "Lights Out". The only one he hasn't managed to do that with so far is Alexander."

That had me thinking. "So if ring names are supposed to incite fear, why is Xander called Pretty Boy?"

Len let out a little snort and shook his head. "That was all Reed. Reed was always riding Xan to get into the fight more. Xander has always been more of a calculating fighter. He likes to think about it, set up his opponent and make every move count. The name was more about getting Xander riled up than anything else." I guess that made some sense when Len explained it like that.

"So it's more a mental game for Xander?"

"Yeah. Xander's skills are almost perfect. Whether he wins will depend on if he has the right mental attitude. Previously he was rock solid."

Alarm ran through me. "Are you worried, Len?"

He ran a hand over his face. "I'm not going to lie to you, Eden, Xander's been out a long time. He's coming back from something horrific and he's never had a fight this big." With every word he said, the dread in my heart got heavier. "But I've never seen him look hungrier or more focused. His condition is spot on and I'm not going to tell him this, but he's got faster and stronger, if I'm any judge. Plus he's got a point to prove. Don't worry; the fight will be pretty even. It'll come down to who wants it more and uses their head. Alexander's always been a thinker when he fights."

"I hope you're right. I'm starting to feel really nervous," I admitted.

"Don't tell him that. But yeah, I know. He'll be fine. My boy's as tough as they come. That's how I raised him."

There was pride in his voice and it was well founded. "He's pretty special Len."

"As long as you think so."

The guys called a halt to the exercises. Seth and Dane towelled off and got a drink. Xander picked up a rope and started skipping. He looked spent and half dead on his feet. His body was now looking gaunt and depleted. Xander looked like the picture he'd showed me that night.

"Doesn't he need to rest?" I asked concerned.

"Today's crucial; he needs to drop the final weight." I wondered how he could do this. The three guys just looked on as he tortured himself. "He'll rest this afternoon. Then see where he's at, weight wise. Tomorrow morning he'll be up really early to see what he has to do to make weight."

That sounded really ominous. "What happens if he's over?"

"He won't be, but if he's tight to the weight limit he'll exercise all morning in a sweat suit or sit in a sauna or both."

Xander took a couple of small sips from the bottle beside the guys. Reed and Xander had both been monitoring his water intake like hawks the last few days. Apparently, that and his diet were the key to stripping the weight off him for the weigh-in while still leaving him rock solid with muscle. Five days ago he was drinking so much water he seemed to be always carrying a bottle or in the bathroom. Now he was drinking so little he was looking at his water bottle like a guy dying of thirst, which effectively he was, from what I could gather.

A few minutes later the guys headed over towards us. Xander looked exhausted. There were dark rings around his eyes and he looked sick. I wanted to go and hug him, but didn't know if that's what he wanted here amongst the guys.

The ride back to the hotel was a fairly quiet one. The driver pulled up to the delivery entrance in the underground carpark that was closed to regular guests. Xander wasn't really in any mood to be fronting the media at the moment. He was liable to say anything. Both Seth and Dane were very subdued around him compared to their normal banter and razzing.

We rode the service elevator to our floor and everyone got out.

Seth and Dane turned to head to the opposite side of the floor to our room. As he was walking away Seth threw over his shoulder, “Make sure you take care of him, Eden. He could use a good rub down.” Then he winked. I felt Xander stiffen beside me, then his mouth tightened into a slash.

“Fuck off, Seth. I’ve still got enough energy left to flatten your arse.” It wasn’t so much what he said, but how he said it. None of us missed the double meaning. Xander very rarely swore around me, but it was the steel edge in his voice that was really telling. He was hurting bad and I suspected he just wanted a shower and to lay down.

Seth merely grinned and walked on.

“Just ignore him, Xan,” I soothed.

He nodded and like I thought he would, he headed straight to the bathroom.

The next twenty four hours were going to drag.

XANDER

The fight promoters had organised a meeting room in the hotel for this afternoon’s conference. If I had to sit through another one of these meetings, then I was damned glad it was in the same hotel and I didn’t have to go anywhere.

There was no getting around it.

I felt like shit.

I had no energy, I was so thirsty, it seemed like I had tunnel vision and I couldn’t wait for weigh-in to be done so I could drink and eat some carbs again. My weight was coming off fine and we were happy I’d make the weight easy but I wouldn’t slack off now. Better to be well under and have leeway than be stressing because

I was trying to get it off in the morning. Exercise was the last thing I felt like doing in this state. My preferred option was to be lying in bed with Eden in my arms. That was about the only thing that could take away the discomfort.

Reed was already there when I walked in and he had a dark look on his face. That wasn't unusual for Reed, and in my current state, I wasn't sure if I was even alert enough to read his mood correctly. I was so damned irritable and grouchy; I couldn't stand to be around me, let alone anyone else but Eden.

He nodded at me as I sat down.

"How are you doing?"

"Okay. I'm here."

He nodded. "Not much longer now."

I gave him a sarcastic little snort. It was always easy to say stuff like that when it wasn't you going through it.

The door to the room opened and Tina and Simon walked in. They both had that slick over groomed look about them. Tina was all gleaming dark hair, flashing white teeth, and fake tits in a suit. Simon was the male version of it. I'd detested them both on sight when I met them last week when we'd first arrived. My views, unfortunately, hadn't changed.

After a round of big flashing teeth smiles, the pair quickly hooked up a laptop to the data projector in the room and pulled up some sort of presentation they wanted to go over.

"This is what we want to focus the final press conference on. It's the last real chance we're going to have to get out to the masses. Tickets for the event are sold out, but there are no limits on what we can take in pay-per views so that's our focus in the last twenty-four hours. The campaign will be focused on social media mainly with good coverage in the TV space as well. We want as many people to click that sign up link as possible."

Yeah, it all made sense and I'd heard it all before. Nothing new there.

"So the press conference needs to really focus on this grudge match between you two. We need to whip up as much excitement as possible. No topic will be off the agenda and the more controversial the better." My stomach turned. If I hadn't already been feeling sick before, then I definitely was now. "We've planted questions with a lot of the press people in the room and we want you and Luke to play up the tensions."

"What sort of questions?" I snarled. I didn't like the feeling I had about this at all.

Tina shrugged a little and looked to Simon as if trying to decide who was going to answer.

Simon suddenly didn't look quite so sure of himself, but covered it with a big cheesy smile. "Oh, you know the usual about The Cobra, how you feel about that, why you've stayed away for so long. That sort of thing...maybe a few around your relationship with the scarred girl." His voice had trailed off so the stuff about Eden was much quieter, which made me hellishly suspicious. The fact that he referred to her as the "scarred girl" pissed me off beyond measure.

"Her name's Eden," I gritted out, my fists clenching under the table. Simon looked to Tina and it was if they shared some sort of personal joke. "And I don't see why my relationship has anything to do with the fight."

I glanced over at Reed. His face was impassive, but I thought even he looked a little pissed about this.

"Well, it's news. The world wants to know how a girl with a disfigurement like that gets a hot guy like you," Tina cooed at me. "I mean they were speculating on whether or not it was even true until those photos of you kissing her when she arrived surfaced." Simon was sitting back in his chair looking smug and I had no doubt who had set up all that. The desire to get up and wipe that smile off his face was running hot through my veins. There was absolutely no point talking to these people. They didn't give a shit who they hurt along the way.

I'd had enough. My temper was at its shortest when I felt as depleted as I did now.

I stood and walked out before I did something I regretted.

It didn't matter what I said. These people would do what they wanted to anyway. They didn't care how much they screwed with peoples' lives because they were "just doing their job."

THIRTY

EDEN

The phone alarm went off at the crack of dawn. Xander reached over and grabbed it from the nightstand obviously trying to get to it before it woke me. I rolled over and cuddled into him and kissed his neck.

"Morning, Gem," he whispered in that rough morning voice that had all my nerves tingling.

"Hey," I managed and snuggled tighter.

He pulled me into his arms. "Not long now, gorgeous."

I knew he wasn't only talking about the fight, but also about being "together" again.

"How do you feel?" I asked cautiously. I knew today would be the toughest day yet for him. He had to be so depleted from all the "cutting".

"Counting the hours. I need to get up and see what the scales say. I should be fine." I noticed he carefully avoided the question. I took that to mean he felt like crap. One thing I'd learned is that Xander never complained; he just got on with what he had to do. He'd worked so hard these last weeks. I hoped for his sake he was under his goal, because I knew he would do anything he had to do to make the weight.

He kissed my forehead and rolled out of bed. I studied his naked body as he walked to the bathroom. Every single muscle was defined but his skin looked pasty and dry. He looked like that photo he'd shown me weeks ago. Fingers crossed he was at the right weight.

A few moments later he was back with a smile on his face.

"A kilo and a half under." He crawled back into bed and sent a text off to Reed, I assumed.

"Well done. That's awesome. So you don't have to do anything more?"

"Nope. Just not drink or eat." He laughed cynically.

"I'm so glad you're not going to do that bath thing again. I have to say that freaked me out. I was panicking you'd pass out and I'd have to fish you out of all that hot water. I still have no idea how you stood that water. It looked like it was almost boiling. I kept thinking your skin was going to peel off."

"As hot as you can stand. The hotter the better. You did look pretty freaked when you looked in and saw me totally under except my nose." He chuckled. "Sorry, Gem. I should have talked you through that one before I did it. It didn't dawn on me that it might have been a trigger for you. I'm not as sharp as I usually am on this cut." He looked remorseful. It had been confronting but I'd managed.

"Can't say there's much chance I'm going to join you but, I guess you know what you can and can't do." I had to be confident that he did. What he was doing was extreme and I knew inherently, it could be dangerous if not done properly.

He didn't get to respond to my comment as the phone rang just then.

"Hey, man," Xander drawled after answering.

"Yeah, all good weight wise. I feel like shit though so I'm going to hang in bed for a bit longer; maybe try to get a bit more sleep."

Reed obviously said a little more and Xander replied, "All good

I'll see you then. I'm not doing anything at the moment. And no, I won't be tearing one off. I'll catch you later." Then he hung up the phone and rolled over and snuggled into me.

"Reed?"

"Yep." He sounded pissed off and it had to be something Reed had said. My guess it was something to do with us.

"Is there a problem?" I asked cautiously.

"Nope. Just that he thinks we're here screwing each other senseless."

That surprised me. "Didn't you tell him we were abstaining, if he's so damned worried?"

"No, I didn't. It's none of his business. I'm not a novice at this fight prep thing. I'll just be so glad when tomorrow's over and he stops sticking his nose into my life. I get that he's my trainer and I knew what I was signing up for, but I'm just about done. So over him up in my business. Jesus, I'll cuddle up to my girlfriend if I want to." As if to prove his point Xander grabbed me tighter and nuzzled my neck. Yep. I'd guessed right. Reed had wanted to dictate terms in every aspect of Xander's life and Xan wasn't happy about it.

"He's just doing what he thinks is right," I said, trying to be diplomatic.

He just huffed and nuzzled closer. His hips pressed up against my backside. There was no mistaking he was aroused. I tried to stay still, when really all I wanted to do was wriggle my hips back into him and entice him more. But I knew Xander was committed to his course and right now he was at his weakest. I wouldn't disrespect his wishes by trying to tempt him. This morning I needed to be strong for both of us because I knew instinctively Xander was struggling with tempation.

"I want you, Gem," he whispered and pressed closer.

"I know, but you're going to have to wait," I said, and kept perfectly still. "You'll only be annoyed with yourself if you break your own rules."

"I know, but my dick doesn't seem to agree with my thinking

and my brain doesn't have the mental capacity to argue at the moment," he admitted.

"From what I hear dicks are like that. They have a tendency to get you guys in trouble. I'm not going to let that happen. As soon as the fight's over you can have as much sex as you want." I was talking a good game and a big part of me was really hoping he'd be up to having lots of sex. There was also a part of me that was terrified he wouldn't be, but there was no way I was going to let him see, or know, my fears.

Xander needed to know I was one hundred percent behind what he was doing. If Len thought he could do it, then I had to believe he was right. No loving father would ever let their only child do something that might be very dangerous regardless how old they were. Certainly not a person like Len.

"I'm going to hold you to that, Gem. That's a great incentive not to get banged up. What am I going to be looking forward to?" His voice came out as a sexy whisper.

"As if I'm going to tell you that? You'll just get hornier. I'm trying to help, not get you worked up more." I went to get up. "Maybe I should just get up and leave you to get some more sleep."

He held tight. "Don't Gem. I'll behave. Stay with me please."

I snuggled back down. "Well, you did say please."

He chuckled a little and his hand came over my waist and was headed to cup my breast. I caught his fingers in time and laced them with mine and rested our joined hands on my hip. "Spoil sport," he protested a little.

"You'll thank me for this later."

"I know, you really are the best you know and that's just another reason why I love you."

My heart swelled. "Well, as long as you think so, that's all that matters. I love you, too, so much."

He kissed the back of my neck.

"Let's try and get another couple of hours sleep," he suggested.

"Okay. Sweet dreams Xan." Immediately complying with his suggestion. Another couple of hours would be that much closer to the weigh-in.

"Always with you in my arms," he mumbled and I wondered if he'd started to doze off already; he had to be exhausted.

I'd just lay here and try not to worry too much.

XANDER

The walls seemed to be rippling as I sat in the dressing room waiting to head out for the official weigh-in. Reed was pacing beside me. For what reason, I had no idea. I was the one that was doing this. Off to the side were a series of bottles that were calling to me more than any alcohol ever could.

There sat the precious fluids I'd drink as soon as this weigh-in was done, to rehydrate my body. Twelve feet away and this pain would all be over.

I'd had no more than half a dozen sips of water since I woke hours ago. I looked like a cliché in a vampire movie.

Finally one of the organisers popped his head in. "Five minutes."

"Right," Reed said. Then he turned towards me. "You okay?"

"No, but I will be in about half an hour."

"How dizzy are you?"

"Sitting down. Okay. Standing up, okay... hopefully."

Reed nodded. "You just need to get to the scales, mate."

"Thanks for those words of advice! Getting to the scales is kind of what I'm focusing on. I'll be fine—I think."

The seconds ticked over and finally we began to make our way down the shoot to the weigh-in area. As soon as I walked into the arena beside Reed, I could hear the fans going wild. The place seemed to be packed for a weigh-in. It wasn't unheard of for a crowd to turn up for a weigh-in, but this seemed to be extreme.

Tina and Simon were standing off to the side with big smiles on their faces which I took to mean that they were happy with the frenzy going on. Music blared from the speakers as I climbed the small staircase up to the weigh-in platform. Every step was a challenge and it took, what seemed to be an inordinate amount of mind control, to make my legs lift on cue.

An even bigger roar from the crowd erupted, signalling "Lights Out" had just entered behind me. I took the spot the officials pointed out to me and stood with Reed beside me. I hoped to hell I wouldn't need to lean on him. I just wished the world would stop spinning, but I knew that wouldn't be the case until I started to drink again.

"Lights Out" greeted me with that big shit eating grin of his as he climbed the stairs. He was trying to make out he was doing great, but I knew he was feeling no better than me. Reed, nor I, missed the way he slightly miscalculated the second step from the top.

He stepped over to the position the official pointed out and threw me a wild eyed stare with a crazy grin. Right here was when all the ring hype and bullshit started—the psyche out and all that crap. "Lights Out" was known for being a dick about this stuff. The PR people loved it, other fighters not so much. It didn't look like he was going to disappoint. I generally loved Americans. Over the years I'd spent a lot of time here and found them to be warm and generous people. Even Luke, away from the fight hype wasn't a bad bloke, but he just seemed to lap it up a little too much.

The announcer started to speak to the crowd explaining about the fight and our records. It was nothing more than background noise in my head. My brain was focused on the unquenchable thirst I had.

Who would have thought it'd take ten minutes to introduce two fighters, but it did, and all the while the crowd roared and hollered.

"God, if it's like this now, tomorrow night will be a zoo," Reed hissed between closed lips to me. He was right, but I wasn't going to think about any of that. It didn't matter. All that mattered was taking down "Lights Out." "Strip off your clothes. You're about to go up." I toed off my joggers, which I'd worn sans socks. Then, pulled the T-shirt over my head and stepped out of the loose tracksuit pants until I was standing in just a pair of ultra-light weight athletic shorts.

The announcer looked over at me. "And now, ladies and gentlemen, from Logan, Australia please welcome Xander "Pretty Boy" Todd." The crowd roared even louder and there were a few jeers. That didn't worry me. It was to be expected. I was in Luke's home town after all.

I stepped up to the scales and glanced over at the digital read out. Seventy five kilos exactly. Two kilos under the required seventy seven. Easy Peasy.

This time I grinned over at Luke, let him feel a bit of the pressure of making weight. I was done, qualified. The announcer went on to introduce "Lights Out" as I stepped back over beside Reed.

"Lights Out" made a big deal of thrusting his arms into the air like he'd won the fight before we'd even stepped into the ring. He stepped up onto the scales and the readout wobbled around before finally settling on seventy six point three kilos. He cheered again and hopped off the scales

There were a few more official things said and then it was all over until the press conference in four hours' time. As the opponent, I made my way from the stage first. I was down the shoot and in the wide corridor on my way to the dressing room when I heard "Lights Out" call. "Enjoy the last few hours with that face, Pretty Boy. Tomorrow night I'm going to fuck you up till you're as ugly as that girlfriend of yours." Anger surged through my veins.

I spun around and was opening my mouth to unload when Reed threw out an arm across my chest and barked. "Xander!" I froze, but every nerve in my body had moved from wanting water to now wanting to rip the arsehole's head off.

"Save it for the cage," Reed snarled. "He's just trying to get a rise out of you."

Reed half guided, half shepherded me back to the dressing room and passed me the first bottle of fluids.

"Enjoy."

I took the bottle and downed the half a litre as quick as I could. My body was screaming for the fluids. It was some sort of electrolyte drink, but I drank it that fast I didn't even taste the flavour.

Then he handed me another half-litre of water which I downed in big gulps and passed back to him. Finally he handed me a litre flask of water.

"Sip this for the next hour." He looked at the time on his watch. "Okay, you can have another at three fifteen." For every hour I was awake from now until before the fight tomorrow night, I'd drink a litre of water; that was about all my kidneys could process. If everything went to plan, I'd step into the cage tomorrow night about ten or twelve kilos heavier. It was crazy how we cut weight, but that was the way the sport worked.

Already I was starting to feel better. My throat felt lubricated again and the dizziness seemed to be passing. I sipped a couple more times from the flask of water. It was time to start eating now.

"Okay, let's head back to the hotel and get you fed."

Oh yeah, that sounded good. I was looking forward to doing some serious food damage. For the next few hours I'd indulge.

THIRTY-ONE

EDEN

Xander came back from the weigh-in with Reed in tow looking much brighter than when he'd walked out a couple of hours ago. The chef Reed had hired for him was just finishing up the preparation for his meals in the compact kitchen the suite offered. This was something that had been occurring ever since I'd arrived. The chef would come in a couple of times a day, prepare a series of meals and leave them with instructions for reheating or whatever.

"How'd it go?" I asked getting up from the sofa and the book I was reading to cross the floor to him.

He pulled me straight into a solid hug and dropped his lips to mine for a kiss that left no doubts in my mind about how he felt about me.

"Seventy-five kilos. Two kilos under." He took a sip from the bottle he carried and grinned. "I'm starved." He took my hand and pulled me over to the dining room table and started in on all the food that was laid out.

There was so much food. All high quality carbohydrate dishes such as brown rice, sweet potato and quinoa; it smelt fantastic and I bet tasted even better. There was grilled salmon and a couple of very juicy looking steaks as well as a huge bowl of beautifully steamed vegetables.

Xander sat down and over the course of the next hour systematically hoovered through the vast majority of the food in between taking sips of water from the bottle. At three fifteen, Reed handed him another and he started in on that one.

It was amazing to see how his body was almost transforming in front of my eyes. The black from his eyes seemed to be disappearing and I watched his skin take on a more natural look. His dad joined us for the "re-feed" and we all laughed and joked a little about everything and nothing. The fight wasn't even mentioned and to be honest it was the most relaxed I'd seen them all since this had started.

When the food was demolished. Xander stretched out and took my hand. "Come watch a movie with me?" He pulled me up from the table and we moved over to the sofa where he pulled me down to lounge with him. Reed and his father got up saying their goodbyes.

"Be ready at five thirty," Reed reminded him as he headed out the door.

"See you then," Xander called offhandedly as he flicked through the movies on the hotels pay-per-view channels.

"What do you want to watch, Gem?"

"Nothing too heavy."

We finally agreed on an action comedy cross over thing that was light on story line and big on easy action and laughs.

The alarm on his phone had beeped once and Xander had gotten up and taken another bottle of water from the fridge.

The movie wasn't all that long, which wasn't at all surprising considering the storyline or lack thereof.

"I guess it's time to get ready for this press conference," he said standing and offering me a hand. "I can't wait till all this is over." He pulled me in against his body and his mouth found mine and his tongue swept in and brushed away all sane thought with his wicked teasing. A low growl escaped from his throat and he pulled me in even tighter to him. My hands curled around his rock hard shoulders and I kneaded the muscles under my fingers. It would be so easy to get carried away.

We both seemed to realise it as we moved our heads back a couple of inches. "Go have a shower, Xan. This is just making things more difficult."

"I'd ask you to come with me but..." He glanced down at the bulge in his pants.

"I know and remember I'd want it a lot colder than you."

"A cold shower might not be a bad idea right now," he said and sauntered off.

A little while later we were both showered and dressed. Xander in a pair of black jeans I hadn't seen before and a plain black T-shirt with an abstract colour splatter over it. It never ceased to amaze me how he could make simple clothes look insanely good. The splatter was the only colour he wore. He had a sexy street look going on.

"You look so much better than you did a few hours ago," I said to him when he'd emerged from the bedroom.

"I feel so much better. Tomorrow, I'll feel even better."

"Good. I can't say I like seeing you like you were earlier. I know you have to do it but I don't like seeing you suffer like that even if it's all part of what you love doing."

"Yeah, the cutting part sucks. But it's all part of making sure I get to the fight in the best condition possible with the greatest amount of strength."

He fussed with his phone for a second before we waited to head downstairs to the press conference which was being held in the Hotel Ballroom.

"What's up?" Xander was fidgety and seemed uncomfortable while we waited for our escort to arrive. This sort of restlessness was out of the norm for him.

"I hate doing these press conference things and I think this one's going to be a doozy. The two PR people from the fight franchise are doing everything in their power to whip up a frenzy of hype and they don't give a shit who they hurt in the process. Unfortunately, there's naff all I can do about it." There was no mistaking the frustration and distaste for the whole thing in his tone.

"Don't worry about it. They're only words and as long as we don't take it to heart, then they can't hurt us." I tried to make my words sound solid and convincing. Maybe if I said it with confidence, I'd believe it, too. That was the point. I did believe it, but it still didn't make it any less hurtful when the barbs flew.

"People just suck. I don't get why they feel the need to be so cruel and hurtful. I guess it's small minds and insecurities."

There was a knock at our door and Xander glanced through the peep hole, then opened it before I could answer, and we were no longer alone. Xander took my hand and led me from our suite. Four official looking guys in black suits immediately moved forward to surround us and we made our way to the elevator. The ride to the floor the ballroom was located on was done in silence. The door opened and we all moved out.

"This way, Mr Todd. We'll take you back to where your party is waiting." The men shouldered their way through the crowd of reporters and other interested bystanders and now I understood why there were four of them. It had seemed like overkill up on our secure floor, but now I saw it for the necessity it was. We moved down through a hotel service corridor and the guys escorted us into a comfortable room with a couple of sofas and a table of refreshments. Reed and Len were already there, as were Dane and Seth. After this we'd all planned to have a quiet dinner before an early night.

Seth made a show of looking Xander over. "Well, that was unexpected. I didn't think security had a hope of getting you through there without you losing your shirt or getting pawed."

Xander chuckled. "Yeah, it's a mob scene." But he still seemed to have that jittery nervous energy about him.

"Calm down, man. It's not the fight, just the press conference," Dane joked.

"Wish it was the fight. I hate this shit." He cast me a glance and I realised why he was so uptight about it. He was worried what they were going to say about me. I tried to give him my best reassuring smile, but I wasn't sure if it worked or not. A few seconds later the four guys were back and escorting him and Reed away for the press conference.

"Come on. We'll watch from the side," Len said getting to his feet.

My stomach was in knots and I wasn't sure I really wanted to see this.

Here goes nothing I thought to myself.

XANDER

The room was awash with the din of what seemed to be a million bees as they led us up to the stage with tables and chairs set out along it. In front of each seat there was a microphone. The room had been darkened a little and all I could see was row after row of media people. But judging by the noise it had to be full. Sponsors' screens had been placed at each side of the stage and there were about ten chairs behind each wall for both camp's entourage. I was just settling into my seat with Reed to my left when I spotted Dad and Eden from the corner of my eye. Seth and Dane were right behind them.

As I glanced to my right I could see Luke moving towards the stage with his crew in tow as well. I looked straight ahead and tried to block it all out. My hands were resting on the table in front of me, but underneath the clothed table, my legs were bouncing.

"Try to relax, will you," Reed said out of the corner of his mouth. I took another sip from the water bottle that was my constant companion—anything to give me something to do. I could feel the animosity flowing off "Lights Out" as he sat down in his designated chair.

A few moments later Parker Cook, the promoter stepped up onto stage and took the seat in the middle of Luke and me. Just like Reed was to my side, so was Barry, Luke's trainer.

An official looking guy let out a piercing whistle and the room hushed. He then explained how the questions would be organised and answered before the cameras started to roll. It really was all about the "viewing and exposure opportunities."

The man walked off to the side and we were away.

"Ladies and Gentlemen, thanks for coming out this evening." Parker started the proceedings and droned on for a couple of minutes. This show was as much about him as it was about the fight. "Enough about all that. Let me introduce you to the fighters you've all come to see. As you know this fight has been touted as one of the greatest grudge matches ever. Xander "Pretty Boy" Todd here is undefeated, but hasn't fought in over three years since that fateful day he took the life of The Cobra." Parker paused for a few moments, letting the full force of those words sink in and the tension build in the room. This was his craft and he was a master at it. Guess it didn't matter that I thought he was a disrespectful arsehole right about now.

"On the other side of me is Luke "Lights Out" O'Donnell. He's a fighter that's won by knockout on every single occasion, bar the fight he lost to "Pretty Boy" here, just over four years ago." The din in the room had become a buzz. "I'm not going to say anymore at the moment, rather, I'm going to turn it over to you to ask these magnificent fighters the questions you're all dying to know the answers to."

The room had been broken into quarters and there was an official taking questions from each section. The front left quadrant was first to go and they were moving around clockwise.

Just like at home the first few minutes were spent asking the easy questions. I'd answered about three of four straight-forward questions about my preparation. I was wondering when the dirt was going to come out. It always did.

"How have you acclimatised to Vegas, Xander?"

"Great. I'm well over the jet lag. I don't mind the climate. So I'm feeling fit and comfortable with all that." I leant back a little from the microphone and didn't miss the snarling.

"You won't be too comfortable after this fight." This comment came from "Lights Out."

The comment didn't go unnoticed by a few of the reporters in the front sections.

"Care to explain that comment a little more "Lights Out"." The reporter whose turn it was asked.

Luke laughed in a smug, sardonic kind of way. "Absolutely. "Pretty Boy" here, won't be so pretty after I've finished with him and he's going to be anything but comfortable with the hurt I'm going to put on him tomorrow night."

The gallery of press all seemed to turn to me. "How do you feel about that Xander?"

I shrugged my shoulders trying to appear as nonchalant as possible. The press were hanging on my every word. "Nothing I haven't heard before. I recall Luke saying something similar before our last encounter. If memory serves me correctly, it was Luke that was damned uncomfortable the next day. Six cracked ribs, a sprained wrist and a torn groin from what I recall, oh, and a hell of a headache from the knockout I gave him." A ripple of laughter rolled through the room.

Once again, I could feel my opponent glaring and sneering at me.

"Xander, Luke's ring name is "Lights Out", but maybe yours should be "Death Punch". The vast majority of your wins have also been from knockouts, not to mention your last fight resulted in the death of your opponent and fellow fighter, The Cobra. How do you feel about that?"

My mind raced as I tried to think of what to say.

"If you're asking whether I'm going to change my ring name.

No. Reed here monikered me with it and it's not something I'm going to mess with. As for what happened to Colton, well, I'm sure you've all read or heard it before. I'm very regretful for the accident that occurred. I really don't have anything more to say about it."

The question moved to the next section. "How do you feel, "Lights Out", getting into the cage knowing you've only ever been beaten by "Pretty Boy" and knowing he killed his last opponent, whether it was accidentally or not?"

Luke laughed almost hysterically and I wondered what he was playing at. Maybe it was some strange ploy? "I've won my last ten fights since then, at a much higher level. "Pretty Boy" here hasn't even been in the cage. What do you all think is going to happen? Come on people do the math..." Oh no, he couldn't stop there could he? He took it a step further and crossed the line. "I'll tell you what's going to happen; he's going to end up looking just like his freak show girlfriend. That way they'll be a matching pair." Luke glared over at me, cockiness and putrid dripping from his lips as he chuckled at his own pathetic attempt at humour.

That was the lowest of low blows. I started to rise from my chair anger ripped through me. Fuck him. Reed slammed his hand down on my thigh and pushed his considerable weight on it.

"Sit down. He's just trying to wind you up," Reed hissed in my ear. I knew it was the truth, but it hurt. No man should have to listen to the woman he loved being attacked; let alone in a public forum being beamed to millions of people. But even more to the point, Eden shouldn't have to go through this. This was hateful and so hurtful.

I was terrified she'd run and I wouldn't blame her. I glanced past Reed to my left and saw they were all standing now. Dad had his arm around her shoulders and Dane was on the other side. Seth was at her back. It was as if they were shielding her from the hurtfulness and all I could think about was that she was going through this because of me. They were shielding her from the crap that she was facing because she was with me. It was my job to protect her as her man. I was doing everything but, it seemed.

I took a deep breath and I realised every eye in the place was on me. It was so silent the place was eerie.

Right then, I made a decision.

I rolled my jaw and took a deep breath to calm the beast that was raging inside me, wanting to tear out Luke's hateful throat.

"I mistakenly thought this fight was between the two of us, Luke." My voice was quiet but steely and I had no doubt everyone knew my level of rage and control.

Luke butted in. "It is "Pretty Boy". Unless you need your girlfriend to help you out. She's looks as scary as hell—you haven't fought in a long time, after all," he joked and there were a few smirks from his camp. Others chose to look embarrassed.

Rage engulfed me but I had to keep it together; I couldn't stoop to his level. I wouldn't degrade myself or Eden like that. My mind whirred with options and possibilities. What should I say? All the while the press looked on like hungry sharks, waiting for me to say or do something. They could smell the blood.

I turned to look my opponent in the eye. "Luke, I don't normally engage in prefight bullshit, but today I'm going to make an exception, because today you've managed to degrade our sport, which is supposed to be honourable, to a whole level that is just all kinds of screwed up."

Luke was almost jumping up and down in his seat now. I wondered if he was on some interesting drugs because he was behaving like a demented madman. "What you don't like us poking a little fun at your girlfriend? It's all part of the deal man. You were the one that decided to go out with her. I would have thought the "Pretty Boy" could have pulled a pretty chick." Gasps went up around the room but Luke kept on carrying on.

I couldn't believe my ears. My temper had moved to nuclear now. My fists were clenching on top of the table and I did nothing to hide it. Reed leaned on my leg some more to stop me from standing. The press were silent, but mesmerised as they looked between us.

As much as I wanted to rip him limb from limb, I couldn't do it now. Right now words were my only weapons and I had to use them carefully—very carefully.

"So you want to bring Eden into this Luke? Then let me tell you a little bit about her." My eyes moved from Luke who almost looked like he was salivating at all this rubbish to glance briefly to my left and Eden's face. It was ashen and grief stricken. I only hoped what I was going to do wouldn't make it worse for her.

"You're right, Luke. Yes, Eden has some scars, as you've so cruelly pointed out. You really think she or I didn't know that? But do you know how she got those scars Luke?"

Luke looked over at me with a stupid grin on his face but said nothing, just shook his head like the belligerent idiot he is. The press remained silent, hanging on my every word.

"I didn't think so because if you'd bothered to do your research there's no way you would have made those comments. Eden got those scars...mate." I gritted my teeth and spat the word. He was anything but friend tonight. "By choosing to head down a staircase into a floor engulfed in flames to find her sister who was trapped by the flames. She walked into a fire to find her sister." Gasps went up around the room and the faces I could see in the half-light were full of surprise, awe and shock.

"I can't think of much of a braver thing to do, but you have the audacity to sit here and fire pot shots at her scars. You're a real hero, Luke." My voice dripped with sarcasm. "It's people like you that disgust me. With your celebrity status, you could be building people up and inspiring; instead you choose to be a bully and try to attack people. Why do you feel the need to do that? I can only think it's because of your own insecurities."

Luke went to say something.

"I'm not finished and I think the only thing left for you to say right now is an apology," I thundered, my voice reverberating around the room. Luke sat back and suddenly looked very small and his crew seemed to not know which way to look.

"Eden makes me want to be a better person every day. I love

her for that, and many other reasons I doubt you'd ever understand. Yes, she has scars, and she doesn't feel great about them. But she also doesn't let them rule her life. Everyday she gets up and works her butt off to be the best sister, daughter, girlfriend and person she can be. She's the bravest person I know and those scars are a constant reminder of just how brave she is. I couldn't be prouder to call her mine."

I got up. I was done. This conference was at an end as far as I was concerned. I was just about to head from the stage when I couldn't resist one last comment.

I leant back over the microphone. "Let me promise you one thing, Luke; the only lights that will be going out tomorrow will be yours."

The press erupted into a frenzy of questions and security had a mountain of a job to manage it. I didn't care.

Simon and Tina came rushing up towards me their faces stricken. I didn't care.

All I cared about was getting to my girl.

That's all that mattered to me.

THIRTY-TWO

XANDER

I pulled Eden into my arms as soon as I reached their spot behind the screens. I didn't say a word just held her tight. The noise from the uproar in the room was overwhelming.

Her tears soaked through my shirt and I hurt for every single one of them. I could only imagine the pain of having all that put out there for the world to see, to pick over and give commentary on. No one deserved that. What Luke had done was unforgivable.

We needed to get out of here. I was still raging inside and I needed to know how bad the wounds to Eden were.

"Let's get out of here," I yelled to my group over the noise. I bundled Eden to me the best I could and the four suits moved as one to form around us. Five minutes later we were all in the safety of our suite.

What a clusterfuck!

I flopped down on the sofa and pulled Eden with me into my lap. I still had no real idea what she was thinking. The only positive was that she hadn't bolted yet. That had to be something, surely?

Reed and Dane sat down on the sofa opposite. Dad prowled in front of the windows and Seth leant against the bar that separated off the kitchen and dining area. I could tell they were all too stunned to really understand what had happened.

"In all the years I've been around fights of all types, I've never seen something like that. Trash talk is one thing that's well just…fucked." Dad opened the proceedings. "Sorry, Eden. I didn't mean to swear but nothing else quite covers this."

Eden sat up a little straighter. "It's okay, Len,"she said quietly reaching for a tissue from the box on the table beside the sofa. "It's not exactly a surprise that it happened."

"No, it's not," Len said, still fuming.

I looked between the two. Shit had just gone down big time with Luke, but there was more to come I was sure. These two knew something more—they were referring to something else. I didn't miss the look between them.

"What aren't you telling me?" I demanded in a quiet voice.

Eden stiffened in my arms and whispered, "Damn." Then she cast a little sideways look at dad. He had a look on his face that screamed "Busted".

"Right. Who's going to spill the beans?"

There was another exchange of glances, before Eden went on. "I ran into a little trouble at uni."

"What the hell, what happened? Why didn't you tell me?"

"I didn't tell you because I wanted your head focused on the fight, not my problems." Her voice held an edge.

"Well, my problems have become your problems it seems. And quite frankly I don't give a fuck about the fight if it means you've had to hide stuff and suffer in silence because I'm involved." I moved out from under her and stormed over to stand by the windows as well. I needed to be on my feet and free to move. I was so keyed up and pissed off.

"Okay, I get your annoyed but I handled it. It was cruel and hurtful and all the usual, but it's also made me stronger. That's exactly when I decided not to let the hateful people win anymore.

That's the point when I decided I wasn't going to take it anymore."

I gritted my teeth. What had happened for her to have this type of epiphany? "Tell me," I pleaded. God, what had she been going through for me?

She nodded her head and had a look of resolve on her face. I couldn't believe how strong she was. I was waiting for her to dissolve into hysterics or something.

"It was my last exam on the Friday before we left. I went in and sat down at my usual seat. When I opened the exam packet it had half a dozen pages that were screenshots from social media pages. There were some pretty ugly photos of my scars and lots of nasty comments."

I couldn't believe what she was telling me. "What the hell? What did you do? How did they get in the exam papers?" My brain was struggling to take it all in and make sense of it.

"Fortunately, I'd studied till it was second nature so I did the exam on auto-pilot. Then I showed the whole lot to the exam supervisor and lodged an official complaint. I'll chase it up when I get home." I was staggered at how calmly Eden was sitting there.

"Do you have any idea who did this?" I asked trying to keep the fury from my voice. Who would do something so horrid? How could this happen?

"I don't have any evidence, only a feeling but I think it was Cindy. I caught her giving me a funny look, kind of like she was expecting me to do something," Eden admitted.

"Trouble making bitch," I snarled.

"She's always been bad news, mate," Dane piped up.

"It's not the first time she'd tried to start shit and not just to you. I know she did some stuff at high school," Seth added.

"It doesn't matter if she did or didn't. I realised in that horrible two hours that the stuff they were writing and saying was their problem. Not mine." Eden's voice was strong and full of conviction. "Because Xan is in the public eye, there are always going to be small minded and insecure people. Yes, it is hurtful and horrible but it's a reflection on them not me. Isn't that basically what you called Luke on tonight? I realised you were far more important to me than taking to heart what people were ever going to say about me, Xander. If that is the price for loving you, then so be it."

Hell, it had been a day for disclosures. It wasn't a secret that we loved each other but I'd declared exactly that in front of millions of people and now Eden was doing the same in front of my father and my closest friends.

"But the point is, you shouldn't have to pay a price to love me," I raged in frustration.

"I don't disagree with you, Xander, but it's not the way the world works. You and I should know that better than most. But what you did down there tonight? Nobody other than my family has ever stood up for me like that, certainly not publically." There was a resignation in her voice, an acceptance of her fate and while I guess, that it was good to know she was accepting things she couldn't change, it didn't make it right. Not one little bit.

"But that's just it, Eden. I shouldn't have to stand up for you like that. God knows I will every time because I love you more than anything but it's just...not right." I was so angry and frustrated I could barely speak.

That's what was killing me.

I just felt so powerless to protect her.

I stormed into the bedroom stripping as I went. I needed to hit something badly. Work off this rage. Figure out what I should do.

A few seconds later I was in my workout clothes.

"Xander, what are you doing?" Reed barked.

"What does it look like?"

"You need to rest, not train."

"Like I can rest and relax when all I want to do is tear the heads off every last fucker that ever dared to disrespect her." I grabbed a towel from the stack and another couple of water bottles.

"Give me an hour, Eden." I pressed my fingers to my lips and threw her a kiss. She gave me a little smile that spoke of acceptance. She understood what I needed to do and she was okay with it. Eden got me. When did she get so damned solid?

"Don't go too hard," she cautioned.

I just gave her one stiff nod.

"Fuck me; this is going to be a circus," Seth muttered, moving to the door.

"Boys," Reed barked and they followed me into the elevator.

A few minutes later we were in the hotel gym. Fortunately, there'd only been one middle aged guy in there using the treadmill. He'd taken one look at all of us and made a bee line for the door which Seth was now standing guard at.

Dane had thoughtfully grabbed some pads and gloves from his room. Now I was pounding away, trying to work out the mad. Reed was sitting on an exercise bike watching on pensively. I could tell he was wondering if the whole fight was about to go down the toilet.

Hell, no!

There was no way I wasn't walking out of that cage as the winner tomorrow night. That fucker was going down in the worst way.

I wanted his blood.

I wanted to take out every last hurtful and hateful comment that had been directed at Eden on his worthless hide. Fuck him and everyone else that thought it was okay to be so damned cruel. The familiar feeling of impact and burn throbbed through me. Nothing ever worked quite like hitting bags or pads.

Twenty minutes in and the anger started to clear enough that a glimmer of an idea sprouted in my mind. Thirty minutes in and I knew what I was going to do. Fuck the PR people. They were at me to post more. Well hell, I now had something I wanted to post about.

I stepped back from Dane and dropped the gloves I was wearing. Reed passed me a water bottle and I drained it in a few long gulps then I reached for my towel.

"Who's got my phone?" I demanded.

"I do," Seth called out from the door. He fished it out of his pocket and tossed it over to me. I plucked it easily from the air and glanced at the screen. It was blowing up with all sorts of messages. FaceBook, Twitter, direct messages, text messages; they were all there.

It was time I went on the offensive. I was sick of defending and ignoring. That only worked so well for so long. Then action needed to be taken.

"What are you doing, Xan? Do you think you should be posting when you're in this sort of mood?" Dane warned me obviously concerned.

"There's no better time."

I typed out a message for FaceBook.

It was simple.

I stand 100% by everything I said. If you don't support what I said and my choice in Eden then I don't want you for a fan or friend. I'll help you find the unfollow or unfriend button if you're confused.
If you support what I said let's start a positive revolution. #Brave

I hit the post button before I had more time to think about it.

Then I copied the same message into my Twitter app and fiddled with the post to fit the character limit.

I stand 100% by everything I said. If U don't support what I said & my choice in Eden then I don't want U for a fan or friend. #Brave

I pressed post on that as well then turned my phone off. What was done was done. The next statement I made would be in the cage.

The guys couldn't hide their confusion and weariness. I didn't blame them; it had been a monumental afternoon.

"Who's hungry?" I asked as I headed for the door. They all fell in beside me.

We rode the elevator in silence.

"Meet you in the private dining room in thirty minutes," I called to Dane and Seth as they headed to the right.

I made my way to the end, but Reed stopped me with a hand on the arm.

"I owe you an apology," he said.

"Oh?" This was very strange behaviour for Reed. Reed didn't apologise. He was the type that was always right. His grey eyes were more stormy than usual and I knew what he was about to say was not easy for him.

"I was wrong about Eden. I'm sorry."

I nodded my head and thought about that. "Yeah, you do owe an apology only I'm not the person you owe it to. You owe it to Eden."

He stiffened and I watched my words process through his head. A few seconds later he nodded. "You're right. I'll make sure I take care of it."

"Appreciate it." I didn't need to say anymore. Reed was a man of his word and he would make it as it should be.

I turned and was heading to the door.

"Xander, one last thing..." I looked over my shoulder at him. Reed's jaw flexed and I knew whatever he was about to say was going to cost him greatly. "I didn't get it before; I do now. I understand why you chose Eden... She's about the bravest woman around."

"I know, mate. Don't tell me. Tell her," I said with a knowing chuckle.

Reed threw me a chin lift and I returned it.

Things were about as right as they could be given the debacle of a day.

Now I just had a girl to check on and a fight to win.

THIRTY-THREE

EDEN

The day of the fight was surprisingly quiet. Xander was very calm and did a lot of eating and drinking earlier during the day. He'd weighed a whopping twelve kilos heavier today. My mind was still trying to get around that. And well, his body could only be described as magnificent as he'd risen from our bed naked this morning.

In contrast to yesterday where he looked desperately ill—today he looked the absolute picture of health and strength. Every muscle looked full and bursting with power and strength. His eyes were back to being bright and intensely sharp instead of dull and sluggish.

After a monster breakfast, he'd spent the morning stretching and a masseuse had come and worked on his body for over an hour. Then he'd eaten another big meal and he'd dragged me off to the bedroom for a nap. He claimed he slept better when he was curled around me. It was no hardship at all. If that's what he wanted, then there was no way I would object. If he was going to fight, then it was my job to make sure I supported him the best I could. Reed had thrown us a bit of an exasperated glance but had said nothing.

Now we were all in full on fight mode.

We were all gathered in Xander's dressing room. Very soon it would be time for Len and me to go take our seats ringside. Reed, Seth and Dane would be with Xander throughout the fight. Xander was stretching out again; his flexibility never ceased to amaze me. Dane was fiddling with hand wraps and I gathered very soon he'd be wrapping Xan's hands.

When we'd gotten up a couple of hours ago, he'd eaten his last meal before the fight. It was some sort of high energy, easy to digest meal, of chicken and brown rice. It smelt divine and tasted even better when he had pushed his fork at me for me to try.

The two of us had sat there at the table with the fight kind of looming between us, like the proverbial elephant in the room.

"Might have to steal this guy and bring him home." Xander had joked and nodded to the chef that was fixing something else in the kitchen, trying to lighten the mood a bit.

"Probably a good idea, seeing I don't cook." I'd agreed with a giggle.

"You'll get there. We'll see what we can do about fixing that when we get home if you want. If you don't, it doesn't matter."

Xander was being very supportive and I appreciated that. But now I was on the path to overcoming my fears, I wanted to rid myself of them all. "I want to give it a go," I'd said.

He head nodded between forkfuls. "Okay, then."

He'd eaten in silence for a few more minutes as I watched on, not quite sure what else to do.

"Are you nervous about the fight?" I'd wondered a lot about this, but I'd never asked him before early.

"Yeah, I am," he'd admitted a little sheepishly. "You need to be nervous though. You need the extra zing that adrenaline nerves give you. I've just got to be able to control the nerves."

"That makes sense," I'd said. I'd been doing my best not to show my nerves then and now. I really hoped I was pulling it off.

Len moved over to where I was standing. "We're going to need to go and take our seats soon. Leave these boys to do their final prep."

Suddenly, it all became even more real and my stomach started to do crazy flip-flops. I didn't say anything, just looked at Len. My face must have said it all.

"It'll be fine. Eden."

"Thanks, Len, but I think I'm going to be a bit of a mess until it's all over."

"Yeah, I often think it's worse for us than it is for him. There's not a damned thing we can do to help. Just be confident that he's done everything he can in prep and he puts up a good show." Len was trying to make me feel better, and I appreciated it, but I knew it was going to be one of the longest hours of my life.

I glanced at my watch. Half an hour until fight time. Then five, five minute rounds with a minute in between.

"Okay, let's go, Len. I don't think I can stand it much longer," I decided. As much as I wanted to stay with Xander, I was struggling to keep my nerves together and I didn't want that rubbing off on him. Len gave me a little pat on the back that said a lot more than words before he turned towards Xander.

"Okay Son, we're going to go take our seats."

Xander stood up and came over. "Okay. I guess this is it."

He sounded fatalistic and I hoped it was all positive.

Len pulled him in for a quick hug. "Proud of you, Son. Kick his arse." I was never more thankful to have a man of few words beside me. Too many words and I knew I'd have been even more of a wreck.

"That's the plan, Dad," Xander said confidently.

When Len stepped back from Xander, I stepped forward into his arms. He pulled me in tight and whispered, "I love you Eden."

"I love you too, Xan. Good luck, but I know you won't need it."

He leaned in and caught my lips with his in a lingering kiss. I couldn't help but capture that full bottom lip between mine and give it a little nibble.

He let out a groan and broke away a little. "I'm so looking forward to later."

I grinned and rubbed my nose against his. "Me, too. Don't get that face messed up and make sure you're not too banged up. I've got plans..." I pressed my lips to his one last time. "I know you've got this. Go tame those oni."

He gave me a grin that I knew he reserved specifically for me. "Count on it, Gem."

God, I prayed he was right.

XANDER

I stood bouncing from foot to foot at the door to the shoot that would lead me down to the cage. The arena was packed to the rafters with fans and they were so noisy, it felt as if the place would fly apart.

"Jesus Christ, these Americans know how to put on a show," Seth said a bit in awe, looking around. Music blared from the speakers, the crowd was cheering and the atmosphere was so intense. There had been four other fights before mine. So, by now the fans really had a taste for some blood and action. They were looking for the climax to the card—the main event.

"You ready, Mr Todd?" a harried looking man with a headset and a clipboard asked my group in general.

"He's ready," Reed ground out, answering for me.

Oh yeah. I was ready.

Two days ago I was fighting demons that I wasn't sure I could put down. They'd been gnawing at the edges of my psyche and confidence when I was physically at my lowest. Not today. Yeah, I was nervous but I was going to win. Nothing else would be acceptable to me.

There was no way I could let Luke disrespect my girl like that.

That couldn't go unpunished. If ever I'd needed a reason to win, Luke had just given me one hell of a motivation. Seemed he was much better at running his mouth than his brain. I hoped that stayed true to form. That would be my edge. My ability to be strategic was what would get me the win.

Being strategic meant that I had to be clear-headed and not let my emotions or nerves get the best of me. I needed to push it all back and just focus on what I had to do. Every strike, kick, grapple and hold needed to work to my advantage.

"Out you go, Mr Todd."

"You ready?" Reed looked me square in the eyes, Dane and Seth looked on.

"Yes." I said and I meant it. I'd never been more ready for anything.

Reed nodded to the guy with the clipboard and he spoke into the headset. The music changed and "I will not bow" by Breaking Benjamin started playing. That was my cue to move.

As soon as I stepped through the doorway, the spotlight hit me and I tried to avoid looking at it. I didn't want my eyesight fucked up. It all seemed so surreal. Every step I took was one step closer to the cage. I've had some big fights before but this was a whole new level. There must have been twenty thousand screaming fight fans in this arena.

Images of The Cobra and Carrie were trying to push their way into my consciousness. I beat them back and focused on what I needed to do. Step by step, I made the longest walk of my life. When I was a short distance from the centre platform the Master of Ceremonies started his spiel. "Ladies and Gentlemen, our challenger for tonight's main event. He's been out of the cage for the past three years since he took the life of one of the sport's greatest champions, undefeated in his professional career..."

My skin was tingling at the words, adrenalin was racing as I put my foot on the first step; this whole show was staged to perfection.

"Please welcome from Logan, Australia..." I made it to the top of the platform as he finished. "Xander "Pretty Boy" Todd." The crowd roared and rose, stamping their feet. The movement seemed to reverberate through every essence of my body.

As much as knew I needed to ignore the crowd, it was impossible. I'd thought it would have been a totally hostile reception. It surprised me that wasn't the case. All over the arena the place seemed to be littered with fans holding up signs that read #Brave.

Seth had let slip this morning that my posts were trending wildly. I couldn't think about it then or now. My focus had to be on bringing down Luke.

Then the music for Luke started. It was some rap song I didn't recognise, full of obnoxious beat and attitude. It suited him to a Tee. I headed over to my crew, trying to ignore what was going on.

"Ladies and Gentlemen our defending champion tonight. With a near perfect professional record of fifteen from sixteen fights by knockout. From right here in Vegas, please welcome your hometown hero, Luke "Lights Out" O'Donnell." The crowd went insane and Luke danced around jeering at me.

"Ignore him," Reed barked at me and dragged my focus back to him as I danced from foot to foot. "Don't get sucked into his bullshit. You know what you have to do." I nodded. I did. "Stay focused on the plan. He's going to want to make this quick by a knock out. You can't give him the opportunity."

Reed patted me on the back and Dane pushed my mouthguard at me. "You got this, man."

"Take out the trash, mate!" Seth called as I moved forward to enter the cage.

I slipped the mouthguard into place with my gloved hand and rolled my shoulders.

I was ready. Bring it on.

The referee called us to the centre and spoke a few words about what he expected. I didn't hear a single one of them. My focus never moved from staring into those mocking blue eyes of Luke's.

We bumped gloves and stepped back. The referee gave the signal to go and it was on!

Adrenaline surged through me and we danced for a few paces, I was eager to get this thing started—dancing wasn't going to do it.

I stepped in and threw a sharp left jab to his head and followed it up with a stinging right leg kick that connected hard on his left thigh. He grinned at me and charged forward with a crisp jab, cross, then hook punch combination that caught me a little by surprise. The hook to the right side of my jaw left me off balance and forced me back. But as I did, he launched himself forward and we both ended up on the floor of the cage—me on the bottom and "Lights Out" on top of me.

I was momentarily shaken. How did that happen so quickly I wondered, momentarily shaken. Luke moved in and covered my body with his across my ribs. Fuck! He had me locked up in a side control and my focus clicked back in. If I didn't do something quick, the fight would be all over before we even got started.

Somehow I managed to get my left arm under his chest and from there I could protect my head from the strikes he pummelled me with. His knees connected with my ribs. I needed to get up off the canvas and fast. To do this I had to set him up.

Fortunately, I managed to keep his body off me just enough with my left arm. This allowed me to bump my hips sideways across, towards the wall of the cage. When I sensed I had enough leverage, I rolled into him and managed to find my feet. Luke followed my movements and slammed his body into my left side. The hatch work of the cage grill bit into my right side as Luke pinned me against the wall.

This shouldn't have happened. To win this fight I had to maintain control of the rounds. I wanted a knockout, but to be safe I needed to win every round on points in case it went to the end and a points' decision. "Lights Out" was far too much of a dangerous opponent to give him any leeway. I needed to get back the upper hand and survive this round.

Three years away from the cage had created a thick layer of ring rust on my moves—something that no amount of training could counteract. It wasn't that I hadn't expected it, I just needed to do something the hell about it.

Luke hammered at my ribs with short hard jabs and he had his other arm wrapped around my left shoulder and back, trapping me there against the mesh in a hell of a Whizzer. My feet were jammed tight against the wall of the cage. I focused on his fist that punched at my ribs. The next time he hit, I latched on to his wrist, giving me control of that arm.

Once I had control of his arm, I circled my trapped arm outwards, over his head to escape from the Whizzer. From there I almost reversed our positions and slipped my body behind his and grabbed hold of the arm I had locked up with both hands.

This was more like it. Now I had the position of power and control, but this round was just about survival and scoring as many points as possible. I wanted some distance from him. I needed to give myself some time to regroup and plan my next attack. Everything was happening a bit too fast at the moment. I needed to slow it down and give myself a chance to get back into the groove of fighting in the cage.

I kneed him hard in the back of the thigh and shoved him forward with my hands into his lower back. He stumbled forward as I skipped back toward the centre of the cage. It was enough time for me to catch my breath and steady myself.

"Lights Out" came at me with a big angry right front kick. I saw it coming in towards me and stepped to my left, pushing it away with my right hand. That set me up to land a whipping left outside leg kick to the back of his thigh. I felt the sting as the top of my foot connected with the hard muscle of his leg. My right fist flew out and connected solidly with his jaw in a heavy cross punch. Then I skipped back a few steps.

The anger on Luke's face was there for all to see. He'd been expecting this to be over in seconds. That wasn't happening. There could only be one winner and I was determined that it would be my fist raised in the air. If it took five rounds, so be it. I was fit enough to go the distance. Our mantra for the last eight weeks had been "Train hard, fight easy." It was never going to be easy, but I had the fitness to last the distance no matter how long it went.

We danced around in the centre for a few long seconds, both of us circled looking for some sort of opening. Finally, "Lights Out" advanced and I slipped my hands from their ready position on my cheek bones to a full cover guard with the heels of my palms pressed high on my forehead.

He threw a jab, cross, hook punch combination. Instinctively, I ducked and weaved. I felt his blows glance against my guard. Luke followed it with a stinging outside leg kick to my thigh. I anticipated it coming. It was a move I'd seen him use many times in the fight footage I'd studied. Automatically, I'd raised my left knee in a leg check to harmlessly intercept the kick.

We traded blows in the centre of the ring for a couple more minutes. My defence held tight until he figured out my ploy and split my front guard with an upward striking elbow. It caught me in the middle of the forehead and I saw stars for a second or two. That was enough time for Luke to lunge forward and get his hands behind my head in a clinch.

Acting on reflex I managed to snake my hands around the back of his head, to complete a neutral position between us. Neither one of us had the advantage. We traded knees with no real gain for either one of us until the bell sounded.

We broke apart and he gave me a snarling growl as he headed to his corner.

I'd survived the first round, but if I wanted to win I was going to have to come up with a far better game plan.

EDEN

Much of the crowd was on its feet yelling and screaming as the bell rang at the end of the first round. Len and I were no different. My throat was hoarse from screaming. Len had been bellowing beside me for Xan to do this or that. I understood very little of it.

All I knew was that my man was still standing and so far looked just fine. He'd jogged back to his corner and the guys had him surrounded, to the point I couldn't see him at the moment.

I'd clutched Len's arm so hard through the whole first round, I was sure I would leave bruises. I'd never seen a live fight before, let alone one my boyfriend was fighting in. My reactions to it shocked even me.

"Looks like we've got ourselves a true blue fight fan," Len chuckled as he peeled my fingers from his forearm. "Probably best you let the blood flow back before the next round, Girl."

"Sorry Len, I'm just so..." I didn't know what to say or how to explain it.

"It's okay. I know."

"How'd he do, Len? Is he winning?" My stomach was in knots.

Len shook his head. "Boy had a serious case of ring rust; he was damned lucky to get out of that first ground control. "Lights Out" is a much better fighter than when they last met. It'd be close on points. Probably too close to call."

His eyes were glued to Xander and the guys. They'd gotten busy and I could now see Xander sitting on a stool. Dane mopped at his face with a towel and Seth was doing the same to his shoulders. Reed screamed in his face, using animated gestures. No doubt barking instructions for round two.

I wasn't sure where Len stood on any of it. "What's he need to do now?"

"He needs to take control. These boys are much more evenly matched than they ever used to be. Alexander needs to stay calm and not let Luke come at him like that. Towards the end of the round he was just bunkered down in defence. That's not going to cut it. He has to set up some attacks of his own. You don't win a fight by defending. Eventually you have to strike."

What Len said even made sense to my very limited understanding.

"What do you think Reed's telling him?"

Len didn't even hesitate. "I bloody hope he's telling him to go on the damn attack. Although the boy does like to plan a strategy half a dozen moves ahead. Drives me bat shit crazy waiting for him to do something sometimes." The frustration and helplessness Len felt was evident.

I couldn't help but grin. Len was just as keyed up and nervous as I was. He just had a different way of showing it.

The clock must have been counting down to the start of the next round when Xander finally looked over in our direction. His eyes caught mine and I gave him my brightest smile and a double thumbs up. Then I blew him a kiss as he headed back to the middle for round two.

I had no idea how I'd make it through five rounds like the one before. This was exhausting and I was just watching.

THIRTY-FOUR

XANDER

"Okay, that should have settled the nerves and chipped off the rust. Now you need to get down to business. You need to frustrate him, Xan. His temper is what's going to win the match for you. He loses form when he's angry. Keep him frustrated and mad. Then when his form drops off, take advantage," Reed barked at me through the din of the crowd.

I nodded, taking it all in.

"He's good, but nothing you can't take. I'm not sure how fit he is either. Rage takes up a lot of energy. Make him pay for that."

The guys mopped at me and gave me a water bottle to sip from. There was a slight metallic taste in my mouth but nothing too bad. Sweat was running freely from my body now and my heart was beating solidly.

I needed to do better.

Just as time was called, I spotted Eden and Dad. She gave me that smile of hers that seemed to block out everything else and a double thumbs up. Then she blew me a kiss.

The most I could manage in return was a nod. I hoped she

understood.

With Eden firmly in my mind I headed back to the centre of the cage. She'd been so brave and strong through all this. I couldn't let her down now. It was my turn to step up.

I watched Luke approach and remembered each and every one of those hateful words he'd thrown at her yesterday. My blood pumped faster through my veins. Time to get serious.

Aggressively, I stepped forward and fired off a quick, crisp punch combination. Luke's guard was good and I only managed to catch a glancing blow. He countered back with a punch combination of his own. He was known for his power punches and strikes. That's how he managed to snare his victims. I'd been working really hard on all my defensive moves and my guard until it was automatic and super sharp. So far everything was holding just fine.

As we went deeper into the round, I could feel his frustration growing. His technique was becoming looser. The strikes were no longer as clean and crisp. I just had to be patient, move him around and wear him down.

I sensed rather than heard the crowd becoming more and more restless. They were looking for a result—something to happen.

Luke must have decided it was time, too. He unleashed with a big cross punch and followed it up with a hook that was just as wild. I used the opportunity of his unguarded open body to shoot forward and grab him around the middle, taking him to the mats in a double pick up. There were just as many opportunities to get a knock out on the canvas as I could from a strike while I was on my feet.

I got him pinned to the mat in a solid side control, my body draped sideways across his. Rather than trying to defend or escape, his temper flared again. He was focused far more on trying to pummel me with strikes from his hands and knees, even though I had him pinned to the mat on his back.

Luke's choice of strike over defence made it easy for me to slip from a side control and spin around over his body until I was in a textbook mount position, my hips over his. Now it was my turn to rain strikes down on him. Time and time again, my fists pummelled down and connected with his jaw, head and his forearms, which he used to guard his face. His facial features contorted in rage rather than pain. He was one tough motherfucker.

I cocked my elbow ready to deliver the most punishing of all strikes to his head—a downward elbow. I'd been in this position before; I had the upper hand and I could finish it now with this one strike. As I started the descent of my strike, a flash of a memory penetrated my fight fogged brain and I saw The Cobra's face morph with Luke's and emotions that have no place in the cage pushed at my resolve. I hesitated just a fraction and it was enough for Lights Outs to harmlessly bump my body forward over his head. The opportunity I had was lost and I'd given him the upper hand again.

My legs remained firmly locked around his waist, but he used my momentary lack of commitment to his advantage. Then the postitions were reversed and I was on my back and he was kneeling on one knee; the other leg was ready to push up with his foot which was planted by my hips. My arms were up guarding my head, but that didn't stop the force of the blows he's barraging me with. If the adrenalin wasn't running so hard through my veins, it would have hurt like hell.

Right then, I felt nothing. But it was only a matter of time before he got a knockout if I couldn't get out of this position. The only thing that'd protected me so far was the lock I had with my legs around his waist holding him back, to a degree, and my unfaltering defensive guard over my head.

The frustration was there again and "Lights Out" pulled back for a monster hit. I used the slightly longer break in the tempo between his punches to scoot my body sideways towards his planted foot. In a split second, I slipped my right hand from my guard and wrapped it around his ankle and rolled my body, using the leverage of my legs around his waist as a pendulum. It was a sweet move.

Sweat dripped in my eyes as I now had him pinned against the wall of the cage. Once again I'd managed to get back to a mount position, but this time I had him jammed against the wall of the cage with nowhere to go. Time seemed to slow as I hammered down on his face and upper body with punches—every one of them deserved for his attacks on Eden.

One, two, one, two...the tempo ticked over in my head as my gloved hands hit down on him. His body wriggled beneath me, trying to dislodge me from the position I held over his hips.

Not this time, Luke. This time, I was hanging on.

If I couldn't get the knock out here I was going to hold the advantage to the bell, which had to be any second surely?

I hit down with my left fist and lined up for a punishing strike with my right, but somehow he managed to free his left arm from between our bodies and the cage. His hand grabbed me tight around the back of the neck and before I could react he dragged me down—forward and hard onto his waiting elbow.

Pain radiated out through my skull and my vision darkened for a second. Then I felt the warm sticky ooze as the bell rang out. Never had I been so glad to hear that damned bell. That was so close to being all over.

The referee sent us back to our corners and called the doc to take a look at my head. It was only blood. I hoped to hell the doctor shared the same belief—otherwise my night was really going to suck.

I needed another chance to get the win.

EDEN

Fear clawed at my stomach as I watched the last couple of seconds of that round. Xander had seemed to be in total control, then out of nowhere "Lights Out" had landed some crazy strike.

Now Xander was bleeding from a cut on his forehead as he headed to his corner. My emotions were all over the place—pleased he seemed to be okay but worried he was injured.

"He's okay, Girl. You can let go of my arm," Len's voice bit out. It was only then I realised I had both hands around his forearm this time, and there were little indentations where my nails had been digging in.

"Sorry," I gushed out, my eyes remained solidly focused on what was happening in the cage. "What's going on?" I demanded, feeling absolutely sick with worry.

"Stop panicking. The Doc's going to take a look at it. Most important thing is he made it through the round." Len stood there shaking his head looking agitated. Then he started muttering to himself.

Same as before, my view to Xander was obscured with the guys and the doctor milling around him. Len was upset about something and I had no idea what I should be doing or feeling. I just wanted it to be over and Xander to be safe again.

"I can't believe he keeps going back to the damned mount looking for the knock out strike. Fuck me, is he looking to replay the whole Cobra thing again with a different ending?" Len vented, not even checking his swearing which he usually did around me.

Then I realised what he was saying. Twice in that round Xander had gone looking for a knock-out strike from the mount position. That was one position I did know. Probably best I didn't mention to Len how I'd learnt that one. I understood the point he was making which was something.

"I have no idea, Len," I shrugged.

"Neither do I, but if Reed doesn't tell him to quit that shit, we are going to have some serious words." Then I started to realise just how critical things were. Len was looking very frustrated. Was that a cover for how concerned he was?

"Is he doing okay, Len?"

Len dragged his hand down his face. "He needs to stay on his damned feet and use his real skills, ground fighting isn't working for him today."

I looked between Xander and Len. The guys had moved away a bit and I could see him sitting on the stool looking mighty pissed off or was that determination?

The only thing that made me feel slightly better was that the doctor was leaving the cage and Xander seemed fine.

"Stop worrying, Girl. He's had worse paper cuts." Len seemed to read my mind.

"But there was so much blood."

"Course there was. Heads bleed like a pisser. Always looks way worse than it really is," Len scoffed at me.

I didn't care what he said. It was still blood and I didn't like seeing it coming from the head of the man I loved.

XANDER

"What the hell were you doing?" Reed demanded as I sat down.

Yeah, excellent question. What the hell was I doing? Twice I'd ended up back just like that last God damned fight. What was that about? I was lucky to still be in this bout.

"You're lucky to still be in this." Okay, either Reed and I were on the same page or that hit to the head was worse than I thought because now he was in my head. "But I don't think I need to tell you that. So I hope to hell you're feeling more confident because there's no way you should have survived that round. Now you've just got to bring it home."

The doctor muscled in and sponged the blood away then slabbed a liberal dollop of Vaseline over the cut—ringside first aid at its best.

"Your vision clear?" he asked, focusing on my eyes.

"Yeah, I'm fine." My pride was hurt more than my forehead.

He nodded and turned away. I guess that meant he was

clearing me to fight on. Thank fuck for that. Reed stepped in and took his place as Seth passed me a drink bottle and Dane wiped away the sweat that kept forming on my body.

"Keep working his frustrations. His strikes are getting wilder and wilder. Stay off the fucking canvas and go for a strike. Straight punches. Stay in his face. Be monotonous, annoy the hell out of him. That's what you're good at. God knows you're annoying the hell out of me! Then go for the knockout when he makes a mistake."

I nodded my head and sipped a bit more water.

Nope, wasn't going back to the canvas for another go-round. The canvas Gods definitely weren't loving me tonight.

"He's never had to go past the second round other than that fight with you. It's new territory for him," Dane urged me on confidently. "Definitely a strike will take him out. Come on, Xan, we've worked on this for so many hours."

"Yeah, buddy. Take it from a ground lover. It's a strike for sure," Seth agreed.

The crowd were restless and I tried to keep my head firmly focused on the job still to be done. One minute was both a lifetime and no time at all in the scheme of a fight.

It was time to get back in there.

"Get to work, Pretty Boy!" Reed barked at me.

I caught sight of Dad and Eden as I made my way back. Dad had his fist clenched and threw a jab in the air. Yeah I knew what he meant—strike.

Eden held her hands together to make a heart shape and then pointed at me.

I bumped my fists together and nodded at her.

She'd know what I meant.

For a fleeting moment I wondered if this was how she felt when, she stood at the top of the stairs and had to gather the courage to walk down into the fire. I'd never know just how much courage that took, but I wasn't going to fail her now.

I stepped into the middle and eyed "Lights Out". This was it.

He looked at me with a belligerent smirk and I knew Reed and the guys were right. Frustration was going to be his downfall. I focused on keeping my face expressionless. That would eat at him more than anything else.

When the referee called time on, we danced around the centre for a few seconds, both of us feigning punches and advances.

"Take it to him." It was rare, I normally didn't hear much when I was fighting but I couldn't miss Reed's bellow from the sidelines. It broke through and rattled around in my head.

As if on autopilot, I lunged forward and delivered a jab, cross, jab, punch combination and followed it up with a lightning fast leg kick to his left thigh, which he was leading with. I felt his head snap back at the impact of my fists against his face and it felt good.

Luke took a couple of stumbling steps to the side, but righted himself and I could see the frustration and rage written all over his face. He bulldozed forward at me with a wild right cross punch that he telegraphed a mile away. I easily caught the punch with my left hand and harmlessly brushed it away. This left him wide open and perfectly positioned for me to throw a straight punch and catch him directly in the nose.

I didn't miss.

Immediately, I threw a left hook punch and caught him square on the right of his jaw. Luke was thrown off balance and lurched forward a little, directly into the path of the driving upward knee I had waiting for him.

His body caved in the middle and I heard the breath whistle from his abdomen as the force of my knee drove him back to the wall of the cage. I knew that hurt him. He was moving a little slower and gasping for breath.

That was too good of an opportunity to miss. I rushed forward and locked my hands around his head in a clinch. The wall of the cage halted Luke's backward progress and I started unleashing hits to his body with my knees. I'd hurt him, but now I wanted to really hammer home the message with more heavy strikes to the body. I couldn't give him a chance to get his breath back.

Luke threw some wild blows of his own into my ribs and I struggled to maintain my knees attacking to his midsection. Finally Luke decided he'd had enough of this and pushed me backwards with one of his fists to my cheek in a cross face move. The leather and sweat from his gloved fist was a pungent smell in my nose.

I had no choice but to step back or have my neck snapped at a funny angle. As I stepped back, "Lights Out" chased me with a heavy cross punch, which he landed to my jaw. The impact pushed me back another pace or two and he kept following me as he landed a step through kick to my ribs.

Fortunately, I'd managed to get my arm down just in time to block and the kick hit more on the outside of my flexed bicep than my ribs. If it had been my ribs then I know they would likely have been busted with the force of that kick.

He might be firing back, but I instinctively knew I was gaining ground. Luke's technique had wandered off and his strikes were no longer precise, true and targeted. They were more on the wild and hopeful side. He'd really thought that rib kick would have done some damage.

The frustration was evident in his eyes and on his face. I let him advance one more pace then lashed out with a snapping front kick to his mid-section. Speed was my friend. The impact immediately buckled him over a little. I decided right then to attack his legs. If he couldn't stand, he couldn't fight.

I didn't give him time to recover from the front kick I'd just delivered before I followed it up with a whipping leg kick to his left thigh. My kick landed perfectly. That would leave a cork on the muscle surely?

He stepped away favouring the leg and I sensed the tide of the fight finally turning in my favour. I'd been holding my own until now. It was time to put the hammer down and really take control of this fight.

I wanted to go after that leg some more, but to do that I needed to soften him up with another heavy combination. The leg had slowed him down enough to allow me to land a very heavy straight punch to his nose with my left hand, then a straight punch to his stomach with my right. I think I heard a crack as my fist connected with his nose but I couldn't be sure because of the screaming crowd. They could sense there was something big about to happen.

Every muscle in my body was taut with anticipation and I knew he was hurting. I stepped forward with my left leg and used the whole force of the rotation of my hip, shoulder and arm to deliver a body blow into his ribs. Just as I planned, the combination of punches had left him tight against the cage wall with that weakened left leg open for another attack.

I didn't miss the opportunity.

I fired in another whipping leg kick with pinpoint accuracy. It was pain on top of more pain for "Lights Out". His left leg was no longer a weapon. He'd be lucky if it kept him upright from here on out.

The wall of the cage smacked him from behind and prevented him from retreating further. Anticipation flooded my body. I knew I had him at my mercy.

I stepped in closer looking for the opening. His arms flailed left and right in wild undisciplined blows. He'd lost his technique and all I had to do was keep a solid guard to my face to render his strikes useless. Guard, I could do all day.

Luke dropped his chin and was trying to attack at me with arms that more resembled a windmill, than the world-class fighter he was. Reed was spot on again. This is what frustration did to "Lights Out". I just needed to time this right.

The split second after his left hand connected with my shoulder, I dropped my right fist from the guard on my face and drove my fist upward into the underside of his jaw. It was a teeth-rattling uppercut.

His head snapped back and this opened him up for an easily landed hook punch to the right side of his jaw.

The force of my punch threw his weight forward and I knew this was it. This was where I could get the knockout. The crowd knew it too—the roar intensified to the point it penetrated my focus. I wouldn't be distracted from my task. He'd just given me the perfect opening I was looking for. It was time to take it.

I stepped to the left, reached forward and slipped my right hand behind his head in a move that cupped his skull. To finish it I pulled him down toward my upward thrusting right knee.

The distance closed and I felt the bone in his jaw give way as my knee drove upwards. His weight crashed forward toward the canvas uncontrollably and I knew it was over.

Numbness temporarily enveloped my thoughts. I looked from Luke sprawled prone on the canvas to the referee, then to his corner men who were now rushing into the cage hot on the heels of the doctor that had seen to my head before.

Dread filled me.

Had I done it again? Was history repeating itself?

The doctor dropped to the canvas beside "Lights Out" and I hovered slightly off to the side, my emotions flooding me. What should I do? I'd won but had I killed him too?

Seconds ticked by as the crowd roared at the knockout, then they'd gone deathly quiet waiting for an official result. Every person in the arena now had their eyes glued to what was happening on the canvas a few feet from where I stood. They were all watching the doctor work on "Lights Out" as his crew huddled around, their faces etched with concern.

I couldn't look towards my corner or Eden. If I'd done it again, I didn't think I could survive that. What would they think? Hell, what would Eden think? That's all that mattered to me.

My heart was in my throat and my mouthguard suddenly seemed to be smothering me. The doctor motioned to the balding referee and he leant in close. There was a little nodding and I had no idea what that meant. Then I thought I saw one of Luke's legs twitch.

Was it good or was it bad?

A few seconds later, the referee stood and strode forward to me. He grabbed my right fist, which was hanging limply at my side and thrust it in the air.

"You're the winner by knockout. He's going to be fine." The crowd picked up on what was happening before the referee had even had time to finish his sentence to me. They were cheering and screaming with even more intensity.

"Ladies and Gentleman. Winner by knockout in the third round, Xander "Pretty-Boy" Todd." The Master of Ceremonies voice cut through the din.

It was all so surreal. I was struggling to believe what the referee was telling me. As is if to confirm what he'd told me, I glanced down and saw Luke moving some more. Relief flooded through me. He really was going to be okay.

Then it hit me like a tonne of bricks.

I'd done it and no one was more surprised than me.

THIRTY-FIVE

EDEN

It all happened in a blur. One moment Xander had him pinned against the cage and the next, "Lights Out" was falling forward to the canvas, his body prone.

"He's done it," Len yelled in pride.

My mind took in what had happened—he'd won.

The crowd hushed and focused on the action in the cage.

Then I saw the look on his face and I knew what was replaying in his head. He was reliving the end of the last fight with The Cobra. My heart bled for him. I could see the pain etched in his face. He thought he'd done it again.

Oh God, I hoped not. How would he ever forgive himself?

I grabbed for Len's arm. "What's happening?"

Len was shaking his head. "Boy's won the fight, but Luke's not moving." I could hear the concern in his voice.

My eyes flew around the arena and back to the cage taking it all in. Concern was written on every face in the arena. After what seemed like eons, but could only have been a few seconds, the referee approached the doctor and they seemed to be conferring.

Then I was sure I saw Luke's leg move as the referee headed over to Xander.

He thrust Xander's arm into the air in victory and the arena erupted in cheers.

I jumped up and down and hugged Len hard.

"He won! He won!" I cried.

"He did!" Len yelled. Then he was dragging me from our seats to where the little gate that opened onto the floor surrounding the cage was. Security stopped us.

"Get out of the way, mate." Len was in no mood to mince words. The security guard looked from Len to me and I clearly saw the moment he realised who I was and opened the gate for us.

Another security guy jogged to keep up as Len and I rushed to the cage. We were up the steps and inside before I realised what was happening. Reed, Seth and Dane had Xander in a massive hug. They were all bouncing around, backslapping and cheering.

Luke was now being taken away on a stretcher his arm up and waving to the crowd. I rushed forward and pushed through the crush of people that seemed to have found their way into the cage.

"Xander!" I called.

His head snapped up and his eyes locked on mine. He muscled his way from the hold the guys had on him and pushed forward to meet me.

My arms closed around his neck and I hugged him to me tightly. Right there in his arms my world felt right.

"Oh Xan, you did it!" Emotion was choking my words and tears were streaming down my face. I was so pleased for him and I knew we were together on an emotional rollercoaster at the moment.

Len stepped up and wrapped his arms around both of us.

"Proud of you, Son. Well done!"

Xander lifted his head from beside mine and looked at his father.

"Thanks, Dad."

His face was starting to swell in a few spots and the cut on his head looked angry but I knew it the moment I really looked into his eyes.

He'd beaten back his demons.

He was free.

•••

The next hour was crazy. People swarmed all over us, which I found disconcerting, but manageable. I thought back to how I would have handled this three months ago and inwardly dissolved into a fit of hysterical giggles. Handled it! I would have melted into a puddle on the spot.

Throughout all the craziness Xander never left my side, other than to take a shower when we finally made it to the dressing room—which now seemed to have become more like an impromptu party room than his dressing room. Champagne was flowing and people were definitely in the mood to celebrate. I'm sure Xan would have dragged me into the bathroom, too, but now wasn't really the time to be testing new ground for me. Although I'm almost positive I would have been fine with Xander there beside me.

I stood to the side of the room enjoying the champagne and kind of catching my breath, while I waited for him to emerge. It was only now I realised how tough and emotionally draining the last few days had been. But I was proud of how far I'd come as a person and the way I'd handled it. I'd made it through, by believing in myself and Xander. Everything else was really just white noise when it was all said and done.

I hadn't noticed Reed move up beside me, I'd been too consumed watching for Xander. He nudged me gently in the ribs with his elbow. "You'd better go rescue him when he comes out. The hoard look hungry!" I'd noticed the bevy of scantily clad women with lots of hair, boobs and short skirts all swarming around. I had no idea who they were or where they came from. They'd just seemed to descend on the room with the PR people and promoters.

"Who are they all?"

"Oh, just the hanger oners. They seem to turn up at every fight. Kind of like flies at a BBQ."

I giggled at that visual. Reed was one hundred percent right. He'd made a point of seeking me out this morning while Xander had been stretching and getting a massage, to apologise for his behaviour. I got the feeling that wasn't something Reed did often, so I appreciated the effort he made. We were on the way to constructing some sort of relationship, which I knew was important to Xander even if he hadn't said so. Yes, Reed hadn't been particularly nice to me, but he'd been acting out of concern for Xander so for that I could forgive him.

But there was something I needed to say to Reed tonight. "Thanks for looking after him this campaign and fight. I know it wasn't easy. You did great."

Reed nodded. "He gave me a few more grey hairs tonight, but he got the job done in the end."

I giggled a little. "Yeah I don't think I'm very good at watching him fight. Len's got my nail prints all up his forearm."

"He's tough, he'll cope," he said shrugging.

"Yes, but I'm not sure my heart can take it. I'm only now realising how much of a nervous wreck I've been for days," I joked.

This time Reed let out a belly laugh. "You haven't been on your own, you know?"

What? These guys had all been swanning around the last few days like nothing was going on. "But you guys have all been so casual about it."

He winked at me. "I'll let you in on a little secret." Reed looked up from me glancing around as if trying to spot someone. His eyes stopped on Len, who was across the room talking to some distinguished looking guy in a tailored suit. "We've been shitting bricks for the last eight weeks. The last few days became particularly uncomfortable for Len and me."

I burst out laughing, not quite believing what I was hearing or who I was laughing with. I was staggered that Reed was telling me this and it must have been written all over my face because he then went on to explain.

"I figure I might as well come clean. Xander made it very clear to the whole world yesterday where he was at, with you two. You'll be part of the next prep so you might as well share the grief from the start."

Next fight! I hadn't thought that far. "Can I get over this one first? Or is there something already in place that I don't know about?" What weren't they telling me? I ended my comment with a giggle of trepidation.

"Na, nothing yet." Reed nodded his head over at Len. "But Len's talking to the money man over there. I'd say it's a very safe bet they're talking about another fight." There was a bit of a pause, before Reed asked the very telling question. "How do you feel about that?"

Wasn't that the question? It was Reed fishing to see what my reaction was. Surprisingly, it didn't take me long to answer. What's more it was the truth as I saw it at least. This was what Xander was supposed to do. He was fulfilling his dreams.

"Reed, fighting and martial arts are a very big part of who Xander is. I know he has some reservations about certain aspects of fighting because he's in a relationship with me, but we worked around them. If he wants to keep fighting, that's totally up to him. I'll support him whatever his decision is. But I have to trust that you and he know what's best for him when it comes to taking fights and what he's capable of doing." I looked him directly in the eye. I wanted to put it on him. Reed needed to know that I would hold him at least partly responsible for whatever happened in the future. "Can you promise me that?"

He nodded and a very serious demeanour came over him. "Yeah Eden, you can trust me. Xander is like a little brother to me. I wouldn't put him in any fight I thought he couldn't handle nor would I let him step into the cage if he wasn't prepped properly."

"Good, then yes I will support whatever he decides." I meant it. That was what relationships were about, supporting your partner.

"Can't say I won't be a nervous wreck, but I'll try to keep a lid on it."

"We all feel the same," he admitted.

Xander emerged from the attached bathroom, showered and looking somewhat refreshed. A shorter redhead with curves that belied gravity, tried looping an arm around him as he came through the door.

He politely removed the arm and said something to her. Her big hopeful smile turned to a nasty looking sneer and I couldn't help but feel amused.

Then Reed turned to study me. "You mentioned he had reservations. He never said anything to me..." Reed was fishing and I could tell it was killing him that he didn't know everything about Xan. Reed was very territorial about his fighter as we'd discovered over the last weeks.

"Let's just say it's something you can't help him with nor do you need to know if he hasn't told you."

Reed stood there looking puzzled. Then he nodded towards Xander fighting his way through the crowd. "He looks like he needs rescuing from the "flies"."

Reed was right. Xander was glancing around the milling crowd looking for us.

"I'll make it easy for him. I'll go try out my own brand of fly spray."

He chuckled and patted me on the shoulder. "Yeah, go look after him. He deserves it."

I placed my champagne flute on a nearby table then negotiated my way through the throng of people. The closer I got to him the more he seemed to be surrounded by "flies". He looked so handsome standing there even with his battered and bruised look. I couldn't resist this wounded warrior so I totally got the appeal and attraction he presented for the "flies" but it wasn't going to work for me any longer. The last few feet towards him proved more challenging. The flies were pretty thick!

Being tall worked to my advantage. Xan saw me coming and he

moved forward toward me. I took the last couple of steps shouldering my way through the stiletto-heeled pack.

I ignored the "Watch it, bitch" and the "Wait your turn." Xander was mine. They'd just have to find another BBQ. The distance between us closed and I threw my arms around his neck and kissed him hard on the lips. He drew back a fraction and hissed, "Steady Gem."

I leant in close and whispered in his ear suggestively, "Someone in need of a little TLC?"

He hugged me tight to his body. "Oh yeah, definitely in need of some TLC but you might need to be gentle with me."

I giggled back and nuzzled my mouth into his ear. "I can be gentle. Let me know when you're ready to start the TLC."

He made a sexy growling sound in the back of his throat and every single nerve ending in my body twitched in readiness.

"That works for me. Let me see if we can bail," he whispered back.

"Sounds good to me."

The "flies" around us had started to disperse when they realised the BBQ was over.

Reed moved up to us and winked at me. "Most effective bug spray around." Then he turned to Xander. "They need you for the press conference man."

Xander let out a pained sigh. "Really?"

"Yep, really. Last one."

"Okay, if I really have to." He sounded like a little kid that was complaining over eating his vegetables.

"You really have to," Reed confirmed. "Part of the contract."

We started to make our way to the door.

"Would have almost been worth getting knocked out to avoid it," he grumbled.

"Don't say that," I chastised. "Don't even think it. It'll all be over soon."

"Then I get some TLC?"

"Yep, then you get some TLC."

"Awesome. It's been a very long two weeks," he said nibbling on my ear lobe.

I couldn't have agreed more.

•••

We were escorted from Xander's dressing room by security to a large room that was filled with the waiting press. Xander had kept his arm around my waist the whole way. Reed, Len and the boys were right behind. This room was set up a little different to the one at the hotel yesterday. This meant Xander had to walk down a central aisle to take to the raised podium stage at the front of the room. There was a table and two chairs on the little stage with microphones behind both. Parker Cook was already sitting on one of the chairs.

Xander turned to walk down to the front and I baulked. Xander was still holding on to me as he turned and looked at me with a question in his eyes. I wasn't supposed to be up there in the open with him.

"I want you with me," he confirmed, pulling me close.

"But it's about you," I protested.

"I would never even be here to take that podium if it wasn't for you. Please?"

How could I resist? I nodded and the butterflies returned to my stomach. We started the walk down the aisle and cameras clicked and flashed like crazy. Reporters kept thrusting microphones in our faces and asking questions. It was a mob scene. I glanced behind me nervously and noticed Len and Reed were hot on our heels. Len winked at me as if to say, "I've got your back, Girl." And I knew it was true and I felt so much better for their support.

At the end of the aisle Xander took me over to the side of the room level with the podium and dropped a light kiss to my lips and whispered for my ears only. "Looking forward to that TLC, Gem." I heard the cameras go wild and I knew that there was a warm glow heating my face. Len moved to one side of me and

Reed the other. Dane and Seth stood behind me forming a solid wall of support.

Xander sat down at the table. Parker leaned over and said something to Xander. He turned and glanced across at me and I wondered what Parker had said. Then Xander nodded and said something back.

The press all seemed to be just as interested in the exchange. The place had hushed considerably. Parker turned on his microphone.

"Ladies and Gentleman, thank you for coming tonight. First up I'd like to congratulate tonight's winner by knockout, Xander "Pretty Boy" Todd." There was applause, cheers and whistles before the press settled down again as Parker went on to talk about what an overwhelming success the night had been and how the fight had really lived up to all that it had promised.

Then the questions started.

"Xander, how do you feel about tonight's win," a reporter from a news station asked.

"I'm very pleased with the result. I've achieved what I set out to do. I've trained incredibly hard during this prep to achieve the win and I got it," Xander said modestly. He wasn't one for a lot of hoopla. "But I couldn't have done it without the support of my team. Reed as my trainer, Dane and Seth as my training partners and, of course, Dad to keep everything running smoothly. Thank you all so much. Their support means the world to me" They all nodded around me. Then his eyes found mine. "But I'd like to give a special thank you to my girlfriend, Eden. This whole prep has been completely new and very challenging for her, but never once has she faltered in supporting me even when she's had to endure what no one should. Thanks, Gem. Your support, courage and commitment is what got me across the line tonight. You reminded me how to be brave again."

My heart was fluttering and squeezing and I couldn't love him anymore, could I? An attractive woman in a suit asked the next question. "You took a few heavy hits tonight; have you sustained any injuries as a result?"

Xander grinned. "Ah yeah, I got myself into a few situations I shouldn't have. But no, I don't have any injuries." He motioned to his forehead. "I've got a few bruises and this little war wound that I'm sure, Reed my trainer, is getting a laugh out of. This one might leave a bit of a scar and mess up my ring name." Xander shot Reed a cheeky grin. "But on the whole I'm fine, nothing that a few days rest won't heal."

A reporter from down the back yelled out, "Were you expecting him to be so tough, Xander?"

Xander nodded. "Yeah I expected it. I knew this fight was going to be insanely tough. Luke's a great fighter and he's got massively better since we last met. He had every advantage with a home town crowd and heaps more recent experience, but I wanted this win badly. I guess I should be apologising for ruining your party shouldn't I?" Xander gave them a mock grimace and they all burst out laughing and responded to his easy personality.

"Xander, you seemed really slow to get going tonight," someone to the side called out, but I couldn't work out who.

"You might say that! The ring rust was damned thick. I won't deny it. I know I was lucky to survive a couple of times, but I guess instinct and training kicked in and I got home tonight."

Then one of the reporters that had been niggling at the last press conference stood up and my stomach dropped with dread. "You seemed really rattled after "Lights Out" hit the canvas. What was going through your mind? It looked like you were reliving your last fight."

I saw Xander's jaw work and I knew this question was one that cut deep. "Yeah, I'd be lying if the past didn't cross my mind. We all know the risks when we step into the cage but that's why we train, to minimise them. I'm just really glad Luke's going to be okay. Regardless of our differences, no fighter wants to see his opponent badly injured or worse."

"Not even when he trash talked your girlfriend?" someone piped up.

Xander didn't speak for a moment and he looked royally pissed. "Trash talking is part of the fight scene. Sometimes it goes too far. Luke majorly crossed the line with his comments, but that's on him."

A young woman in the second row stood. "What are your thoughts on the social media storm that's been blowing up the web since your posts yesterday?"

Xander shrugged nonchalantly. "I really have no comment because I haven't looked. I turned my phone off as soon as I made those posts. To win tonight's fight I needed to fully concentrate on my job."

"Well then, let me give you a few stats." She looked down and read from her notepad. "The video footage of your press conference has been viewed over twenty million times. Your hashtag Brave has been trending on all platforms since about an hour after you posted it. You've received over one hundred thousand tweets of support, your fan numbers have quadrupled on both twitter and Facebook and just about every major media outlet in the country and overseas has picked it up!"

Oh my God! Was this true? I'd been living in a self-induced bubble. If I didn't know about it, then it couldn't hurt me.

Xander laughed a little in disbelief and stared at the woman. "Are you serious?"

The woman grinned at him obviously enjoying being the one that broke the news to him. "Absolutely. What you said at yesterday's press conference then what you posted last night seems to have really resonated with people. How do you feel about that?"

He sat back in his chair and ran his hand through his short cropped dark hair. "Wow."

"Did you mean to start a social media tsunami? Because that's what has happened. It seems people are sick of the social media trolls and are posting that hashtag Brave in response to and on everything they see as being derogatory, hurtful or degrading."

The room was silent except for the cameras that were all

focused on Xander looking stunned. “I never realised. I just felt so helpless last night. Eden was coping all this backlash she didn’t deserve because of me and I’d had enough.”

“But isn’t that exactly the point?” the woman insisted. “You gave a voice and support to everybody that has ever felt or been bullied and been unable to stand up to them.”

Xander looked shell shocked. None of the hits he’d taken tonight seemed to have left him as dazed as this. The press and every person in the room were waiting patiently for him to respond as was I.

Finally after a few long seconds he spoke. “I guess… As I said, I did it because I felt frustrated and helpless that people were being cruel and were taking cowardly pot shots from behind the protection of their screens or phones at Eden. To me, that said so much about them as people since they were attacking others that they didn’t even know. If what I did gives people hope and support to fight their own demons and the courage to go on when some insecure people will knock them down for being brave enough to have a go, then I guess I’ve had an even bigger win with those posts last night, than I did tonight.”

What happened next shocked the hell out of me.

A woman from the back of the room stood and started to clap. Every head in the room turned and looked then another and another stood clapping until every person in the room was clapping in support of what Xander had said.

Somewhere in the whole surreal experience my hands had joined as had those of the men around me. Tears streamed down my face and I grabbed at Len’s arm. I’d been so proud of Xander when he won tonight. I couldn’t be prouder now. Xander was the type of person that made a difference by just being himself and doing what was right.

He knew what it was to be brave and he’d shown me and the rest of the world.

THIRTY-SIX

XANDER

I was stretched out on the bed naked. It was a forward and in your face move but Eden and I were way past freaking out over a little nakedness now—it was just another little reminder of how far our relationship had come. How much she had grown.

Adrenaline had left my body a long while back. Now the bone weariness had overtaken me, but no way was I too weary for my girl. After the press conference, the doctor had put a couple of stitches in my head. Then my dad, Reed and the guys had come back here for a few quiet drinks. We'd finally managed to kick everybody out of the suite ten minutes ago. I was still struggling to actually believe the events of the night.

This fight and the prep had been tough mentally and I just felt like I needed some time to decompress and relax my body and mind. All I wanted to do was chill out and hang with Eden for a bit. I'd had enough of being on show for the last few weeks, particularly the last two days. I feared my life was going to be a three ringed circus for a while after the events of the last couple of days. Some people loved being a celebrity; I was a reluctant celebrity, at best. I found it more to be a necessary evil and part of the territory, than something I craved or needed.

I didn't have any more time for contemplation, because every functioning brain cell I had suddenly focused on Eden crossing the floor from the bathroom to the bed. Fuck she looked like a runway model as she glided across the floor to me.

I loved her long loose, limbed figure, with all those soft curves that just called to my hands. I needed to be with her, in her, on her more than I needed my next breath. She wore a little camisole top and loose satin shorts in a shining dark grey colour. The contrast on her golden skin tone and hair looked incredible. Her hair was all thick and falling in lush waves around her face and shoulders. But her eyes? There was something new there. There was all the beauty of Eden I was so used to seeing now, but that wasn't it. It was something deeper.

She took another couple of steps and then it struck me. It was a confidence in herself as a woman. My woman. God, she did it for me. Other guys might like the cheap, the obvious and the fake. I'd take Eden every time. I loved the genuine integrity that was an essential part of her soul. It wasn't there on show for everyone to see, but it was there if you bothered to look.

Not for the first time, I thanked whatever higher power had prompted me to get off my arse that day in the café.

"Are you ready for some TLC?" She looked at me with a sultry and suggestive smile.

"Oh yeah, Gem. Come love me up, sweetheart." I held out my hand to her.

She moved around to the end of the bed and crawled up over me on all fours. Her hair draped down around us like a silken curtain and the light from the lamp threw shadows over her face as she looked down at me.

"You're so beautiful Gem—inside and out." The words caught in my throat with emotion. I meant every one of them.

"Thank you." She smiled and lent down to press her lips to mine. This time she went carefully. Her lips brushed mine in a caress that was so soft it could only be described as a tease. She pulled back a fraction and ran her tongue along my bottom lip. It still stung in places.

I must have winced a little or something.

She pulled back. “Does that hurt?”

“It stings a little but I’ll gladly pay the price to have you kiss me, Gem.” I reached up and pulled her head back down to mine. Her lips found mine again softly. Then she drifted to the sides and kissed both corners of my mouth. Then she placed little kisses along the line of my jaw, and around my eye.

“What are you doing, gorgeous girl?” I wriggled and chuckled a little under her ministrations.

“I’m kissing all your booboos better. Where else did you get hit?” Her silky lips had just about covered all my face and were making their way down my neck to my chest. She ran her tongue around the dragon on my chest and I couldn’t help the shiver that ripped through my body more than any punch “Lights Out” had landed tonight.

Her head dropped to the side and she found a few bruises that were now visible on my ribs. They’d be black and blue tomorrow before turning a rainbow of colours over the next week. It was all part of the game.

Once she’d kissed and petted all over the right side of my ribs she headed for the left. I couldn’t resist it anymore. Her beautiful breasts were right there teasing me from under that floaty little top. I slid my hands down her back and grabbed the hem of it, sliding it back up and over her head.

“I love that colour on you, Gem, but nothing compares to seeing your beautiful skin.” I trailed my hands up and down her rib cage. I loved running my hands all over her. My hands briefly found one of my favourite places to rest —her breasts, until she dropped lower and started trailing kisses across my abdomen.

I was so turned on. My cock was so hard and now cradled between her breasts as she draped herself over the lower part of me.

"What are you doing to me, Gem?"

She looked up with mischief in her eyes. "I thought that would have been perfectly obvious. I'm showering you with tender loving care."

"Is that what it is? All I know, Gem, is that I'm so hot for you right now." There was a pained tone to my voice.

A knowing little giggle escaped her throat and the breeze tickled my stomach. "Is that right? Then I guess I'd better do something about that."

Before I could say another word or even figure out what she had in mind those silky lips wrapped around my cock and her tongue stroked around the head. It was some kind of heaven. The little minx seemed to hit every sensitive spot with laser like precision.

She sucked me down deep and caressed her tongue up the underside of my cock and I sucked in a hard breath to keep from coming. My hips rocketed off the bed and I tried to blank my mind to the exquisite sensations she was reeking on my dick. It had been too long and now I was so close.

Once again she did it and my reaction was just the same, but this was not how I wanted to finish tonight.

"Gem," I pleaded in a strained tone. "Baby, you've got to stop or I'm going to come like this. I want to be buried deep inside you when I do." To emphasis my point I grabbed her shoulders and pulled her up.

My rock hard cock left her mouth with a distinctive "pop" and she giggled a little. She pressed up to her hands and knees again over me and I wriggled down the huge bed a little more so I could pull one of those rosy nipples of hers into my mouth.

I lapped my tongue across the hardened peak and her back arched, then I circled my tongue and a little moan escaped her throat. Enjoying this game I grazed my teeth across the bud and this time I was rewarded with a little squeal and she pressed her breast harder into my mouth.

"Oh, you like that, Gem?" It wasn't really a question. Her

answer had been obvious but she let out a breathy "Yes" anyway. I slid my hands down over her back until I found the fabric of the cute little shorts at her hips. I hooked my fingers in and pushed the fabric over the curve of her butt and down her thighs. Eden kicked them off the rest of the way. My hands returned to that rounded butt I loved so much and squeezed the globes tight in my fingers. I loved everything about this woman but I needed more than just my hands on her. I wanted her wild and wanting.

I pulled her body forward. "Wriggle up, Gem. I want a taste. I've missed having my mouth on your pussy. I've missed your taste."

"I thought I was the one supposed to be smothering you in TLC?" she complained but complied none the less.

"Oh this is TLC, Gem. Just being with you is all I need." I didn't say anything else; just drew her hips down over my lips and ran my tongue the length of her slit. The flavour of her arousal burst on my tongue like sherbet and I lapped at the wetness, wanting more.

She cried out and bucked her hips into my face. It was the sort of hit I'd never get tired of feeling. Every ache I had from the fight was fast disappearing. I found the little tight nub of her clit and focused my attentions there until she was panting like she'd run an Olympic sprint. When I felt her tense in readiness for release I sucked her clit into my mouth and paused, drawing out the sensation. Should I let her come? Or should I make her wait?

Decisions, decisions.

"Oh, Xander, please!" she begged and the decision was made for me.

How could I resist Eden anything, much less something that would bring us both so much pleasure. I kept up the suction and flicked my tongue over her clit.

Immediately her hips bucked and grounded against my face and her body flung about wildly. Her breath was coming in harsh pants between agonising groans of pleasure as she screamed my name. I held her tight to me, dragging out her pleasure with my tongue and lips. Finally, she slumped forward towards the head of the bed looking all sexy and satisfied. The look on her face was a huge stroke to my male ego. What man didn't want to see his woman looking like this and going nuts at what he did to her?

I ran my hand up and down her thigh, as I let her catch her breath. Suddenly I realised the weariness had disappeared only to be replaced by a hunger for her that was raw and basal.

Her head lifted from the pillow in surprise as I rolled from the bed. I could see the question in her eyes.

I rounded the bed and leant forward to hook her knees in the crook of my arms. I dragged her back down the bed and the surprise in her eyes had turned to a hot look of need. She might have been shy to start with, but not anymore. Now Eden was open to anything and everything. I knew it was because she trusted me in everything we did and not just in the bedroom. Eden knew I'd never betray that trust. The feeling it gave me, knowing how much she trusted me, was something that just seemed to overwhelm me at times.

She grinned up at me as her hips came level with the end of the bed. "I thought you were tired and a bit battered and bruised tonight."

I chuckled and returned her grin. "I am. But suddenly the part of my body that is hurting the most is my cock and I know exactly how you can make that pain go away."

She giggled and raised her eyebrows at me suggestively. "Well then, what are you waiting for?"

I tightened my grip around her thighs and nudged my hips forward. Like a missile guidance system, my cock immediately found the target and I thrust home. The sensations of her hot wet pussy surrounding me flooded my senses. I sucked in a breath and gritted my teeth trying to push back the need to lose my head in a few quick violent thrusts to oblivion.

Eden wrapped her long legs around my hips and locked them at my waist pulling her tight to me. It was so fucking good. I rocked my hips in long firm thrusts until we had a rhythm that seemed to suit both of us. Her hands clutched at the sheets and she was rolling her hips to meet mine.

"Oh yeah, Xan. There. Right there." I retraced the arc my hips had travelled and she panted, "So good," in reply. Oh yeah, she was so right.

My balls were sucked tight to my body screaming for release as I felt her walls start to squeeze me.

Then her back arched up and I released the brakes on my control. I slammed my hips hard into her, both chasing and pushing her to release. The harder I thrust the wilder she thrashed on the bed. She met my thrusts one last time with a roll of her hips and cried out her release. I could hold back my own orgasm no longer.

My hips hammered into her in short sharp strokes while her walls drained every last drop of pleasure from me.

Somehow I managed to hold my feet, even though the bone-tired weariness had returned and my head was spinning.

We both looked at each other and laughed. It had been so intense and earth shattering, but there really was no elegant escape from this position.

"Get up here, Pretty Boy, and give me a cuddle before you fall on your butt." She held out a hand to me. Now there was a demand I knew I'd be smart to follow.

EDEN

The next morning I woke to find him missing from the bed, and a hum and gurgling noise coming from the bathroom. I rolled over and edged to the side of the bed before padding across to the bathroom.

I couldn't keep the smile from my face as I found him lying, eyes closed in the monster tub with the spa jets running. The bruises on his face were a little more prominent this morning, but he was still sexy and handsome to me. The bubbles were playing peek a boo with my ability to see his hard cut body. Just when I caught a glimpse, they'd reform over where I'd been looking, obscuring my view.

Xander must have sensed me there and his eyelids slowly rose and a lopsided grin formed on his face.

"Morning, gorgeous," he said.

"Hey, you. You feeling okay?" I asked, concerned that he'd got up to sit in the spa because he was hurting.

"I'm okay, a bit stiff and sore, but on the whole I'm fine. I should have done more recovery work after the fight." His hands broke the surface of the water in a move that spoke of the impossibility of that with everything that went on. "I woke up a while ago and you looked so peaceful, I thought I'd come hang in here for a while."

His eyes were trailing my body and becoming increasingly hungry. I knew that look and it was a thought I shared. An idea popped into my mind and I suddenly felt nervous. Could I go through with it?

"Stay right there. I'll be back in a sec." I headed to the separate toilet off the bathroom and closed the door behind me. After I did what I needed to do, I washed my hands in the basin and looked at my reflection in the mirror.

The face I saw looking back at me still had those same scars yet it was very different from the one that used to look back at me. This one was the face of a woman who was no longer controlled by her fears. This was the face of a woman who was brave enough to take what she wanted from life and make it hers. Fears were something that just needed to be faced and pushed at. None of it was easy, but nothing worth something ever was. The man lying in that tub was more than worth conquering any fears I might have

The thought of enjoying being able to share it with him, and the need to do so, was more than my fear of the warm water in the tub. I pulled my hair up off my face and secured it on the top of my head in a messy knot with an elastic I'd left on the vanity.

This was it. I headed back to the bathroom and moved to the tub. Xander hadn't moved but he was watching me curiously.

"Want to join me, Gem?" He held his hand out for me to take, seeming to understand what I wanted.

I reached my hand out and took his. His fingers closed tight around me as a peace and strength descended over me. It was all I needed.

"It's not very hot. It won't burn. Just put one foot in at a time." His voice was calm and reassuring.

As if on command at his voice, my left leg rose and my toes, then my instep and finally my heel descended into the warm water. The water actually felt surprisingly comforting and I stepped forward until my leg was submerged to my knee. Then I brought the other leg over the edge and into the water.

"You okay, Gem? You're doing great."

I placed my other hand on the edge of the tub and took a deep breath. This was it. I didn't think about it anymore. It wouldn't hurt me. I lowered the rest of my body into the water and I felt the warm resistance coupled with the tickling bubbles of the spa jets. It was surprisingly good and my mind raced back to a time when I used to love having a bath.

Xander let go of my hand and pulled me back against his body, wrapping an arm around my chest. That was all I needed. Any previous fears of warm water now seemed ridiculous and foreign.

"How's that, baby?"

"Feels good," I admitted.

He chuckled. "Can you be a little more precise? What feels good? Beating the hot water demon? The spa? Or being cuddled close to me?"

"Can I be greedy and say all three?"

"You surely can."

"Then I'm saying all three."

He brushed a loose strand of hair back from my face.

"I love you, Eden. Thanks for sticking by me through all that crap. I know how difficult it was for you."

"I guess that's the thing I've learned about love, Xan. It makes you want to do things you don't think you're capable of, or even want to, for someone else. Case in point, I'm sitting in this bath and it's pretty damned good." I turned my head and kissed his jaw.

"You're right. I didn't think I'd ever get in the ring again and I did because I needed to." He seemed to be in a quiet and reflective mood this morning. I didn't mind in the least. The last few days had been insane.

"Are you going to take another fight?" I asked not sure whether I was ready for the answer or not.

"Yeah, I think I probably will. Dad mentioned to me last night there's a shot at the world title after that win last night. I'll give it a few weeks, then make a call." He went quiet again for a little while. "How do you feel about that?"

I laced my fingers through his free hand. "I'll tell you what I told Reed last night." I felt him stiffen under me. "I told him that it was totally up to you. If that's what you want to do I'd support you; the same thing applies if you don't ever want to step into the cage again. The decision's yours, Xan. I'd never stop you from doing something you felt the need to do. That's not what loving someone is about. It's about being part of what they're trying to achieve. It's about supporting and being there for them. You've done that so much for me and I want to do the same for you."

He squeezed me tighter to him. "God, I love you, Eden."

"Whatever you want to do is fine by me."

"I haven't made any decisions. I need to think on it some more, but it is something I've always wanted to do."

"I know." I squeezed his hand.

"You do realise our life is probably going to be a little crazy from now on out? I've no idea where all this press and social media shit is going to go," he warned.

"One thing I've learned Xan is that you can't help what other people think, say or do. Trying to second guess them will drive you insane and stop you from achieving anything. You can only be true to yourself and the ones you love, no one else really matters in the scheme of things."

"When did you get so wise?" he joked.

"Um, I kind of met this guy who demanded that I stop hiding and come out to join the world with him."

"Really. Must have been a hell of a guy."

"Modest, too." We both laughed for a bit.

I pulled our joined hands out from under the water and examined the pads of my fingers. "Will you look at that? We've even got matching prune wrinkles."

"Definitely a match made in heaven," he agreed.

"So what are we going to do today? I'm not sure we can sit in here much longer."

"Nope. That would probably be a bad idea, but I do have an idea that I think would be much better." His voice had gone to that low growl tone that I loved; every one of my nerves was back on high alert.

"What did you have in mind?" I asked a little breathlessly with anticipation.

"How about we take in the sights?" It wasn't exactly what I thought he'd suggest but I didn't mind as long as I was with him. "There's something in Vegas that I'd really like to try on for size."

The place was full of casinos and to date we'd done very little other than focus on the fight; a little flutter at the tables might be fun. "Are you looking to see if you can increase your winnings?"

"That wasn't exactly what I had in mind; I'm a lucky guy to have you. It'd probably be really pushing my luck to think I could win at the tables as well." He shifted his body a bit and his very hard erection probed at my hip.

I dragged our linked hands to his cock and closed my hand around him. His hand cupped mine over his engorged flesh. "This is something that I'd be happy to try on for size, if this is your much better idea."

He chuckled. "You can try that on for size as much as you want, Gem. But getting back to my idea before you remove all rational thought from my head... we're in Vegas and I'm a firm believer in taking in the whole experience. There's one in particular I think we'll really love, but it's kind of a leap of faith."

I was getting suspicious. I'd seen the brochures for that bungee jump off the hotel on the coffee table just yesterday. In fact, Dane had been talking about it. That experience looked horrific. "Xan, I'm all for facing fears, but I'm not inclined to want to jump off a perfectly good building and I'm not sure the jolt would be great for you at the moment."

He burst out laughing. "That's not what I had in mind. Dane and Seth can go do that shit."

I had no idea what he was talking about then. "I give up. What's this great idea?" I wished he'd hurry up and get on with it, because I had ideas of my own. I closed my fingers to give him a little reminder.

Then he removed our joined hands from around him and caught my chin in his fingers and turned my head so I could see his eyes. They were dark and serious and full of emotion. "I love you more than anything, Eden. I thought the leap of faith we could take was marriage. Will you do me the honour of becoming my wife?"

My stomach felt as if it flipped over and my heart leapt into my mouth. I took a great gulping breath and gave him the only answer that made any sense.

"Yes, Sensei."

EPILOGUE

six months later

EDEN

I laid back and tried to clear my mind and relax as the needles of Jarryd's tattooing machine moved over the raised skin on my side. Today was the last of the ten sessions I'd endured in order to transform the ugly scars of my side into a true work of art. It had been five months and lots of pain but I knew it would be worth it. I grimaced and let out a little squeak of pain. Some areas just hurt like a bitch!

Xander squeezed my hand in support and I glanced over at our matching wedding rings. "Nearly done, Gem. Hang in there, gorgeous." His voice was calming but I knew he felt every jolt of pain that I felt.

"When do you start the prep for the World Title fight?" Jarryd asked in that low calm voice of his.

"Monday week," Xander answered. I could hear the excitement in his voice. He really did live for this stuff.

"Feeling confident?"

"I wouldn't have taken the fight if I didn't. It's a huge commitment for not only me, but my whole team and Eden. I wouldn't do it unless I was one hundred percent committed," he explained.

I winced again as Jarryd hit another tender spot. "How do you feel about it, Eden?"

Jarryd was trying to take my mind off it, bless him. "If that's what he wants to do then he should do it. I'll support him one hundred percent."

"You're lucky to find someone so supportive of what you do, Xan. It can't be easy being a fighter's wife," Jarryd commented.

"It has its moments. Although, it might be different for all I know this time. Last prep I was his girlfriend. This time I'm his wife."

Oh, how things had changed since then. Five minutes after the shock of Xander asking me to marry him had worn off, we'd sprung into action. He'd found a "traditional Vegas Chapel" and the plans had swung into action. Later that afternoon I'd walked down the aisle on Len's arm to be met at the altar by Xander and his groomsmen—Reed, Dane and Seth.

I'd found a gorgeous designer dress in the hotel boutique that was an ivory silk and stunningly beautiful in its simplicity. It was completely unadorned by anything other than the beautiful long lace sleeves. The rest of the dress was absolutely plain but clung to every plane and curve of my body like it had been custom designed for me. Xan wore an impeccably cut dark suit with a snowy white shirt and he couldn't have looked more handsome. The bruises and slight puffiness of his features only seemed to give him more of a "bad boy" air. Oh yeah, but he was my own version of a "bad boy." I'd take respectful, honourable and committed over anything else. There was absolutely no doubt in my mind he was the man for me.

We'd left Vegas that night and spent the next week quietly exploring the beauty of the Grand Canyon and surrounding areas. When we got home with me sporting a three carat solitaire diamond set in platinum with a matching wedding band, my family had been surprised and pleased for me. But I could tell they regretted not having had the opportunity to share the day with us.

That was something we were going to rectify on our one year anniversary. We were going to do it all again. Only this time it would be planned rather than spontaneous, and all our family and friends would be in attendance. Beth and my sisters would stand up with me. In fact, Beth was now talking about moving to the city for a bit and I couldn't be happier. I loved that we spoke every day via technology, but I'd love to see her in person more often. Sophia and Tori has also been busy. If everything went to plan Sophia would be trying for her black belt just before our "Wedding take 2" and Tori would be going for brown. But my husband had a fight to win first and that was where our primary focus had to be.

"How would it be different?" Xander asked, obviously curious.

"Well, this time I'll be living with you twenty four seven rather than heading home. That's one thing."

He gave me a cheeky wink. "I can definitely see the pluses to that."

A smirk crossed Jarryd's face, but he didn't lift his head from studying my skin.

"Well, I guess there is that... but I'll also have to put up with him being bone tired and let's not even talk about the diet," I jibed back.

"I don't recall you being this mouthy last time, Gem. Is that what happens when you become a wife?"

"No. That's what will happen when I'm deprived of junk food for eight or ten weeks," I informed him.

Xander chuckled. "I never stopped you from eating what you wanted before," he corrected.

"True. But I'd feel bad sitting down to something yummy while you're eating chicken and rice for every meal. Besides I could afford to drop a few pounds," I said offhandedly.

"Don't you dare! You're perfect just the way you are. If you need junk food to maintain that figure, then I'll happily watch you eat it while I force down some more chicken and rice." Jarryd and I both laughed at the visual.

"Can you just imagine the look on his face, Jarryd, as I sit down to a bowl of ice cream? Have you got any idea how much he likes ice cream?" I tormented. It was a common thing for us to chill out on the sofa with a carton of ice cream and one spoon while we watched a movie, or at least until something more interesting came up.

"Ooooo! That one would be hard to take; Xander pissed is never a good thing," Jarryd agreed.

We joked about the fight prep for a few more minutes then Jarryd asked me about school. "Are you going to be stuck here doing exams this time while Sensei here, heads off to Vegas again?"

"Not this time. Exams are in a few weeks. Then, I'll have a couple of months off before I start the next semester. That'll give me time to be with Xan through the fight and for us to have a couple of weeks' holiday somewhere before I get stuck into it again." I explained. "At least studying for exams gives me something to do while he's training."

Jarryd nodded, then lifted his head from his work. "Hey, I'm not sure if you heard but Cindy moved to Melbourne last month. Seems she decided a fresh start was in order."

Xander rubbed the back of my hand with his thumb. "I can't say I'm sorry to see her go. She caused a heap of grief for you Gem." He was referring to "ExamGate" as it became known. We'd come back from Vegas and the media was still hyped about everything we did, including our whirlwind marriage. It seemed I couldn't go to the bathroom most days without it being reported. I'd even had a few agents contact me with offers for my story. Xander and I were currently thinking it over. If my story could give people hope then I'd consider it, but it had to be the right offer and handled sensitively before I'd finally accept.

The local press had got wind of "ExamGate" and Cindy made more crazy statements on social media, all designed to discredit me when things started to heat up. The only problem was I had the evidence. It didn't work out so well for her. Xander's celebrity status had turned the tables on the social media thing since the fight and now his millions of fans seemed to hang on every word or comment he posted. There hadn't been any more problems with internet trolls, well, at least none I was aware of.

Eventually the Dean of Faculty ordered a full investigation and video footage showed one of the tutors slipping into the exam hall and tampering with the papers. Finally, he'd confessed when questioned. Apparently, he had been infatuated with Cindy and thought it would score points with her. It resulted in both of them being expelled and funnily enough, the relationship didn't go anywhere either. How surprising!

"I just hope she figures out what she wants and findssss it." I hissed out the last bit.

"Almost done, Eden. Just a little more shading here," Jarryd assured me. "So is Len going to be running things again this prep?"

"Yeah, dad will step up again. He and Eden do most of the admin work, accounting and organisation now. I just don't have time anymore," Xander admitted.

I looked up at him and gave him a knowing stare. "It wouldn't have anything to do with the fact that you hate bookwork and everything accounting, would it?" I asked innocently.

"No idea where you got that thought from? I just figured you could use the practical experience seeing you're so still hell bent on getting your accountancy degree. I'd have been happy to buy a few houses you could renovate, decorate and flip," he answered just as innocently.

"Once again, thank you for offering. But seriously Xan, how many times do I have to tell you that I'll do the decorating and design thing once I've finished my degree? I did drop the IT but I want to finish what I started with accountancy. Besides it'll save us a fortune in accountancy fees in the long run," I argued.

"My wife, ever the practical one. But you love decorating and design," Xander pointed out.

Jarryd chuckled and we both glared at him and said "What?" in unison.

"You two sound like such an old married couple!"

Then, we all ended up laughing. It was pretty funny. Fortunately, Jarryd managed to lift his hand away before my ribs started to wriggle from the laughter.

He wiped away a little blood and studied his work. "I think that about does it, Xander. What do you think?"

Xander studied it with him and I held my breath. Every time I had a session, I fell more and more in love with the design Jarryd had created.

When we'd gotten back from Vegas we'd come in to see him and he'd shown me the ideas he'd drawn up for me. I knew immediately he got where I was and what I needed. Xander had added a few ideas of his own and had declared he wanted to get a tattoo that complimented mine. Jarryd had gone away and come up with a connected pair that I knew would look amazing, but still uniquely represented our individual challenges and struggles. When we'd seen them, we both decided then and there they were perfect for us.

"Yeah, man. It's awesome," Xander, agreed a big smile on his face.

My impatience was starting to really get the best of me. "Can I see it yet?"

"Sure. Time for the grand unveiling," Jarryd said, moving over to the large mirror on the wall of his studio. He worked alone in a little upstairs studio not far from Onigashima.

Before I moved, Xander pressed my shirt that I was using to strategically cover my breasts to me, and took my hand to help me from the chair. Once I was upright I pressed my hand against my chest to hold the shirt in place and moved to the mirror.

I'd loved my Anime inspired warrior princess the minute Jarryd had introduced me to her, but now I was speechless. She was so beautiful, fighting through the flames and slaying oni left and right.

Xander moved up beside me and stripped off his shirt. His design had been finished weeks ago because working on his perfect body had been a cinch for Jarryd compared to my scars.

He stood beside me, his left side to my right. His Anime warrior prince fought back the grim reaper; a cobra poised to strike was coiled behind him. Both our figures wore matching uniforms of black and red and the Onigashima logo was emblazoned on their chests.

Jarryd had drawn them so that if we were standing side by side. Our prince and princess had their backs to each other to symbolise the fact we always had each other's backs. Then, when we were facing each other, our warriors were looking at each other.

Finally, I found my voice. "I love it, Jarryd. Thank you so much." I couldn't help the tears that slipped from my eyes. Xander put his arm around my shoulders and pulled me in tight, side to side.

"Great job, man. Never thought it would look so good," Xander turned his head to say to Jarryd.

"Glad you're happy. Take your time. I've just got to move my car. Then I'll be back to dress it for you," he said and disappeared realising we needed a moment alone.

Xander ran his finger down my cheek. "Now, you just need to decide about this."

I'd already decided what I was going to do. I was going to try cosmetic tattooing first. I'd seen some of the results on burns and it was amazing. We had the money for the surgeries, but I wasn't so keen anymore.

What I really loved was that Xander didn't say get it "fixed". The scars no longer mattered. He'd fixed me. Well, I'd done it, but he'd shown me how to be brave again and supported me every step of the way.

Now Jarryd's art had turned something ugly into something that looked incredible and made me happy every time I saw it.

"I love my little princess almost as much as I love you," I said holding his eyes in the mirror.

"And I love you, my brave warrior princess." There was so

much feeling in his voice that my heart overflowed with happiness and I knew he felt it too.

I loved our finished tattoos and I knew that would never change. But it was what we'd finally decided to inscribe across both tattoos that really linked them. On the bottom of each, in identical script, Jarryd had written.

"Defeat the Demons Inside"

then under that he'd inked

"Brave"

I hope you enjoyed
Xander and Eden's story.

Dane's will be along very soon.

A GIFT TO YOU

I hope you enjoyed reading Brave. I have a gift for you.

For those of you who would like a little more of Xander and Eden, please sign up for my newsletter "GayleForce" and you will receive the bonus chapter. (The Vegas Wedding!)

http://eepurl.com/brHOPv

PLEASE NOTE: If you choose not to take up this offer the story will not be impacted. I just thought you might like a little more!

Thank you so much for reading!

BRAVE BOOK TRAILER:

Seany Olsen, Chloe Hughes, Kim and Seila Pear, Remedy X and I, had a little fun playing and put together this book trailer for Brave. See what you think.

www.youtube.com/watch?v=MxfeVobySQQ

ACKNOWLEDGMENTS

This is the bit of the book that gets bigger every single time, and it's not a bad thing! What it means, is that I'm just so fortunate to have met and to have great people supporting me and for that I am very thankful.

Let's start with the book. So this one was a bit different. I had a little team of beta readers helping me here. First off, Karen Harper who not only beta read the novel but also edited it—thank you so much for your support and believing in my vision for what I wanted to do with this book. It isn't Centre Games and it was something very new for me to try! I'm hoping you will love Xander and Eden as much as I do. Bring on the next one...Dane and ?

Thank you to Seila Pear and her husband, Kim. Kim took not only the cover photo for the novel but also all the images for the teasers and the trailer. It was a labour of love from his perspective and he did an amazing job. Nothing was too much trouble and he is a true perfectionist. Love your work! Check out his work at Kim Pear Photography on Facebook at www.facebook.com/pages/Kim-Pear-Photography/200554700077377?fref=ts.

To Seila—well gorgeous, you kept me motivated and totally "got" the whole book. You read every single scene over and over. I think you know the book better than me! Thank you for your help with styling and just being there. It means the world to me. You guys are great.

Tamia Simons, my American sister. Girl, you were there for me every step of the way. You provided every single playlist. You read every word I wrote about a hundred times. You're encouragement and critiquing was just incredible. Thank you so much. This book really was a big team effort and you're a major part of that team.

To my muse—Seany Olsen. Well not only are you an incredible fighter, martial artist, instructor, model and all-round amazing guy— you're also HOT, humble, respectful and genuine! I can't thank you enough for all the help you've given me with the technical aspects in this book as well as giving me ideas for names and other stuff. You've let me photograph and video you. You've stood for hours at a book signing. You'll always be Xander Todd to me. Or maybe Xander Todd is you! Thanks you from the bottom of my heart. You can follow Seany here: www.facebook.com/seany olsenmodel

Chloe Hughes, you are the closest girl to Eden I know—the girl next door that doesn't really know just how stunning she really is. Thank you so much for helping out with the video. You'll always be family. I hope you had as much fun as I did making it! Now I just need to find you a real life hero....

To Letitia from Romantic Book Affair, thank you for taking Kim's amazing picture of Sean and turning it into a cover that I absolutely adore. Loved it from the second I saw it. Thanks so much.

I'd like to thank the gorgeous Ariel May. Thanks so much for organising with Remedy X for me to use "Bells" as the soundtrack to the book trailer. I really appreciate it. The song was just perfect for the book. I can't wait to catch up with you and the band (hopefully next year) and the boys can play it live for me! I'm also going to give a thank you to your mum and my great friend Pati May. I know this one was tough for you and I appreciate your honesty. Maybe next time!

To all the bloggers that help myself and every other indie authors, thank you so much. This would not be possible without you!

And now another big thank you to a few of my author friends. A special thank you to Nina Levine, for taking the time to explain the finer points of this whole crazy author marketing thing for me. To River Savage, Melissa Jane, Liz Lovelock, Kirsty Dallas, Dzintra

Sullivan, Max Henry, Carly Grey, Gwyn McNamee, Dawna Raver - you girls are always there for a chat and to lend a hand. Thanks so much I really value your friendship.

To Kim, my aunt, well this one has had a few rough patches.... but we got there. I'm sure there's someone looking down on this one and feeling very proud. We make a great team! Thanks so much.

Last but not least—my family. It's been a very tough six months for us, but we got through and the news is good. So glad to have you home, mum and dad. To Vic, Froglet and Super Duper—yep I wrote "The End" finally and it was a mission and yes, we will be doing all this again...I love you!

Love

Nat

ABOUT THE AUTHOR

A confessed readaholic and romantic junkie, Natalie spends her time juggling a busy career as an IT professional and author. In between staring at a computer screen (she spends lot time doing that!) Natalie, enjoys living the Gold Coast life with her very tolerant husband and two school aged children.

She loves spending time with family and friends, hitting the beach, cooking, working out and curling up with a good book. Her pet hates are cleaning and anything else that can be considered "domestic dullness". If she could have one wish it would be to be able to fit 48 hours into 24.

Natalie is the author of the **Centre Games Series**. A fast paced, romantic suspense series set on the Gold Coast, Australia. The series tells the stories of the Centre, a quasi government agency established to fight environmental, biological and agricultural threats. The Centre Games books are filled with hot alpha males and the feisty independent females strong enough to capture their hearts. Natalie's books pack lots of action, hot romance and surprises.

Natalie is currently working on her fifth instalment for the Centre Games Series and a brand new series for 2015. Look out for a couple of surprise projects coming soon.

CONTACT NATALIE

WEBSITE

www.nataliegayle.com/

FACEBOOK

www.facebook.com/NatalieGayleAuthor

TWITTER

@NatalieGayle1

GENRE: Contemporary Romance / Romantic Suspense / Paranormal /NA

ALSO BY NATALIE

CENTRE GAMES SERIES

Finding Trust (Book 1)

Finding Judgement (Book 2)

Finding Freedom (Book 3)

Finding Resolution (Book 4)

More titles to be added soon!

ONI FIGHTERS SERIES

Brave (Book 1)

Dane's Book (untitled coming soon)

Made in the USA
Las Vegas, NV
19 January 2023

65913615R00275